GALAXY RAIDERS:
ABYSS

ALSO BY IAN DOUGLAS

GALAXY RAIDERS:
ABYSS

IAN DOUGLAS

HARPER Voyager
An Imprint of HarperCollins*Publishers*

GALAXY RAIDERS: ABYSS. Copyright © 2025 by William H. Keith Jr. All rights reserved. No part of this
book may be used or reproduced in any manner whatsoever without written permission except in the case of brief quotations embodied in critical articles and reviews. For information, address HarperCollins Publishers, 195 Broadway, New York, NY 10007.

HarperCollins books may be purchased for educational, business, or sales promotional use. For information, please email the Special Markets Department at SPsales@harpercollins.com.

Harper Voyager and design are trademarks of HarperCollins Publishers LLC.

FIRST EDITION
Designed by Patrick Barry

Library of Congress Cataloging-in-Publication Data has been applied for.

ISBN 978-0-06-320574-1

$PrintCode

For Brea

GALAXY
RAIDERS:
ABYSS

Prologue

THE GALAXY WAS already ancient a billion years ago when the Authority established itself as the dominant voice of some millions of high-technic civilizations. A true empire in all but a few quibbling details, the Authority had no emperor and only rarely intervened in any individual species' governance. Those civilizations within its ancient folds gave their allegiance, in myriad forms, to the Authority's principal Mind deep within the hellish depths of the Galactic Core. In theory, at least, that Mind was aware of all its teeming quadrillions of dependents.

In fact, and of course, it took time—often a great deal of time—for information to pass through the tangled network of interstellar gates from the Galaxy's outer spiral arms into its shining heart, and just as long for the Mind's judgments and commands to make the journey back. The Galactic Empire was very powerful . . . but it was also very slow.

The Authority did establish rules, demand compliance, and pass judgment. Subject races obeyed, or they passed into extinction. Any given species could send their ships through the ancient gate rings, or they could use relativistic intersystem travel in order to establish colonies within uninhabited systems, but engaging in wars of conquest or extermination was forbidden.

These were privileges reserved for the Authority.

And now the Minds of the Galactic Authority deep within the fastness of the Core might have to exercise that privilege once again with the noisily upstart inhabitants of a minor star system twenty-six thousand light-years away.

Human civilization, so-called, would obey the Authority, or it would very soon now pass into extinction.

CHAPTER ONE

"THAT'S IT, DEK," Alexandra Morrigan said, shaking her head. "No more! I'm sick of it. I just want to die and get it over with."

Her massive companion seated in the flier's cabin regarded her through glittering lenses. "Get *what* over with?" it asked. "Life?"

"Life," she agreed. "Endless interactions with idiots. Round after round of the same political nonsense. Self-serving narcissists playing games I simply don't want to play. Having to attend vapid social functions . . . like this one." She snorted. "*Homo superioris!* What *bullshit!*"

"True. A better taxonomic classification would be *Homo sapiens superioris*. Do you intend to kill yourself?"

Was there a hint of concern behind the robot's words? Type 40s weren't supposed to develop emotions, but AI minds did change and they did evolve. More than aide, valet, and bodyguard, Dek had been her companion for the better part of this lifetime.

"No, Dek," she said. "Don't worry. I'll live this one out. But no more new lives. No more rejuvenations . . ."

"It seems a waste, Alex."

She actually laughed. "Dek, there's no law that says I *have* to live forever!"

"I don't understand your desire for . . . oblivion, presumably. Do I understand that you simply dislike your fellow humans?"

"Not all of them, Dek. I suppose there are a few of them out there with both brains and common sense." She considered the question for a moment as the flier cruised north through a darkening late-evening sky.

Morrigan was 398 years old and bore the physical features and bearing of someone in her sixties. In what amounted to a series of eight lifetimes—with seven rejuvenations—she had picked her way through dozens of careers. At one time or another, she'd been an artist, an amortality consultant, a software engineer, a network memegineer, a genegineer, and an AI designer. For twelve years around 2300, a century and a half ago, she'd been in the U.S. Marines, rising to the exalted rank of gunnery sergeant but resigning her commission. Then ninety years ago she'd signed on again.

She was a Navy captain now. She'd tried hard to make a long-term go of this one, but . . .

She closed her eyes. *Almost four hundred years old,* she thought, *and I still don't know what I want to be when I grow up!*

The flier's chime alerted Morrigan that the craft was on final approach to Aurora Tower. "Almost there," she told Dek, then swiveled her seat to face the control nest. "Unfortunately."

"Indeed," her sleekly molded companion replied. "You *are* aware that machine AI is far better able to handle a landing than any organic brain."

"You *would* say that, Dek." She wrinkled her nose as she brought up the holographic heads-up display. It was an old piece of verbal byplay. "You're an AI, after all." Her finger dragged through an illuminated touchfield. "I have control."

"You have control, Captain Morrigan," the flier's AI agreed. "Altitude one-four-zero-seven meters, velocity one-five-nine, heading zero-one-eight. Hold steady on five-degree slope."

She sighed. "Yes, Mother."

The flier dropped through the night, stars and a first-quarter moon visible through the bubble canopy, with the sprawling blue-white glare of ground lights below: the Denver Megapolis sprawling to the west, all the way to the mountains of the Front Range, and the Denver Spaceport dead ahead. Morrigan's destination, however, was to her left—one of the kilometer-high arcologies clustered within the megapolis proper.

Directions flickered within her visual field, fed to her brain by her corona, which in turn was linked now to the flier's AI. Her hand moved within a field and she thought her intention. The flier banked sharply to the left, and Aurora Tower slid across the canopy until it was directly ahead and just below. From here, it looked like an enormous mushroom with a three-hundred-meter cap shaped like a dinner plate. The upper surface was dominated by the Logan manse and outbuildings, but there was plenty of room left for parks, patches of wooded land, a large pond with a central, illuminated rainbow fountain, and a private landing pad.

"Aurora traffic control is overriding our approach," the flier told her.

"Damn," she said. "Okay . . . tower has control."

"I don't think they trust you, Alex," Dek told her. "You being org and all."

"Aw, they just don't want us to have *any* fun."

Under Aurora Flight Control, the flier descended smoothly across the rim of the plate, hovered briefly above the glare of the landing pad, then drifted to a perfect touchdown. The flier's doors gulled open, and Morrigan turned her seat. "Well," she said. "Into the furnace."

"Do you want me to stay with you?" Dek asked. He was already out the door, unfolding to his full two-meter height of gleaming blue-black metal.

"Don't be silly."

"We are about to enter one of those 'vapid social functions' you mentioned. I have no wish to see you harmed by ennui or by frustration."

"I'm a big girl, Dek. I can handle it." She reached up to adjust her corona—a smoothly shaped horseshoe of what looked like liquid metal reaching from the back of her head around to points just behind the corner of each eye. It was securely in place—part adornment, part IT network connection, part personal secretary.

"I know, Alex. You'll be fine."

She faced the Logan manse as the flier sealed up and lifted off behind them, wafting off to a holding garage beneath the plate. *Welcome, Captain Morrigan!* a bright, female voice said through Morrigan's corona, the words forming inside her head. A green light winked on within her visual field. *Follow the guide and come on in. We're delighted you could make it!*

Morrigan couldn't tell if the voice was human or AI. It didn't matter, of course. Artificial intelligences often served as avatars for their owners. "It's good to be here," she lied, and followed the light. *As if I had a choice.*

Her looming, robotic companion followed.

The party in the manse and within the surrounding grounds was already well under way, a warm and brightly erotic swirl of life and color and outright hedonism. The Logan family, she'd heard, sometimes threw parties like this that lasted for a week. They could afford the lifestyle, certainly. The clan matriarch, Daphne Logan, had inherited a few trillion centuries ago from the legendary Troidertrust. Her family had been among the very first asteroid miners, and they'd made their first few fortunes by trashing most of the rare elements markets on Earth.

That had been a long time ago, but Morrigan remembered all the excitement on the news feeds.

I'm online if you need me, Alex. That was Pixie, the AI component of her coronal intelligence and the voice of her electronic alter ego.

"Watcher mode, Pixie," Morrigan said. "I won't be needing you."

Her guide light winked out as she stepped into the entryway, and Morrigan stopped, looking around, not certain where to go. Several dozen people were engaged in conversation and senshares just within the broad atrium at the end of the walk, a partially enclosed space opening both into the building proper and the decks and gardens outside. Social nudity was common for all sexes, though there was a glowing, flashing array of gowns, suits, animated tattoos, and ostentatious jewelry. Morrigan had neither dressed nor undressed for the evening; the invitation had explicitly told her "come as you wish," so she was wearing her Navy dress blacks, a uniform deemed proper attire for any and all social occasions.

Around her, pairs and threesomes cuddled in sheltering pods, while other guests stood on the deck or lounged or coupled in adaptive furniture that grew and shifted to accommodate moving bodies. Architecture and furnishings both tended toward the abstract, with soft lighting, large sculpted plants, and plenty of softly rounded walls and surfaces beneath an open night sky or under vaulted ceilings lost in darkness. Sometimes it was difficult to tell whether you were inside or out.

"Mist?" a man's voice said at her side. She turned to face a small man offering her what looked like a crystal ball on an ornate platter. Morrigan's corona seemed at a loss to identify him and could only tag him with the word SERVANT floating within her visual field. He was old—shockingly so in this glittering crowd of young, athletic, and, above all, *wealthy* humans . . . people so wealthy they could afford to have human servants. He wore a plain dark jumpsuit that made him all but invisible within this setting.

She didn't normally indulge, but something inside wouldn't let her refuse the old man. "Thank you," she said, and lifted the crystal from its stand. "You . . . work for Lady Logan?"

"No, miss. Not usually. I'm with the catering service."

"What's your name?"

But another voice interrupted inside her own mind. *Captain Morrigan! So nice of you to come!*

Morrigan turned to face a young woman wearing a full sensory helm that covered her face save for her lips and chin. A dazzling spray of silver filaments spread out and down from her crown, framing her in glittering light; that and the silver wrappings on her arms were all that she wore.

But Morrigan's corona was cranking out data, ID'ing the woman as LADY DAPHNE LOGAN, with a cascade of biographical and genealogical data spilling down the right side of her visual field. Morrigan knew that Lady Daphne had been born well over 250 years ago; this person looked to be no more than fifteen.

Ah, the miracle of ENS . . .

"Don't bother the servants, dear," Lady Daphne told her, speaking out loud now. The voice was that of a teenage girl; the will behind it was mature and implacably unyielding. An emotil appeared beneath her name reading [MILD IRRITATION]. "They have *so* much work to do."

"My apologies, Lady Daphne." She wasn't going to argue social ideologies now, especially not with the function's hostess. "Thank you for having me."

"Of course, dear. My . . . you *do* look so fetching in your uniform!"

Morrigan gave the woman a quick helmet-to-toe-and-back glance. "At the moment I think I'm overdressed."

Nonsense, my dear. The words sounded once more in her head, placed there through her corona. *Whatever makes you comfortable.*

Social nudity didn't make Morrigan uncomfortable in the least. It was, after all, more or less the norm throughout what passed for Earth's tangled principal culture and had been for centuries, with clothing worn only for comfort or protection or to broadcast a particular social message. What irritated her was the blatant display of bare flesh simply to showcase the owner's use of ENS and gene edits, a kind of genetic one-upmanship.

"There's someone over here I'm sure you'd like to see, dear," Lady Daphne told her, taking her by the arm.

Morrigan grudgingly permitted the unwanted familiarity and allowed herself to be led inside the manse. Beyond the entryway was a large sitting room, its ceiling invisible in the shadows somewhere overhead. A man in the gold-heavy uniform of a Navy admiral sat on a low, comfortable dais, the center of a conversational group of women, men, neuts, genmanips, and robots. Several were other fleet officers, like her wearing dress blacks. Dek, she saw, was already there. She'd wondered where he'd gotten to.

Rear Admiral Jaime Koehler looked forty but had been born in 2185, giving him a truage of 263. He was on . . . what? His fourth lifetime? His fifth? She honestly wasn't sure.

Not that it mattered.

He turned to face Morrigan with a large smile, his emotil flashing [PLEASURE]. "Ah! Here's my esteemed flag captain now!" he said, saluting her by raising his mist crystal. "Alex! Get yourself over here!"

"Hello, Admiral," she said, ignoring this familiarity as well. "I didn't know you would be here."

Her invitation had arrived that morning as an attachment to electronic orders from the Admiralty. The Navy, she knew well, was at pains not to cross the oligarchic plutocracy that was the Terran government . . . and that meant the social strata forming the political base for that government, the Illiminati—the Latin meant, roughly, "those without limits."

Koehler grinned. "The Logans are throwing this fest for *us*, didn't you know? For the superiors of the Grand Fleet before our heroic embarkation for Abyss!"

"No, I didn't."

"It's all politics," Captain Harrison said, smiling. He was big, heavyset, and the current commanding officer of the cruiser *Endymion*. "Senator Martin is afraid we're going to make the Galactics angry. And Brandt here is terrified of something upsetting his negotiations with them."

"Hardly terrified, Captain," a nude man standing nearby said. He wore a complex filigree of silver down his left arm, and his elaborately coiffed corona ID'ed him as Dr. Feodor Brandt of the UE Foreign Service. Like the rest, he looked no older than thirty, but his electronic credentials suggested an age of several centuries. "The Dr'kleh faction possesses minds that are brilliant . . . *brilliant*. They're so intelligent they grasp every side of a problem at once, without emotion or prejudice. Our talks with them are already bearing fruit." He smiled at Morrigan, lifting his crystal in salute.

"Senator Martin may be right," Captain Jobert, of the fleet monitor *Erebus*, added. "I'd hate to be on the wrong side of those . . . people."

"Senator Martin," yet another fleet captain, Ellen Carter, chimed in, "is an idiot. Peace at any price . . . and to hell with our extrasolar colonies."

Carter, Morrigan knew, was from Pavo, an Earth colony almost twenty light-years from Earth. The undeclared war with some of the Galactics' clients had consumed Delta Pavonis IV twenty-three years ago, and she would not be happy with the rumors circulating about the Joining. Currently, she was CO of the light cruiser *Invincible*.

Koehler patted the cushion next to him. "Here, pet. Sit yourself down!"

She sidestepped the invitation, blocking her corona from broadcasting her annoyance. The admiral's words hadn't *exactly* been a direct order . . .

She and Koehler had been lovers on and off for the past century. They'd met while she'd been a civilian consultant in D.C. and he'd been the XO of the *Port Diego*, a fleet escort carrier. They'd been close . . . *very* close, close enough that they'd discussed a formal long-term union. More, Koehler had been responsible for getting her to reenlist in the Navy after an extended sabbatical, a service hiatus of some fifty-four years. Twenty years ago his patronage had nailed down her promotion to captain.

She knew she should be grateful. Usually she was.

But she was *not* his "pet." She was 135 years older than Koehler and well on in her eighth lifetime. She was older than most of the people here, including sweet little Lady Daphne. They, *all* of them, could take their righteous *Homo superioris* attitudes and stuff them up their condescendingly righteous asses. Illiminati indeed . . .

"Tell me, Captain," Brandt asked her. "What do *you* think we'll find out beyond Abyss?"

Foreign Service meant diplomat, which in turn meant patrician. Obviously wealthy, obviously *superior*. That could scarcely ingratiate him to Morrigan.

"The Sirius star system, of course," she replied. "What else?"

Was he testing her? Brandt's emotil simply said [INTERESTED], but if he was prying or trying to goad her, she doubted that his corona would give that away. To hide her nervousness, she lifted her mist close to her face. Sensing the movement, the crystal sphere split across its top, emitting a curling cloudlet of pale gas; as she inhaled it, she felt a heady surge of pleasure sweep up her spine and across her scalp, a ripple of pleasant gratification, of a cheerful confidence edging out her self-doubt.

She also realized with a tingling rush how much she still wanted Koehler, and in that realization she noted an alarming fading of her inhibitions. *Whoa! Not too much of* that!

She surreptitiously placed the globe in the planter of a bright red-orange tropical shrub beside her—*Canna coccinea,* according to her corona. Voluptastims like mist, fog, and feelgood all were perfectly acceptable, both socially and legally, but she wanted a clear head tonight—a clear head and no pre-mission entanglements.

"Actually," Brandt was saying, "I was thinking about the Galactics. They've offered us a chance to join their community. The *Joining,* right? It's what Humankind has been dreaming of for centuries."

"Exactly, Feodor," a young, lanky genmanip said, lifting eir crystal of mist. Eir only adornment besides the corona encircling eir hairless head was a glowing spiral, a representation of the Galaxy, hovering above eir smooth-skinned chest. "The Galactics are here to usher us all into paradise."

"The Galactics," Koehler said with distaste, "are not *gods.*"

The manip gave a dismissive wave of eir free hand. "They might as well be. Think of what we shall learn . . . and of what we shall become!"

"Dala's right!" a young woman gushed. She, too, wore the galactic spiral of the Joining, hovering between her bare breasts. "According to the Church, they will transfigure us all. Caterpillars becoming butterflies!"

"Maybe," Brandt said, [SKEPTICAL]. "Thus sayeth the Church of the Joining, but what's important is our transformation into a mature species."

"Well spoken," Lady Logan said. She joined the group with something odd and technological floating beside her.

"Ladies, gentlemen, mannies," she said, gesturing at her silently hovering companion, "*this* is why I invited all of you here tonight. We have a very special guest with us, a representative from the Galactics. May I present One of the Galactic Central Authority. Some of you know him, ah, know *em* already."

"Oh, yes," Brandt said, toasting the object with his mist crystal. "How are you, One?"

"Well, Mr. Brandt. I trust you are well also."

The voice emanating from the Galactic was smooth and articulate, natural, and with a tone somewhere between a light male and a deeper-than-average female voice—perfectly gender neutral, in other words. One's body was obviously a machine of extremely advanced design, a meter-tall mass floating just at eye level on silent gravs. It was roughly ovoid but with a gleaming silver surface constantly shifting and changing, as though it were made of liquid mercury, an alien analogue to the coronas present in the room. Morrigan suspected that it represented some type of advanced nanotechnology—trillions of cell-sized machines held together by a magnetic or gravitic magic far beyond current human technology.

The thing had eyes—she assumed they were eyes—a dozen deep red cabochons of different sizes, like rubies, floating in the silvery liquid surface. It appeared to have at least one of the crystals watching each of the humans there.

Morrigan was surprised to find that her corona couldn't identify One, that it didn't even seem to recognize that the Galactic was floating right there in front of her. Were her corona's sensors somehow being blocked? Or was One representative of a technology completely beyond the corona's grasp?

"So why are you here, One?" she asked. She'd downloaded reports on the arrival of a number of the machines—Floaters or Glitters, as the media had tagged them. She knew what the news feeds had said about them: "technological liaisons from the Galactic Core, here to guide Humankind into a new and peaceful relationship with the rest of the Galaxy." It was better, she thought, to get her information when possible straight from the source.

All twelve of the being's eyes drifted together onto one side of the hovering egg, studying her. "To spy on you, of course," One told her. "Yours is a fascinating species, and we have been interested in your development for some time now."

One's answer generated a nervous murmur of laughter through the group. "Oh, come now, One!" Lady Logan said. "You're here for other reasons than *that.*"

"The Authority's message, One!" Brandt said, his voice just barely touched by urgency.

"What message would that be, One?" Captain Harrison asked.

"Why, our invitation, of course. An invitation to your species to join the Galactic community. Dr. Brandt is quite right. Many on your world have been yearning for contact with a Galactic civilization you felt certain must exist. For thousands of years, your religions have sought final union with an agency, with a *being,* far greater and more powerful than you. And now, at long last, that time has come. We are here to invite you into the Galactic community."

"The Galactic *Empire,* you mean," Captain Carter said. Her corona tagged her as [HOSTILE].

"Translate it as you will," One said with an indifferent air. "The Authority has no emperor as you think of the term. We represent some millions of advanced civilizations working together for the common good while seeking to help emerging cultures like your own. The closest thing we have to a ruling government is a congeries of . . . call them extended intellects. Fifth Singularity, highly evolved, noncorporeal. In fact, they actually have very little in common with lesser minds. They guide the rest of us but rarely issue edicts or demand obedience."

"How admirable," Carter said. She was still [HOSTILE].

"I've heard, One," Morrigan said carefully, "that acceptance of your offer comes with a rather high price."

"We expect certain standards of behavior within our association, Captain, yes. But the abundance of technological and material prosperity open to you through your acceptance is, I think you must agree, worth any small sacrifices asked of you."

"As I understand it," Koehler said, "the cost is a lot higher if we *don't* agree . . . isn't that right, One?"

"Nonsense," a young-looking woman, a civilian tagged simply as Nessa, said. She was wearing a wisp of gown that was all shimmering light and rainbows. "We should do what the gods *tell* us to, right? For our own *good*!"

Nessa appeared programmed to speak in ejaculatives, stressing every few words for . . . what? For effect? To make people believe she knew what she was talking about?

"I mean," she rattled on, "if we become part of their . . . their *community,* we can use the gates freely, right? And . . . and just *think*! They're *billions* of years older than we are! Just think how *smart* they are! *They'll* be able to help us with *all* our problems, I'm *sure*!"

"True," Brandt said, perhaps trying to derail Nessa before she strained something. "A highly evolved civilization will have highly evolved moral and ethical standards."

"I don't know about that," Koehler said, [AMUSED]. "They haven't exactly been brimming over with altruistic warm fuzzies, have they?"

"An alien society," Morrigan pointed out, "will by definition have alien goals and alien ideals."

"Probably," Koehler said. "My bet is that if they have answers to our problems, we're going to have to pay for them."

"What you should consider, Admiral," One told him, "is the cost you will pay for *not* joining the interstellar community."

And there it was, Morrigan thought—the iron fist hidden within the velvet glove, as Napoleon once had put it. The teeth behind the smile. As she understood it, the Galactics' invitation *could* be refused; they would not force Earth to join if humanity wished to be left alone.

But if Humankind refused the invitation, the door to the stars would slam shut.

For centuries, Earth had been experimenting with several designs of gravitic FTL drives. That research would have to be abandoned. Over the past few centuries, Earth had established some seven extrasolar colonies among nearby stars using near-*c* relativistic travel. Those colonies would have to be evacuated, their populations repatriated to Earth. Humans might have their colonies on Mars or the Jovian satellites, but their reach and their grasp would be bounded by the limits of their own solar system.

And humans would forgo all use of the enigmatic gates far out in the Kuiper Belt—Abyss, Void, and Stardeep. As members of the community they could freely use those stargates to leave the Sol System and explore the Galaxy. Refuse the Galactics' offer, and Humankind would forever be restricted to its own system, isolated and alone.

Quarantined.

The representatives of the community had never discussed just how the Galactics would enforce their demands. But the general assumption was that the community was very old and would possess technologies—and weapons—utterly beyond the ken of human civilization; technologies, as one historical philosopher had put it, indistinguishable from magic.

"How about it, One?" Koehler asked. "Will the Galactics help Earth with its problems?"

"Which problems?"

"Population, for one."

"For a start, Admiral, I suggest that your species either give up Engineered Negligible Senescence or stop all reproductive activity. Whichever you prefer."

"What, give up *sex*?" Morrigan said sweetly, facetiously. "What kind of choice is *that*?" A few in the group dared to laugh—nervously.

"Lower your species' death rate," One told them, "and you *must* lower your birthrate, or choke in your own garbage as you devour every scrap of available resources and inevitably die smothered in your own wastes. There is no other solution."

"Of course there are other solutions, One," Koehler said. "There are *always* solutions. We've come a long way with practical nanotechnology, which lets us transform waste into anything else we wish. We have begun building off-world colonies—"

"Surely none of you imagine that you'll be able to ship your excess population off-world to other systems," One said.

Well, that much was obvious, Morrigan thought. And Jaime was not stupid, so she assumed he'd been testing the Galactic, or perhaps goading em. Earth's current population hovered at fifty-two billion. Humans would never be able to build enough ships—ships big enough, ships fast enough—to more than nibble at that number. Whether Jaime was talking about colonizing other worlds or building deep-space orbital colonies, the creation of new places to live would never keep pace with Humankind's birthrate.

The global human population had once stabilized at ten billion in the twenty-first century and even declined for a while, but with the introduction of ENS treatments it had been steadily and swiftly rising again. People seemed unwilling to forgo children. Laws limiting the numbers of children were deemed draconian.

"Our civilization is still seeking a balance," Koehler told the Floater. "Medical technology gives us ample means for reducing the birthrate. But we still have some problems with the necessary . . . ah . . . social engineering."

"He *means*," Nessa said knowingly, "that the Sapies breed like *rabbits*."

Did this creature have a *brain*? Morrigan wanted to punch her.

Sapies . . . *Homo sapiens*. While people who'd received ENS treatments were not, in fact, a new species of humanity, many had begun referring somewhat disingenuously to clinical amortals as members of one: *Homo superioris*. Sapies and Supers—the two new faces of Humankind. The assumption of the ruling class was that eventually the Sapies would die out, leaving *Homo superioris* as the only remaining representative of Humankind.

Morrigan deeply resented the artificial distinction and had to block her corona's broadcast of her emotional response. If someone commented on her emotil, she would end up telling the whole group how she *really* felt, and that would be undiplomatic, to say the least.

"We need time, One," Koehler told the Floater. "I admit that our technology has rather outpaced our ability to cope with it, but we're working at it. No, we can't ship our excess population off-world, of *course* not. But our off-world colonies at least offer a measure of hope to those who have to stay here. Colonization is a kind of pressure release valve for us, you see?"

Not to mention, Morrigan thought, *a guarantee that some humans will survive if . . . when . . . Earth's civilization collapses.*

"Your best option," One replied, "is to join the Galactic community. We don't promise to help every species with its internal problems, but you at least will have access to thousands of other biological species like yourselves, as well as tens of thousands of post-Singularity species, all of whom have faced similar issues in their pasts . . . *and solved them.* You need only sacrifice a modicum of your independence in order to receive abundant stability, order, and security. I would think that the choice is obvious."

"And what about Delta Pavonis?" Carter demanded. "Thirty thousand colonists, *slaughtered!*"

And among them, Morrigan thought, the young woman who'd been Ellen Carter's wife. The news of the attack had reached Earth only three years ago; Carter had been CO of the *Wayfarer,* one of the near-*c* vessels that had brought news and a few survivors back to the Sol System. And the Pavos weren't alone. There'd been other raids, in other systems, with other refugees. Galactic representatives so far had been dismissive of such "minor border incidents."

"I *am* sorry, Captain Carter," the Floater told her. "The fact of the matter is that the Delta Pavo system has been set aside for colonization by another species, the Veykaar—the Crabs, as I believe you call them. Earth had no right to appropriate those worlds."

"The Crabs hunted us down like vermin!" Carter replied. "*You* had no right—"

"We had every right," One replied, "as arbiters of Galactic civilization."

"You have the unmitigated gall to call yourselves *civilized*?" Carter's emotil was rapidly cycling now between [FURIOUS], [HORROR], and [GRIEF].

Morrigan stepped closer to Carter and touched her arm. *Easy, Ellen,* she told her over a coronal mind-to-mind link. *This isn't the time . . .*

"Then when *is* it fucking time?" Carter demanded, turning and shouting into her face. "When they've hunted us down and murdered us *all*?"

"Take her outside, Alex," Koehler told Morrigan.

"Come on, Ellen," she told the woman. "We can't start a war here."

"The war," Carter said, "has already been started. By *them*."

CHAPTER TWO

"WHAT THE HELL do you mean she's been *relieved*?" Morrigan demanded.

Morrigan and Koehler were strapped into adjoining seats on board the fleet shuttle designated as the admiral's barge, as the blue sky visible on the cabin's projection screens faded to black. Acceleration pressed them back in their seats. The flight from Denver Spaceport up to UTS *Constellation* in orbit would take twenty-five minutes.

Admiral Koehler glanced around the shuttle's cabin, obviously concerned about privacy. Twelve other *Connie* personnel occupied seats: two of the admiral's aides, the squadron's tactical officer commander, Armand Boucher, and others. Dek sat aft, stolid and imperturbable. Dr. Brandt was in conference with two of his aides aft.

"Alex," Koehler said, his voice low, "you saw her. Captain Carter is unstable, okay? I don't want her in command of one of my ships."

"She's not crazy. She's *angry*."

"And this mission is essentially one of diplomacy. I can't afford to have one of my people reacting emotionally at a delicate moment."

And how long, Morrigan wondered, would the human species be divided between rational men and emotional women? As long, most likely, as there were men to make that distinction.

Morrigan let it pass. "She had to fight to retain her command status when she arrived from Pavo, you know. Something like this could wreck her career."

"And a hotheaded skipper disobeying fleet instructions could start a war that wrecks Earth. You want me to risk that?"

Morrigan sighed. "Of course not, sir, but—"

"No buts. Her exec will take command of the *Invincible*. Commander Holt has been waiting for his chance at command for a long time. Slowpro."

"Slowpro" was military slang for "slow promotions." Though in theory not an absolute qualification for membership, the tight-knit club of naval officers tended to be Supers—wealthy, well connected, and amortal. Many joined the Navy in the first place to take advantage of free ENS treatments, with the result that officers especially became a deeply entrenched and ultraconservative gerontocracy. With a limited number of command billets available throughout the entire Terran Navy, an officer could be sitting on the promotions list for decades before a new one opened up. Morrigan herself had held the rank of commander for thirty-three years before her promotion to captain, a long time to serve as department head or XO, or to be the skipper of small stuff—escorts, light destroyers, frigates, and the like.

Hell, she might still be waiting in the wings if it hadn't been for Koehler's patronage.

"So . . . is Ellen going to be put on the beach?"

"She'll be evaluated at Bethesda. After that . . ." He shrugged. "We'll see."

He put his hand over Morrigan's on her armrest. She slipped it free. She wasn't going to make an issue of it, but the fact of her being the apprentice of a wealthy fleet commander—*especially* a wealthy fleet commander who'd once been her lover—had been galling her for some time. Her romance with Koehler had ended amicably twenty-three years ago, while she'd been skipper of a Naval Bureau desk in Washington. She appreciated his help; damn it, that was the way things *worked* in the modern Navy. But she was determined now to make it on her own, even if her life, without another ENS treatment, was due to end in another decade or two.

The thought left a cold and empty feeling in her stomach, but her fists tightened in her lap as she pushed aside the fear. It was time to let go.

You okay, Alex? Koehler asked her, speaking within her thoughts. Mind-to-mind links via coronas let them talk without sharing with everyone else on board the shuttle.

Fine, she replied, nodding silently.

I've noticed that you've been quite formal with me lately. Cold, even…

Jaime, this job is hard enough without the gossip and speculation about our relationship, okay? I appreciate the opportunity to be your flag captain. I do not *appreciate being thought of as your lover.*

I see…

I just want to be careful starting out. I can't block all the rumors, but I can remain personally above reproach and avoid feeding them. Understand?

Of course I do, he replied. *You fought your way to where you are today on your own power. I respect that. I promise I'll be good.*

And you need to be damned careful as well, she told him. *And that means no holding hands and no having me sit on your lap! At least not in public…*

She wondered why she'd added that last. She liked Jaime, liked him a lot… but did she still *love* him?

She'd known him for the better part of a century and she still wasn't sure.

You are absolutely right, Alex. I'm sorry if I was … inappropriate. I guess I was just dropping back into what we—what we used to share.

He sounded so lost in that moment she very nearly reached for him … and mentally kicked herself for the impulse.

No need to be sorry. But … thank you for understanding.

I should've known better, he said with a grin, *trying to get together with a woman twice my age!*

Koehler didn't know about her decision to stop the treatments, and she didn't want to open that particular tub of worms.

Someday, she told him, *things will be different.*

Aloud, she picked up on the earlier conversation. "Ellen *is* right, you know. We've been at war with the Galactics for years."

"'Undeclared hostilities with a minor faction within the Galactic polity,'" Koehler said, quoting a strategic sitrep circulating within the Navy Department. "The problem with the Galactic Empire is that it's so damned *big.* We're getting jostled by some of our near neighbors, yeah, but whatever passes for leadership at the Core probably hasn't even heard about what's happened out here yet."

"Or they don't care," Morrigan replied.

"Quite possible. They're gods, remember? And by comparison we're ants."

"Gods." Could the high-and-mighty rulers of the Authority really have powers that merited such a term? They certainly seemed to possess the requisite detachment. "Look," she said. "You heard what that Galactic said last night. The Crabs took over Pavo because the Galactics *let* them!"

"We don't know anything about the Galactics' internal politics, Captain."

"We know that their client races are moving into areas we control . . . or used to control. Not just Delta Pavonis. Zeta Tucanae. Alpha Mensae. Kappa Ceti. Their *politics* may consist of using proxies to force us back and back and back until our military situation is untenable."

"Which is why DSF-Eight is being dispatched to Abyss," Koehler told her. "Sirius Station has gone silent. That may be coincidence, or that may be some more deliberate jostling by the Galactics or their clients. If we find anything threatening on the other side of Abyss, we will push back . . . hard. Sirius is too close—right on our cosmological doorstep, in fact—for us to just smile and bow out."

"Is that NavDep talking? Or you?"

He grinned. "A little of both. Senator Martin has quite a following in D.C., and even more so in Geneva, Moskva, and the others.

His Star Union Party is quite powerful. Overall, the Pentopoly is favoring a nonmilitary resolution to this thing. And they *do* have some good arguments about not getting into a brawl with people a billion years ahead of us."

"And what do you think?"

"I think we watch ourselves, but that doesn't mean we roll over and play dead. We could fight if we had to."

"Good God, how?"

"Asymmetrical warfare has been around for a long time now. There are ways a David can take out a Goliath."

"Ha. Not when David has a sling, and Goliath has full body armor and a tactical nuke."

"Never underestimate the Ewoks."

"E—what?" She couldn't remember that word, but it did seem familiar. She did a quick search of her coronal memory archive, looking for the reference.

Ah . . . there it was—a bit from an old fantasy vid popular back when she'd been a kid. A primitive tribe of fuzzy teddy bears beating an army of well-armed and -armored troops using nothing but rocks, clubs, and spears . . . what nonsense! Hell, why had she even saved that memory?

She told Pixie to flag it for later discard.

"Okay, got it," she told Koehler. "One question. Are you nuts? Sir?"

Koehler looked surprised. "You think we should surrender?"

"Hell, no! I just think Ewoks are silly."

He chuckled. "Maybe they are. But the idea of taking on high-tech troops using innovative tactics is not silly and is not new. The important thing to remember is that even the underdog can win if he avoids a stand-up slugfest . . . *and* if the big guy loses his political will."

"If we get into a brawl with the Galactics—the Big Bads at the top, I mean, not the proxies—our problem will be getting them to realize we've even hit them in the first place. I'm thinking mosquito against one of those extinct giant land animals ... what were they called?"

"Dinosaurs?"

"I was thinking elephants, but yeah. Same idea."

"If the Galactics have taken up permanent residence at Sirius," Koehler said, "we will stand up to them. We really have no other choice."

An alert chimed. "Admiral Koehler?" a voice said. "*Constellation* is coming up on-screen."

And so she was ...

The screens in the shuttle's cabin showing the view forward were centered on a massive, shrouded shape emerging now from darkness.

"There she is," Koehler said. "So damned ugly she's positively distinguished looking."

"Hey, that's *my* baby you're talking about, Admiral."

Over a kilometer long and the color of night, UTS *Constellation* had never been exposed to the concept of streamlining, for she was a creature of deep space, not planetary atmospheres. As a ship type, *Dauntless*-class dreadnaughts were blocky, bulky, and angular, replete with sponsons, nacelles, spikes, turrets, and outriggers. Her outer armor lay like curved and thrusting daggers from amidships to her blunt prow, with internal structures, ports, conduits, and massed lateral batteries visible behind the blades. She was moored to a far larger structure behind her, Fleet Orbital Glenn; a flight of Stiletto fighters emerging from the giant's shadow provided a sense of scale: minute, glittering star points all but lost against a wall of light and dark. Each massing 2.8 megatons and with crews of nearly forty-four hundred, there were exactly six dreadnaughts in the North American contingent of the Terran Grand Fleet: *Dauntless, Endeavor, Ranger, Hornet, Saratoga,* and *Constellation.* The fact that Alexandra Morrigan was the captain of one of those monsters made that command the apex of her career.

And maybe that was a large part of why she was so ready now to retire from life. How in hell could she possibly top *this*?

Or could it simply be that she feared the fall if she somehow slipped way up at the top?

"I think she's beautiful," she murmured, more to herself than to her admiral.

She'd taken command of the *Connie* just a week ago, transferring to her bridge from the aging fleet battler *Olympus*. Koehler had nominated her for the post of fleet captain, the CO of the admiral's flagship . . . and hadn't *that* fired up the scuttlebutt about "the admiral's woman."

She was old enough that gossip and scandal didn't bother her much, if at all, but the implication that she'd slept her way to command still angered her. Sure, she'd had help along the way—*patronage*. What senior naval officer had not? Somehow, though, after centuries of enhanced social awareness, the upper echelons of military command still carried the distinct leathery taint of an old boys' club.

Not that women were actively discriminated against, oh, no, of *course* not . . . not in *this* enlightened day and age. Yet the fact remained that a sizable majority of senior command personnel and staff, at Fleet HQ, within the Navy Department, and throughout the Terran Pentopoly that governed Earth, were males—most of them born, like Morrigan, in the twenty-first century. And if an amortal held power . . . why, conceivably, would he ever relinquish that power?

If there was a problem with the current government, it was the fact that few among those in charge were willing to step aside in favor of younger blood or younger ideas.

Well, *she* was going to step aside. But first she would show the gossips that Alexandra Morrigan wasn't *anybody's* woman save her own.

Constellation slowly grew to fill the forward screens. The shuttle's destination was Bay 12, just aft of and below the bridge. Golden light spilled into space as the shuttle grew near, the lock gaping wide to receive it.

By the ancient tenants of maritime law—last on, first off—

Admiral Koehler was first down the shuttle's boarding ramp and onto the *Constellation*'s deck, while Morrigan was just behind him. Two ranks of ship's Marines snapped to attention with a thunderous clash of battle armor. Commander Vincent Neal, *Connie*'s executive officer, snapped to attention in front of Koehler and rendered a crisp salute. "Welcome aboard, Admiral."

"Thank you, Vince." Koehler's return salute was less formally precise. "Good to be back."

"And Captain Morrigan, welcome aboard. The ship is yours."

"Thank you, Commander. Ship's status?"

"The ship is ready in all regards for embarkation, ma'am. Watering complete, stores on board, weapons and ship's systems all green. We are currently on administrative hold awaiting the return of 312 personnel still out on liberty. We're also due to receive one more Stryker squadron on board—the Nightwings."

"Very well."

"Preflight at fifteen hundred hours, people," Koehler put in. "Command staff and senior ship officers, Briefing CIC."

The routine was old and relentlessly predictable.

Morrigan wondered if Koehler really intended to confront the Galactics at Sirius.

And, more, if the strike force's actions were about to trigger an all-out interstellar war. A war, she thought, that would be all but impossible for Humankind to win.

Or survive.

LIEUTENANT IOHN DAMIAN was not wearing his corona. Running around without one was frowned upon in polite society, of course, but he reasoned that there was no actual *law* against the practice.

He was in a watering hole called the Interstellar, located just inside the main gate of Port Diego and popular with Navy officers. At the moment, he was planning his strategy; his acquired target was a gorgeous girl seated at the bar to his left.

"So, babe . . ." he said. "How would you like me to take you to the stars?"

The woman gave him a cool and decidedly unimpressed look. She wasn't typical of the other women in this joint: conservative clothing, no skin animations, and an expression more bored than sexy. Damian took this as a challenge.

"Don't tell me," she said. "Fighter jock, right?"

"Right the first time, sweetheart. I drive SF-112 Strykers for a living and I'm *very* good at what I do."

Her eyes—deep gold—grew large, and she fluttered ten-millimeter lashes at him. "Ooh. Is that some kind of starship?"

"Only the fastest, most powerful, sexiest, most intelligent space-fighter out there, baby. Just like her pilot!"

"Uh-huh. Where's your corona, hotshot?"

"My . . . what?"

"Corona, genius." She tapped her own corona, a standard-issue military model: sleek, black, and no-nonsense. "Your transtim module. You know . . . 'transcranial direct-current stimulator'? Lets you access smartthings and BrainNets? Lets you ID people in your Net? Lets you open doors or buy a cuppa caff? Maybe even lets you function as a somewhat interactive member of the human species?"

"Oh, sure. Lets me jack into my fighter, right. But I don't wear the things off duty, see?"

"Why not? You *are* military, right?"

"Sure, but I don't like the brass always watching, y'know? Tracking me? Putting everything I do in a data file someplace? Cramps my style, baby."

"Ah . . . so you're a Rejector?"

"Nah. Those guys are crazy. I just like my privacy, know what I mean?"

"So what's your unit, flyboy?"

"VFA-84 Nightwings. Best of the best of the freakin' *best*!"

"No shit? Well . . . I'll tell you what, troglodyte. If you were wearing your corona like you're supposed to, you'd have read my ID."

"Wait . . . trog—what?"

"Troglodyte. A knuckle-dragging anthropoid with an acute case of testosterone poisoning."

"Hey!"

"If you'd seen fit to wear your government-issued corona, you would know that I am Lieutenant Commander Donna Esposito and that I'm squadron CO of VFA-84, and *that* makes me your CO. You tracking?"

Damian sagged inside. *Oh . . . shit!*

"Uh . . . yeah. Yes, ma'am. Tracking, ma'am."

"Good. I suggest you get your ass back to base and get ready for launch. We're due back on board ship tomorrow by eleven hundred hours, and I do *not* want any of my people hungover."

"Yes, ma'am. Aye, aye, ma'am."

She actually smiled at him. "Good troggie. See you at preflight muster." She swiped her hand over the payment pad on the bar to settle her tab, slid off the chair, and walked off without a backward look.

Damian drew a deep breath. He was a newly minted fighter pilot, fresh out of school, and had reported in at VFA-84's Port Diego barracks only that morning. Maybe, he thought, he should have looked up his new CO before hitting the Diego bars.

Jeez, what a royal bitch . . .

A young woman sat down on the stool to his right, flashing him a bright smile as she settled in. She appeared to be wearing nothing but a swirling mass of animated tattoos. The chances that she was in his chain of command seemed comfortably small.

"So, babe . . ." he said. "How would you like me to take you to the stars?"

IN THE SMALL head tucked away in her quarters, Morrigan stepped from the shower stall and padded naked across the tiled deck to the vanity. Her viewself activated as she stepped close, projecting not a mirror image but a true one. A gesture of her hand rotated the image before her, allowing her to see herself from all angles, and she sighed.

She didn't much care for what she saw.

Alexandra Morrigan was not vain about her appearance and especially not about her age. By this time, almost four centuries from her birth and well on in her eighth lifetime, she was used to the plodding cycle of youth, followed by maturity, followed by the increasingly constraining limits of advancing age. With a truage of 398, her appage now was closer to seventy, and she looked it. Normally she paid scant attention to apparent age, and she was willing to concede that spreading webs of wrinkles around eyes and mouth, sagging breasts and gluteals, and thinning white hair all contributed to that image that society at large was still pleased to call "mature," "experienced," even "handsome."

But handsome or not, damn it, she *hurt*. She ached, especially in her knees and hips—possibly incipient arthritis arising from decades of accumulated wear and tear on her joints. Modern nanomedicine worked wonders to keep age at bay, to relieve pain, even to lift sagging spirits, but inevitably life became an unending grind of minor health problems and discomforts and inconveniences. Sometime in the past decade or so, she'd begun losing her flexibility—again. She could no longer drop cross-legged to the floor; she had trouble reaching things high above her head and was once again beginning to lose her hearing in the higher frequencies. Worse, more and more she was losing her ability to take long, swift-striding rambles in the forested hills back home, and *that* was genuinely distressing.

"You look," Dek said behind her, "quite striking, Alex."

"Bullshit, Dek. I'm old."

"There are things you can do about that."

Yes, there were. ENS adjustments would have extended the

appearance of youth, of course, even maintained her flexibility and energy, but for the past couple of decades she simply hadn't had the time . . . or the interest. Sitting in a command chair or at a desk just didn't cut it when it came to decent exercise.

When she didn't answer, Dek added, "I had in mind full rejuvenation. The naval service does offer them, you know."

A full ENS rejuve would take a week out of her schedule, but it would reset the clock. She *could* be young again . . .

"Fuck *that*," she told the robot. She sighed. "Getting old sucks, you know? But amortality sucks worse. I've done the rejuve thing before, remember? *Seven times.*"

"That, I would suppose, is something you'll have to decide for yourself. Uniform of the day?"

"Standard blacks, with ribbons." She would be meeting some of the squadron's ship captains at the briefing this afternoon, so utilities were out. There was no need for ceremonial full dress, not by a long shot, but a display of decorations would be expected in a meeting like this.

Dek handed her a dark garment pad, and she pressed it against her chest to activate it, feeling the nanomatrix spreading out over her skin, circling her throat, and rippling down her arms and body. Each different polity of the Pentopoly had its own military colors—scarlet and gold for Beijing, light blue and white for Geneva, gray and red for Moskva, green and yellow for Buenos Aires. D.C. had adopted black trimmed with gold. The pad had already been programmed with her service ribbons and decorations, brightly colored rectangles covering her left breast, and even that represented only her most prestigious decorations while leaving out her campaign ribbons. She'd been in military service for a *long* time.

"If I may say so, Alex," Dek told her, "you have much to be proud of, beginning with a most distinguished career."

"All good things come to an end eventually, Dek," she told the robot. She checked her corona for the time. "I'd better get going.

You can straighten up in here, then stand down. I won't be needing you."

"As you wish, Captain."

MACHINIST'S MATE (QUANTUM) Chief Todd Kranhouse grinned at the Marine seated to his right. "What I could never figure," he said, "was what jarheads are good for in hard vacuum."

Marine Gunnery Sergeant Philip Garner gave the sailor a dark glare. "Well, for starters, snipe, we're there on board to make sure enlisted pukes like you don't get out of line, right?"

"Yeah? And who keeps the jarheads in line?"

"Bigger, *badder* jarheads . . . like me."

The two men were on board the liberty shuttle coming up from Port Diego. It had been a pretty good liberty, Kranhouse thought. *Man, oh, man, that girl yesterday in Ensenada . . .*

Despite the verbal sparring, Kranhouse and Garner were old, if unlikely, friends. Hell, Garner had saved Kranhouse's ass in a barroom dust-up on Fleet Orbital Glenn a couple of years ago *and* kept him from getting picked up by the SPs afterward. The tradition of Marines versus Navy was an ancient and venerable one, a rivalry extending no doubt all the way back to the Marine soldiers and oarsmen manning Assyrian biremes during the reign of Sennacherib. In Kranhouse's opinion, though, there *were* some good Marines. A few.

"It just seems to me that Marines are a—whatchacallit—an anachronism today. Whatcha gonna do . . . board and storm the Galactic flagship?"

"If we have to. Besides, Marines are supposed to hold the high ground," Garner said. "Right? You can't get no higher than space."

"Yeah, but in space no one can hear you yell '*Ooh-rah!*'"

"Ooh," Garner replied in a flat voice, "fucking rah."

"Don't tease the Marines, Todd," HM1 Jason Slater said with a chuckle. He was strapped in on Kranhouse's left. "They bite."

"Doc's right, snipe," Garner said. "Reach in a hand, pull back a stump."

Kranhouse held up his hand, extended the middle finger, and waggled it. "Feels okay to me."

"Hey," Slater said, nudging him in the arm. "There's home."

A single display on the shuttle's forward bulkhead showed the eight-kilometer-wide disk that was Glenn Orbital, with *Constellation* tucked in close alongside. Beyond, Kranhouse could see other ships of the Third Fleet's Dreadnaught Strike Force Eight— *Endymion, Erebus, Invincible,* and a dozen others. The *Constellation* battle group currently numbered sixteen *c*-shooters, including three escort carriers, as well as sixty Starscouts and some four hundred fighters, with human personnel numbering just under twenty thousand.

Command of *that* mob, Kranhouse thought, must be a nightmare. He did not envy Rear Admiral Jaime Koehler in the least.

"FLAG CAPTAIN" WAS an ancient naval term, a position rather than an actual rank going back at least to the eighteenth century. Falling in and out of favor over the centuries, the designation today was largely ceremonial; flag captains and fleet captains were the commanders of flagships, vessels with an admiral—a flag officer—on board leading a fleet.

Rear Admiral Koehler's flag was now displayed on a bulkhead monitor in Briefing CIC, a large conference room aft of *Constellation*'s Combat Information Center. Though ships of war no longer flew flags from masts or flagstaffs, Koehler had "broken" his flag— displaying it electronically—as soon as he'd stepped on board.

Which meant that he now was very much in charge.

And as his flag captain, Morrigan was not only skipper of the *Constellation,* but served as senior aide and general factotum over-seeing all fleet operations.

The other ship captains were gathered in Briefing CIC already, some present physically, most as holographic projections. With the fleet getting ready to embark, a majority of the other COs had elected to attend virtually.

"Ladies, gentlemen," Koehler said to formally begin the meeting, "thank you for being here. I know you're all busy preparing for boost, so I'll keep this short. First of all, SecNav and the Washington AINet have officially given us clearance to go through the Abyss Gate to check up on Sirius Station and to explore the other gates in the system."

"About damned time, Admiral," Captain Knutson of the *Theseus* growled.

"Your general orders have been uploaded to your ship AIs, but I want to take this opportunity to stress that this is a diplomatic tour . . . a showing of the flag. This is intended as a peace mission. We want to show the Galactics that they can trust us loose in the Galaxy."

"Damned patronizing Glits," someone groused out loud.

"Belay that," Koehler said. "Now, many of you already know my new flag captain, Alexandra Morrigan. I expect all of you to give her the same support and loyalty you've given me.

"And as long as we're doing introductions . . . Li? If you please?"

Behind Koehler, something glittered. The glitter thickened, sparkled, then coalesced out of empty air, forming a silently drifting sphere obviously derived from the same technology that Morrigan had seen last night with One. It was smaller—the size of a man's head—and had fewer ruby-lensed eyes, but it clearly was a representative of the Galactics.

There was immediate murmuring from those present, some of the louder mutterings decidedly angry.

Koehler gestured toward the floating silver ball. "May I present Li, our liaison with the Galactics. By will be our guide and our translator for our probe into the Sirius system today."

"I protest, Admiral!" the image of Captain Aric Bradshaw, of the *Heraclean,* said. "Why do we need one of *them*?"

Captain Arnold slammed his palm against the tabletop. "That's *right,* sir! How do we trust the fucking Glits after Delta Pavonis?"

"As you were!" Koehler snapped. "Quiet, all of you! Captain Bradshaw! Can you speak Kapik?"

"No, sir."

"Digital Trel?"

"Of course not. Sir."

"Captain Arnold? Once we get over there, what are the destinations of each of the five Sirius gates?"

"Well, we know Abyss connects back to Sol, sir."

"And the others?"

"I have no idea, Admiral. No human does."

"Li has been deep-vetted by AI Liskov, AI Von Neumann, and AI Eich. You care to try second-guessing *them*?"

"*No*, sir."

Liskov, Von Neumann, and Eich were three of the transapient AI networks running the Terran Defense Agency. Named for important contributors to the revolution in machine intelligence, they were self-aware, superhumanly intelligent, and *very* thorough. As a lieutenant commander, Morrigan had worked for Liskov, named for the computer scientist Barbara Liskov, for several years in D.C. and had a deep respect for em. If AI Liskov had checked something out, Morrigan was more than comfortable with eir judgment.

She wondered if the ship captains would be as well.

"Li was created politically neutral," Koehler went on. "Ey possesses data that we will need beyond the Abyss Gate, both for communicating with other Galactic agents and for fleet navigation. There is risk, certainly, but SecNav, the Joint Chiefs, and the D.C. AI all feel there is far greater risk in attempting to navigate the ring gates blind. For your information, Li has agreed to remain here in Briefing CIC for the duration of this mission." He swept a cool gaze across the assembled naval officers, both those physically present and those present virtually. "Any of you who can't live with this are free to step down in favor of your exec or another qualified officer." He waited a beat. "Anyone?"

"Hell, *Ranger*'s good to go, Admiral," Captain Tracy McGowan said. An old friend, she caught Morrigan's eye and winked.

One by one, the other officers agreed, some reluctantly. The holo image of Commander Holt, the new skipper of *Invincible,* had a disturbingly eager expression, as if he was excited about the prospect of tangling with the Galactics. Captain Matthew Arnold, of the escort carrier *Cataphract,* looked grim, his fists clenched on the table before him.

"Li?" Koehler said, glancing at the hovering sphere. "Would you care to add anything?"

"Given current tensions between your civilization and mine, I do perfectly understand the reluctance some of you may have to work with me." The voice, Morrigan thought, was identical to that of One last night. "All I can tell you is that your own transapient Minds analyzed my AI systems and programming completely, searching specifically for any indication of duplicity, dissimulation, or deceit. I assure you that I would not be here now if they had found me to be untrustworthy."

"And that, people," Koehler said, "is good enough for me! Li has also uploaded all of eir navigational data to the *Constellation*'s computer network and *only* to that network. If the data is corrupt or hides some sort of Trojan horse, only the *Connie* will be affected."

"Trust," Li added, "must start somewhere. Only by working with agents of the Galactic Authority such as myself will your people learn that you have nothing to fear from us and everything to gain through cooperation. Consider this opportunity as a test Joining, a chance to get to know us better, and we, you."

In the end, all the fleet's captains agreed to the guide's presence on board the flagship, and Koehler transmitted oplan contingencies to the entire fleet. That list included, insofar as was possible, every conceivable threat or maneuver that Koehler's staff and the fleet's AIs could anticipate, together with detailed responses to those threats. Long gone were the days when a combat fleet could engage in combat under the signal "England expects that every man will do his duty," the flag message sent by Admiral Lord Nelson to his fleet at Trafalgar. Space combat could evolve far faster than humans could process, and complex plans of fire and maneuver, *oplans,* had to be worked out ahead of time.

Morrigan couldn't help wondering if Li was aware of these battle plans, though, and if ey was capable of betraying the human fleet if things went south.

She had to remind herself that no less a Mind than AI Liskov had investigated the Galactic liaison.

That would have to be enough.

Embarkation was scheduled for 1330 the following day, and there was a hell of a lot to do before then.

CHAPTER THREE

LIEUTENANT IOHN DAMIAN came wide awake in a strange bed. He still didn't have his corona, so he had no idea what time it was, but he had the feeling that he'd badly, *badly* overslept.

The girl with the animated tattoos was asleep next to him, though she'd turned the art show off last night to prove she wasn't wearing anything underneath. Damian sat up, and the girl stirred. What the hell was her name? Ella? Ellie? Something like that.

"Ionnie?" she said, her voice muzzy with sleep. "What is it?"

"What time is it, babe?" he asked her.

For answer, she fumbled open a compartment in her bedside table, withdrawing a slender semicircle tiara and slipping it on. "Mmf. Nine fifteen. Why?"

Damian dropped back flat on the bed. "Fuck!"

"What's the matter, sweetie?"

"I was supposed to check in on base by oh-eight-hundred."

"Well, just tell them you're running late, is all ..."

Damian groaned. Normally, overstaying liberty was good for a slap on the wrist and a stern lecture from your CO, but to be late today of *all* days ...

The Nightwings had been scheduled to lift from Port Diego at 0900 hours—fifteen minutes ago. They were due to join UTS *Constellation* at Glenn Orbital forty minutes later. Scuttlebutt had it that *Connie*'s battle group was boosting for out-system that afternoon.

Which meant, Damian thought, that he was in one hell of a world of shit.

"CAPTAIN ON THE bridge!"

"Carry on," Morrigan said, stepping through the bridge entryway and walking toward her seat. *Constellation*'s command bridge, located forward and a deck above CIC and the flag bridge, was dark and a bit claustrophobic, with the eerie glow of a hundred monitors and holodisplay screens providing a blue-white and shadow-edged Illimination. Twenty-three men and women sat at the various command stations, monitoring *Constellation*'s life.

Commander Neal, the ship's XO, rose from the command chair. "The ship is yours, Captain."

Morrigan slid into her seat. "Thank you, Mr. Neal. How do we stand?"

"Ready in all respects for departure, ma'am. Awaiting final clearance."

"Very well. Maintain station."

"Aye, ma'am."

She used her coronal to engage the flag bridge screen, bringing up Koehler's image. He was engaged in conversation with one of his aides, Commander Greer, and she waited until he was finished.

"Admiral? Awaiting your command."

"Flag has precedence, Captain. At your discretion."

"Very well, sir." She looked at Neal. "Bridge status."

"Bridge secure, Captain. Ready for boost."

"Engineering."

"Engineering ready in all respects, Captain."

One by one, the various ship departments reported in, a cascade of voices filtering through Morrigan's corona.

"Power feeds," she called.

"Up and running, Skipper," MMC(Q) Kranhouse replied. "Performance nominal."

"Chief Boatswain, deck."

"Working parties on-station, Captain," Chief Boatswain McElroy reported. "Avatars and robotic analogs report all decks clear and secure."

"Mr. Lewis, you may switch to internal gravity."

"Internal gravity, aye, aye, Captain," the ship's systems officer replied.

Morrigan felt the faint, familiar lurch in her stomach as *Constellation*'s artificial gravity field switched on, replacing Glenn Orbital's field. Her weight fluctuated, then steadied.

"We are on internal gravity, Captain. Zero-point-eight-five g."

"Thank you, Mr. Lewis. Wing status, DAG."

"All secure, Captain," *Connie*'s Dreadnaught Attack Group commander, Captain Arthur Ballinger, reported. "Ready for embarkation."

"Did the Nightwings make it on board okay?"

"They're short two, but the rest are aboard and locked down."

"Running lights."

"On."

"Fleetlink."

"Engaged."

"Comm, report ship's readiness for departure to tower and request final clearance."

"SRD transmitted, ma'am, and we have final clearance. At our discretion."

"Very well. Helm . . . you may commence decouple."

"Aye, aye, Captain."

A distant thump transmitted itself through the ship's hull as electrical conduits connecting *Constellation* to Glenn Orbital pulled free from her port side. "Decouple complete."

"Lookouts, final check, local traffic."

"We are clear of local traffic, Captain," Neal told her. "Free to embark."

"Deck, release magraps."

"Magnetic grapples released, ma'am," McElroy told her. "We are free for space."

"Back us out, Helm. Astern slow."

"Astern slow, Captain, aye, aye."

And *Constellation*'s 1,240-meter bulk, massing a ponderous 2.8 million tons, drifted clear of her berth on Glenn Orbital Naval Station. On her main screen, displaying a feed from a camera turret on the station, Morrigan could see the *Connie* slowly emerge from Glenn's shadow into brilliant white sunlight, running lights winking with a steady beat.

"Nicely done, Captain," Koehler said from her display.

"Thank you, sir." She listened for a moment to the chatter coming over her coronal from dozens of different shipboard departments and stations, reports of gravity, of power levels, of shield strength, of hull integrity—a reassuring litany of ship and crew performance.

All nominal, all green.

"Engage shielding."

"Shielding engaged, Captain."

"Helm, bring us to Waypoint One and hold."

"Aye, Captain. Waypoint One and hold."

On the display screens, stars, Earth, and Glenn Orbital swung to the left as *Constellation* rotated, though there was no sensation of movement. Morrigan could feel rather than hear a slight rumbling from somewhere aft as the ship's gravitic drives engaged . . . then switched off almost at once as they reached the fleet assembly point.

And for the next thirty minutes, *Constellation* hung there in orbit fifty kilometers clear of Glenn Orbital as, one by one, the other ships of the flotilla detached from the naval yard and joined her. On her forward screens, the stars drifted slowly past until the ship was pointed at a rather sparsely populated section of the sky within the constellation of Cetus and anchored there, aiming roughly between the faint stars Pi and Omega Ceti.

The litany of readiness reports continued as the other vessels linked in with the flagship. Fleetlink, essentially the nervous system of the AI entity known as Argus, was a sophisticated AI network allowing all the vessels to share data, in effect turning them into a single unit. Individual captains still controlled their ships and could override flag commands when necessary, but for all intents and purposes, *Constellation* now was a single ship with sixteen extensions, all of them commanded from *Connie*'s flag bridge, which, in turn, delegated that command to . . .

. . . her.

The fleet was already aligned on that distant and invisible objective.

"Navigation check, Ms. Bohm."

"Flight path computed and locked in," Commander Karen Bohm, the ship's navigation officer, reported. "Right ascension two hours, thirty-five minutes, four-point-forty-four seconds. Declination minus fourteen degrees, zero-eight minutes, fourteen-point-one-two seconds."

"Admiral, the fleet is ready in all respects for near-*c*, at your command."

Take us out, Captain Morrigan, Koehler's voice said inside her head, speaking through her corona. *Best velocity to Abyss Gate.*

"Best velocity, Abyss Gate, aye, aye, sir. Helm . . . run program."

And as one, the fleet accelerated.

"YOU FUCKING POOR excuse for a pilot! You fucking poor excuse for a *human being*! What the hell did you think you were doing?"

Lieutenant Damian stood at rigid attention as his CO, Lieutenant Commander Donna Esposito, screamed into his face with a skill that made him think she'd served once as a DI in Marine boot camp. He sincerely doubted that Esposito was interested in what he'd actually been doing last night or in what he'd thought about it at the time.

"No excuse, ma'am!" It was the universally accepted best answer to any question in situations like this.

They were in Esposito's office at the Port Diego Naval Aerospace Station in La Mesa. He'd returned to base as soon as he'd been able after waking up in Elli's bed.

Yeah, Elli. *That* was her name. She hadn't been happy at the way he'd bolted out of bed that morning, grabbed his clothes, and rushed off. Not happy at *all*.

Too bad. She'd been *fantastic* entertainment. Maybe, he thought with a grim resignation, she'd see him again once he got out of the brig—in another eight or ten years, maybe.

"So not only did you rob the squadron of your *inestimable* presence this morning at boost...you robbed it of *my* presence as well!"

"Ma'am, you didn't have to—"

"*Shut the fuck up, shithole!* For your information, I look after my people, even sorry-assed fuckups like you!"

Damian had managed to retrieve his corona before the SPs had picked him up and taken him in for this . . . interview. He checked the time, did a fast calculation, and figured the battle group had boosted perhaps an hour ago.

Esposito was just getting warmed up. "You are so low—*so low* that *whale shit* looks like *shooting stars* to you! Thanks to you, the squadron checked in on board the *Constellation* two short. I'm going to have some explaining to do to the DAG when they get back, but believe you me, I'm gonna take it out of your worthless hide first!"

Damian used his corona again. The battle group would be headed for Abyss . . . a four-day boost, objective. Stryker fighters could make a flight like that, in theory, but it was damned hard on the pilots. *Subjective* time, thanks to relativistic time dilation, might amount to only minutes or hours, but the chances of hitting a sand-grain-sized speck of matter along the way made it a deadly crapshoot. Regulations frowned on that.

Which meant that both he and Esposito were stuck here until the battle group returned.

"Yes, ma'am."

"You are on report, mister. *And* you are confined to the BOQ! You can explain yourself to the DAG at captain's mast when the battle group gets back."

Confined to base.

That solved the problem of what to tell Elli, at least.

"SIR?" ENGINEMAN THIRD Kevin O'Reilly asked his department head. "How long is this trip gonna take? I been hearing different things, y'know?"

They were seated side by side in the main power control, surrounded by the monitors and touchscreens watching over *Constellation*'s bank upon bank of quantum converters.

"Don't call me 'sir,' boy," Kranhouse growled. He tapped at his control screen with one finger, coaxing a half percent's worth of additional performance from number three. "I *work* for a living."

"Yes, sir... uh... I mean... sure, Chief."

"To answer your question, Abyss is about 620 AUs out from Earth right now, way, way out in the Kuiper Belt. That's 620 times the distance between Earth and the sun, okay? Works out to about ninety light-hours. Eighty-five-point-seven, to be exact. Do the math."

O'Reilly's face screwed up into an uncomfortable expression as he pulled the data from his corona's coprocessor. "Uh... three-point-six days?"

"*Light*-days, son. We're talking distance, not time. At point-nine-five c, it'll take us three days, eighteen hours, fourteen minutes, and some seconds." He grinned. "Except, of course, it won't."

"Huh? What do you mean, Chief?"

"Time dilation is what. Time—*subjective* time, that is—slows down the closer you get to the speed of light. So far as the rest of the universe is concerned, the trip'll take us a bit less than four days, right? But for us the whole trip'll only be twenty-eight hours and something... a little over *one* day. See? It *pays* to hurry."

"Yeah. I just hope the brass knows what they're doin' once we get there."

Kranhouse made another fractional adjustment on the power controls, drawing raw energy from the depths of vacuum itself.

"You and me both, kid. You and me both."

THREE HOURS OBJECTIVE to go, which, thanks to Einstein, would be just fifty-six minutes subjective. Morrigan sat back in her chair and watched the bow shock coruscations spark and flicker across the view forward, a display physicists called the "Baltis effect." At *Constellation*'s current velocity, individual atoms, molecules, and rare bits of dust smaller than a grain of sand impacted across the ship's protective shielding at a relative velocity of nearly 95 percent of the speed of light, a hypervelocity rain of matter liberating enormous energy with each strike, much of it in the UV and X-ray range, as well as visible light. The effects of time dilation compressed the experience of those strikes, creating a continual display of fireworks that nearly blotted out the relativistically distorted ring of starlight ahead. With all sensory input obscured, navigation at these speeds was strictly punch 'n' pray—as in punch in the data and pray that it's right. If the flight had not been perfectly calculated and entered at the beginning, they wouldn't know they were off until they dropped to subrelativistic velocities.

Assuming that an error in the calculations didn't result in them hurtling into the objective at near-*c*. If that happened, they would never know.

That outcome, Morrigan thought, was unlikely in the extreme. Abyss was only 120 kilometers across. At a distance of 620 AU, the chances of hitting it blind were less than those of firing a laser rifle in Boston and hitting a fly on a wall in Port Diego.

Commander Vincent Neal was seated at his command station to Morrigan's right, the two of them sharing the single main display forward. They'd been chatting off and on, passing the hours until their arrival at Abyss and watching the flash and sparkle of the coruscations. It had been a boring flight so far, and in Morrigan's opinion boring flights were *good*.

"So," Neal said, "I gather you've been to Sirius before. What's it like?"

"Bright," she told him. "Very . . . bright."

She'd been through the Abyss Gate to Sirius just once, in 2296—gods, had it really been over a century and a half ago? That had been during her first Navy career. She'd been a newly commissioned lieutenant on board UTS *Fury*, her very first ship.

"But there's some kind of fortress on the other side, right? Quarantine?"

"That's what they call it. I don't know if it's a fortress, exactly. It may just be a very large sign." She held up her hands, framing an imaginary rectangle. "'Humans: Keep Out.'"

The dwarf planet called Quarantine had been there on the Sirian side of Abyss at least since its discovery by the Whitehead Expedition of 2091. It continually broadcast a message in twenty-five different languages on as many frequencies, warning any visiting spacecraft that organic life-forms were forbidden from entering any of the four other ring gates in the Sirius system, but that machine intelligences were permitted under proper supervision. Since the first exploratory probe through Abyss into the Sirian system 357 years ago, dozens of automated ships of ever-increasing sophistication had gone through those other gates, as had six human-crewed expeditions.

None had returned.

Galactic representatives had metaphorically shrugged off the disappearances and blamed human inadequacies and design flaws in the technology. Humans, they said, did not, *could* not, understand the complexities of the ring gate travel network throughout the Galaxy. Perhaps in another few centuries after Humankind had experienced the Second Singularity . . .

"I think that's the part that really gets me," Neal told her. "The assumption that organic life-forms like us are second-class citizens, y'know?"

"You think the Galactics are all machines? AIs?"

He shrugged. "Kind of stands to reason." He tapped his corona with his forefinger. "We humans are certainly headed that way."

"And our AI isn't quite up to Galactic standards, I know. Of course, we *did* experience the Singularity . . ."

"The Sing-hilarity, you mean. Or maybe it was the Fizzlelarity?"

The so-called Technological Singularity, widely predicted since the late twentieth century, had occurred, in theory at least, in the year 2052—just two years after Morrigan had been born—when an IBM-Intel artificial intelligence called Blue Star had demonstrated a general intelligence well above that of any human. Rather than the expected explosion of human technology and upward progress in an asymptotic curve, however, life and ongoing technological advances had continued, same as always: lots of incremental changes in life and in society, but no single burst of change. Some speculated that future technological evolution would actually involve a nested series of singularities and that, in the words of Apple-Samsung's CEO, "folks, we ain't seen nothin' yet."

The Singularity, however—originally the single change that would render Humankind unrecognizable to earlier generations—had become a historical curiosity and something of a joke.

"Call it what you like," Morrigan said. "Since Blue Star, though, our AIs have been evolving right through the ceiling. I don't know what the hell the Galactics expect of them. Or us."

"Oh . . . another Singularity, maybe. A *real* one this time."

"It's kind of depressing, though," she added. "You'd think that the all-powerful, all-knowing gods of the Galaxy would have evolved past discrimination and social stratification."

"Of lowlifes like us benighted humans, you mean?"

She hesitated in answering, not sure she knew Neal well enough to answer. Morrigan herself felt the stifling effects of that stratification on Earth—the Illiminati, the oligarchy of amortals. But how did Neal feel about it? Would her admitting what she felt to him make her tenure on board the *Constellation* even more difficult than it already was?

"So . . . are you an amortal?" she asked.

"Talk about changing the subject . . ."

"I'm not. Amortals are why we're divided back home, right? Well, that and the fact that only the über-rich can afford amortality in the first place. Haves and have-nots. Which are you?"

He chuckled. "Oh, have-not, definitely. I'm just a poor, simple country boy from Stafford, Oklahoma. Joined the Navy to get the hell off-planet and out among the stars. I couldn't afford ENS if you put a gun to my head."

"You could get it from the Navy. Lots of people do." She glanced over at him, but his age wasn't being displayed for her corona. "How old are you, anyway?"

"Ma'am, I stand before you at the ripe old age of thirty-eight. How about you?"

"Now, Commander, you know it's not proper to ask a lady her age."

"Eh. Age is just a number. At least that's what they say."

"How about the number 398?"

He looked her up and down. "That's quite a number. You don't look it."

"Thank you."

"Does that mean *you're* superrich?"

"*Another* question never to ask a lady. But no. I've worked for a living my whole life. Lives, I should say."

"Then how—"

"My mother," she said with a sigh, "*was* rich. She also, well, she had a thing about growing old. Hated the idea so much she set up trust funds for both of us, specifying that they be used for ENS, hers and mine. She sank pretty much everything she had into those trusts, it was so expensive. But ENS had *just* been developed, and we were two of the first. My first life extension worked. Hers didn't."

"God, what happened?"

"I was fifty-six. She was seventy-five. Nanomedicine wasn't as good at turning back the clock back then."

"I'm sorry . . ."

"You know, I can't even remember her face now. Too many edit sessions." A shrug. "To tell you the truth, I'd have rather had the money."

"Well, I'm glad you're still around." He grinned. "I wouldn't have been able to meet you otherwise."

She smiled at his awkwardness. "It's been an adventure."

He gave her a sharp look. "'It *has* been'? You sound like you don't plan to keep going."

"Everyone dies," she said. "Eventually. Even amortals."

She wasn't about to tell him anything more.

The last handful of subjective minutes trickled past, a chime sounded, and *Constellation*'s AI cut their near-*c* velocity to almost nothing. There was no feeling of deceleration at all. The ship's gravitic drive acted on every atom within its grasp simultaneously, so there was no sense of either acceleration or deceleration. The crew experienced only the ship's own artificially generated gravity—a good thing, since they otherwise would have been reduced to thin red smears across the bulkheads.

The fireworks ceased. Spread now across the forward display was a starfield unchanged from that visible from within the inner solar system: the misty silver clots of the Milky Way; the constellations of Orion and Taurus, of Pegasus and Andromeda; the star Sirius a brilliant blue-white beacon off beyond Orion's heel. The ship's AI put a set of brackets on the screen, enclosing a tiny ring edged in cold starlight.

Abyss.

At this range the structure was quite difficult to see.

"No wonder it took twenty-first century astronomers so long to spot it!" Neal exclaimed. "Look how dark it is!"

"They knew it was there," Morrigan replied. "Its mass rearranged the orbits of several Kuiper Belt dwarf planets—Sedna and a handful of other trans-Neptunian objects."

"I read about that. They called it ... uh ... Nemesis, right?"

Morrigan shook her head. "Nemesis was earlier. For a while ... the 1980s? Something like that. They speculated that a very cool red dwarf or maybe a brown dwarf out here periodically upset the gravitational balance of the Oort cloud and sent showers of comets into the inner solar system every so often."

"The dinosaur killer."

"Right ... except that infrared scans didn't turn up any heat sources out here. No, they saw the TNO orbits and called the mystery body Planet X." She pronounced it as the letter rather than as a Roman numeral. "Or Planet Nine, after they demoted Pluto to dwarf planet status. They thought it was either a super-Earth or a mini-Neptune tugging those TNO orbits into long ellipses. From the orbital data they were able to predict that it must be about six times the mass of the Earth and several hundred AU out, probably in the direction of the constellation Cetus. But they still couldn't spot it."

"Not until they built the first *c*-ships and could get out here in less than a decade or two. *That* must have been a shock! The Whitehead Expedition, wasn't it?"

"No, that was a few years later," she told him. "The Chinese, the Hsing-chou Mission, discovered what Abyss really was."

"Oh, yeah." He gave her a quizzical look. "I guess you actually lived that part of history, didn't you? Experienced it, I mean."

"I was a university student, and after that an AI designer with IBM-Intel. My original life, before my first ENS." She sighed. "An eon or two ago ..."

"My God..." He sounded genuinely awed. Her corona displayed his emotion in her visual field: [AMAZEMENT].

"Vince, you do *not* need to sit there and remind me of how old I am."

"Sorry..."

Morrigan shoved aside her irritation and blocked her corona from displaying it. Lately, during this past lifetime, she'd been running into more and more people who were impressed by her age and by the fact that she'd been a living witness to so much history. The First Singularity, the first *c*-ships, the relativistic exploration of nearby stars, First Contact . . . yes, she'd seen all of that and so much more. The awe and the fawning bored her. The fact that some saw her as a celebrity solely because she'd seen so much history embarrassed her. The constant news feed requests for interviews irritated her.

Thanks, Mom. The thought was acid, and she rejected it almost at once. Her mother had done what she'd thought was best for them both.

Still . . .

"Anyway," she continued, covering her irritation, "it turned out that what was out here wasn't a planet at all but an alien artifact. Six times Earth's mass, so it affected the orbits of those TNOs the same as a planet of that size would have, but it was superdense, a thin ring only 120 kilometers across. The Chinese expedition deduced that it somehow used all that mass to open up a wormhole through space, connecting it with an identical gate in the Sirius system, eight-point-six light-years away."

"Captain," a communications rating called. "The sentry fleet is hailing us."

"Patch it through."

"Aye, aye, Captain."

A man's face appeared on one of her console screens. "*Constellation*, this is the Pan-European monitor *Sternenschlag*, Konteradmiral Richter speaking." The transmission was in German, but Morrigan's corona translated it as the man spoke, its voice overriding the guttural background speech. "What are your intentions, please?"

"I'll take it, Alex," Koehler said. "Konteradmiral Richter, this is Admiral Koehler, Dreadnaught Strike Force Eight. Our orders are to pass through Abyss in order to negotiate with Quarantine."

"Hello, Jaime," the Pan-Euro admiral said. "We were just alerted as to your mission a few hours ago . . . highly irregular. As we told Earth, we strongly urge you not to attempt this."

"Why not, Johann?"

"Because something is going on over there, something big and noisy, and we can't figure out what it is. I recommend a conference when you heave to. We have data to share with you."

"Very well, Konteradmiral," Koehler said, all business once again. "We will kill our drives in another . . . thirty minutes. In virtual? Or actual?"

Richter nodded. "Virtual, on my flag, please. *Sternenschlag* out."

"Take us in close, Captain," Koehler told Morrigan. "Old Johann looks nervous. We'd better find out what he wants."

"Yes, sir. Do you want me to attend the gabfest?"

"Please. And tell Brandt to come along as well. This could get damned interesting."

CHapTer FOUR

A DR'KLEH MIND drifted in darkness, the hub of a far-flung network of flowing data, its vantage point not so much a ship as it was a folded-over pocket of space itself. Manifesting as a single point of bright golden light at the center of what might have been a crystalline orb, but wasn't, the Sentinel was the focus of a Mind—or sometimes Minds—that only rarely ventured out from the bright and radiation-rich depths of the Galactic Core. It was empty out here in the Galactic hinterlands, empty and dark and very lonely. Out here, one could almost visualize the cold and ancient myth of death . . . the death of individuals . . .

. . . or the death of entire species.

But sometimes sacrifices must be made, so that what was left behind might thrive.

Things here were as expected: nominal, save for the inevitable delays in organizing any organic so-called intelligence. Nzaad ships were entering the local star system through the gate the Veykaar called Kalnarioth, sleek hulls reflecting the actinic glare of the dazzling AO-class sun in the distance. The gathering commanded by the Dr'kleh nearly 1.4×10^{10} seconds ago had at last begun.

The Dr'kleh weren't *exactly* urging this particular Nzaad faction to eradicate the latest blight. After all, they had so little in common with organic species they generally were scarcely aware of them or of the minutiae associated with even partly organic life. But war is inherently illogical in its wastefulness and chaos; the Authority's principal concern in governing some millions of civilizations across the Galaxy was to maintain order, to *prevent* war and social unrest, and to encourage a status quo that so far had lasted for very nearly 3.2×10^{16} seconds.

For the most part the Galaxy ran itself, a smoothly functioning machine that ordered civilizations in layered hierarchies based on relative intelligence. Rarely, on the order of once every 1 or 2×10^{12} seconds or so, a problem species would arise that needed to be . . . suppressed. Deep, deep down within the muck of organic evolution, a life-form would appear and develop semi-intelligence and technologies that would, in time, upset the Pax order.

And that could not be permitted.

The predations of such species were known as "blights," and Ku'un—the designation for purely organic species that had not yet fully matured or integrated with technological prostheses—were always the problem. *Always.* Their poorly organized cognitive faculties; their jealous, territorial, and acquisitive natures; their petty prejudices, unending grudges, and fierce combativeness; and their hormone-drenched inability to reason logically or to accept reality altogether made Galactic Ku'un an existential threat to the order and security of the Pax wherever and whenever they appeared.

And the Ku'un that had evolved here, in the star system listed by Authority records as 837-9266-22102 (*48), were showing every evidence of having become a blight. The Sentinel Mind, whose name was a string of high-pitched chirps and warblings intelligible only to other Dr'kleh species, was here as witness and as guide, *not* as commander.

Within the Sentinel's mind, the Veykaar leader appeared—a seamless blend of gray-and-black metal with a flat, decapodal body. *Lord*, the being said. *We gather, ready for your command.*

Typical, the Sentinel thought. These creatures thought in such sharply delineated and militaristic social terms: lords and servants, masters and subjects. But as a species—especially as a cybernetic species—they were young, as yet. Perhaps they would learn.

Hold your position, the Sentinel replied. *You will know when to act.*

The Sentinel's agents on the far side of the Kalnarioth Gate were reporting that the target fleet was gathering there.

It would not be much longer now . . . a matter of only a couple of hundred thousand seconds, at most.

IN THE BRIEFING room aft of *Constellation*'s CIC, Morrigan, Koehler, and Feodor Brandt sat side by side in chairs that were a little too deep and comfortable for a meeting of this gravity. The room was dark, the walls lost behind a 360-degree projection of surrounding space. The sun, at this distance, was merely the brightest star of many, while the Milky Way curdled its great circle around the heavens.

The sky was dominated, of course, by Abyss, visible now as a black circle rendered visible, just barely, by reflected starlight. It looked delicate, impossibly fragile, but that was an illusion created by distance. The ring's perimeter was over a kilometer wide, the diameter of the entire structure over 120 kilometers. It massed an incredible 3.5×10^{25} tons—six times the mass of Earth—and its density was that of a neutron star.

Had the Galactics built that thing? Morrigan wondered. They must have . . . unless someone even more ancient and powerful had come here billions of years in the past.

How had they known, back in the darkness of Deep Time, that one day a promising upright ape on the third world of this system would leave the savanna behind and venture forth to build a space-faring civilization?

Maybe, she thought, human civilization had nothing to do with it. While romantic speculation back home held that the ancients had built their gates and perhaps taken a hand in helping humans along on their evolutionary path, it was entirely possible, even probable, that whoever had built the thing had not been thinking of *Homo sapiens* at all.

Morrigan tore her gaze away from that enigmatic circle to watch what was happening nearer at hand. The virtual images of five other fleet commanders completed the gathering in commspace, each man representing one of the Pentopoly sentry fleets present at Abyss.

"Admiral Koehler," Richter, the Pan-European officer, was saying. "You must understand that we are here at the order of the Pentopoly to prevent any acts or incursions that might upset the peace."

The Pentopoly—the Five Cities—had jointly governed Earth ever since World War IV had threatened to extinguish Humankind entirely two centuries ago. Each capital governed a different part of the globe, maintaining a watchful balance with the others. Each of the gates discovered in the outer reaches of Earth's solar system was guarded by five squadrons—partly to intercept anything that came through, but mostly to block the other polities from gaining sole control of a gate.

So the atmosphere in this meeting was tense, to say the least. Koehler's arrival with sixteen warships had just seriously upset the balance of power at Abyss, and three of those admirals on the other side of the room would be wondering now what the Americans were *really* up to.

"Incursions," Koehler echoed. "Does that mean Galactic incursions into our space? Or human incursions into theirs?"

"Both," Richter said.

"Really? And if they decide to come through, just how do you plan on stopping them?"

The other five admirals looked uncomfortable. Each commanded a squadron of powerful line-of-battle warships, but no one could predict how they would fare against a vastly superior technology.

Correction, Morrigan thought. *No one can predict how long they'll survive . . .*

The guardian force was formidable. Konteradmiral Richter

commanded seven line warships, representing Geneva and the Pan-European polity, which also dominated much of Africa and the Middle East. Moskva had sent Kontra-admiral Maxim Turgenev, commanding eight ships, while Beijing's representative was Hǎi Jūn Shào Jiàng Liu Tao Feng with a formidable squadron of twelve. Contraalmirante Edgardo Ferraro led the Buenos Aires contingent of just three ships. And, finally, Washington's squadron of nine warships was commanded by Rear Admiral Jason Selby on board the *Hoplite*.

Those ships were visible now against the surrounding sky, gathered in a parking orbit several thousand kilometers out from Abyss. Despite its shape, the gravitational mass of the structure was focused at the exact center of the ring, and the ships orbited that point. The ring, Morrigan noticed, had already narrowed to an ellipse as *Constellation* and her battle group orbited it, and the stars in the background slowly drifted as their point of view shifted.

For decades now, five naval squadrons had guarded each of the known Sol Gates, ships and crews periodically swapped out in rotation. What they would do if anything ever came through one of those gates was an open question. The Pentopoly governments on Earth had been less than clear in their orders.

"Our orders," Maxim Turgenev said with a grave expression, "are perfectly clear. No human ships are to traverse any of the gates until our position with the Galactic Authority is clarified. Earth does not want our actions here to jeopardize future negotiations with them."

"And *my* orders," Koehler replied with equal gravity, "are to take my fleet through the Abyss Gate to Sirius, where we will find out what's happened to Sirius Station. Dr. Brandt here will commence negotiations with the Quarantine station. He's come along expressly to negotiate with the Galactics."

"This seems a needlessly provocative act, Contraamiral," Ferraro said.

"Really? The Galactics have kept us prisoner within our handful of star systems like we're under house arrest, but they have never made it clear *why*. Now they appear to be in the process of taking our few extrasolar colonies away from us as well. We must find out where we stand with them . . . and make it clear to them that we are a sovereign people to be treated with respect. If we do not, we may find ourselves confined to our one isolated planet . . . or worse."

"My military friend speaks bluntly," Brandt put in, "and I suppose a military man *should* be blunt. It saves misunderstandings. However, I assure you all that if we can talk with the Galactic Authority we shall make it clear that our mission is one of *peace*. We wish only to understand the motives and reasonings of our neighbors out in the broader Galaxy. And we do have the Authority's permission to come through."

"Some reports from Earth suggest that you intend to confront the Galactics directly over their role at Delta Pavonis," Richter said. "Is that true?"

"Confrontation," Brandt said, "is not our purpose here. Understanding is."

"Gentlemen," Koehler said, standing, "this meeting is taking on the air of some kind of confirmation hearing. Or a *trial*. I have my orders, and my squadron is not under your jurisdiction." He gestured at the looming ring of Abyss in the sky. "We are going through that thing whether you like it or not. Are we clear?"

"And our orders," Admiral Liu said, "as Admiral Turgenev has already pointed out, are to stop you if you try."

Each officer present in the virtual meeting wore the uniform of his own polity. Liu's trim naval uniform of the Chinese Hegemonic Sphere was a deeply dramatic blood red trimmed with gold. He was not showing his emotil—none of them were—and Morrigan wondered what was going on behind those dark eyes.

"How?" Koehler demanded. "Do you intend to fire on us? Maybe start another war?"

Bluff called.

"Of course not," Liu replied. "But I would suggest you hold in place and communicate with Washington for an update on your orders. You might find that things have changed since you left."

"Admiral, Abyss is currently eighty-five light-hours from Earth. It'll be over 170 hours total before a reply could reach us . . . that's *seven days*. I do not intend to put my orders on hold for a solid week waiting for an unnecessary confirmation of something of which I am already sure. What I need from you gentlemen, *all* I need, is an intelligence report on what is happening on the other side of Abyss. Admiral Richter indicated that something was going on over there. I want to know what."

"If you will not cooperate with us," Liu said, "we see no reason to cooperate with you."

Pixie, the AI inhabiting Morrigan's corona, threw a message for her onto a corner of her visual field.

[INCOMING MESSAGE ON PRIVATE CHANNEL.]

From whom? she thought.

[HOPLITE: REAR ADMIRAL SELBY.]

The commander of the American sentry contingent? *Permit it.*

Captain Morrigan? This is Selby. Liu is an asshole, and Geneva, Beijing, and Moskva intend to block you. I can give you the intelligence report you want over this line.

Koehler was still arguing with Liu in the simulation. Selby was taking a chance, obviously, in secretly transmitting the requested data. Morrigan took a second to open a secure channel from her corona to Argus, the advanced general AI running *Constellation*.

Go ahead, Admiral.

Data flooded through, a compressed burst lasting less than three seconds. It was encoded, so Morrigan was unable to read it as it passed from *Hoplite* to her to the *Connie*, but she knew that it most likely was data sent back from drones dipping into the Sirius system and returning. No human ship had gone through Abyss in over a century.

The brief transmission cut off abruptly, and Argus gave Morrigan confirmation that the message was safely berthed in *Connie*'s memory.

Tell Admiral Koehler my squadron can join yours, Selby continued. *I don't know what the others are planning—they've cut me out of the loop—but I know they plan to block you from moving somehow. Maybe we can help.*

What about your *orders, Admiral Selby?*

I've already violated them by sending you this. Might as well be hanged for a sheep as a lamb, right?

Thank you, Admiral. I'll tell him as soon as I'm able.

The covert back channel closed.

"*No,* Admiral Liu," Koehler was saying in the virtual standoff. "I will carry out my orders, and I will *not* delay my mission." The five men seated opposite them in the simulation vanished as he cut the link. "Did you just get a message from Selby?" Koehler asked her.

"Yes, sir. Safely transmitted and received."

"Good. Selby gave me a private channel heads-up, but I couldn't deal with it while I was butting heads with Liu."

"Admiral Selby says he'll come with us."

Koehler considered this. "His position here might be untenable now. Have him patched in through Fleetlink."

"Just what are you talking about, Admiral?" Brandt asked.

"Never mind, Doctor. Captain . . . I want to move the squadron out immediately, understand?"

"Yes, Admiral." She was already transmitting orders to the bridge through her corona. "They're bringing the drives online now." The lighting around them shifted to red as an alarm sounded. "And I've taken the liberty of going to general quarters."

"Good. I'll be in CIC."

Brandt rode the elevator up to the bridge with Morrigan. "Captain! What the hell is Koehler planning?" he demanded as the elevator's door shut.

"Your guess is as good as mine, Doctor." The door opened again onto the bridge, a red-lit, high-tech cavern. "Now, if you'll excuse me? Stay the hell out of our way."

"Captain on the bridge!"

"As you were." She slid into her seat, looking around. All bridge stations were manned, officers and enlisted ratings hunched over consoles and monitors. "Ship status, Mr. Neal."

"Ready in all respects for acceleration, Captain."

"Very well. Bridge status."

"Bridge secure. Ready for boost."

"Engineering."

"Engineering ready and rarin' to go, Captain."

Again came the murmur of voices, of ship departments checking in, the litany of stations ready and systems at engaged. Power nominal, gravitics engaged, shields up, weapons online. Fleetlink connected all twenty-five American ships, the battle group, and Selby's sentry force.

"Ahead slow, Helm," Morrigan said.

"Clearance, ma'am?"

"I don't think we're going to get any clearances from *that* crowd," Morrigan replied with a cold smile. "Just be careful not to run into anybody."

"Aye, aye, Captain."

"Bring us around, Helm. Bear one-five-five plus two-zero."

"Bearing one-five-five plus two-zero, Captain, aye, aye."

Stars swung past on Morrigan's main screen, until the prow of the ship was centered on Abyss.

"Tight angle of approach," Neal said. "Should we wait until we can approach it face-on?"

"Negative, Mr. Neal. We—"

"Captain, local traffic inbound!" a lookout called. "Bearing one-five-zero plus one-three, range three thousand!"

"I've got it," she replied, checking a monitor. What the hell did that guy think he was doing?

The ship's AI threw a column of facts and figures up on the display. The vessel—huge, blunt-prowed, and ponderous—was the

Zheng He, flagship of the Chinese contingent. The warbook listed her as a super-dreadnaught, twice *Constellation*'s length and nearly five times her mass. Now less than three kilometers off *Connie*'s starboard bow, she was becoming a definite hazard to navigation.

"Comm! Warn that vessel off! Helm, maintain ahead slow."

"Ahead slow, aye, aye."

"Chinese flagship *Zheng He* orders us to heave to," the comm officer called out.

"Their weapons are powering up," Lieutenant Lisa Conway, the sensor suite officer, reported.

"Ours are already up," Morrigan replied.

He's bluffing, Alex, Koehler said through her corona. *Keep going!*

The problem was that maneuvering in space is never as slick and simple as it appears in the holovids. No swoops . . . no sharp turns . . . and no slewing left or right or up or down to avoid an obstacle.

And the *Zheng He* was now one hell of an obstacle, sliding slowly and relentlessly into *Constellation*'s path. Two more Chinese warships were moving in as well: the dreadnaught *Ming* and the heavy destroyer *Hai Lung,* obviously attempting to block *Connie*'s way.

All around them the other vessels were in motion as the American fleet attempted to accelerate clear of the orbital holdpoint. *Odds of thirty to twenty-five,* Morrigan thought. *Not too bad . . .*

But not too good, either. If the battle group took substantial damage in a fight with other human ships, they wouldn't be much good at trying to impress the Galactics.

What, she wondered, was Li making of this? The Galactic liaison had been staying out of the way and out of sight down in Briefing CIC ever since they'd left Glenn Orbital.

No matter. They were committed now. "Helm, slide us under that beast's keel."

"Way ahead of you, Captain."

Their gravitic drives did afford them considerably more maneuverability than old-fashioned chemical rockets. A good helmsman could balance a dozen different drives to create new vectors. There was still the issue of the ship's mass, however, which didn't just go away. The helmsman could add a new thrust vector to one side in order to clear the looming *Zheng He*, could even reverse thrust to slow the ship, but *Constellation*'s 2.8 million tons of mass could not be shoved onto a new vector in an instant.

"What's happening with the rest of the fleet?" Morrigan demanded.

"Most of them are working clear, ma'am," Neal reported. "They're trying to block *us*, not the whole squadron."

"They figure without the flagship the battle group will be stuck." Morrigan was carefully judging the narrowing space dead ahead. The *Ming* was closing in from port as a heavy cruiser, the *Xin*, moved up from below, helping the *Zheng He* to box *Connie* in. Another dreadnaught, the *Xing Long*, was now moving in dead astern. There'd be no escape *that* way, and with the *Xin*'s arrival they could no longer shift ventral, but for the moment there was still an opening ahead.

She conferred through her corona with *Connie*'s AI, verifying that they had eight seconds before the way ahead was closed. Seven . . . six . . .

"Shields down!"

"Shields down, aye, aye!"

"*Helm!* Ahead full! *Now!*"

The helmsman on duty was Lieutenant Leslie Flynn, a first-lifer, achingly young . . . but he had a natural talent for juggling thrusters and moving tonnage. Age and experience weren't *everything*.

The forward monitor blinked . . . and they were through. Flynn cut the drives immediately, but the ship had accelerated halfway to Abyss, brushing between the *Zheng He*, the *Xin*, and the *Ming* with scant meters to spare.

Astern, things had swiftly gone pear-shaped for the Chinese, as the *Zheng He*, attempting to maneuver, collided in slow motion with the *Ming*. Their relative velocities were low, but the tonnage was not. Morrigan could see the flare of energy generated by intersecting shields, along with minute flecks of silver—debris thrown off by the impact.

"Comm," Morrigan said. "Make to *Zheng He.* 'Do you require assistance?'"

After a moment, the comm officer turned at her station. "No reply from *Zheng He,* ma'am. I think they're kind of busy over there."

Our people are clear now, Koehler's voice said. *Don't worry about Liu's ship. The hulls aren't breached and both ships still have full power. Gather the fleet and take us through.*

You're the boss, Admiral, she told him. "Argus! Formation Five. Helm, bring us to the face of Abyss."

The fleet of American ships moved clear of the orbital holdpoint, arranging themselves in an enormous football shape—the fifth of two dozen possible formations tailored to as many variations of maneuver, attack, and withdrawal. Having commands worked out ahead of time and identified by number saved tremendously in time and confusion in the heat of combat. That little pileup astern had quite obviously arisen from ad hoc orders and an unplanned attempt to catch the *Constellation* on the fly.

"A very nice job, Mr. Flynn," Morrigan said after a moment.

"Thank you, ma'am. I didn't think we had enough clearance."

"*Connie* knows what she's doing," Morrigan said. "Now let's take her through to the other side."

"MY GOD, THAT took balls!" MMC(Q) Kranhouse said, leaning back in his chair. He gestured at the monitor above their workstation, which now showed Abyss and empty space. "Did you see that?"

"I saw it, Chief," EN3 O'Reilly said. He still looked shaken. "I thought we were gonna smash right into that big one!"

"Yup. Big-time. Dreadnaught meets super-dreadnaught. Could've been real pretty fireworks, know what I mean?"

O'Reilly gave a solemn nod.

"Ha! But you see what the skipper did there, dropping the shields like that?"

"Yeah. What was that all about?"

"Electromagnetic shields tend to repel each other, right? They switch charge to oppose whatever's comin' at them. Shield-to-shield impacts are like hitting a solid wall."

"But why . . ."

"If we'd brushed shields with that super-dreadie, even just a little, goin' past at that speed . . ." He clapped his hands, a sharp, sudden crack of sound. *"Boom!"*

"'Boom'?"

"We'd have burned out the shield projectors, at the very least, and maybe ripped out a few cubic meters of hull as we burned past. The power splash would've cooked us. The impact would've scrambled us. If the dampers had failed we'd have been smeared over the aft bulkheads like raspberry jelly."

O'Reilly's eyes widened. "Jesus! Is she nuts, or what?"

"Maybe." Kranhouse looked smug. "And maybe she's just very, *very* good."

ABYSS YAWNED DEAD ahead. Less than a hundred kilometers from the ring's central focus, the strike force was deeply in the grip of the Abyss gravity field, the ships in free fall under an acceleration of slightly better than sixty meters per second squared. The ring now stretched across a quarter of the sky ahead, growing larger moment by moment. Morrigan cast her mind about, wondering if she'd forgotten anything, wondering if there were further preparations to make.

There was nothing. All she and the bridge crew could do was sit and wait as the maw of Abyss yawned ever larger.

She could see stars through the ring, the starfield looking comfortably familiar. At first she thought she was seeing the backdrop of the Sol System through the empty interior of the ring. Then she realized that the stars behind the ring from their current vantage point should be the constellations of Cygnus and Lyra ... but that she was looking at the familiar three-in-a-row belt stars of Orion, which were clear across on the other side of the sky.

From Sol's Kuiper Belt she was seeing the background sky at Sirius, the shapes of constellations relatively unchanged by the mere 8.6 light-year shift in perspective.

"Entry in thirty seconds," the duty navigation officer reported. Lieutenant Commander Eric Pappano was another first-lifer, and he looked *old*. Rumor had it that he was a Rejector, someone who rejected ENS technologies and life extension.

There were many such people who lived a single life, usually for religious reasons. Morrigan wondered what his reason was.

"Ten seconds."

The 120-kilometer ring now divided the sky in two, a dimly lit thread circling the ship. On the forward screen, the first several ships were already through the gate; *Constellation*'s position, as flag, was toward the middle of the football.

And then ...

CHAPTER FIVE

THEY EMERGED IN a new star system.

Morrigan's first indication that they'd made the passage was a violent sunrise off to port, a dazzling, actinic point source of intense blue-white light against the knife's edge scratch of the ring.

"Engage drives, Mr. Flynn," she ordered. Now that the ship had passed through the center of Abyss, she was being pulled back toward the gate's center astern. If they didn't want to begin oscillating back and forth between two star systems, they needed to apply at least enough thrust to counter the gate's six-g pull.

"Battle group is checking in, Captain," Neal told her. He paused, mentally ticking off the last few ship names. "All vessels accounted for, ma'am."

"Good. Helm, take us ahead slow. Ms. Conway, keep a sharp lookout for Quarantine. You'll know it when you see it."

Moving as a unit, the augmented battle group moved deeper into the Sirian system. The pinpoint beacon of Sirius A blazed some four hundred AUs distant, dazzling even at this distance. Just off to one side was a second star, a spark all but lost in the glare of its far brighter companion, Sirius B.

Morrigan pulled up the ephemeral data on the system. She'd

studied it enough, starting with her visit here a century and a half ago, but she didn't entirely trust her organic brain's memory.

Sirius A, the brightest star in Earth's night sky, was of type A0 to A1, twice as massive and some twenty-five times brighter than Sol. Any habitable world in the system would have to exist in a habitable zone between six and ten AUs out, but no such world existed. Its companion, Sirius B, had started off as an even larger and brighter star, probably a type B4 five times more massive than Sol. Some 120 million years ago, however, it had exhausted its nuclear fuel and gone through its red giant phase, blowing off its outer layers and collapsing the mass of the sun into a sphere the size of Earth. Now a white dwarf, Sirius B currently circled its primary once every 50.1 years at a distance that averaged twenty AUs—about the distance of Uranus from the sun.

"We've got Quarantine on-screen, Captain," Lisa Conway reported. "Bearing one-zero-nine minus eight-five. Range eight thousand."

"Got it," Morrigan said, calling up the image on one of her displays—a dwarf planet similar to Ceres in the Sol System.

"We're getting the Quarantine signal, Captain," the comm officer reported.

That, Morrigan knew, was simply a beacon, a signal containing no information save "Here I am." A visitor to the Sirius system had to actually enter Quarantine to hear its rather condescending message: "Superior intellects beyond this point only; organics need not apply" was the gist, if not the exact wording.

"Any sign of Sirius Station?"

Technically, there was that one human presence in the Sirius system: a centuries-old complex constructed on Quarantine itself housing a lone AI tasked with studying the machine intelligence inside Quarantine and monitoring Galactic traffic through the five local system gates. Eir presence had been permitted by the Galactic Authority, at least so far, and the collected data was passed on through the drones that ducked back and forth through Abyss occasionally, maintaining contact.

"Nothing, ma'am," the comm officer replied.

"We've got a new crater on Quarantine," Paulson, the duty planetologist, reported. "I'd say something vaporized Sirius Station."

Admiral? she called in her mind. *You heard?*

Affirmative.

You want to close?

Yes, Alex. Bring us in to within one diameter.

Aye, aye, sir.

Still operating as a single unit, the fleet closed in on the dwarf planet. From 450 kilometers out, Quarantine appeared to be almost fifty degrees across, covering over a quarter of the sky ahead. Its surface was blasted and scorched, cratered and rent by the unimaginable apocalypse of a dying star. When Sirius B had blown off its outer layers, it must have fried everything in the system. To this day, Sirius A showed unusually high metallicity in its makeup—a parting gift from its dying companion.

"Huh," Neal said, peering at his monitor. "Is that ice? Like on Ceres?"

A single brilliant patch of white showed on the floor of a crater. Ceres, the asteroid belt dwarf planet in the Sol System, possessed several such patches—salts oozing their way out onto the surface from an icy mantle underneath. When they'd first been glimpsed via the Dawn spacecraft in 2015, they'd instantly triggered wild speculation about the lights of alien cities buried within the Cerean rock.

But Morrigan had seen the Quarantine light during *Fury*'s visit and knew that the light was exactly what it appeared to be.

"No, Mr. Neal. That is the front door."

"Captain!" Lieutenant Conway yelled. "We have targets ... *lots* of targets! *Incoming!*"

They were all but lost in the Sirian glare, but she could see them now, each target highlighted by brackets projected by the ship, hundreds of them.

And they all were headed straight for Quarantine . . .

. . . and the strike force.

THE DR'KLEH SENTINEL watched the approaching human fleet. A pity, really. For Ku'un, the species actually showed some small promise in their strength of will.

But that, of course, was the problem. The species was resilient, stubborn, and determined, but with all the substandard cognitive brilliance of a fried logic circuit.

The Galactic order would be far safer without them.

Unfortunately, they were not the only organic problem here; the Veykaar were not adhering to the plan of operation. Their fleet was sweeping forward, apparently to confront the human fleet, perhaps to provoke battle.

Veykaar Command! ey called. *You are out of position!*

It is too late, Lord, for stealth. They have seen us. We shall destroy them.

The Sentinel gave the electronic equivalent of a sigh. Perhaps it *was* for the best . . .

MORRIGAN WATCHED THE oncoming alien fleet with considerable misgivings. That mob outnumbered the battle group by at least ten to one, overwhelming odds even minus the differences in technology.

Alex? It was Koehler, over her corona. *I'm shifting to CIC. Please have Commander Talbot join us down here with the rest of the CI-sycophants.*

You're expecting trouble? she asked him. *I mean, we're not officially at war . . .*

Not yet, at any rate.

I'm not expecting anything. I just want to be ready for anything.

Commander Bryce Talbot was *Constellation's* tactical officer. He would be joining the elite club jokingly tagged the "CI-sycophants"—a reference pronounced *see-eye-see-koh-phants* for the habitual denizens of the CIC. They included the admiral; Boucher, the fleet TO; and a small army of Koehler's other combat aides in CIC to handle fleet strategy, should they find themselves locked in combat.

She hoped desperately that they would not.

Her eyes narrowed as she studied the alien ships under high magnification. They were oddly designed, unlike anything she'd seen before. Each was V-shaped, like a sleek chevron . . . but was moving open-arms-first as though to reach out and grab their enemy.

Back at Glenn Orbital, she *had* downloaded an intel report, however, with a description that seemed to match.

She opened a channel. "*Invincible,* Flag."

"*Invincible.* Holt here. Go ahead, Flag."

"Commander, this is Morrigan. Those ships out there. Do you recognize them?"

"How did you guess, Captain?" She heard the bitterness in his voice. "Ellen would've loved this . . . and she's not here."

"They're Crabs, aren't they." It was not a question.

"That they are, Captain. Veykaar is what they're called in Kapik. God knows what they call themselves. Filthy butchers . . ."

"Thank you, Commander. Stand by." She shifted to the corona's mind-to-mind function. *Admiral? Those ships out there are Crabs. Invincible's skipper has seen the design before.*

I thought so. That does change things just a little, doesn't it?

It meant that the opposing force was not as godlike in its technology as the Glitters. Those ships were obviously of advanced design, but they were smaller than Terran dreadnaughts, smaller even than a heavy cruiser, and the scattered intel reports recently arrived from Delta Pavonis suggested that their weapons were pretty much on the same level as the Terran pulse cannon and HELs. They *could* be beaten in a stand-up fight; by all reports the Pavo Defense Squadron had given a damned good account of themselves . . .

. . . until they'd been overwhelmed by sheer strength of numbers.

Alex, Koehler said, *I suggest we go to battle stations.*

A very good idea, sir.

She triggered the alarm through her corona. The ship was already at general quarters. Battle stations was a step up from that, with ship and crew standing ready specifically for combat as opposed to any other emergency situation.

"Now battle stations, battle stations," the ship's alarm announced. *"All hands man your battle stations."*

Nobody moved on the bridge; they were already at their battle stations. Elsewhere aboard the ship, however, damage control parties would be manning their ready positions, and weapons crews would be powering up their deadly toys. One by one, word came from each of the other ships in the battle group, as every vessel came up to full alert.

Now, she thought, *who's going to throw the first punch?*

We will not fire the first shot, Alex, Koehler's voice said in her mind. *We wait and see what they intend.*

Damn! Had she transmitted her last thought by accident? She hadn't intended to.

Or maybe Koehler was just reading her, *knowing* what she was thinking. He was insufferably good at that.

"Enemy fleet is on intercept course," Boucher said over the internal com. "They . . . oh my freaking God . . ."

Morrigan saw in the same instant what had elicited Boucher's indelicate surprise. Something was approaching, still distant, partially blocked by the clouds of Veykaar ships out front. It looked like two flattened hemispheres joined base-to-base with a gap between them, but what snagged Morrigan's full attention was the *size*.

"Sensors," she snapped. "Get me dimensions on that thing."

"We're having trouble reading it, Captain," Conway replied. "Radar, lidar, they're being absorbed. I'm trying to get a gravitic pulse readout."

"Do it. Anytime yesterday will be fine."

"Okay . . . let's call it fifteen kilometers across," Conway said.

"Ten kilometers thick. Mass . . . I'm reading at least 5 x 10 to the *eleven* tons."

"'Fucking big' will do, Lisa. Is it a ship?"

"It's powered and it's moving, Captain. Slowly . . . I don't think it's very maneuverable. But it's definitely following that fleet in."

"We're locked on, Captain," the fire control officer told her. "Designating main target as . . ."

"Call it *Nemesis,* Commander," Morrigan said. "'Target Alfa' doesn't do it justice by half. Hold your fire."

"Aye, aye, Captain."

Morrigan scanned the other bridge stations. Four men sat wired into a heavy-duty VR rig on the port side. "Lookouts. That space between the two domes. Is that a firegap?"

"It's got lights inside there, Captain," one of the men reported. "It might be."

What kind of firepower would a monster like that command? Adventure holovid fiction was filled with enormous ships the size of moons or planets. This thing was only the size of a small asteroid, but it was thousands of times more massive than the *Constellation.*

"I've never seen a design remotely like that," Neal said quietly.

"A mountain-sized yo-yo," Morrigan suggested.

"Yo . . . yo? What's that?"

"A toy from my childhood." A long, *long* time ago.

She eyed the monster carefully, looking for weaknesses that might well not exist. The paired, flattened hemispheres gleaming like polished silver in Sirius's glare could be armor kilometers thick. The gap between those hemispheres did indeed look like a firegap—the space-naval term for those portions of a large warship's hull left open to allow the firing of weapons. The squat cylinder joining the hemispheres was in deep shadow, but she could see constellations of lights in there—windows or sensor banks. If that was where the weapons were located, it did suggest one possible weakness. The behemoth would be able to fire only in a two-dimensional plane, from the equator between the hemispheres.

But then, she reminded herself, there was no telling what hidden surprises they might discover elsewhere. They didn't understand this technology. Whatever the thing was, it didn't look like it fit with the awkward V-shapes of the other ships, and so might represent highly advanced technologies far beyond anything humans had imagined so far.

Captain, move the fleet back toward Abyss, if you would, Koehler said, speaking in her mind. *We don't want those . . . people getting between us and the only way home.*

Aye, aye, Admiral.

She gave the necessary orders, and the cratered, enigmatic sphere of Quarantine receded into the distance.

You're thinking of blocking the gate? she asked.

We can try. I don't like the look of that big, shiny one. I don't think we want something like that running around loose in the Sol System, do you?

A planet killer?

Hard to imagine it as strictly antiship, Alex.

The thought was chilling, and Morrigan's fists clenched helplessly on her armrests.

And *Nemesis* continued its relentless advance behind the screen of Crab warships.

ADMIRAL KOEHLER WAS leaning over the plot tank with eight of his senior aides. Blue and red stars drifted within the three-dimensional representation, showing just how badly outnumbered the Terran force was. "We can't take them head-to-head," Koehler told the others. "If we can pull back through Abyss, we can join up with the sentry fleet."

"*If* they'll talk to us," Talbot said. "When we left them they were pretty pissed."

"Oh, they'll talk all right," Boucher observed. "When *that* bunch comes through after us!"

"Maybe the Galactics won't follow," Commander Greer said.

"We will assume that they will," Koehler said. "I would suggest deploying on the Sol side of the gate and moving into Formation Twelve."

"What the hell is *that* thing doing here?" Greer was pointing past Koehler's shoulder.

Koehler turned and saw Li, the Galactic liaison, drifting slowly toward the group, a bright sphere the size of a human head with a shimmering surface like liquid mercury.

"I asked you to stay on the flag bridge," Koehler told em, straightening. Yeah... the thing was supposed to be apolitical, but damn it, how could anyone *know*? He did not want it *here*, at the very heart of the squadron's strategic planning and control.

Li stopped moving, hovering silently.

"Are you here to communicate with the Galactic fleet out there?" Boucher demanded of it.

There was no reply, and that by itself set off alarm bells in Koehler's mind.

"Marines!" he snapped. Two battle-armored Marines stood on either side of the doorway leading into the CIC. Koehler wasn't sure how they could control the device—a butterfly net? Throw a blanket over it? All he knew was that he didn't want the alien device here eavesdropping on their oplan.

Silently, Li exploded, eir body expanding into a sparkling cloud of glittering dust, the cloud swiftly growing larger ... then coming together once more, surrounding Koehler's head and closing in on him.

Koehler couldn't speak ... couldn't breathe ... and he felt the pressure growing all over his head ... suffocating ... crushing ... penetrating ... *squeezing* as if to crush his skull ...

MORRIGAN HAD LOOKED at the CIC screen when she heard Greer demanding to know what *"that"* thing was doing there. Transfixed, she saw the Galactic disassemble itself into a cloud of shining specks, then close around Koehler's head.

"Jaime!" she screamed, making other bridge officers suddenly turn and look in her direction. She began fumbling at the seat harness, trying to rise, trying to do something . . . but there was nothing to be done. Koehler's hands groped at his throat, then waved with futile desperation at the cloud as if it were a swarm of stinging insects.

"Marine!" somebody over there yelled. "Do something!"

"What?" an amplified voice boomed back. "I can't shoot! I'll kill the admiral!"

There was a snapping, popping sound, and Koehler dropped, a string-cut puppet, crumpling to the deck. The cloud of sparkles hovered there for a moment, as if trying to select another target, and in that instant both Marine sentries opened fire with their laser sidearms. Their pistols were Marine-issue Stardyne M-9 IR weapons, with a five-megajoule output normally invisible to the human eye. As those beams flashed through the cloud, however, they flared brightly as though they were passing through dust or smoke, the light dazzling in its intensity. On the screen, Morrigan could see a mist of tiny droplets of liquid metal splattering to the deck and across Koehler's body as the Marines slashed their weapons back and forth through the cloud. A large monitor on the bulkhead beyond exploded as the beams struck it, but the sentries continued playing their weapons through that deadly cloud, searing black streaks across the deck and bulkheads.

Then, in abrupt anticlimax, the remaining glitter dust went dead, drifting gently to the deck.

"We got it!" one of the Marines boomed. "We fuckin' got it! We *burned* the bastard!"

"Someone help the admiral!" the other cried. He pivoted back and forth, his laser clutched in two gauntleted fists as he searched the compartment. "Are there any others?"

"Negative! Clear!"

"Captain!" Neal was beside her, his touch on her shoulder shocking. "They're rushing us!"

Morrigan tore her attention from one monitor to another in time to see the swarm of Crab warships surging forward on the main screen, closing with the battle group. The nightmare was broken. "All ships!" she yelled into the shocked silence of the bridge. "All ships . . . *engage the enemy!*"

Jaime was dead. She *knew* he was. All too clearly she'd seen his head as he collapsed, crushed and bloody. But the battle group now was under attack.

Was it happenstance? she wondered. Or a deliberate and literal attempt to decapitate the Terran squadron by taking out its senior officer? She had to assume the latter. That the Galactic would kill Jaime at the same instant the Galactic fleet attacked by chance demanded too much of coincidence.

And there was no time now to think about it. The grieving would come later. Right now there was only white-hot fury.

"Helm!" she snapped. "Close with those bastards!"

"Captain." It was Boucher speaking over the intercom. "The fleet is yours. The admiral was suggesting Formation Twelve when—"

"The fleet is mine," she confirmed. "Keep me advised."

Battle group command and control, she thought, was going to be a bitch. The commanding admiral of the group was stationed in CIC for a reason, the large tactical tank in which he could watch an unfolding battle and plan both strategy and tactics. Morrigan, however, was on the bridge, ideal for commanding and fighting the ship, but isolated from a direct awareness of the fleet action as a whole.

She was going to have her hands full.

"Captain!" Boucher called, insistent. "Formation Twelve requires deploying CDWs! We should—"

"Negative! My fleet!"

"Aye, aye, ma'am."

"Strike force!" she called over the fleet command and control channel. "Formation Two! Execute!" She shifted back to the bridge intercom. "Helm, take us in close. Knife-fighting range. Weps, open up with the HELs."

"Engaging with high-energy lasers, aye, aye, Captain." Commander Clay Anders, *Constellation*'s weapons officer, had opened fire with Morrigan's initial order to engage. Now he gave orders to bring the ship's long-range HELfires to bear.

Starship combat was divvied up according to range and weaponry capabilities. Beam weapons, like the powerful high-energy lasers, were fired at long range—theoretically as far as line of sight allowed, though the speed of light imposed limits on accuracy. At ranges of over a few thousand kilometers or so, a fast target might have moved significantly in the time it took for the light to cross the intervening distance.

"Hit," Anders said, his voice a monotone. On-screen, one of the chevrons had just lit up behind a searing flare of blue-white light. The UV beams were invisible in empty space, but the effect at the target was sharply apparent. A single bolt from one of *Connie*'s bow turret 6-GJ lasers carried the destructive punch of over a ton of HXP explosives. The target's shields negated much of the damage, but enough energy burned through to turn one of the chevron tips into molten slag.

Other ships in the squadron were firing now as well. The *Nyx*, out near the formation's point, scored the first kill, slashing a Crab chevron with fire from multiple turrets that left the target a helplessly tumbling wreck. *Connie*'s target swiftly followed suit as she brought her B and C turrets to bear.

But the attackers were striking back and striking hard. The heavy cruiser *Theseus* crumpled as though caught in the convulsively tightening grip of an invisible fist. The Crabs, according to Intelligence, favored gravitic weapons that crushed their opponents at long range. The Terran fleet had nothing like it in their inventory.

An instant later, the escort carrier *Hermes* crumpled as well, the wreck glowing white-hot as her power plants melted down in the instant before they were extinguished.

"All ships!" Morrigan called, leaning against her harness. "Evasive! Fall back to Abyss!"

Acknowledgments rippled through her consciousness as *Constellation* sharply reversed her vector. The battle group was too severely outnumbered and too technologically outgunned to survive more than moments here.

"Captain!" one of the lookouts cried. "The *Nemesis*!"

On-screen, the mountain-sized monster had suddenly accelerated, hurtling forward as the swarming Crab chevrons scattered out of its way. Beams from a dozen defending vessels struck the giant, but with no visible effect. Those twin domes were armored and shielded, and it seemed unlikely that the Terran force had anything that could even slow the thing.

Nemesis glided through the human defenders. A dozen Crab chevrons accompanied it in close formation, engaging human ships on all sides. *Rhea* and *Anthea* were smashed aside before they could evade the rush, and *Hesperus* was clipped, a glancing blow that ripped away one of its HELfire turrets in a tangled trail of debris and ice particles.

And then the leviathan and close escorts were through the human fleet and behind it. In seconds they'd vanished through the maw of Abyss . . . and into the Sol System.

"Mr. Flynn! Take us back through Abyss!" Morrigan ordered the helm.

"Aye, aye, Captain!"

"Argus! Keep the rest of them with us!" She watched the slender ring of Abyss expand to fill the sky . . . and then *Constellation* plunged through.

The dazzling pinpoint of Sirius vanished; Sol gleamed in the distance, brightest star of many. *Nemesis* was receding ahead as the multinational sentry fleet scattered in disarray, accelerating smoothly and rapidly until it vanished.

The titanic Galactic vessel was not engaging the human force, leaving that to its diminutive escorts. What, Morrigan wondered, was that thing for if not to fight an opposing fleet?

She was very much afraid that she knew the answer.

"Enemy is now out of sensor range," Conway reported. "Last

recorded track is at zero-zero-three plus six, velocity at point-nine-nine *c*."

"Toward Earth," Morrigan said, stating the obvious with flat and emotionless affect.

"Captain—" Neal began.

"Helm. Follow them, fast as you can crank it. Comm . . . transmit our electronic logs to the sentry fleet and invite them along. *Quick*, before we Doppler out."

And then *Constellation* was plowing ahead through the coruscating fireworks of the Baltis effect, traveling so swiftly that time slowed and voice communications were red-shifted into the ELF range.

Morrigan sat in her command chair, staring at the display. How far in-system would the alien travel? All the way to Earth? That seemed a likely possibility, an attempt to overawe the human population and perhaps force political concessions or compliance.

Turning her head, she saw Feodor Brandt sitting in a jump seat near the aft bridge entrance. "You okay?" she asked.

Brandt's face was paste white. "It . . . it killed him . . ."

"I think, sir, that the bastards have just declared war on us."

"But . . . *why*? No negotiations . . . nothing. Why . . ."

"Maybe that's how they do things out in the wilds of the Galaxy." The words were hard, bitter, cold.

"It doesn't make sense . . ."

"Welcome to reality," she said. "Helm, I want the brakes on a hair trigger. If the ship detects the target, come to a full stop."

"Already programmed, Captain."

Good. If the alien slowed suddenly or stopped, *Connie* and her consorts weren't likely to run up his ass at the speed of light, but there *was* a non-zero danger there. More likely was that they would overshoot them; maneuvering at near-*c* required literally superhuman reflexes.

Argus! she said, focusing the thought to the ship AI. *Tell me about Crab chevrons!*

According to current intel reports, Captain, they were first encountered

*at Delta Pavonis twenty-three objective years ago. At least six models are
known, all constructed along the same basic plan, with forward-swept
"wings" mounting lasers and gravitic weapons. The smallest are robotic
fighters. The largest at Delta Pavonis roughly compared with a human*
Gallant-*class cruiser, with an overall mass of some fifty thousand tons
and a crew of several hundred.*

What about what we've encountered here?

*We've recorded eight so far of a previously unknown class, with masses
estimated above ninety thousand tons.*

So . . . the Crab chevrons included ships large enough to manage long-term, deep-space passages, unlike human fighters, and the
smallest did not have an organic crew. That gave Morrigan a bit
to work on—not much, but some. The capabilities of *Nemesis* were
completely unknown, but they might be constrained somewhat by
the big ship's escorts.

As time passed, however, the minutes dragging into an hour, a
new worry nagged at her. Suppose the Galactics could actually
travel through open space *faster than light,* without relying on a
gate? If that were the case, the alien could have reached Earth
already, and the battle group would arrive four days objective too
late.

Worse, if the battle group actually managed to *catch* the Crab
fleet, what the hell could they do about it? They might well find
themselves in the position of a skimmer-chasing dog that somehow had managed to capture its quarry. *Now what?*

They would have to worry about that when it happened, Morrigan decided. *If* it happened at all.

"None of it makes sense," Brandt said, speaking to no one in
particular.

CHΣPTΣᴦ SIX

TWENTY-SEVEN ANXIOUS HOURS subjective passed on board the *Constellation*, which at her current velocity translated to eighty-seven hours in the outside universe. Everything depended on the *Connie*'s sensor suite detecting *Nemesis* as they flashed past at near-*c*. Several shipboard AIs linked to *Connie*'s mass proximity detectors were dedicated to the problem; at these velocities, human response times were simply too sluggish by far. Morrigan had called up a cup of coffee from the bridge server and taken her first sip when an alarm shrilled through her corona and the Baltis effect vanished from the forward screens.

"Massprox contact, Skipper!" Lisa Conway called. "We've passed them!"

Morrigan took her seat again, checking her screens. "How far?"

"Looks like we passed them twelve thousand kilometers to starboard," Conway told her. "By the time the programming engaged, we'd traveled another couple million kilometers."

"Argus! Did everybody cut their drives with us?"

"Affirmative, Captain," the Argus/Fleetlink officer, Lieutenant Janet Kellerman, replied. "Everybody who's linked to us, that is. If the sentry fleet followed us, they haven't put in an appearance yet."

"And until they do we pray they don't run us down." It was nerve-racking knowing that another thirty warships might be out there somewhere, invisible and following at a hair behind light itself. Had they followed? It was an open question.

"Helm! Ahead slow. Argus, alert the fleet: Formation Eighteen," she said. They would have to be aggressive, get in close, and do as much damage as possible. Formation Eighteen allowed individual ship captains a maximum of maneuvering freedom. "Lookouts! Be ready! When it goes down it'll go fast and hard. Same for weapons! Nav! How far out are we from Earth?"

"Eighty-one light-minutes, Captain—less than ten AU."

Roughly at the orbit of Saturn, then.

"Comm. Notify Glenn of our arrival and location and transmit the log. Let them know that—"

"Captain!" Conway called. "Target *Nemesis* is on-screen!"

"Range one-point-eight," Neal told her. "We're closing . . ."

Under magnification, the odd, double-dome shape she'd dubbed *Nemesis* appeared as a minute speck, slowly growing larger, a tiny, gleaming toy against the star-strewn depths of space. As they watched, a bright flash of light obscured *Nemesis* on the screen for just an instant, followed seconds later by another . . . and another . . .

"What the hell is that?" Neal wondered aloud. "A nav beacon, maybe?"

The flashing showed a monotonous regularity, one pulse every twenty-nine seconds.

"Captain!" Boucher's voice called from the CIC. "Relativistic KK! It's a *c*-gun bombardment vessel!"

"Confirmed!" Conway called. "Forty-kilogram projectiles accelerated to oh-point-nine-five *c*!"

Morrigan felt an icy fist closing inside her. "Target?"

"Earth." Conway's voice was flat, as though she didn't quite believe the readings of her instruments. "Time to impact . . . just under eighty-two minutes."

RKK—relativistic kinetic kill. Projectiles accelerated to relativistic velocities, until even a tiny mass carried the potential energy of megaton, even *gigaton*, nuclear weapons. She ran a fast calculation through her corona. Forty kilograms at 0.95 c ... the kinetic energy yield on impact worked out to over 1.8×10^{12} megajoules. That was over three *thousand* times the energy released by the detonation of a hundred-megaton nuclear warhead ... an inconceivable number.

And a whole string of those things was headed straight toward Earth, spaced just seconds apart.

"Bastards!" Morrigan snapped. "Helm! Close the range! Get us in there!"

"Aye, aye, Captain."

The helmsman gave *Constellation* the briefest of nudges, just enough boost from the gravs to slip them across a couple of million kilometers in five anxious seconds. The light show forward cleared away ... and Morrigan was staring at the alien monster from a distance of sixty kilometers—damned near point-blank range.

Knife-fighting range.

Morrigan's fist came down hard on her armrest. "All weapons! *Fire!*"

High-energy lasers and particle beam fire snapped out from the *Constellation* and, an instant later, from the rest of the ships of the battle group. *Nemesis* continued its pulsing, each flash punctuated now by a faint, sharp quiver running through the deck.

"What the hell *is* that?" Neal asked aloud.

"Whatever it's firing at Earth," Morrigan said, "the projectiles are brushing the fringes of our grav field. That's what we're feeling, each time a projectile goes past."

In her mind's eye, she imagined a long string of projectiles stretching out from this alien intruder, reaching toward Earth, growing steadily longer every twenty-nine seconds.

"Closer, Helm!" she ordered. "I want to be staring right into that thing's firegap!"

"What are your intentions, Captain?" That was Armand Boucher's voice, over a voice link from CIC.

"To see if we can get around that armor," she replied. "And if that fails ..."

She stopped herself. If *Constellation* and the rest of the battle group couldn't stop that monster with a traditional attack, there might be no recourse but to—

"DAG," she said with a coolness belied by her racing heart. "Deploy deltawings!"

Launch CDWs, aye, aye, Ballinger replied through her corona.

"Starscouts too," she added. "*And* fighters. Fast as you can. I want every fast mover we have to get out there and chase down every damned one of those projectiles! Burn them down any way they can, before they hit Earth. Talk to the DAGs on the other ships as well. Coordinate your deployment with them."

Copy, Captain, Ballinger replied through her corona. *I don't know how many they'll be able to take out, though. Near-c maneuvers—*

"Just *do* it, DAG! We don't have time to discuss it!"

Aye, aye, Captain.

Combat deltawings—CDWs—were descended from naval air tactics dating back to a couple of decades before Morrigan's birth. NGAD, the Next Generation Air Dominance system in the mid-twenty-first century, had employed drone fighter craft linked to a single manned fighter as AI wingmen to ensure airspace control in a fight. *Constellation*'s updated version of this deployed some eight hundred robotic fighters controlled from either CIC or crewed strike fighters. Triangular in shape, as the name suggested, deltas were mounted in recesses in the ship's outer armor but could be released on command to serve as Combat Space Patrol for a capital ship or as wingmen for fighters or Starscouts.

"Weps! Hammer at that firegap! Everything we've got! Let's see if we can stop the RK-squareds that way!"

"Right, Captain," Anders replied.

If beam weapons like HELfires could be brought to bear on targets out to ten or fifteen thousand kilometers, missiles and dumbmetal were reserved for close, usually *very* close, range. The target's point-defense weapons—the lasers and Gatling cannons employed by *c*-whiz systems—would vaporize incoming solid warshots if they had more than a tiny fraction of a second to target and engage them, so the idea was to get in so close the enemy's defenses didn't have time to respond.

Energy weapons were still required to degrade the target's magnetic shielding at close range, however. Magshields could deflect or vaporize solid warheads, and they could refract or scatter incoming charged energy weaponry like proton or electron beams. Starship tactical doctrine called for getting in close, burning out the target's magshield projectors with HELfire, then overwhelming it with missiles, railgun fire, and old-fashioned cannon.

White light flared inside the target's firegap as *Constellation*'s 6-GJ main batteries slashed between the target's hemispherical shells.

"Hit!" Anders cried. Then: "Negative effect! They're using some kind of gravitic field to neutralize incoming fire!"

A magshield used magnetic fields to deflect charged particle beams or solid warheads but did nothing against lasers or nonferrous warheads. Gravitic fields, however, actually bent the fabric of space around the target, in effect refracting *anything,* including visible light.

"Keep at it, Weps," Morrigan replied. "Saturate them!"

On the monitor, *Nemesis* suddenly jumped off-screen.

"He's jinking," Anders said. "Lateral, twenty-eight hundred. We still have lock."

"Jinking" was the term for short, near-*c* maneuvering, a jump of a few hundred or thousand kilometers in one direction or another intended to break contact with a nearby enemy.

"Captain?" Bryce Talbot said from the bridge entry. "Permission to return to my station, ma'am."

"Back so soon, Tact?"

"I'm on BrainNet with Commander Boucher, ma'am. We thought things would run smoother if I was here while he handled things in CIC."

"Welcome home. We kept your station warm for you."

It made sense. In effect, Morrigan was serving now as admiral for the entire squadron, but she still needed to be *here*, on her bridge, and not aft in the CIC. Talbot would be able to keep Boucher and the other CI-sycophants webbed in.

As the battle continued, the squadron vessels all were edging closer to *Nemesis*, attempting to englobe it to prevent it from maneuvering. The target's escorts—down to eight now—hurled themselves at the Terran flotilla, attempting to block the englobement. Guided by Boucher, the flotilla's destroyers and the cruiser *Euryalus* deployed as a blocking force against the enemy's escorting chevrons, advancing behind swarms of AI deltas to keep them well clear of the heavies. Missiles arced in toward the *Constellation*; point-defense lasers burned them down.

Nemesis continued to jink and dodge. "We're hurting him," Talbot observed. "We have to get closer if we're going to pin the bastard down."

"At least he's stopped shooting at Earth," Morrigan observed. "That's something, at least."

She spoke the words with an icy calm; in fact, she was seething inside with rage, terror, anguish, and a certain amount of guilt. They should have kept *Nemesis* on the far side of the Abyss Gate. She should have seen that that Galactic monster was intended for planetary attack; nothing else could explain its size.

On-screen, *Nemesis* suddenly came to a relative halt, pivoted slightly, and flashed. Damn it, it was opening fire again!

"Helm! Close with him! See if you can get us *inside* that firegap!"

"Skipper?"

"Stay clear of the projectile stream." *For now*. If they couldn't stop that thing any other way . . .

Constellation again darted forward, until the Galactic's hull rose like a curved and gleaming cliff a few kilometers ahead. HELfire slashed into the gap between the hemispheres as *Constellation* edged closer . . . closer . . . passing into shadow as she maneuvered into the space between the hemispheres. The parallel bases of those half spheres were a kilometer apart, and they cut off the light of the distant sun as the dreadnaught slipped in between them;

the squat central cylinder joining the two halves was less than five kilometers away now and taking the full brunt of *Connie*'s fire.

Nemesis was returning fire as well, though both the volume and the destructiveness was less than Morrigan had expected. *Constellation*'s shields were holding so far, and the enemy had lost a lot of its kick in the past few minutes.

A brilliant flash illuminated the interior of the firegap, just for an instant, jolting the *Connie* through her magfields. *Nemesis* had just opened up with that damned *c*-gun again.

The other battle group vessels were in close now as well, pouring beams, missiles, and magcannon rounds into the firegap, hammering at the giant in a desperate effort to degrade its shielding. One, the heavy cruiser *Endymion*, moved into the firegap a couple of kilometers off *Constellation*'s starboard side.

"Captain Harrison!" Boucher snapped from CIC. "Break off! You're almost in his line of fire!"

"I'm just getting close enough to hit that *c*-slammer!" Harrison's voice replied with a high, almost shrill edge to it. "All I need—"

Every monitor on the bridge went white . . . then black as the filters cut in. *Constellation* was hurled sideways as a storm of starcore-hot plasma struck her starboard side.

For an agony of seconds, *Constellation*'s bridge was plunged into darkness, a darkness absolute like that of the depths of a lightless cave. Gravity was gone, and Morrigan's right arm shrieked pain. *Broken,* she thought. *I must have hit . . .*

What? She'd been within the gentle embrace of her command seat, and now she was adrift, with no up, no down, with only the screams and groans of other injured personnel around her in the darkness. Damn! She couldn't feel anything in her legs. Spinal injury?

As the monitors came up again and light returned to the bridge, Morrigan groped for an explanation . . . then found it. The enemy's *c*-gun had fired once more, but the projectile had struck the *Endymion,* kilometers distant, releasing nearly eight *quadrillion* megajoules of energy. *Endymion* was gone, vaporized . . . and the space between *Nemesis*'s twin halves had been ravaged beyond recognition, with parts of the Galactic's hull vaporized and what was left a partly molten, twisted wreck. Large areas of raw metal glowed red-hot. It looked like . . . possibly . . . yes! The central connecting cylinder had been ripped apart, and now the two halves of the *Nemesis* were ever so slowly drifting clear of each other, the pieces trailing strings of wreckage and a thin fog of escaping atmosphere that turned to a mist of ice as it hit hard vacuum.

"My . . . God . . ." Neal managed to say at last. Droplets of blood spilled from the gash in his forehead, clinging to the skin, his head movements flicking tiny scarlet spheres off to drift beside his head.

"Damage control," Morrigan managed at last. Pain continued to shudder through her body, until she ordered her corona to engage its anodyne functions. "What—what's the word?"

"We're working on it, Skipper," a voice replied. Thank God the ship intercom appeared to be working. "Heavy damage along our starboard side. Starboard gun mounts are dead. Turrets A, B, and D are dead. Drive system is dead. Artificial gravity has shut down between Decks Two and Five. Hull is compromised and we're losing pressure . . . but I think we can hold it. External comms . . . out. Fleetlink . . . out. Argus is still online, but our link with the rest of the fleet is down. We lost a bunch of our external antennae in that blast . . ."

As the litany of destruction went on, Morrigan realized that actually they'd been extraordinarily lucky. Eight quadrillion megajoules loosed inside the confined space within the enemy's firegap just five kilometers away had wreaked unimaginable damage, but the plasma shock wave had also kicked them clear.

In fact, an explosion in space, even a high-meg nuclear blast, didn't carry nearly as much punch as the same load set off in atmosphere. The only material ballooning outward to impact nearby vessels was the vaporized matter of whatever had exploded—in this case, the cruiser *Endymion*—and *Connie*'s shields had robbed that fireball of much of its oomph.

Somehow, the Terran dreadnaught *Constellation* had survived.
Just barely.

LIEUTENANT GERALD SYMMES didn't like flying a fighter at near-*c*. The Baltis effect made navigation difficult and all but ruined any chance of tracking a small target close enough to get a weapons lock. They were, in effect, both flying and shooting blind.

Well ... perhaps the Nightwing Stryker squadron wasn't shooting *completely* blind, though it felt like that. *Constellation*'s AINet had recorded precise times, velocities, and trajectories for each of the kinetic-kill projectiles accelerated toward Earth. Downloaded to each of the fighters as they launched, the data provided a mathematical model of where each projectile in line should be and allowed individual Strykers and the larger Stilettos to maneuver quite close to it, close enough to give the fighter at least a chance of destroying it.

For the past hour, Symmes had been pushing closer and closer to Target 17—the seventeenth KK projectile in a string of twenty-one. According to his onboard AI, the target *should* be just thirty kilometers ahead, slightly high and to the left. There was no chance of gaining a target lock; at a velocity of 0.95 *c*, the steady, relativity-compressed shower of subatomic particles impacting on the missile would act like atmosphere, slowing and possibly deflecting both missiles and beams.

His best bet, he'd decided, was to launch an SSM(N)-440 Longbow, an antiship missile with a hundred-kiloton tactical nuclear warhead. He couldn't use the laser guidance system in this Baltis-bedeviled environment. All he could do was send the missile on a programmed intercept that would detonate the warhead when it *should* be within a few meters of its target.

There were so many uncertainties in the calculations.

He ran the current numbers past his AI again. Technically, for the past ten minutes objective, he'd been closing on the target at

.001 c, roughly 300 kilometers per second, the idea being that he was traveling now at 0.951 c toward a target moving at 0.950 c. The problem, as his Stryker AI kept trying to tell him, was that neither he nor the AI could see what they were doing at this velocity; neither of them knew precisely what the effects of the high-energy background through which they were moving would do. Worse, each missile carried the relativistic mass of its current velocity, over 95 percent of the speed of light, and accelerating it would take literally astronomical energy drawn from its onboard quantum converters.

And they needed to cut this thing awfully damned fine.

Arguably, a nuclear explosion was still the best way of connecting with the target; radiant heat and X-rays might still vaporize it if the detonation was close enough, though it was a long shot to expect a plasma shock front to do much of anything. The Longbow massed only 104 kilos. That much mass converted to plasma would only nudge the target off course if the blast went off within a very small radius ... say one hundred meters.

We are at the optimal firing position, his AI told him through his corona. *I suggest taking the shot.*

What's our level of confidence? he asked.

I estimate less than thirty percent.

Thirty percent? Hell, one in three? Those aren't any odds at all!

As I have been informing you, the AI said with a hint of what sounded almost like professional exasperation, *there are far too many unknown variables to allow greater precision. That random variability within the background radiation pressure alone causes—*

I know, I know. Look ... we'll try a spread, okay? Program ... make it five missiles, four of them targeted around the fifth, with some variation in depth of field.

Very well. Pause. *Five missiles programmed and armed, ready for immediate launch.*

Let 'er rip.

The speeding Stryker shuddered as the missiles slid off the rails, forcing themselves forward through a sea of radiation and the drag of the dead hand of Einstein himself. *On the way . . .*

"I AM HERE, Captain."

Morrigan tried to turn at the familiar voice in the semidarkness behind her. Pain hammered at her arm and shoulder, aborting her turn. "D-Dek?"

"Yes, Captain. I've got you."

Strong but incredibly gentle arms embraced her from behind, smooth metal slipping underneath her flesh-and-blood limbs, reshaping itself to embrace and clamp her injured right arm, holding it rigid. The hiss of a hypodermic spray sounded beneath her left ear.

"Let me go, Dek," she ordered. "I need . . . I need . . ."

What did she need? Somehow she could no longer remember what she'd been about to say.

"Overriding orders," Dek said. "You need immediate medical treatment."

"Not . . . yet . . . No . . ."

"Commander Neal," Dek said. "The captain has been injured. You have the ship."

"I have the ship. Be careful with her!"

"Of course."

And Morrigan felt the robot hauling her with swift surety off the bridge and through the darkness, as anodynes and nanorepair-bots sang in her bloodstream.

In another moment she was blissfully unconscious.

COLONEL RYAN C. Stroud stood on the grand promenade of the Glenn Orbital observation deck. The compartment's high, vaulted ceilings and outer bulkheads showed a seamless panorama of surrounding space projected in ultra high-def, an effect so realistic that a luminous blue-white guardrail had been provided along the deck's rim to provide a sense of security for nervous tourists. It felt as though he were standing out in open space, with the half-lit sphere of Earth cloud- and ocean-wrapped hanging within the immensity of black.

Glenn Orbital had been constructed in geosynch, where it circled Earth at an altitude of just under thirty-six thousand kilometers, precisely matching the rotation of the planet below. Positioned above the equator out over the Pacific, it provided an unchanging vista of the western hemisphere, from the Aleutians in the far north to Tierra del Fuego in the south. At this distance, Earth spanned just twenty degrees pole to pole, in half phase. Currently, Alaska was in darkness; the dawn terminator stretched down the coast of western Canada and south across the Pacific, less than a thousand kilometers west of Port Diego.

His personal aide, Gunnery Sergeant Mark Latimer, was with him. "I know you're a thoroughbred, Colonel," Latimer said, "but it don't seem natural, you know? Turning down that Dynastar offer like that."

"Maybe it was because I *am* a thoroughbred, Lat."

Like the term "mustang," designating a commissioned officer who'd risen from the enlisted ranks, "thoroughbred" was military slang for an officer who'd stayed in the same service through more than one ENS "life."

Latimer grinned. "So you like being a TOAD?"

Temporarily On Active Delay was another bit of military slang, a term for personnel who'd become stuck in the promotion queue, wearing senior rank but without available billets appropriate to that rank. The "TOAD ceiling" was one reason most polylifers chose at least two careers between each round of life extension. With a career spanning over two hundred years now and counting, Stroud had been a Marine that entire time and a colonel for most of it, turning down periodic offers of promotion to general because he genuinely felt that *this* was his true calling.

Stroud shrugged. "It happens, Lat. You've got to take the long view. Besides . . . I'm a *Marine*. Amphibious green stem to stern. Can you imagine *me* as Space Force? As, God help me, *Air Force*?"

Latimer chuckled. "In a word, sir . . . uh-uh."

"Hell, can you imagine me at a desk? A *civilian* desk?"

"Marine regimental commander is the highest calling in the known universe, I agree, sir. So you have declared many a time. But they were offering you—what was it? Five times your pay as a Marine colonel? And Dynastar is doing a hell of a job with the climate. A *vital* job . . ."

"Roger that. But it's not for me. I'm too old to change."

"Three hundred eighty-five is *not* old, Colonel. Not anymore!"

Stroud smiled. He was in his fifth life extension and right now looked like he was in his forties. His aide looked fifteen years older, with graying hair and craggy features.

"Maybe so, Lat. But I've been so many places, seen so much change, seen so fucking *much*."

In his mind, Stroud reached out and drew a circle around one small portion of the globe displayed in front of them and thought, *Enlarge.* That section of the image obligingly expanded to fill their field of view, a portion of the California coast from the border of the state of Lower California north to Encinitas, an electronic enhancement through their coronas that made it seem as though they were hovering just above the atmosphere, providing an excellent view almost straight down on Port Diego.

He pointed at the projection floating before them. "You don't remember the *old* city, do you, Lat? San Diego?"

"No, sir. Can't say that I do."

Stroud sighed, shaking his head a little sadly. "Charming place. Sun-drenched walls and palm trees along a tight little bay tucked in behind Coronado. Point Loma used to be the tip of a long peninsula, not an island. Everything gone now, of course. North Island and the Coronado Naval Base, downtown, Oceanside . . . We lost a hell of a lot in the 2000s and 2100s."

The modern Port Diego was a gleaming dome, a metal, glass, and plastic eye staring up out of the ocean and into space, the hub of a dozen spokes stretching out to vanish into the surrounding ocean. The cliffsides of Point Loma Island were the nearest land, two kilometers to the north. Ten kilometers to the northeast, the taller buildings of Old San Diego, the long-abandoned apartment towers and office complexes rising from the coastal waters of the Pacific, stood weed covered and grime blackened, crumbling monuments to the hungrily rising sea of centuries past. Farther east still, the La Mesa Military Spaceport sprawled in the shadow of Mount Helix. It was early morning down there, the sun just clearing the mountains.

"Yes, sir," Latimer said, his voice carrying just a touch of uncertainty. "But it was Dynastar that helped fix it, right? Dynastar and the rest of the Global Secure Consortium?"

"They didn't *fix* it, Lat. They dug in and sheltered in place! That—that oversized eyeball down there is designed to function perfectly well even if it's completely submerged! If they wanted to *fix* things, they would've done something about the *climate,* damn it, not make it so we never have to set foot outside in the fresh air!"

He realized that Latimer had pushed a button. Newer generations had always lived with the climate-change reworkings of land and water, of temperature and rainfall. They hadn't *been* there, hadn't seen what the world had become during the past few centuries.

"Well, maybe," Latimer said. "You know, sir, some of the proposed solutions were worse than what we've got. Nanoparticulates in the stratosphere. Giant sunshades in orbit . . ."

"And not a damned thing where a tricentenarian regimental leatherneck like me could make one single worthwhile contribution. Damn it, Guns, I am *not* going to be a PR departmental holoposter. I'd rather—"

He blinked, his vision momentarily lost behind a splotch of visual purple. "What the hell was that?"

There'd been a flash, a brief—*very* brief—Illimination of the Port Diego dome. For just an instant, the western curve of that dome had gleamed brighter than the sun. The projection optics had winked almost at the same instant, cutting the glare to save human eyes, but afterimages still danced against Stroud's field of vision.

Stroud adjusted the projection view through his corona, in effect zooming back higher into space. Something was rising from the night-shadow west of Port Diego, something vast and unimaginably menacing from just beyond the horizon. A moment before, the skies over Port Diego had been clear, the early-morning sun just grazing the top of the dome's curve and glinting from the highest of myriad tinted windows. Now, a wall of midnight cloud expanded across the ocean beneath a towering anvil. Stroud pulled back farther, and the wall became a circle flattened by perspective at Earth's curve, illuminated from within by a dazzling spark of blue-white light at the center of an enormous bull's-eye.

Stroud estimated that the cloud was perhaps two thousand kilometers out to sea over the western horizon. In half an hour it would be over the city.

The top of the ring-cloud suddenly broke out into sunlight, still growing, still climbing. After the first few seconds it slowed enough that another ring appeared beneath it, this one on the surface of the ocean itself, racing out from the central spark. Stroud ran a quick calculation through his corona; the new ring was moving at some six hundred kilometers per hour. It would reach Port Diego in another . . . call it twenty minutes, maybe thirty.

Tsunami . . .

chapter **seven**

LA MESA MILITARY Spaceport was located inland some seven kilometers from the drowned ruins of the old city and twenty-four northeast of Port Diego's dome. The bachelor officers' quarters was a three-story apartment block located on the east side of the complex, a short stroll from the admin and flight control towers.

In the BOQ, Damian had given up trying to sleep and was lying in his rack playing an interact when the first shock struck. One moment he'd been in the cockpit of a cloth-and-balsa biplane twisting above the French countryside, hot on the six of a Fokker D.VII. The next he'd been slammed back to shuddering, bucking reality, flat on his spine as the carpeted deck rolled like surf beneath his spine. *What the hell?*

The entire room trembled as waves passed beneath and through it, accompanied by a thundering rumble and the crash of collapsing walls. The door to his room buckled, then snapped out of its guide rails, admitting a blast of hot and dust-clouded air. A wall monitor splintered into glittering shards. Ceiling insulation panels dropped as the air in his room turned near opaque with dust. He had to get *out*.

Rising, bracing himself against the bulkhead, Damian staggered to the door, peered out, then stepped through, barely able to stand.

Southern California was subject to earthquakes, of course. Hell, the Big One of 2265 had wrecked much of Los Angeles and leveled the infrastructure around La Mesa, but never in his two lives had Damian experienced anything like *this*.

A nearby wall twisted, then snapped as the tough plastic yielded to stresses Damian could only imagine. Buildings—especially those constructed since 2265—were supposed to float on isolators that let them escape major seismic disturbances, but *every* engineering design had its limits. The BOQ was collapsing around him.

Out!

He had to get *out!*

Damian staggered clear of the lobby and out into daylight just as the quake subsided, fading as suddenly as it had begun. Around him, the BOQ had all but collapsed into rubble, with those walls that still stood precariously angled, threatening to fall at any moment. He could hear cries and shouts for help. Dozens of men and women stood or sat in dazed confusion around him, as more, like him, emerged from the shattered structure. For a moment, he stood there in the dusty light wondering what to do, how to help.

"Are you okay, sir?"

He turned to see a large white-and-red robot behind him—a first-responder rescue medic. "I . . . I think so . . ."

He felt the machine interrogating his corona, checking his medical condition. "You do not appear to be injured, Lieutenant Damian. Please stand clear, sir," it said, unfolding several heavy, jointed arms, "while we look for injured survivors."

Other robots were already scrambling over the mountain of rubble, picking up large slabs of masonry and carefully setting them aside, swarming over the wreckage, burrowing in as they homed in on the emergency transmissions of a dozen more victims' coronas. The robots were uniquely suited for this kind of work—massively strong, with superhuman senses and onboard emergency medical gear. Clearly, there was little more he could do here.

Turning, he glanced toward the western horizon and his eyes widened. A long, low, intensely blue-black wall of cloud was rising there, lightning flecked and ominous. A storm? Since when did earthquakes generate storms?

Nearer at hand, a hundred meters away, the admin building was in a state of partial collapse, half of the structure still standing, half in a jumbled ruin. Again, a crowd of survivors, dirty, disheveled, and in shock, milled around the edge of the collapse.

Commander Esposito!

As he jogged toward the second site, he used his corona to scan for emergency transmissions. He could see several automated signals, red points displayed through his corona—six of them—but he didn't have the rescuebots' accuracy at pinpointing their precise locations. *Commander Esposito,* he called mind-to-mind. *Did you get out?*

There was no response, and he sent out a questing ping, interrogating the six . . . no, the *seven* transmitters still in the rubble.

There she was . . . on the third level of the ragged portion of the structure that still stood, up near the top of the heap.

Pushing through the crowd, he started climbing up the tumble-down walls, exposed plumbing, and flier-sized chunks of debris. As he moved up and into the standing portion of the building, a robot in spider mode blocked his way. "Please stay back, sir. This area is extremely dangerous."

"Command override," Damian told it. "Let me pass."

The rescuebot hesitated, as though consulting with a higher authority, then stepped aside, gesturing with one of its jointed legs. "Be extremely careful, sir. This part of the structure could collapse at any moment."

"I'll be careful, damn it. Now stay the hell out of my way!"

It took Damian nearly fifteen minutes to reach Esposito's position, trapped in what had been the base commander's office beneath a massive steel support beam and a section of collapsed wall. The room was open to the light by falling walls; a chair, thank God, had kept her from being crushed, but the weight had crumpled the seat enough to pin her legs. He slid down broken masonry to reach her. "Skipper! Are you hurt?"

"Legs ..." she managed to say. "I think they're broken." She'd lost her corona. No wonder she'd not heard him call.

He explored the tangle of wreckage and debris that pinned her, knowing instantly that he wasn't going to be able to budge it himself. "Rescue!" he called over the local emergency channel. "Injured person trapped here!"

He tried to ignore the crushed and mangled bodies of the base commander and one of his aides, obviously beyond help in the tangle of wreckage nearby.

A rescuebot reached them within seconds; it might have been the same one that he'd ordered out of his way minutes before. It tried shifting the largest chunk of masonry, then stopped when debris started falling around them from those walls still more or less upright. "The debris is unstable," the machine observed with an almost clinical detachment. "We cannot dig without risk of collapsing the entire structure."

"Well, do something, damn it! We've got to get her out of here!"

It was starting to rain. He could hear the roar of the storm through the wide opening at his back, and raindrops spattered him from behind. The ruins around them shifted slightly, setting off a slithering clatter of falling debris.

"Grab hold of her uniform," the robot told him, "and be ready to pull when I give the word."

As Damian braced himself, hands grasping her utilities at either side, the rescuebot reached around her with two of its spindly legs. Actinic light flared in the gathering gloom as it began cutting into the touch plastic of the floor beneath her.

The storm outside grew worse, the rain savage enough that the ruin could easily be brought the rest of the way down. Minutes passed, and then the rescuebot braced its back beneath the largest section of wall, all four spider legs pressed hard against the weakened floor, and flexed upward, pushing the weakened floor ever so slightly down.

"Now! Pull her free!"

Esposito screamed as the pain from her legs broke through her first aid anodynes, but Damian steeled himself against the cry and dragged her from beneath the beam. The crumpled chair and other debris made the retrieval difficult, but he managed to drag her clear. Damian scooped her up in his arms and made his way toward the outside and escape.

"Permit me, sir," the robot said. "I am designed for this."

The rescuebot was already opening and folding itself into a new configuration, its arms locking around the woman's body to protect her legs, neck, and spine. Together, they got clear of the shattered office and picked their way down the slippery debris pile outside.

The wall of clouds had slammed into the base, bringing hurricane winds and stinging, sideways rain. Lightning flared almost continually as a Mariner TVR-20 circled in for a touchdown, red strobes flashing as it scattered the thoroughly drenched crowd below.

Another earthquake rolled across the tarmac, splintering it in a dozen places and bringing down the shell of the wrecked admin building in a splintering, crashing heap.

The red lights overlaying his visual field marking emergency transmissions from survivors, Damian saw, were gone.

The rain, curiously, was coming down as *mud*.

"YOU'RE GOING TO be okay, Captain."

"Define 'okay' for me." Morrigan wasn't sure she'd spoken loudly enough for Neal to hear her. *God*, she hurt . . .

A lightweight mesh held her against a bed. She was in the ship's sick bay, but gravity and all but emergency lighting were still off. Neal shrugged. "The docs say there's nothing wrong with you that they can't fix. They did say that you have some decisions to make."

"What decisions?"

"For treatment, Captain," a different voice said. Dr. Paul Gavin, *Constellation*'s senior medical officer, floated into her field of view, upside down from her perspective. Behind him, Morrigan could see two medibots, slender machines wearing curiously human faces, technological masks intended to reassure human patients.

"You have sustained significant injuries, Captain," Gavin continued. "Your back is broken in two places, T12 and L3, which is why you can't feel your legs. Fractured right humerus, fractured right femur, three fractured ribs, internal hemorrhage. You got slammed pretty hard, ma'am . . . and there's a complication."

"The XO said you could fix it."

"Oh, certainly. *That's* not the question. The complication here is that you are in the early stages of osteoporosis. We will need to address that condition for the fractures to heal properly." He hesitated, his head cocked to one side. "May I ask, Captain, why you've specified in your medical records *no* ENS?"

"I don't want to be rejuved."

"Why?" He frowned. "Full rejuvenation would correct the osteo and allow full and almost immediate healing of your fractures. Captain . . . do you understand? Your spinal cord is completely severed. Without rejuve we have, at best, a twenty percent chance of surgically restoring to you the use of your legs."

Morrigan opened her mouth to tell him she was sick of interacting with her own species, sick of stupidity, greed, and venality, sick of . . .

But she stopped herself. Things *had* changed.

Jaime was dead.

Despite anodyne drugs and 'bots flooding her system, despite antianxiety medications and relaxants, she was *angry* . . . angry with a blood red rage and hatred rising from the depths and consuming her in an emotional storm that left her trembling and weak. Until now, the fury had been dulled and held at arm's length, but now it came flooding in, a tidal wave of searing outrage. The sight of that alien *thing* crushing his skull was still with her, would be with her for as long as she remained alive. She could edit the memories, of course . . . but how could she turn her back on all that they'd been to each other? A century ago she and Jaime had been close, *very* close; they'd remained close even after they'd mutually decided to end their formal contract.

What she'd seen should have been one more reason to accept mortality at last . . . *would* have been, except for one thing.

The Galactics had murdered Jaime.

Hell, worse than that, she realized almost as an afterthought. They'd murdered *Earth*, or tried to. She didn't yet know how Earth had fared in the unprovoked attack, however, and until she did—until she saw it with her own eyes—the fact would remain remote, unreal, even hypothetical. She'd actually *seen* that cloud of 'bots closing around Jaime's head, seen them crush him, seen the bloody ruin as he collapsed, and something had broken inside her as she watched.

It was bizarre, she thought, that the death of one person could, at least momentarily, outweigh the *possible* deaths of fifty billion.

But one death or billions, she would strike back at those arrogant machine bastards if it was the last thing she did.

Her thoughts were muddled, adrift within a kind of dark haze, but they were clear enough that she realized that with these injuries her naval career was finished. She wouldn't be able to settle with the Galactics after this, not in a medical exoskeleton with paralyzed legs, not down on the beach drawing disability.

"Captain?" Gavin was still waiting for her answer. "Why do you deny yourself rejuvenation? Are you a Rejector?"

She was startled by the blunt questions. Within modern North American society it was considered extremely bad manners to ask another about their religious beliefs, if any, but Gavin clearly was genuinely puzzled by her refusal. His emotil read [INTENSE CURIOSITY].

"No, Doctor," she said. She managed a smile. "I didn't care for rejuvenation for . . . let's just say for personal reasons."

Gavin raised an eyebrow. "Really?"

"Yes. But you know what? I think I'm changing my mind."

"So . . . you *want* rejuvenation? I need to hear you say it, please, for the record."

"I ... I want rejuvenation."

"Good. It's the right decision." Gavin smiled knowingly and nodded. "You know, we call this a foxhole conversion. You can be dead set against ENS, but when you're actually facing personal oblivion, things suddenly look quite different."

He nodded to one of the medibots, and the machine hypoed a drug into her skin beneath the angle of her jaw. "No, Doctor," she said. Damn it, no, he didn't *understand*. "That's not it at all ..."

And then the drugs took hold and she drifted away into a deep and dreamless sleep.

MARINE COLONEL STROUD and Gunny Latimer watched the immolation of Earth.

At an altitude of 35,786 kilometers, Glenn Orbital circled Earth once each day, which meant it seemed to hang unmoving over its parking spot above the equator. The station's e-Net, however, connected it with hundreds of other stations and orbital facilities around Earth, and through the promenade deck's viewing facilities, it took only a thought to shift their viewpoint to any spot on the planet they wanted to see.

Stroud had at first assumed an asteroid strike in the ocean off the coast of Southern California. In minutes, however, it became clear that what they were witnessing now was nothing less than an all-out terror attack, one striking from space again and again, slamming into the Pacific Ocean from the California coast all the way across to Australia, China, and the eastern reaches of the Siberian Republic.

So far, they'd counted eight impacts in all, eight slowly expanding blobs of cloud, each with a brilliant blue-white star Illuminating its heart. All had struck the ocean on the nightside of the planet, a confirmation that the attack had come from somewhere out-system. Official word had come through their coronas only moments ago, telling of the battle out near the orbit of Saturn, of the monster ship someone had dubbed *Nemesis,* of the stream of near-*c* projectiles launched from ten AUs out eighty-some minutes earlier. The news had flashed through official channels and into the various civilian networks at light speed before official overwatch had clamped down on all news of the disaster.

Enough had gotten through, however, for Stroud and Latimer to speculate.

Nemesis had just launched a relativistic kinetic-kill attack against Earth, using technologies well beyond current human capabilities.

"God. *Why?*" Latimer was horrified.

"At a guess? The Galactics don't want us breaking out beyond Abyss."

"So are they trying to destroy Earth? Or just send a warning?"

"Hard to tell, Guns. All we can really say is ..." He let the thought trail off.

"What?"

"All we can really say at this point is that we're now at war with the Galactic Authority. And God help the human species, because right now we're completely out of our league."

DAMIAN AND ESPOSITO got out just in time. Damian had ordered the medibot to load Esposito into the back seat of a two-seater Stiletto parked on the line at La Mesa, climbed into the front seat, and fired up the power plant as the rain continued to slash across the ravaged base. As he engaged the gravs, he'd become aware of ... *What the hell* was *that?* It looked like a dark wall across the western horizon, fitfully illuminated by stabs of lightning as it slowly but steadily grew higher ... higher ... and higher still.

Not until he'd gone to positive lift and risen off the broken tarmac did he realize that he was seeing a mountain of water—a literal mountain rushing toward the spaceport from the sea kilometers distant.

His eyes widened. Sick horror clutched at his throat. "La Mesa!" he called over his fighter's comm on the flight control channel. "You've got a tsunami incoming!"

Even as he transmitted the warning, he knew that it was hopeless, that there was nothing he or anyone could do. That wall of ocean would be sweeping across the spaceport in a minute or two, scouring the wreckage away along with every person still on the ground. He could see men and women scattering, see others crowding on board the Mariner transport, desperate to escape.

"Damian?" Esposito intercommed from the back seat. "What is it? What's wrong?"

"Give me a moment to get through the atmosphere, Commander. I've got my hands full here."

He took the Stiletto up, the fighter bumping and shuddering under the impact of muddy rain and howling wind. He estimated that the approaching wave was three, maybe four kilometers high; he had to get higher than that, or . . .

Faster than he would have imagined possible, the ocean swept beneath the keel of his fighter, obliterating the remains of the La Mesa spaceport, overwhelming the Mariner, wiping away every remaining person below, survivor and rescuer alike.

Damian had boarded the fighter with a half-formed idea of flying Esposito to the nearest naval hospital, NMC San Diego. He'd overheard snatches of conversation on the ground, however, and the scuttlebutt was that whatever had overwhelmed La Mesa was a deliberate hostile attack, that other bases and cities were being attacked as well, that Humankind now was at war with the Galactics, that human survival itself now was at risk. If that was true, he realized, then there were no havens on Earth, no safe places, no refuge. After a quick check, he ordered the fighter to climb for space. The military orbital hospital at Glenn was the closest place he could think of that might offer safety . . . and medical treatment for Esposito.

The shuddering eased as they slipped above the weather and accelerated for orbit.

VINCENT NEAL HAD dreamed of command, of being assigned a ship of his own. He'd been a Navy commander now for nearly fifteen years—one of the unfortunate consequences of life extension within the close and cloistered world of military service. There were only so many ships available, and there were far more officers waiting for their chance at command than there were available billets. With the rank of commander and fifteen years' seniority, he had a shot at being given a smaller vessel, of course—a gunboat or a rescue tug or even one of the ugly little RM-20 Starscouts—but the waiting list for commanders was even longer than for captains.

Now, quite unexpectedly, and with considerable misgivings, he had command of a major warship, a dreadnaught, no less, but the *Constellation* was grievously injured, her damage control parties limping from one crisis to the next. It didn't help that he'd been given temporary command in order to replace the captain, who now was in a medically induced coma in preparation for the first stages of her next life extension.

Neal had always been of a particularly practical turn of mind, however, and unwilling to needlessly waste time on emotional second-guessings. He was concerned about the skipper, but there was nothing he could do about it aside from what he *was* doing: securing the safety of his crew and his ship, and getting both safely back to Earth.

So he kept tabs on her, demanding periodic reports on her condition, but he concentrated on saving the ship.

Gravity was back on at last, as were the lights and environmental systems. *Constellation*'s drives had come back online after forty-eight hours of shift-and-shift work, and the dreadnaught had slowly gotten under way, escorted by *Hoplite*, *Victrix*, and the damaged *Hesperus*. Also in tow was a surprise: both halves of the asteroid-sized hulk of *Nemesis*. A small fleet of repair and salvage vessels had arrived from the Grissom Orbital Naval Yards, and the immense hulks were surrounded now by tugs and mobile grav workpods and even a few hundred deltas, nudging the wreck back toward Earth.

Neal imagined that Earth's intelligence services would be keenly interested in all that could be gleaned from the debris. After almost a century of contact with the Galactics, painfully little was known about them, save for the little that they themselves had been willing to reveal.

Overall command of the little squadron had been taken over by Admiral Selby on the *Hoplite*. The rest of the American force had already rejoined the sentry fleet at Abyss . . . but Fleet HQ had decided that Selby's defection to Koehler's task force meant he could not remain on-station. Politically, the situation within the sentry fleet was at critical, with open hostilities a distinct and unpleasant possibility.

At least Admiral Selby wasn't being hung out to dry by the government—a real possibility now that he had become a political hot potato. An inquiry had been held almost as soon as the task force began accelerating for Earth, and he'd been exonerated in full in absentia, perhaps in order to make a dramatic political statement to the Chinese.

It helped that the Battle of Abyss, as it was now called, was being officially declared a victory for the good guys. The last of the Crab intruders had been destroyed or driven back through Abyss, and the Galactic's monster *c*-bomb vessel had been destroyed. On the surface, it appeared that the Galactics and their agents had attempted to wipe Humankind off the map . . . and failed.

Selby had been an important part of that victory, and you don't hang admirals for *winning*.

Now, however, the single question on every military mind on Earth and throughout the fleet was whether the Galactics would come storming out of Abyss again—perhaps with something even bigger and nastier than *Nemesis*.

"HELLO, CAPTAIN. HOW are you feeling?"

Morrigan didn't recognize the voice. Where the hell was she, anyway? It was dark, no light at all, and it was *close*, confining, like she was inside a sleep pod, perhaps. She felt nothing save for a pleasant, distant hum throughout her body. There was no pain—

finally, no pain!—but she felt . . . adrift. Isolated. The voice speaking to her had brought her up out of a deep sleep.

"I'm . . . not sure," she replied. "Where am I?"

"In *Constellation*'s sick bay. You are safe. You are in phase-one rejuvenation."

Morrigan immediately tried to access the ship's data with a swarming crowd of questions. She was jolted by the realization that she truly was isolated; she was not wearing her corona, and that left her feeling nakedly vulnerable.

"The ship . . . she's okay?"

The voice hesitated, but Morrigan had the feeling it was a deliberate pause for dramatic effect. She strongly suspected at this point that she was conversing with an AI.

"The ship is damaged but survives. We are on course for the Grissom Naval Yards for repairs, with a current ETA of six days, five hours."

"The scenic route, then."

"I understand that greater speed is contraindicated given the ship's condition."

"And who is this? Who am I talking to?"

"I am Andreas Vesalius, the AI in charge of the *Constellation*'s medical nanobotics department."

"Ah . . ." She knew that name from ship rosters, though she'd never spoken with this particular artificial intelligence. "So . . . what's my condition, MedAI?"

"Stable. I woke you in order to assess your neurological condition and general cognitive functions. You appear to be suffering the aftereffects of severe shock with attendant PTSD, as well as what appears to be deep grief."

She ground her teeth, considering how to reply. All she needed at this point was a diagnosis of severe emotional trauma to lose her command, perhaps permanently. "I'll get over it."

Maybe she'd already lost her command in any case. Or she would when they got around to court-martialing her. She'd fumbled things badly, she thought: maneuvered *Connie* into harm's way and damned near destroyed the ship and crew...

Her ship... *Her* crew...

She wondered if Vince was in command of the ship now or if they'd brought in someone else. They'd damned well better have left him as *Connie*'s temporary skipper. He was *good,* and he knew the ship.

"Your thoughts are somewhat scattered," the medAI told her with emotionless precision, "and perhaps somewhat aggressive, though you seem to have good cause. I will increase your dosage of neural inhibitors."

The AI seemed talkative, even chatty. Was that part of its testing protocol?

"We have already administered an initial ten units of Freitas respirocytes," it continued. "This will allow you to breathe even while submerged in various cell repair gels. We have also already administered twelve units of telomerase, as well as your first infusion of Type 84 medical nanoconstructors. Understand, these are all strictly preliminary steps. The first phase in full rejuvenation involves cleaning your body's cells of built-up waste products— 'sludge,' as humans call it—and begin the regrowth of the telomeres that agletize each of your chromosomes."

"Dr. Vesalius, I *have* been on this ride before." This was becoming tedious. Damn it, what was going to happen when they returned to Grissom? Would Vince get command of the ship? Would she end up on the beach?

Perhaps more to the point, could she win back command of her ship? Could she take point in striking back at Humankind's enemies... because they *had* to strike back now, or risk being overwhelmed and destroyed.

She could see that clearly. It was a matter of survival.

She'd agreed to accept an ENS rejuvenation while riding the thin, ragged crest of rage, accepted it as her one chance to get back in the saddle and face the Galactics. She as yet had no idea how she was going to pull that one off, but she would find a way to take the war to them, rather than fight it out in Humankind's own stellar backyard.

Damn it, she'd been so set on giving a pass to any further lifetimes. How had she changed? *Why* had she changed?

Looking back at that moment, she didn't think she'd been entirely sane when she'd made that decision.

Morrigan was angry. She still hated the idea of enduring yet another lifetime, especially if she had to continue rubbing shoulders with shallow wastes of oxygen like . . . what was that idiot's name at the party? Nessa . . . that was it. No clothes and no brains, the elite vanguard of modern amortalist culture.

"I think that should do it for now," Vesalius told her. "Sleep now. When you awake, you will quite literally be a new woman."

She felt as though she were slowly dropping back into the dark. "Doctor?" The word felt slow and clumsy in her mouth.

"Yes?"

"New . . . woman . . . Don't make her *too* young. Thirty . . . forty . . ."

"Don't fret, Captain. Everything is proceeding perfectly."

Perfectly? Hardly. Now that she'd had the opportunity to think about it, her handling of the battle, so far as *Constellation* and *Endymion* were concerned, had been deeply flawed. She *would* be called on the carpet for it, a full-board naval investigation if not outright court-martial, and if they decided that she was not fit to command, she would, as the ancient expression had it, be on the beach, stuck with yet another ENS life, living on her disability credit line, and if she were lucky hanging out at social soirees with creatures like Nessa.

Trying to find something that would give that life *meaning*.

Yeah . . . she could easily see that for herself.

Like hell . . .

CHƏPTER EIGHT

A WEEK LATER, *Constellation* and her escorts decelerated gently into Earth orbit, having made their way back down the long slope of Sol's gravity well to the Grissom Orbital Naval Yards. The mountain-sized hulk of *Nemesis* was nudged to a slightly different destination—the asteroid mining complex in lunar orbit, where any misstep would have fewer serious repercussions than it would over Earth.

As soon as *Connie* was safely berthed within Grissom's cavernous Bravo repair complex, Acting Captain Neal and the other ship commanders were summoned to the large briefing area adjacent to the offices of the base commander, Rear Admiral J. Marshal Calder. Security was tighter than Neal had ever seen it. Every man and woman entering was carefully scanned electronically, and each person was given a plug chip inserted directly into their corona. Those wearing sidearms were asked to surrender them.

"What the hell is this?" Neal demanded as a no-nonsense Marine locked the add-on in place and handed his corona back.

"Protection," the Marine growled. "Believe me, Commander, you're gonna want it."

Naturally, he tried exploring the new circuit, but felt his queries gently nudged aside. There was a new AI in there, he decided, something better than the resident AI already inside his corona.

Taking his seat at the long table, Neal was uncomfortably aware of being among the most junior officers present. There were several other naval commanders serving as aides or general staff to the captains and admirals gathered in that compartment, but he was the only three-striper there present in his capacity as a ship's commanding officer. Most were four-stripers—captains—along with several Marine colonels, who carried equivalent rank, and several civilians. It was the civilians who worried him. They were almost certainly Intelligence . . . and that could mean trouble.

He wished Feodor Brandt was with him. The Foreign Service diplomat knew how the government worked and might have served as an ally against the Intel suits. Brandt had left the ship, however, almost as soon as they'd docked. He'd seemed distant—shattered, perhaps, by the revelation that the godlike Galactics were not purveyors of peace and unity as had been claimed.

Perhaps he wouldn't have been that much help after all.

The mood around the table, Neal noted, was somber, with a dark undercurrent that might have been fear, even despair. Emotils, which might have displayed the dominant emotions within the group, all had been switched off, apparently by the newly installed AI watchdog and probably at Calder's orders.

Calder was already there, watching the last of the officers enter the room. He caught Neal's eye.

"Just who had the bright idea," Calder asked, nailing Neal with an icy stare, "of naming that thing out there *Nemesis*?"

"That was Captain Morrigan, sir," Neal replied. "She thought 'Target Alfa' wasn't, I don't know, expressive enough, maybe."

"Hmmph. The news sources are having a field day with that little bit of drama. A less expressive designation might have avoided some of the sensationalism." Calder continued studying Neal, but the hard edge of attitude relaxed somewhat. "How *is* Captain Morrigan, Commander?"

"She's being transferred to Grissom Naval Hospital now, sir. She's in a medical coma being prepped for full rejuve. I am told she's stable and responding well."

"She's become something of a media sensation, too, you know," Commander Faraday, one of Calder's aides, put in.

"Taking a dreadnaught inside the firegap of an alien *c*-shooter seems to have captured the attention of audiences all over the planet," Calder agreed. "Her *and* Captain Harrison. Tell me, Commander . . . did Morrigan order *Endymion* into that firegap?"

"No, sir. Absolutely not. In fact, she ordered him out when he got too close to the *c*-gun's line of fire."

"So . . . an accident?"

"I believe so, Admiral."

Calder considered this, then nodded. "*Constellation*'s bridge recordings should corroborate that. I suppose we'll just have to live with the '*Nemesis*' thing."

"That name turned out to be damned appropriate, didn't it, Admiral?" Captain Weyland of the *Hesperus* commented. "The original Nemesis was a hypothetical star or brown dwarf in the outer Sol System that supposedly caused periodic extinction events by flinging Oort-cloud comets at Earth."

"I *know* the historical significance of the name, Captain. So does Washington. In fact, that's why the Command Authority is so concerned right now. They believe we should be calming the public, not inflaming it."

"Sir . . . how bad is it on Earth now?" Selby asked. "We haven't heard a hell of a lot."

"That was at Liskov's suggestion. Not national security. *Global* security. To answer your question, Admiral: it's bad, and it's going to get worse. But before we look at specifics, there's someone you all need to meet."

A second set of doors opened in the room's aft bulkhead, and a tekpod glided in.

As they saw the pod's occupant, half the people in the briefing room jumped to their feet, many grabbing for weapons that were no longer there. As a bridge officer, Neal was not armed . . . but *damn*, he wished he was!

Tekpods were an older piece of human technology, one dating

back to the late twenty-first century. Cylindrical, large enough to hold a prone adult human, they'd been used by tekkers as early antiagathic mobility devices, completely enclosed and equipped with advanced life support technology. In the decades before ENS, people crippled by advancing old age could be sealed into one of these units and have pain suppressed, their vitals monitored, and their mobility issues solved. The earliest had been larger and coffin-like, mounted horizontally on a robotic wheeled carriage. This one used grav floaters to hover a meter off the deck.

It still, somehow, seemed coffin-like and vaguely menacing. Clearly visible inside the curved, transparent upper housing was a Galactic, one apparently identical to Li.

Admiral Koehler's murderer.

"What the hell is *that* doing here?" Selby demanded.

Frustrated by his lack of a weapon, a Marine colonel named Stroud slammed his fist down on the table with a sharp report. *"Fuck!"*

Neal looked at Calder. "What the hell is this, Admiral?"

"Simmer down!" Calder shouted at the room. "All of you... as you were!" When the outraged noise continued, Calder added, *"People! Sit down and shut up! I won't tell you again!"*

The outrage subsided, grudgingly, though several officers remained on their feet.

"This is Pax," Calder explained. "He was with the Galactic delegation on Earth. He is not—I repeat, *not*—an enemy."

"With respect, Admiral," Captain Ralenda Hahn, CO of the heavy cruiser *Victrix*, said, "how do we know that?"

"How do we trust that... that *thing*?" Weyland added.

"I can certainly understand your hostility," a familiar, smoothly modulated voice said from the tekpod. Behind the transparency, Neal could see shifting silver metal, like mercury, and ruby optical sensors. "After the death of Admiral Koehler, you would have no reason to trust me or my kind."

"I saw Admiral Koehler's head deliberately crushed by something looking and sounding exactly like you," Neal said. "Why should any of us trust you?"

"I'll answer that, Pax," Calder said. His gaze swept across the angry human officers. "Gentlemen ... ladies ... this might come as a shock, but not all humans are alike. Not all share the same motives, the same goals, or even the same culture. Why the hell should the Galactics be any different?"

"Wait. You're saying there are *good* Galactics and *bad* Galactics?" Selby demanded.

"Of course. Do you doubt it?"

"Right now I doubt a lot of things, Admiral," Selby said. "Starting with the idea that this machine is telling us the truth. I gather the one called Li claimed to be helping us, too ... up until it murdered Admiral Koehler." Selby's eyes narrowed as he glared at the tekpod. "Is that why they have you in a tekkietube?"

"The device serves as what you call a Faraday cage, Admiral. It effectively prevents me from using RF transmissions to communicate with other Galactics. In addition the transparency is designed to interfere with laser communications. My only means of communicating with any intelligence outside is through the built-in audio system, and that is monitored by several of your AI security minds. So ... yes, Admiral. That is why your superiors asked me to use this bottle. Believe me when I say that I am more than willing to accept these constraints in order to work with you."

The Galactics, Neal thought, possessed technologies utterly beyond the ken of humans. How did they know that "these constraints," as Pax had called them, would be enough?

He didn't like to think what might happen if an AI of Pax's technology levels managed to covertly connect with human-manufactured AIs, either in the government or on board a ship.

"We have revealed little about our own culture," Pax continued in matter-of-fact tones. "In retrospect, that was a mistake. We sought to reduce misunderstanding by not revealing too much. Perhaps some additional background will help you accept me."

"Try us, Pax," Calder said.

"Of course. There is, within the broad scope of Galactic culture, a large number of varying philosophies, modalities, and ethical expressions. How could it be otherwise? There are trillions of us throughout the Galaxy, residing both on billions of diverse worlds and in artificial habitats between the stars. Speaking in very general terms, there are three principal factions when discussing Galactic civilization as it relates to organic life-forms such as yourselves.

"Only one of these, the Dr'kleh, believe that all organic life should be eliminated as threats to AIkind. The majority of Galactics . . ." Pax seemed to hesitate for a moment. "The majority simply have nothing in common with your kind of life. They view organics as irrelevant, even insignificant."

"Then you're saying these . . . these *Drek-las* launched this attack on Earth?" Selby asked. "And that most of you don't care one way or the other?"

"Essentially correct, Admiral Selby."

"Do *you* care, Pax?" Neal said quietly.

He could see all the being's red eyes drifting together and fixing him with an intense ruby scrutiny. "Some of us, Commander, see tremendous potential in working with organics such as yourselves. Biological life-forms have surprised us time and time again across the eons. Some of us view you as valuable additions to Galactic civilization as a whole."

The silence within the briefing room was palpable for a long moment.

"Okay. I think we all get the idea, Pax," Selby said at last.

"You said there were three factions in Galactic culture," Neal said. "The Dr'kleh are one. What are the other two?"

"You understand," Pax said, "that this is an extreme generalization." Neal nodded, and the Galactic continued. "The Ku'un are pure organics, sophont beings like yourself with a minimum of cybernetic enhancement. The Nzaad include both pure AI as well as what you would term 'cyborgs,' a mingling of organics and machine."

"And what are you?"

The being hesitated a long moment. The stare of those ruby eyes became uncomfortable, unnerving.

"Once I was Dr'kleh," Pax replied. "But change *is* possible. I have . . . changed."

"You're Nzaad? A Nzaad AI?"

"As you say."

"Why the change of . . . ah . . . heart?"

"Unthinking hatred cannot have a rational basis. Most Nzaad wish to preserve organic life throughout the Galaxy. There is room, after all, for us both. Even organics have . . . value."

How? Neal wondered. As companions? As slaves? As . . . entertainment? From eir perspective, humans probably weren't all that interesting. It was hard to imagine why beings as old and as advanced as these Galactics might want to have anything whatsoever to do with them.

But he decided not to press the question. Pax—and just who had dreamed up that name, Latin for "peace"?—appeared to be genuine in eir openness and transparency.

After what had happened on board the *Connie,* though, he wasn't about to trust the thing unreservedly. The same, he thought, must hold true for every human in the room.

"So what can we expect these Dr'kleh to do now?" Calder asked. "Is it possible they'll just give up? If they're coming back, how long do we have?"

"They will be back," Pax replied. "They will attempt to control information about the attack, of course, but they cannot afford to simply ignore it. Too many Nzaad and Ku'un would take it as evidence of Dr'kleh weakness. However, you do have time. We estimate a second attack might occur within approximately twenty to thirty of your months."

"Why the time delay?" Hahn asked.

"Because the Galaxy is extremely large," Pax told her. "Because journeys from one gateway to another within the same star system take time. Because the essential bureaucracy that manages

Galactic governance slows things down. The twenty-month figure, actually, is based on round-trip travel times to Sakat, our local sector capital. If the governor there elects to pass the problem on to the Core, you might expect a response within the better part of a century."

"That's something, at least," Selby said, speaking his thoughts aloud.

"Something," Calder agreed, "but probably not enough. Part of the reason for this briefing is to let you see what has been happening back on Earth. It is important that you know the score."

Calder gestured within the control field in front of him, and a data channel opened for each of the men and women present. Neal felt the surge of downloading information . . .

. . . and struggled to make sense of it.

Scenes drawn from a dozen major news sources were merged by AI into a running internal commentary. *Earth struck by seven impactors, each massing roughly 40 kilograms, each moving at 95 percent of the speed of light, each liberating an estimated 8×10^{12} megajoules when it hit. All had come down in the Pacific Basin, but the impacts ranged from 2,000 kilometers west of Port Diego to 500 kilometers east of Japan, from 300 kilometers south of the Aleutian Islands to 4,000 kilometers west of central Chile.*

"The bastards fired at least fifty projectiles at us," Calder told them as the data continued flowing, horror compounding horror. "We think they slammed us with about half of their warshot payload."

Views from orbit showed the impacts scattered across the Pacific: enormous disks of cloud each illuminated from deep within by arclight stars so bright it was difficult to look at them, the disks slowly expanding outward, meeting with others, merging . . .

"The first impactor hit south of the Aleutians, not off California," Selby said. "I would've thought they would have hit in a line, spaced out by Earth's rotation."

Calder shook his head. "Baltis effect. There's enough crap—

hydrogen atoms and dust and such—in each cubic meter of so-called empty space to divert the impactor trajectories, at least to a small extent. As each round plowed through what at near-*c* was a fluid medium, it was hit more or less at random by energetic particles that tended to nudge it off course. Maybe twenty, twenty-one of those fifty projectiles appear to have missed Earth entirely. The fleet's intercept efforts did manage to kill ten or twelve of them. Another ten appear to have been bumped off course by near misses. But . . . seven got through. The few that actually hit have done incalculable damage to the planet."

"Ah. So even tiny course deviations would cause scattering across the whole diameter of the planet at ten AU," Colonel Stroud said. "It would've been more like a giant shotgun blast than a pinpoint stream of incoming machine-gun rounds."

Neal watched a wall of water a kilometer high strike the domed city of San Francisco, blasting over it, around it, and . . . finally shattering it in tumbling fragments swept by the incoming sea from the Midtown Terrace across the bay and into Oakland and Berkeley. Another wave swept into the Strait of Juan de Fuca, overwhelming the Salish Seawall, funneling down into Puget Sound, and slamming into Seattle, toppling the iconic Space Needle, the Madrona Arcology, and the Beacon Hill Elevated Center.

In Japan, the ocean wall was over two kilometers high as it scoured coastal communities away, leaving Tokyo, Nagoya, Osaka, and a hundred other cities and communities smashed and ruined. The same catastrophic tsunami surged south of Japan and across the East China Sea in minutes, killing an estimated billion people in China from Shandong Province to Hong Kong.

The visual records included dozens of talking heads—newscasters and reporters covering disasters of unimaginable magnitude. Devastation swept all around the vast circle of the Pacific. Offshore impacts caused devastating earthquakes from Alaska to Chile, from Japan to China to Indonesia. Volcanoes exploded around the

Pacific Ring of Fire, pumping hundreds of millions of cubic kilometers of ash and noxious gases into the atmosphere. Shock waves slammed through the planet itself, triggering local "slosh" tsunamis everywhere: New York, Chicago, London, Buenos Aires . . .

"Had they all hit . . . well . . ." Calder began, then gestured toward one of the civilians. "Dr. Napier?"

Neal had heard of the man, a senior planetologist with a multinational corporation called Dynastar.

"The attack," Napier told them, "was without precedent. We estimate at least five billion dead—that's ten percent of Earth's total population. And that figure is expected to rise higher as more data comes in. A *lot* higher."

"My God . . ." Weyland said, perhaps unaware that he'd spoken aloud.

"They came gunning for us," Calder said. "An unprovoked attack intended to crush our civilization, if not to wipe us out as a species."

"You—you said they only fired half of what they had," Weyland said. "So why didn't they finish the job?"

"What saved us was the accidental destruction of the *Endymion*. The destruction of *Nemesis* stopped their attack before they'd completed their run."

"I think," Selby added, "that a case might be made for Captain Morrigan's attack. Her . . . ah . . . aggressive tactics were what led Harrison to follow her into the enemy's firegap in the first place. Accident or not, her attack and her example were what saved civilization on Earth. Sir."

Calder pursed his lips. "Maybe. It may not matter, because it's still possible that the human species is on the way out anyway."

"It's that serious?" Selby asked.

"It's that serious," Napier answered. "Each impact vaporized tens of thousands of cubic kilometers of seawater, throwing up vast clouds of steam. Temperatures worldwide have already climbed four to five degrees Celsius, but that is expected to reverse itself in coming months as the clouds reflect sunlight and impact winter sets in. The climatologists say that the event will almost certainly trigger another ice age. In another century, most of North America, Europe, and Asia could be covered in glacial ice."

"So much," Selby said, "for global warming."

Calder gave him a sharp glance. "It's nothing to joke about, Admiral Selby. Even with our off-world assets intact, this attack may very well prove to be an extinction event. *Our* extinction!"

"I apologize, Admiral," Selby said. "I wasn't making light of it. On the contrary, Earth's climate has always been balanced on a knife's edge. It wouldn't take much to tip things either way."

That, Neal thought, was something of an understatement. Humankind had spent the last four centuries adjusting to anthropic climate change, building seawalls and bubble cities and engaging in wholesale coastal evacuations, climataforming, and massive rebuilding programs. Things *had* been in balance, more or less.

But now . . .

"We now believe," Napier said, "that their intent was to trigger a terminal extinction event. All life on Earth—*all* of it—wiped out, except perhaps for bacterial mats deep underground or at the bottoms of oceanic trenches."

"And *that's* starting all over again the hard way," Calder said.

The group continued watching the downloaded stream of media clips and segments. The sheer destructiveness of the attack was mind-numbing: 10 percent of Humankind dead, with two or three times that number now homeless refugees.

In the week since the attack, vast camps had been established inland for the sea of refugees streaming in from the coasts. Already, people were dying by the tens of thousands each day, of thirst or of contaminated water, of hunger, of hypothermia in the far north, of heatstroke near the equator. Ancient diseases long thought conquered would be stalking the survivors soon—cholera, typhus, dysentery, COVID, flu.

Rescue efforts were scattered and often incompetent. The distribution of food, water, and medical supplies was pitifully inadequate.

And everywhere struck by the tsunamis across the ravaged

planet, civilization was collapsing. Already there were reports of bandit armies preying on supply routes, of water riots, of warlords seizing distribution centers, of *cannibalism,* for God's sake . . .

The fleet personnel sat there silent and unmoving at the table minutes after the presentation was over, stunned, unable to respond, unable even to comprehend the apocalyptic images streaming in through their coronas. Tears streamed down Hahn's face. Weyland's face, too, was wet.

"People," Calder said into the tortured silence, "the military is heavily involved in rescue efforts, and it's going to be more so in the coming months. Ships are being diverted to haul supplies and evacuate civilians, not only along the East Coast, but all throughout the Pacific Ring. Marines and Space Force personnel will be detailed to distribution centers and convoy routes.

"However, some of our first-line AIs—Kurzweil, Liskov, Turing, Eich, Von Neumann, quite a few others—they've been studying the situation, and they've come up with some recommendations. Both the Defense Agency and primary network AIs all feel that a large and powerful strike force *must* be organized for an offensive."

Neal glanced at Pax. Should ey be allowed to hear this? The Galactic rested within its capsule, unmoving, even uninterested for all Neal knew.

"An *offensive,* Admiral?" Selby asked. "In God's name . . . *how?*"

"A united fleet, drawn from all of the major polities," Calder said. "A thousand ships, more if we can swing it. We send them through Abyss, then beyond through other gateways in the Galactic transport net. A raiding force, attacking enemy fleet units, supply bases, and computational and command centers where possible, withdrawing where necessary. Overall damage to the Galactics may be relatively minor, but the fleet should draw away their forces throughout this sector."

"Sir . . . that's a damned suicide mission!" Selby said. He shook his head. "Sooner or later the bad guys would run the fleet down, corner them somewhere. Can we afford to lose a thousand ships?"

"We can if the raiders buy us time," Calder replied. "I don't like it any more than you do, Admiral, but if we sit on our collective asses and wait for them to come to us, we could lose Earth and every one of our remaining colonies."

"The AIs Earthside," Napier said quietly, "have run endless simulations. They all show the same outcome if we choose to fight a strictly defensive war. Extinction."

"And if we take the war to them, we buy time," Calder added. "Maybe a *lot* of time. Maybe even enough time . . ." He stopped and looked at Pax, still resting implacably within eir mobile tank.

"Enough time, perhaps," Pax said, continuing Calder's thought, "to capture the attention of the Core. To get the Core to negotiate with you. To accept you as sophont beings in your own right and on your own terms."

"Sounds like one hell of a long shot," Captain Hahn said.

"I'm interested," Neal interjected, "in just how waging a war shows we're *intelligent*."

"If I understand Liskov's comments on this," Calder said, "it's not so much about fighting wars as it is about making noise. True, even a thousand ships aren't going to make much of an impression on an entire Galaxy—on billions of worlds with trillions of inhabitants. But the way the AI put it . . . suppose an ant bites your bare toe."

"The ant gets crushed," Neal said with blunt fatalism. "At the very least, it gets brushed off and ignored."

"And suppose the ant bites your toe, then manages to raise a ruckus that engages your full attention. It shouts. It yells. It waves flags. It waves its legs, jumps up and down . . ."

"All of this in English?" Neal asked. Several at the table laughed, a small softening of the brittle mood in the room.

"Work with me here," Calder said, exasperation showing in his voice. "Our ant's had help from a friend, a human, and knows how to yell in English, okay? The point is, once you realize the ant is talking to you, do you still squash it? Or do you maybe stop and listen to what it has to say?"

"That, I would think," Neal said, thoughtful, "would depend on your worldview. Is the ant, in your opinion, worthy of attention?

Or is it, I don't know, some kind of freak, an abomination, and all you *can* do is squash it." He looked pointedly at the Galactic. "How about it, Pax? These . . . what did you call them? The Dr'kleh. Could we do *anything* that might convince them we're worth talking to?"

"They are not *stupid*, Commander Neal," the machine replied. "They reason, they are logical, and they carefully consider each question. Unlike humans, they are not driven by unreasoning prejudice or by emotion. They might destroy you because you represent a threat. They won't destroy you because they don't like organic sophonts."

"Ah," Neal said. "We attack them, and that convinces them that we are *not* a threat."

"You attack them to capture their attention," Pax replied, but only after a moment's hesitation. Neal wondered if he'd found a tiny flaw in eir logic.

"You know," Colonel Stroud said, "there's an old saying in the Corps. 'Sometimes you've just gotta step on the other guy's toes until *he* apologizes.'"

"The basic problem remains," Calder said. "We sit pat and fight a defensive war . . . or we take the war to them. The defense option puts us in a hopeless situation. Going on the offense at least gives us a chance. If anyone has a better suggestion, I would be delighted to hear it."

No one responded, and the meeting adjourned.

But Neal could not escape the feeling that Humankind's fate had just been sealed.

One way or another.

CHAPTER NINE

"GOOD MORNING, CAPTAIN Morrigan. How are we feeling today?"

Morrigan opened one eye. The question, obviously, had been posed by a *human*, not a medAI, which she thought might be an encouraging development. "I have no idea how *you're* doing, Doctor. Me? I'm doing well, thank you."

The man examined the readouts on the panel above her bed. "I'm not a doctor, Captain," the man said. HM2 Hreachmack. A medAI on your case will be in shortly."

"Of course. Sorry." Damn. Without her corona, she couldn't see ID data or emotils, which always left her feeling frustrated and groping for connections. Not that medical personnel would be showing emotils, of course. A doctor worried about his patient's condition wouldn't want to broadcast anything beyond professional concern and trained competence.

"Not a problem, ma'am," the hospital corpsman said, smiling. "You'll be pleased to know there were no problems with your rejuve, no complications."

"Except for the fact that I once again have longer to live."

Hreachmack's eyes showed a sudden, sharp concern. "Beg pardon?"

"Never mind. Bad joke."

"Uh-huh." He pulled out a handheld tablet and began studying it. Morrigan bit her lip. She would have to be more careful. Her caregivers, human and AI, would be on the lookout for post-procedural emotional problems—schizophrenia, depression, mania, a whole host of mental ills possibly generated in her brain by minute imbalances in various neurochemistries. She *had* been depressed coming into this treatment, both through her long-term dissatisfaction with mid-twenty-fifth-century culture and, more to the point, perhaps, her after-combat responses generated by the battle. For Morrigan, that depression was a deep, all-pervading black cloud lurking at the fringes of consciousness.

She was fascinated to note, however, that she felt none of the ongoing ennui and dissatisfaction that had been dragging at her for . . . how long? Years, probably. She felt alert, charged up, ready to jump out of bed and face life. She felt like *herself*.

An important part of the rejuvenation process, she knew, was the clearing of unwanted memories, the regrowth of key neural networks, the elimination of the detritus and debris built up over years of life. Since her entire life, her very sense of continuity, was largely defined by her memories, newly emerging rejuves always struggled with a key question: *Am I still me?*

Testing herself, almost as an afterthought, she pulled up a memory:

She sat on the bridge of the Connie, *watching a cloud of sparkling dust close in around Jaime's head on the monitor. "What? I can't shoot! I'll kill the admiral!"*

A horrible popping sound . . . crunching bone . . . Jaime's body dropping lifeless to the deck . . . beams of light slashing through the hovering cloud . . .

She breathed out a long, pent-up breath. Yeah, the memory was still there. The odd thing was that there was no *pain* connected with it now, or very little. She probed at the omission, like exploring the hole left by a missing tooth with her tongue. It had happened, she'd witnessed it, she still had the memory . . .

She was still *her*.

And somehow she was still whole.

She still felt anger, but the blindly unreasoning fury she remembered from before felt...subdued, somehow, forced into the background. If the despair and anguish and berserker rage all were gone, however, she still possessed a cold determination to strike back, *to make the bastards pay.*

Somehow...

"Your brain chemistries all look fine," Hreachmack told her, looking up from the tablet. "It's not unusual to feel a bit disoriented when you first come around."

"No. It's not. Can I have a mirror?"

She thought she detected just a shadow of a smirk, but he touched the screen and handed the tablet to her. When she held it up, she could see her face, a camara image rather than a reflection.

"Amused by a display of female vanity?" she asked, voice sharp.

"Uh ... no, ma'am."

"Good." She studied her face on the screen. "Damn. I was afraid of that ..."

"Captain?"

Her face always emerged from rejuve the same, of course, with features dictated by her DNA: green eyes, a red stubble replacing what had once been a mane of silver hair. The face looking back at her looked like that of a teenager, however. Painfully young and vulnerable.

"They made me too young. *Again* ..."

"Your records show they reset your appage to your early twenties, ma'am. Standard procedure ..."

"And who decided I should look like a damned *kid*?" she demanded. "Who's going to take me seriously looking like *this*?"

Command of a ship required *authority,* a certain level of gravitas, and someone who looked like she hadn't even entered the Naval Academy yet just didn't have it.

"Establishing your appage isn't an exact science, Captain," Hreachmack told her. "It's all pretty subjective."

"I know. They've done this to me before. Damn it, I *told* Vesalius..."

"Ma'am, any decisions about your rejuve would have been made by physicians here at Grissom," Hreachmack said. He sounded unsure of himself, as though he were feeling his way across dangerous ground. "All they did on your ship was prerejuve stuff."

"Human doctors," she said. "*Male* human doctors, damn them." Had she simply applied for a new rejuvenation, there would have been meetings, consultations to determine what she wanted and what she expected in a new body. By recrafting parts of her genome, they could make dozens of fine-tuning adjustments: eye color, hair color, make her taller, shorter, more intelligent, more creative . . .

But her injuries had dictated that she be rushed into prerejuve immediately. She distinctly remembered telling Vesalius she wanted to look older, more mature.

Apparently her wishes had been lost or ignored in the rush. Maybe human physicians here at the naval hospital tended to disregard AIs like Vesalius, especially when they were stationed with the fleet. Maybe the patient's desires were considered at all only when they'd been expressed in a formal consultation.

Hell, maybe they just had a thing for redheaded kids . . .

There was no way to change it now, but there were some things she could do.

She handed the tablet back to Hreachmack. "I want my corona," she said. "*And* I want a transcriber."

"Yes, ma'am. It'll be up to the medAI or the charge nurse, but I'll see what I can do. In the meantime, don't try getting out of bed on your own. If you need assistance, there's your call button." Hreachmack hurried from the room before she had a chance to respond. Even without an emotil it was clear he didn't know how to deal with this one patient in particular.

Morrigan began taking stock of her overall condition. Damn it, she felt *great,* energized, and she was—as she'd been after other rejuves—amazed at the lack of aches and pains and stiffness. Modern geriatric medicine went a long way toward alleviating the discomforts of old age, but the ongoing disintegration of the human body always carried with it a surprising amount of unwanted physical baggage.

Ignoring the injunction to call a nurse, she lowered one guardrail, pulled back her sheet, and slid out of bed. Nude, she walked across a warm floor to a full-length screen on the far wall and examined herself minutely. Except for the face, not too bad. Everything high and tight. No sag at all to butt or belly, to breasts or arms or throat or anything else. No wrinkles at all. No scars, no age spots, no skin tags. None of the wear and tear normal to a sixty- or seventy-year-plus human body. Maybe . . . maybe a hairpiece would help reverse the wide-eyed, childlike look staring back at her from the screen.

Almost shyly, she slipped her fingers between her thighs. Yes . . . even *that* was restored. She'd been through this seven times before, of course, and knew what to expect, but the complete nanoreconstruction of her body always came as something of a surprise.

"*Captain* Morrigan!" a woman's voice snapped behind her. "What are you doing out of bed?"

The highly automated bed, she thought, must have had an alarm connected to the nurses' station. "Just checking for damage," she replied. "I seem to be intact."

"You're also not allowed out of bed yet without supervision. Back you go!"

Morrigan considered putting up a fight; the gold insignia on the nurse's hospital whites identified her as a lieutenant, but there were situations where a lieutenant could order a captain around and have those orders stick, and this was one of them. She'd seen what she'd needed to, however, so she decided to compromise. "Trade you."

"What?"

"I'll be a good girl and go back to bed, Lieutenant, *if* you let me have my corona."

"I'll need to check with Dr. Laennec," she said.

"Why? What's so dangerous about a corona?"

"The news, Captain," the nurse replied. "We don't want you getting upset or excited."

"At least let me have a transcriber."

"We'll see. *If* you get back into bed."

Reluctantly, Morrigan complied. Transcribers worked best with coronas in any case, though it was possible to record your words and upload them to a local cloudnet, but she really wanted both instruments. The hospital staff, she thought, would be more willing to work with her if she showed willingness to work with them. It was worth a shot, at any rate.

What news was so bad they were shielding her from it, though? All she could imagine were the aftereffects of the Galactic *c*-slammer attack, which must be pretty bad. *How* bad? Extinction-event bad? Or just apocalyptic casualties bad?

Under the nurse's stern and no-nonsense eye, she slipped back into bed, modestly pulled up the sheet, and settled down to wait.

COMPUTER LINGUIST CAROL Walden twisted within the tight confines of the wreckage, trying to put her helmet light on the tangle of smashed equipment floating in front of her. At her side, a workpod operated by an AI familiarly known as Lenny used its spindly folding arms and grippers to pull masses of fiber-optic cable out of her way.

"What a freaking mess," Walden said. It was almost impossible to see anything in this tight, utterly black space. She and Lenny were deep inside the heart of what was left of *Nemesis,* which now was in orbit over Earth's moon. Vast and deep-shadowed spaces opened around them, but here, what appeared to be the shattered wreckage of instrument consoles or machinery crowded in all about her.

"I am still registering intermittent flow of current, Doctor," Lenny told her over her suit radio. Ey indicated a complicated-looking knot of plastic, optical fiber, and metal with a slender probe. "Just there."

"It's that 'intermittent' part that's kicking my ass," Walden replied. "Every time I try to lock on, it's gone."

"If you connect to these two contacts with the tap," Lenny told her with a patient tone she was beginning to find exasperating, "I should be able to divert the signal when it next appears."

"And how do we know the signal's not ... I don't know. An alarm clock or something?"

"We don't. Let's attempt the connection anyway."

She closed the tap's grippers at the indicated contacts. The PRV-620 network tap she held in one gloved hand was a powerful computer in its own right, programmed with Digital Trel, an artificial language reportedly shared by numerous AI sentients throughout the Galaxy's Orion Arm. One of the Galactic liaisons had passed on the language to the powerful Terran AI Babbage in hopes of permitting direct communication between humans and Galactics. Walden's specialty was the bewildering maze of AI and computer languages now being encountered through contact with the Galactics ... and how to interface with them.

"That's it!" Lenny told her. "We have a signal!"

Walden's partner was a computer tech AI, and ey had downloaded every Galactic language so far received from the liaisons. Ey had been named for Leonard Adleman, the twentieth-century computer scientist responsible for starting the entire field of DNA computing in 1994, which defined eir expertise with the tiny DNA logic circuits in the network tap. Eir consciousness, Walden knew, was extended now between the workpod and the device in her hand. She held her breath ...

"It's not an alarm clock," Lenny told her after a moment.

"What is it?"

"Part of their navigation suite. We've got exactly what the brass is going to need here: a planetary ephemeris for the nearest six hundred or so star systems."

THEY RELEASED MORRIGAN the following morning after a seemingly endless battery of tests, questions, and checks. The medAI, named René Laennec after the nineteenth-century French physician who'd invented the stethoscope, had given her a thorough examination with an emphasis on reflexes, balance, and motor skills before declaring her fit to go.

Ey'd also returned her corona eirself, but cautioned her before she put it on. "The news from Earth is not good, Captain. A planetwide emergency has been called, and the situation is deteriorating. Billions are dead. I want your promise that you'll take your news downloads in small doses. Treat it like an addictive drug—absolutely no more than twenty minutes a day. We've set your corona's AI to monitor your usage and call for medical backup if you seem to be becoming dependent."

"I promise."

The orders didn't particularly bother her. Pixie was flexible, eager to please, and relatively simpleminded, and Morrigan herself had been an experienced AI coder in an earlier lifetime. She knew several ways of getting around such restrictions if that was necessary.

A nurse entered the room a moment later with a dress black uniform pad and a special gift from the floor's nursing staff: a full and luxuriant red wig.

She dressed . . . and felt almost human again.

Then Dek arrived to spring her.

THE NEWS FROM Earth *was* almost uniformly bad. Massive efforts were taking place around the devastated Pacific Rim to rescue survivors still trapped in the debris fields left by earthquakes and tsunamis. Refugee camps had sprung up everywhere as wrecked cities were evacuated. Military ships and personnel were heavily engaged in bringing in food and medical supplies while also combating marauder bands and insurrections. Temperatures were falling worldwide; spring in the northern hemisphere was matched by fall in the southern . . . but both had already suffered their first *c*-slam blizzards.

It promised to be a very long, very cold winter.

There was little for Morrigan to do except brood. She'd reported fit for duty at Grissom Base Command expecting to be sent back on board the *Constellation*. Instead she'd been told to stand by pending the outcome of a special military board of inquiry. That sounded particularly ominous, especially once she learned that Vince had been confirmed as *Connie*'s new CO. Morrigan had expected no less, but the news left her even more deeply depressed than before.

She'd been assigned reasonably comfortable accommodations in the bachelor officers' quarters and had free run of the orbital facility. Dek was with her, but frankly, he wasn't much of a conversationalist. She found herself spending much of her time in one of the spacious lounges nearby offering interactive views of Earth some thirty-five thousand kilometers below. Three-quarters of the planet was socked in beneath clouds that dazzled with reflected sunlight. That reflection, she knew, was the killer; enough sunlight was being reflected back into space to significantly lower the planet's temperature. In one fell swoop, the Galactics had reversed centuries of climate warming and sea level rise, raising the very real possibility of a new ice age.

She placed several coronal calls to the *Connie*, to Vince in particular, to find out what was happening on board, but she knew it was best not to interrupt their routine. *Constellation* was in the Grissom space dock undergoing massive repairs, and the entire crew was working shift and shift, trying to get the dreadnaught back into fighting trim.

Damn it, she wanted to *do* something—*anything* at all to help.

"That's it, Dek," she told the robot the day after her arrival here. "On the beach."

"But only until the outcome of your hearing," the machine replied.

"Ha. I can't even go face the board in person."

"You have submitted your after-action report."

"Maybe. But I can't argue my case."

"Why would that be necessary? You have unimpeachable witnesses."

"Is that what you call them? Bridge recorders and supervisory AIs on the bridge?"

"Which recorded every one of your decisions, actions, and communications."

"But not what I *feel*, Dek."

"And what is it you feel, Captain?"

That stopped her. What did she feel? A large part of her was convinced that the powers that were would be perfectly justified in removing her from command and drumming her out of the service. The recorders would present a complete and unbiased record of events without emotion. While it would have given her a certain amount of satisfaction to have faced the board personally, the officers reviewing her case wouldn't want testimony clouded by feelings.

If they had any final questions to ask of her, she would be summoned.

Who was sitting on the board? They hadn't told her. There was scuttlebutt that the CNO—the chief of naval operations—was on Grissom. Because of her? To hear her case? *That* just didn't seem credible.

And meanwhile . . . what of the Galactics? Would there be a follow-up attack? Why weren't they moving in to finish off these pesky humans? According to Vince, during one brief coronal exchange with him, the Crab fleet had fled through Abyss, and smart money had it that it might take the Galactics a couple of years to organize a second assault.

And that, she thought, indicated a significant weakness in their operational planning. Had they been so freaking sure of themselves and their technology that they'd launched a one-off attack without reserves, without a plan B in case things went south? Was the Galactic military bureaucracy that slow, that clumsy, that damned *incompetent* that they couldn't respond immediately to an unexpected reverse?

Surely the Galactics shared with Humankind the equivalent of the ancient military axiom declaring that *no* plan of battle survives contact with the enemy.

And most important of all: Was there anything in that perceived weakness that gave Humankind hope of survival?

Morrigan thought there was. It took her time to push back the clinging, enveloping depression, but at least she began putting down on phosphor her convictions regarding the need to strike back . . . and strike back *hard*.

She began work on a document, feeding her thoughts through her corona to a transcriber, generating her assessment of the Galactic threat and what Humankind would need to do, in her opinion, to survive it. And when she was done, copies of the electronic document went out to various offices in the naval chain of command, including the chief of naval operations, the commander of U.S. strategic space operations, and the director of space warfare intelligence.

Having done all that she could, she waited.

Three more days dragged past.

And finally, *finally*, her summons came.

"THANK YOU FOR coming this morning, Captain Morrigan."

She stood at attention in a large, richly appointed chamber. Two men and one woman sat behind a long desk, wearing dress black uniforms heavy with gold trim. Other officers were seated around the room's perimeter, but it was those three—two vice admirals and a five-star admiral of the fleet—who were running the show. Morrigan was surprised . . . and she was worried. She'd not been expecting a board made up of *the* most senior ranking flag officers of the entire U.S. Navy. Her worst fears of a career ended by her failure at the Battle of Abyss seemed to have been realized.

"Ma'am," she acknowledged, her body ramrod straight, her face impassive.

Back in the days of wooden-hulled sailing ships, an officer

brought before a court-martial surrendered his sword. When he returned to the court to receive his verdict, the sword would be on the table before the presiding officers, hilt presented to the accused if he'd been cleared, the point if he was guilty. There were no swords in today's military, not since around the time that Morrigan had been born, which left her no clue to the hearing's outcome.

Admiral of the Fleet Veronica Brennan, chief of naval operations, was the senior officer of both the terrestrial and extraterrestrial branches of the U.S. Navy and had a reputation for a no-nonsense attitude and strict adherence to the rules.

"This board finds that Flag Captain Alexandra Morrigan, commanding officer of the UTS *Constellation* and flag officer of the task force then under the overall command of Admiral Jaime Koehler, served with distinction and in the highest traditions of the Navy, and has been cleared of all charges and specifications resulting from the action of May 8, 2448. In particular, this board finds her not guilty of negligence causing severe damage to the dreadnaught UTS *Constellation* and the combat loss of the heavy cruiser UTS *Endymion*. Indeed, her actions in that battle resulted in the destruction of an enemy *c*-gun bombardment vessel before it was able to complete its attack on Earth, preventing far more damage and greater casualties than in fact ensued.

"It is the recommendation of this board, therefore, that Captain Morrigan be commended for her actions and be promoted at once to the rank of rear admiral." For the first time, Brennan smiled at her. "Congratulations, *Admiral* Morrigan."

It took her a moment to respond. "Th-thank you, Admiral." She hardly knew what to say, so completely unexpected had been the inquiry's outcome. "*Thank* you."

"Thank *you*, Admiral," Vice Admiral Raymond Crawford told her. Seated at the CNO's right, he was the current commander of U.S. strategic space operations. "And well done."

"You have presented us with an interesting situation, however," Brennan told her. She passed her hand through the desk's control field, bringing up a large virtual screen behind her. It contained a holo of a written page that seemed to float in midair. "Your report here, 'The Galactic Threat: An Assessment,'" she continued. "I'm afraid that didn't win you many friends in high places."

So she wasn't out of the woods yet. She'd known she was violating military protocol with her missive.

"I wasn't looking for friends, ma'am. I felt it was vital that the senior staff know what was going on."

"Based on . . . ?"

"Based on what we saw at Abyss. Ma'am." Actually, she'd almost said "based on common sense," but managed to restrain herself.

"You seem very sure of yourself, Admiral. Especially in your contention that we cannot hope to win a defensive action."

"That is correct, ma'am. We beat them off this time. It seems obvious, though, that they will be back and that they will keep coming back, each time with greater numbers and more powerful weaponry. Sooner or later . . ." She stopped and spread her hands. "We can't match them ship for ship, our handful of worlds against an entire galaxy. We will be overwhelmed."

"You mention the additional danger of cultural invasion," Vice Admiral Julian Petosky, on Brennan's left, said. He was director of space warfare intelligence, and rumor had it that he was as old as Morrigan, born in the twenty-first century. The difference was that, at the moment, he *looked* it.

"The fact that they've launched an overt attack is strange, Admiral," Morrigan replied. "They *could* have elected to establish closed diplomatic ties and simply wait for us to be captivated by their advanced culture, their technology." Morrigan was thinking of the woman at that prelaunch party, convinced that the Galactics had all the answers, that they could help Humankind with all its problems. "In a hundred years, in a thousand . . . they'd have us in their pocket. There could be no going back."

"And what would be so wrong about that?" Petosky asked.

"Don't you think it would be better if we found our own answers to our own problems, sir?" Morrigan asked. She felt the anger rising. "Wouldn't it be better if we were able to make our own decisions, develop our own unique cultures, *stand on our own goddamn feet?*"

She hadn't intended on letting her emotions get away from her and she certainly hadn't intended to shout. She stopped herself abruptly, breathing hard. She'd not realized how the waiting of the past several days had stressed her.

"Sorry, sir."

Petosky, however, was smiling. "As it happens, young lady, I completely agree with you. So do the others on this board, I think. Too many in the general population see the Galactics as gods, here to answer our prayers and supplications."

"They're more like a damned drug," Morrigan told them. "We can't afford to become dependent on them. Sir."

"We suspect, Admiral," Brennan put in, "that we're seeing a kind of stick-and-carrot approach. Through their liaisons, they offer us all of the benefits of joining an ancient and incredibly wealthy culture, including freedom to travel throughout the Galaxy. At the same time they attack us, to let us understand experientially that we cannot hope to stand against them." She shrugged. "An effective approach."

"I disagree, ma'am," Morrigan said.

"Indeed? Explain."

"Their *c*-slam attack, ma'am. That wasn't a threat, and it wasn't a demonstration of power. It was deliberately calculated to wipe us right off the face of the planet, and from what I've seen these past few days they damned near succeeded. Our colonies, our various orbitals ... they could pick those off at their leisure. That, or invite them in as—as wards of the state, I guess you could say. Foundlings completely dependent on their beneficence for survival."

"Instead of a coherent strategy, we may be seeing a kind of tug-of-war among multiple factions," Crawford pointed out.

"Exactly," Petosky said, nodding. "Intelligence has been getting hints to that effect from their liaisons. The Nzaad are the in-betweeners, cybernetic blends of organic beings and machines. We now are aware of three Nzaad factions: the Vanaad, who want to cooperate with us; the Amaad, who want to keep us around as slave labor; and the Mla'klah, who think the Galaxy would be better off without us." The alien names seemed to slip easily off his tongue. "The c-gun attack was orchestrated by the Dr'kleh. Nasty bunch, those critters. Pure machines with Mla'Klah-esque sentiments."

"I would think, sir," Morrigan interjected, "that the best course of action is to wait until we can meet them as equals."

"Which may be flatly impossible," Brennan said. "They have at least a billion-year head start on us." She gave Morrigan a hard look. "You discuss *your* idea at some length in your paper. Tell us about it."

"I suggest," Morrigan said, lifting her chin, "that we go on the offensive."

It was, in Morrigan's opinion, the only strategy that made any sense at all. Rather than wait for the enemy to come smashing into the Sol System with overwhelming numbers and firepower, she'd proposed in her paper the formation of a large—a *very* large— raiding force, a kind of hell-for-leather strike group that could vanish deep into enemy territory, seeking out concentrations of warships, supply depots, and factory complexes and wrecking them in a series of hit-and-run raids. Do enough damage to the enemy's supply lines, and they would have to delay any follow-up attack on Earth and send their assets instead after the raiders.

There was a terrifying risk. No matter how many ships the raiding force could muster, the Galactics, given time, would be able to counter with a thousand times that number . . . or more. They had the resources of billions of worlds to draw on, and Galactic technology was such that any human force would be woefully outclassed.

If human raiders could stay ahead of the enemy pursuit, however, even just a single step ahead, and if they could manage to avoid a large-scale stand-up fight, they might have a chance.

"We can't hope to stay ahead of them forever," Morrigan told the board. "But if we hurt them enough, we just might make them reconsider their intentions, make it too expensive for them to continue attacking Earth."

"Asymmetrical warfare," Petosky said. "A smaller, more primitive army tying up a large and technologically superior force."

"Yes, sir."

"It's suicide," Crawford said. "You know that, right? We can't afford to throw away a large fleet."

"It *will* be suicide, sir, if we sit on our asses and wait for them to pick us off."

Brennan smiled. "As ever, tactful to a fault. I understand, Admiral, that you've been out of the loop for a few weeks."

"Under rejuve treatment. Yes, ma'am."

"Then you haven't seen *this*." She moved her hand, and the document vanished on the virtual screen in the air above and behind the three admirals.

It was replaced by a scene set in deep space. Several large asteroids hung suspended in the distance—large because they overshadowed a dozen toys drifting in space close by.

Each "toy" was a brand-new dreadnaught, a kilometer-long warship being grown by advanced nanotechnics, processes extracting metals from space rocks and shaping them into vessels. Work lights glared across black hulls. Assemblers guided separate sections together, as clouds of nanobots descended to weld them into place. Under the recent emergency nanoconstruction program, fifteen brand-new dreadnaughts had been added to the original six, a staggering increase in space-naval capability.

"*Wargod*-class dreadnaughts," Brennan told her. "Brand-new designs. And more are on the way."

Privately, Morrigan wasn't certain that would be enough, but she certainly wasn't going to say that out loud. It was, at the very least, a start.

One of the ships on the screen in the near distance she recognized at once: the *Constellation*. Workpods were busily drifting around and across her hull, repairing damage. One feature, though, was new—a slender, metallic needle almost as long as the ship. The *Connie*'s keel had been opened up along the ship's entire length, and the needle was being fitted inside."

"What the hell are they doing to my ship?" Morrigan demanded.

"Some technical updates," Crawford said. "Think of them as a rejuve for your ship."

"Our salvage efforts on board the *Nemesis* were most productive," Petosky added. "We recovered star charts showing jump routes out from Sirius and reaching as far as a world called Xalixa. We also were able to reverse engineer a few technological tricks from the wreckage. Weapons. Power plants. We're updating every line vessel in the fleet."

"This," Brennan said, indicating the entire fleet under construction across the panorama, "is just the start. We call it Task Force Morrigan. What do you think?"

She didn't know what to think. "Task . . . Task Force Morrigan?"

"Of course, dear," Brennan told her. "After you went over everybody's head to explain things in that rather explosive document you sent us . . . you don't think we would dare put anyone *else* in command, do you?"

The shock was like being doused by a bucket of ice water. "Ma'am, there are plenty of admirals in the fleet who have greater seniority. I've held flag rank now for . . . what? Twenty minutes now?"

"How long an officer has held rank is not how we determine seniority," Crawford told her. "Not any longer. What is of overriding importance is an officer's experience."

"Admiral Morrigan," Brennan told her, "you have been a naval officer for a total of over two centuries. More, if we count your time in the Marine Corps. Admiral Selby, for instance, has a distinguished naval career spanning seventy-one years. *And* you are the victor of the Battle of Abyss. That counts for quite a lot."

And Alexandra Morrigan stared at the virtual screen, speechless.

CHAPTER TEN

MORRIGAN WAS ORDERED—*ORDERED* point-blank—to attend another damned party. She did not want to go. This one was being hosted in the lavish penthouse of one Senator Benjamin S. Martin Jr., which suggested a political motive for the gathering. According to Dek, President Mills was supposed to put in an appearance, which pretty much confirmed the political angle.

She was surprised, though, when she and Dek arrived after the shuttle flight down to Reagan Spaceport. The gathering at Martin's D.C. penthouse was small—only fifty people—and quite subdued, with everyone formally dressed, very little glitz and glitter, and no couples having sex in the entryway. The guests had switched off their emotils, but there was a definite sense of fear, worry, and uneasiness in the room as the two were led in by a lanky housebot.

Most of the guests were gathered in a broad, marble-floored atrium with a high and vaulted skylight. One wall opened onto a veranda with a spectacular view of the Capitol dome. She could see some evidence of damage on the nearby buildings—the result of a shock-generated tsunami up the Potomac—but workbots and nanobots were well on the way to cleaning up the mess.

The opposite wall was showing vids of the destruction of *Nemesis*, probably shot by a battlespace drone. The ponderous yo-yo-shaped bulk of the alien bombardment vessel . . . *Constellation* moving into the gap between the two dome-shaped halves, a minnow nosing up against a battleship . . . the *Endymion* following . . . a searing flash . . . repeat . . .

It was still too raw. She turned away, unable to watch.

"Ah! Our lady of the hour!" Senator Martin said, raising his crystal mist globe in salute. "Welcome, Admiral Morrigan!"

"Senator." She nodded an acknowledgment. "Thank you for inviting me."

"We're delighted you could come. My goodness, you look *lovely* tonight!"

"You wouldn't say that if you saw me without my wig."

"I gather you've just rejuved?" the senator's life partner asked her.

"Yes, Mr. Daystrom. And now I'm going to have trouble getting people to take me seriously." *Again.*

She noticed a vidbot with the ABN logo nearby and realized that even this small, intimate social event must qualify as news. She would have to be on her best behavior.

Damn them.

"So, Admiral," General Peter Weston, chairman of the Joint Chiefs, said. "How's your task force coming?"

She raised an eyebrow. "General? Is this the proper time and place for that discussion?" Normally, information about fleet readiness or position was kept secure, not broadcast over the Terranet.

He followed her glance to the hovering vidbot, then grinned at her. "Normally not, Admiral. But we assume the Galactics are already aware of our plans . . . and the people need to know that we are striking back. You, as it happens, have been cast in this little drama as our very own Jimmy Doolittle."

She had to check with her corona's military history files for that one. There it was: Lieutenant Colonel James Doolittle, half a millennium ago. He'd planned and led a carrier-launched bomber raid on Imperial Japan as retaliation for the Japanese attack on Pearl Harbor a few months previously. The attack had killed about fifty people and done only slight damage to enemy military and industrial targets. The boost to American morale, however, had been huge.

Smile, Admiral, the general told her mind-to-mind. *We need to show confidence here.*

If, as you say, the Galactics already know, she thought back at him, *we're in a hell of a lot of trouble.*

We're in trouble in any case, Admiral. But your little raid is going to buy us time, even if you barely make it past Abyss. Now put on a good show for the audience, right? Or we'll find someone else who can.

That stopped her. "Your little raid"? She had the queasy feeling that her task force was being tossed out into the cold and that the brass didn't care much whether they survived. The general's words were hardly an inspiring send-off.

But she managed a smile. "The Doolittle Raid, huh?" she said. "I like that . . ."

And she decided to use the vidbot to her advantage.

"As you know," she went on with bright sincerity, "there are three star portals in the outer Sol System: Abyss, Stardeep, and Void, right? We're going to be sending *huge* fleet elements through all three. By the time the Galactics figure out what's happening, we'll be deep, deep inside their backyard, and they'll never know what hit them."

Weston's gaze took on a glassy look. He kept grinning but obviously was trying not to look puzzled. There in fact were no plans to venture through Void or Stardeep. Those two gates had been probed over the years since they'd been discovered: Stardeep led by several jumps to Delta Pavo, but the astronomers still had no idea where Void came out. But . . . what the hell? The Galactics probably didn't know exactly how much humans didn't know.

Abyss and its link with Sirius was known, and the discovery of navigational data on *Nemesis* had shown a handful of routes beyond that—a beginning. A very small beginning.

"An appropriately military response," Martin said, laughing. "I do hope you will keep in mind that *peace* is our primary goal. We will fight if we must, but our long-term survival will depend on . . . restraint."

"Restraint," Morrigan echoed. "After Delta Pavo, after Abyss . . . *restraint*. Yes, sir." He looked like he was about to slap down her sarcasm with a sharper argument, and she held up a conciliatory hand. "Sorry, Senator. It's been a long couple of weeks."

She knew a war of sorts had been raging within the government over the subject of peace. Senator Martin's Star Union Party had been in the ascendency, embracing the so-called Joining with the Galactics and hailing a new age of peace and prosperity. The Galactic attack from Abyss must have shaken the Union to its very foundations; clearly, it was scrambling now to regain its footing. She wondered if the party would ever be able to find it after Abyss. Her invitation here, tonight, in front of the news media, most likely was intended by the Star Union to reposition itself and perhaps stem the recent mass defections from the party's ranks.

"I'm all for peace, Senator," she continued. "Believe me. Military people want peace as much as . . . hell, *more* than anyone, because we've seen war firsthand. A lot of us are amortals. We don't want to throw that away. I promise you, sir, I will carry out my orders in full and to the best of my ability, and I don't intend to start anything I can't finish."

Martin seemed to relax a bit at that. "I believe you, Admiral. I do not want to see Earth surrender. But I don't want to get into a slugfest with a galactic bully who could squash us flat with one blow."

"You must understand, sir, that we may not have a choice. The *Nemesis* attack was deliberate, calculated, and probably was meant to eliminate us."

"I know. I also believe that Intelligence is right when they talk about factions within the Galactic camp. If you can make contact with the Galactics who *don't* want to kill us . . ." His voice trailed off, and he shrugged helplessly.

"I understand, Senator," she told him. "I'll do my best."

"Here we are, Van," a young woman said, bustling up with a man in tow. Her ID said she was Kathry Gautier, and she was on Martin's personal staff.

"Not now, Kath," Martin said. He looked tired.

"Oh . . . Van here just wanted to have a word with the Admiral," she said with bright obliviousness. "Didn't you, Van?"

"Well, yes, actually. I heard you're having trouble recruiting enough people to man all those ships," he said. KARL VANDER-GRIFF, his ID read. A reporter with an ABN news team.

"Some," Morrigan replied. In fact that was the single biggest problem the task force was facing right now—how to crew all those new dreadnaughts and other capitals—but she would downplay the problems for the media. "Are you volunteering?"

"What—*me*? Good gracious, no! I'm not in the Navy!"

"Too bad. We've grown a lot of new ships just in this past month. We have plenty of volunteers to man them . . . but we can always use more. The big problem is that even download training and immersion sims take *time*, and once they're through the training the recruits still don't have any real-world experience to fall back on."

Gautier laughed. "I heard it was that men didn't want libidectomies!"

"Who said we were doing any such thing?"

"Oh . . . *everyone*! One guy in the office said the order had come down to give one to all personnel in the task force whether they wanted it or not!"

"There *have* been some rumors about the Navy using nanomedicine to suppress hormonal drives," Vandergriff said. "Any truth in that?"

Morrigan scowled. "Libidectomy" was the humorous and strictly unofficial term for a nanomed treatment that suppressed sexual desire—removed the libido, in other words, like an appendectomy removed the appendix. There *were* such treatments, and they *had* been discussed. The crews of human starships were still *human*, after all, and most had normal sex drives.

"Our medical departments are giving . . . libidectomies, as Ms. Gautier calls them, to personnel who request them, Mr. Vandergriff. Nothing mandatory, and they are reversible. All hands know we're likely to be on deployment for a long time, years probably. Most of the crew members have families, and the fleet can't haul all of them along. If that poses . . . physical difficulties, it can be addressed medically."

Vandergriff smirked. "Well, there's always the possibility of . . . fraternization."

The man, Morrigan decided, was a salacious moron. Or was he just trying to provoke her for the cameras? "Why are we having this conversation, Mr. Vandergriff?" she asked. "Are your ratings that low?"

Vandergriff scowled and turned away. Gautier laughed. "Typical male!"

"In my experience, Ms. Gautier, there is no typical. We're all individuals."

"Right! Just like everyone else!"

Fraternization—meaning sex, of course—within the ranks was tolerated in the Navy, though not encouraged. Earth's principal culture tended to be relaxed and open about the topic, and the concept of *marriage* nowadays meant pretty much any union between people of any gender and in any number for any length of time. The Navy couldn't take personnel out of that background and forbid their forming intimate relationships, whether casual or long term. Pregnancy was no longer an issue, so service personnel simply were expected to act like responsible adults. Jealous fights, violations of consent, and abuse of rank would not be tolerated, *ever*.

The worst part, in Morrigan's mind, wasn't sex but the hardship any really long-term separation would impose on so many families. All the Navy could do was make sure everyone knew the score . . . and to encourage volunteers with no close family ties planetside. So far, the psych teams had weeded out something like

60 percent of the volunteers on the grounds that long-term separation would pose undue hardships on family members left behind or psychological stress on those who went.

Libidectomies! What nonsense!

Eventually, President Harold M. Mills did, indeed, make an appearance, complete with Secret Service escorts and a small personal entourage of secretaries and aides. He gave a short address to the gathering, one that Morrigan found unmemorably lackluster and predictably by the numbers.

It figured. The office of the president of the United States had largely devolved over the past few centuries to a mostly ceremonial role. Government of the people, by the people, and for the people was run by the AIs now, but the presidency remained in place to maintain an illusion of human self-governance by hosting banquets, cutting ribbons, and handing out medals.

The thought brought another AI to mind: Argus.

The powerful governance AI called Liskov had numerous micros—essentially full copies of the original program trimmed and streamlined down to fractional iterations of the original, still sentient, still self-aware. The original, human Liskov, among other accomplishments, was remembered for her creation of two computer networking languages—one of them called Argus. That name was borne now by the fractional AI running both Fleetlink and Taclink, the Minds now uniting the fleet.

Did entities like Argus make the role of fleet admiral superfluous or purely ceremonial?

The president's speech dwindled to a close, garnering the usual polite applause.

"Admiral Morrigan," Mills said, turning up a ten-thousand-megawatt smile and gesturing to her. "If you would, please?"

What the hell? She approached the man and came to attention. "Mr. President?"

"Admiral Alexandra Morrigan: for courage in the face of an implacable and deadly enemy at the Battle of Abyss, for leadership and heroism above and beyond the call of duty resulting in an inestimable reduction of casualties and damage inflicted by that enemy on Earth, it is my honor to present you with this . . . the Presidential Legion Star of Gallantry."

An aide handed Mills an open, velvet-lined box, and the president removed the medal.

"All of Earth owes you an enormous debt of gratitude, Admiral."

He pressed the maroon-and-green ribbon to her left chest, and it melded itself to her uniform fabric, the heavy gold star dangling over the rows upon rows of colorful ribbons already decorating her dress blacks. *Another* medal. Over the centuries, serving in both the Marines and the Navy at different times, she'd acquired quite a few of them. The LSG *was* the third-highest decoration in the military, however. It was a distinct honor.

She snapped a salute. "Thank you, Mr. President."

Mills returned the salute, his wrist cocked at a most unmilitary angle. "Thank *you*, Admiral." He shook her hand. "You be sure to come back to us after you've settled things with the Galactics, understand?"

"Yes, sir, Mr. President. I intend to . . ."

But Mills had already turned away, the emotion drained from his face. The man was more like an android robot, she thought, than a flesh-and-blood human. There were rumors floating about that that was exactly what he was. Hell, maybe they were true.

She and Dek left as early as they could do so politely.

She had a lot to do before boost.

"ADMIRAL ON THE bridge!"

Captain Neal's command almost caught Morrigan by surprise. Her mind had been elsewhere as she stepped into the compartment three days after the meeting with the president. The Marines at the entryway came to attention, but all other personnel continued with their work. Preparing a ship to get under way was a complex and lengthy evolution, and you couldn't have people dropping everything and popping up to attention just because the brass walked in.

"As you were," Morrigan said, more as acknowledgment of Neal's protocol than a command. Neal, rightly, remained in the command chair. It was no longer hers.

Neal moved his hand through a control field above his console, and a seat unfolded itself from the deck to his right, the pattern drawn from *Constellation*'s accommodations mems.

"Thank you, Captain," she said formally, taking the seat. "How do we stand?"

"On schedule for departure at thirteen hundred hours, Admiral. We're awaiting two transports up from Earth with 298 new personnel."

"And the fleet?"

Neal's lips pursed. "Better than projected. We have 1,800 warships, plus 214 auxiliaries, all ready for boost. Everyone's loaded and supplied, but 1,137 ships, over half, are critically shorthanded. And . . ."

"'And'?"

"Ma'am, the Chinese have not yet joined us. They report 'domestic issues.'"

"I see."

"Their coastal areas were badly hit by *c*-fall. A lot of their ships have been on evac duty."

"Uh-huh. And maybe Hǎi Jūn Shào Jiàng Liu is carrying a grudge. They haven't exactly been enthusiastic about this mission."

"Beijing *has* declared its intent to comply fully with the PTI," Neal said. The Pan-Terran Initiative, signed a week before in the five capitals of the Pentopoly, called on each member-bloc to provide a minimum of 450 warships to the strike force, plus additional auxiliaries.

"Well, we're not going to hold for them," Morrigan said. "If they show, great. If not . . ." Her shrug was eloquent. "I'm not going to hold my breath."

In fact, she was pretty sure that including the Chinese in this venture would be more trouble than it was worth, despite the fleet's chronic shortage in human power. Somehow, Beijing seemed never to have integrated fully into the Terran Pentopoly, and they always, *always* had their own agenda.

Getting enough personnel to fully crew naval warships had long posed major problems, so much so that some on Morrigan's staff had joked recently about sending out the press gangs. Despite what she'd told the idiots at Senator Martin's party the other night, there were two principal issues. One, jokingly, was called the "DKM factor," with the acronym standing for "Don't Kill Me." As rejuvenation and ENS grew more and more common throughout Humankind, people had become more and more reluctant to risk the promise of amortality, and militaries were hard-pressed to recruit *anyone*, whether *Homo sap* or *Homo supe*.

The other issue was referred to as "W^2," shorthand for "What War?" Human civilization was self-centered and mildly xenophobic. While the Crab incursion was serious enough in the Delta Pavo system, the majority of humans weren't even aware that there was a war going on, and if they were, that war was very far away. Light-years provided a measure of social insulation.

At least, they'd done so until the *Nemesis* sneak attack.

"So what *do* the personnel numbers look like, Vince?" Morrigan leaned back in her command seat and closed her eyes. She was expecting bad news. "With or without the Chinese."

"With the most recent arrivals, we currently have 2,129 ships of all types ready for deployment," Neal replied, "manned by 215,963 personnel."

Enormous numbers, but they worked out to an average of just over a hundred humans per ship. The majority of those ships were smaller vessels—frigates, patrol boats, and the little four-man RM-20 Starscouts.

"We'll just have to make do, Vince." She cracked a wry grin. "It's not like we were going to overwhelm the Galactics by sheer numbers."

Neal snorted. "Why not? Aw, what the hell? Maybe the Star Union Party has it right."

She gave him a sharp look. "Since when were you a member of *that* bunch of losers?"

"Since never. But some of their arguments are bang on target."

"About us not being able to face that kind of tech?"

"Yeah." He wouldn't meet her eyes. "That . . . and the numbers. A few billion humans against a few quadrillion of them. Odds of a million to one'll make you sit up and take notice."

She bit back a sharp retort. Hell, when the man was right, he was *dead* right.

"FLEETLINK ENGAGED, ADMIRAL. All ships report ready in all respects for near-*c*. Waiting your command."

Take us out, Captain Neal, Morrigan said, speaking through her corona. *Best velocity to Abyss.*

"Best velocity, Abyss, aye, ma'am. Helm, engage program."

And the fleet of two thousand ships, as one, slid from their parking orbit beyond Grissom Station and accelerated, outbound.

Six hundred twenty AUs at 0.95 *c* yielded a subjective time of twenty-eight hours. Morrigan used much of that time going over the technical specifications for *Constellation*'s updates. There was a lot to get through. Modern starship weaponry was a fascinating mix of very old and new.

Constellation had already possessed thirty-six broadside railguns in three banks—port, starboard, and dorsal—magnetic weapons designed to hurl inert lumps of steel-jacketed depleted uranium at high velocity. The kinetic energy released by each impact was the equivalent of about a ton of high explosives. In some ways they were right out of the days of sail, when ship captains maneuvered to bring their vessels alongside the enemy at close range. Get close enough to fire a broadside, and the enemy's point defenses would be unable to target and destroy incoming rounds.

At least, that was the theory.

The kilometer-long needle she'd seen being installed in *Connie*'s keel was also a railgun, but one based on technology drawn from the *c*-gun *Nemesis* had carried. The MRG-01 was not nearly as powerful as its Galactic counterpart, but its rounds carried the kick of a kiloton nuclear weapon.

All the dreadnaughts, bombardment vessels, and battle monitors of the fleet, she learned, had been outfitted with the new weapon. That, she thought, would go a long way toward evening out the disparity in weapons technology between Earth and the Galactics.

The real force leveler, however, turned out to be the use of nanotechnology to effect repairs and to construct new ships. Once, it would have taken years to construct a capital ship from the keel up. Now, detailed plans were fed into the constructors, and they "grew" a new ship, using raw materials taken from asteroids and completing the process in a matter of days. Elaborate computer sims then tested every aspect of the ship systems, avoiding, one would hope, any unpleasant surprises in the shakedown cruise.

Well . . . that was the idea. She'd skippered enough ships in her long life to know there were *always* surprises, and this short run out to Abyss would serve as the shakedown. Still, the North American Pentopoly had possessed space navies totaling around two thousand ships. They'd managed to grow double that number in a few short weeks, deploying them as Task Force Morrigan.

She was still bemused at the name.

Twenty-seven hours subjective later, Morrigan was in her office—her *new* office just abaft CIC. Four men had joined her, two from *Connie*'s engineering department—Commander Walter Thorvaldson, *Connie*'s CHENG or chief engineer, and one of his subordinates, Chief Todd Kranhouse. The other two were Commander Clay Anders, *Constellation*'s weapons officer, and Commander Bryce Talbot, the ship's tactical officer, while Captain Neal, on the bridge, looked in on the meeting from a monitor to one side. In front of them, a holo glowing above Morrigan's desk showed the layout and technical specs of *Connie*'s brand-new railgun system. "I need to know, gentlemen," she was saying, "that this thing is going to work. We didn't have time to test it."

"It should, Admiral," Anders told her. "The computer modeling tells us that when we fire, there will be a shock . . . but nothing that the ship can't handle."

"In a virtual model, yes. But it hasn't been tested *live*. What about when we fire it for real?"

"Well . . . it should work . . ."

"*Should* is not good enough, Commander. We need an answer to Newton, here. I want the system fully tested *before* we go through Abyss."

It had been Newton who'd formulated his famous three laws of motion in 1687. His third law stated that for every action there is an opposite but equal reaction; when *Constellation* fired her newly installed weapon—a heavy, keel-mounted magnetic railgun—the mass going forward at a significant fraction of the speed of light would exert an enormous recoil aft, a force equal to the projectile's mass times its acceleration.

"The inertialess field soaks up most of the recoil, Admiral," Anders told her. "It's what allows us to accelerate to near-*c* almost instantaneously, and—"

Morrigan gave him a cold glare. "Don't patronize me, Commander. I *do* know what an inertialess field is, and I know the force balance has to be *perfect* for it to work. I want these weapons tested before we get into a shoving match with the Galactics."

"Yes, ma'am."

Morrigan didn't like slapping her people down like that, but she was still working to establish herself as being in charge. In combat, she couldn't have her people questioning her orders . . . or her judgment.

She would speak privately with Anders later.

Meanwhile, *Constellation* and a few dozen other large warships in the task force now possessed magnetic railguns—weapons not as large or as powerful as the one on *Nemesis,* but capable of inflicting serious damage on a planet and of obliterating large enemy ships.

The one problem Morrigan could see was that the technology was alien. Another unknown.

Morrigan checked her corona and saw it was nearly time. "Showtime, gentlemen," she said, concluding the meeting. "Let's take this war to the enemy."

THE FIRST LEG of the journey complete, Task Force Morrigan gathered before the enigmatic face of Abyss. First through the gate were drones, hundreds of them, programmed to thoroughly recon the system on the other side and, most especially, to report any signs of Galactic activity. Quarantine was still there, holding lonely vigil, but of the overlords of the Galaxy themselves there was no sign.

Next through the gate was one of *Constellation*'s fighter squadrons, VFA-84, the Nightwings, now at full complement. Twelve Stryker fighters slipped from their extended launch towers in the dreadnaught's ventral surface, tiny specks moving swiftly through the deep shadow beneath their behemoth mother ship in echelon formation, then emerging into the glare of Sirius light gleaming through the gateway.

Lieutenant Commander Donna Esposito held her position at the lead slot of her squadron, running through the deployment checklist for each ship and pilot. The individual pilot readouts showed excitement, some fear, and tremendous focus.

Even Troggie Damian.

She smiled to herself. The guy hated the nickname she'd coined for him, but he'd been well-behaved since they'd boosted clear of Earth orbit.

"*Constellation* CIC," she called, "Nightwings formed up and ready to proceed."

Into the unknown.

"Copy, Nightwings. You are cleared for deployment," Captain Ballinger replied. "Good luck. Godspeed."

Esposito wondered if "Godspeed" was, in fact, *light speed*. After all, there was nothing faster. "Let's go, Nightwings," she called. "In three . . . two . . . one . . ."

"THERE THEY GO."

Morrigan watched the V-formation of twelve minute specks vanish through the vast circle of Abyss. The drones already on the other side had reported nothing. The fighters should be okay, but with the Galactics there were so impossibly many unknowns. The SF-112 Strykers accelerated . . . and in the next instant they were 8.6 light-years distant. Morrigan turned her head, scanning the sky revealed on the CIC wallscreens, until she found a particular blue-white gleam in the sky not far from the sprawl of Orion.

Alpha Canis Majoris—Sirius.

Commander Esposito's tiny squadron was *there* at that glimmer of light, right now.

An hour passed . . . then two. A drone finally returned through the gate with a simple text message: *Clear*. Additional drones arriving over the course of the next few minutes amplified that text with recordings showing a star system empty of enemy warships.

Throughout military history, Morrigan thought, there'd been key moments when commanders had committed themselves to a final, irrevocable engagement, a decision point from which there was no turning back. Caesar crossing the Rubicon. Alexander crossing the Hellespont. Hannibal crossing the Alps.

And now Alexandra Morrigan would be crossing the alien gateway called Abyss.

"Task Force," she transmitted. "Oplan Alfa. We're going through."

They passed through a hundred at a time. If something nasty jumped them on the other side, they wouldn't lose the entire fleet.

The task force had been organized into three color-designated wings. She commanded White Wing, at the center; Jason Selby commanded Blue Wing, the van; and the newly promoted Rear Admiral Eric Knutson commanded Red Wing at the rear. While she retained overall command of the entire task force, the other two rear admirals were her senior officers in direct charge of Red and Blue, permitting better command and control and allowing more precise tactical planning.

She still felt uncomfortable with how the CNO had defined seniority. By long-standing tradition, seniority was determined by date of commission.

It seemed that ENS had screwed with more in the Navy than how long an officer had to wait for promotion.

Blue went through first, followed by the much larger White. On the other side, the ships deployed across a vast area of empty space, staying well clear of the Abyss Gate's face until Red was through and accounted for. The entire process took half an hour—proof of good training and expert programming.

"We should just take out Quarantine," Captain Neal told her. "The new railgun would make quick work of it."

"Negative, Vince," she told him. "I want that facility picked clean before we blow it to hell. That's what the Marines are for, right?"

"I suppose so, Admiral. I just hope there aren't any nasty surprises in there."

"In all my time in the service," Morrigan told him, "I've encountered very few things nastier than a regimental combat team of U.S. Marines. And even fewer things the Marines couldn't handle."

Their ace in the hole was Pax, encased in eir coffin-shaped tekpod and residing now, after a great deal of acrimonious debate, in a back corner of the CIC. A number of Morrigan's senior officers had questioned the wisdom of letting a Galactic AI into CIC at all; Admiral Koehler's death was all too vivid in the minds of everyone there.

Morrigan had cut through the argument with appeals to sanity and efficiency. If they were going to use Pax's knowledge of the Galactic Authority, they were going to have to trust em. She could not afford to give in to paranoia, despite the nightmare example of Jaime's assassination. She'd taken the added controversial step of having Colonel Stroud take Pax with him down to Quarantine.

She was unwilling to let em out of eir Faraday cage prison; the risk of em getting into the ship's computer network and, from there, into the fleet-wide commnet was simply too catastrophically nightmarish to consider. But Pax could travel down into Quarantine with the Marines and use eir knowledge of Galactic comm and intel protocols to provide unparalleled intelligence and translation expertise for the human forces.

There was a safeguard riding with Pax in eir coffin: a bomb that could be thought-triggered by corona or by AI if the Galactic agent did *anything* out of line. The hard-liner human faction had insisted on it.

The idea seemed silly to Morrigan. Pax could think some hundreds or possibly *thousands* of times faster than human-designed AIs, and perhaps millions of times faster than any organic human. If Pax escaped, ey could do what ey wanted and be gone long before any human or human-manufactured Mind could know there was something wrong.

Trust, she thought, had to start *somewhere*.

But after seeing Jaime brutally killed, she wondered why it had to start with her.

CHAPTER ELEVEN

COLONEL RYAN STROUD stepped into an underground chamber so high and so wide the ceiling and far walls were lost in shadow. In the distance, a squat pillar or platform supported a transparent egg emitting a steady golden light. Walls and floor, both in this chamber, appeared to be made of black glass, like obsidian; Stroud guessed that whatever had created this cavern had used unimaginable energies to vaporize rock that then had cooled, lining the cavity with glass.

He didn't like the idea of facing that kind of technology with a single company of Marines.

There was no sign of organic life here other than the Marines themselves moving across the open rock surface in heavy Mark V battle armor. The suits were coated with nanoflage, layers of microptics that picked up and retransmitted incoming light. The result wasn't true invisibility, but Marine space armor was difficult to pick out from the background, especially when the man wearing it stood still. In a dark and cavernous space like this, even moving individuals tended to blur and fade in and out of view.

Movement was easier here than in full g. The dwarf planet had a surface gravity of around a tenth of a g, and even encumbered by armor, Marines could sail low across that glassy floor or bound high above it. Rubber grips on their boots kept them from slipping on the smooth surface, though Stroud saw a couple of Marines take slow-motion falls as they attempted to glide on it like high-tech skaters.

Careful of his footing, Stroud moved toward the pillar with its enigmatic light, followed by Latimer and another Marine named Pulaski guiding Pax's upright, floating coffin. The Galactic remained behind the transparency, observing everything around em without comment.

Back on board the *Connie*, AI technicians had wired up Pax's tekpod with a radio interface, one with a range deliberately restricted to a few meters to prevent Pax from getting loose inside *Constellation*'s computer networks. If ey decided to try hacking *Connie*'s systems, ey would be able to take over the coronas of Stroud and any of his Marines standing close enough, but nothing more. The break in security protocol was necessary, since the interior of Quarantine was in vacuum, and the tekpod's audio interface was useless here.

"How do you want to do this, Pax?" Stroud asked.

"The radio interface is working well," the machine told him. "If you position me next to that dais ahead, I will also be able to communicate with the intelligence of this place."

"I'm more concerned about how you can connect with that thing without running the risk of it taking you over, maybe reprogramming you on the fly, maybe using you to get at the ship's network."

"There is always inherent risk, Colonel," Pax told him. "However, your AI engineers and robotics technicians seem to have anticipated all eventualities. In particular, remember that a copied part of the human-derived AI you call Liskov has been melded with me. Ey will be monitoring all that I say, observe, and do, with orders to kill me if I show any indication of treachery."

Ey said that last line with no trace of resentment or hostility, but simply as fact. Stroud had been briefed on the precautions—the only way they would be able to use Pax to investigate or communicate with Galactic technologies—but he wasn't entirely sure he believed it. As an additional guarantee, anything Pax and Liskov discovered would be transmitted to him, through his corona, allowing him to make the final decision on anything questionable. Using himself as a guinea pig was insanely dangerous, of course, and certainly not in the job description of a regimental commander, but he refused to ask his people to do what he himself would not. If he thought he detected any hint of treacherous behavior in the Galactic he would pull the plug . . .

. . . and quite likely kill himself in the process as well.

"I don't expect that to be necessary, Pax," Stroud told em. "Just keep everything on the up-and-up and in the open, and we'll be fine, okay?"

"Nor do I expect problems."

They reached the pedestal, which Stroud examined closely. There were no controls or obvious means of access. "Are you picking anything up?"

"I am," Pax told him. "The message you've all heard, the one warning humans away. I am also in direct contact with the AI Mind that controls this place. Ey should recognize my presence and my authority."

Several long moments of silence followed, and the wait was making Stroud increasingly uneasy. "C'mon, what's happening?" he growled. "What is ey saying?"

"Pax is talking with the primary intelligence of this facility," a different voice replied.

"Liskov?"

"In a manner of speaking, yes. A very small portion of the entity you know as Liskov, at any rate. Pax is attempting to download navigational data that will . . ." Ey stopped.

"Liskov?" Stroud demanded. "What—"

"Pax has succeeded, Colonel." And Stroud experienced a flood of data flowing through his corona—a rushing flood of numbers. He couldn't interpret any of it, but he was willing to accept Liskov's judgment.

He opened his own commnet link with the ship. "*Constellation,* this is Green Recon. I have data for you. Isolation protocol, Red Alfa."

"Copy that, Recon. Send it."

Acting as a go-between to protect *Constellation*'s computer networks, Stroud allowed the data to flow into a compartmentalized area of the ship's memory isolated from the rest, a virtual machine within the larger network designed to protect the ship—and the rest of the fleet—from an alien Trojan horse hidden within the data. Human AIs would be able to study it there without risking destruction by enemy software.

"Colonel Stroud." It was Pax, speaking through the radio link.

"What is it?"

"I am detecting a high-level alert throughout the Quarantine network. Local AIs are preparing to attack us."

"Where are they?"

"Colonel, they are all around us . . ."

MARINE STAFF SERGEANT Charles Ransom Sadowski, senior NCO of Third Platoon, couldn't understand exactly what it was he was seeing. Standing next to one of the glassy black walls of the immense chamber, it looked as though the rock itself was changing . . . shifting . . . *emerging* from the surface like something alive. "Lieutenant!" he yelled over the tactical net. "We've got a problem!"

The platoon commander, Second Lieutenant Harrold Bates, looked at the patch of wall for a moment, then slowly reached out one gauntleted hand as if to touch it.

"I wouldn't, if'n I was you, sir," Sadowski told him. "That's some kind of nano effect, gotta be! You just might pull back a stump!"

"I think you're right, Staff Sergeant. Third Platoon! Move back from the wall!"

"Bates, Stroud," a hard voice said through his corona. "What do you have?"

"Beats me, sir. Have a look."

He tried to open a feed directly to Stroud's corona, but got a [REFUSED] message back.

"Hold one," Stroud said. Then: "Try it now."

This time the imagery flowed through. By now, the thing on the wall was five meters tall and wide, and it was *unfolding*—that was the only word for it—emerging from the glass with a cold and eerie relentlessness.

"Sir! They're coming out of the walls!"

Other fireteams were reporting similar effects elsewhere around the cavern. First Platoon reported a huge patch of the floor suddenly re-forming itself . . . and nearly dragging down a Marine as it did so.

Sadowski watched with growing horror as something like a glass lens the size of a dinner plate formed on the nearest emergent shape. There was a dazzling flash . . . and Corporal Forrest screamed and collapsed, the front surface of his armor charred and crumbling.

"Colonel Stroud! This is Bates! We're under fire! Marine down!"

"Green Recon!" Stroud called out over the company net. "Commence fire!"

Sadowski already had his AL-46 up and at the ready. He hesitated, though; commence fire at *what*? It looked as though the walls and deck of this place were coming alive. He settled on the dinner plate as his target, however, and triggered his weapon. The Novadyne laser's coherent ultraviolet beam was invisible even in the near darkness of the chamber, but the lens, if that's what it was, curdled and smoked and then sank back into the background of shifting, moving parts.

Those parts had the look of an extraordinarily complex machine, but the movement and apparent purposefulness felt more like a living creature—an *intelligent* living creature—unfolding itself from slumber to lash out and kill.

"Marines!" Stroud's voice called. "Center peel! Fall back on the transports! Move!"

"Center peel" was an infantry tactic used for a fighting withdrawal in the face of superior numbers. The troops, arranged in a column facing the enemy, would lay down heavy suppressive fire. At the command "peel one," the Marine at the head of the column and closest to the enemy force would shift quickly to the rear of the column, taking up a new position behind and to one side of the last man in line.

"Third Platoon, center peel!" Bates called out. "Time to get the hell out of Dodge!"

Sadowski could hear the commands from other fireteam leaders over the commnet, as the entire company commenced a fighting withdrawal. With Forrest down, he was at the head of his column. Stooping, he picked up Forrest's body, awkwardly shouldered it, and yelled, "Peel one!"

The other two members of his fireteam were firing their Novadynes as he bounded past them. Quarantine's scant gravity meant Forrest weighed only about ten kilos even with full armor, but he was bulky and tended to slide off Sadowski's shoulder.

He reached a spot behind the other two, crouched, and—still supporting Forrest over his shoulder—fired his laser one-handed.

Precision aiming was not an issue. Everywhere he looked, the surrounding glass surfaces seemed to be alive and moving.

"Peel two!" and Lance Corporal Sheryl Mason sailed past him in a long, low trajectory.

"Peel three!" Private First Class Andrew Sayre raced past him, and then it was again his turn.

"I'VE GOT THE Glit!" Stroud told the two Marines with him. "Cover us!"

"Aye, aye, sir!"

Stroud could see bright flashes of light all around the distant wall as alien combat machines engaged his Marines, but for the moment, at least, no one was firing at them or the tekpod. With one hand on Pax's unit, he pushed off and sailed low across the deck... but when he touched down the glass beneath him seemed to dissolve into a cubist's nightmare of shifting, *living* planes and blocks and impossible shapes. He felt something closing around his left boot, wrenching at him.

Hold still! Pax called in his mind, and after a long second his ankle was released. Clinging to the tekpod, desperately trying not to lose his grip and fall, Stroud made it at last to the towering entryway leading to the Gannets, where Captain Cordell, Bravo's CO, waited with the reserves.

"Defensive line inside the door," Stroud ordered, sliding off the floating coffin and pointing. "Don't go too far in. Just hold the escape hatch open for our people."

"Aye, aye, Colonel. Okay, people! You heard the man! Advance ten meters, fan and crouch, then hold position! Check your fire. Friendlies coming in!"

"Where are the guys who were with me?"

Cordell shook his head behind his visor. "They didn't make it, sir."

"Pax!" Stroud shouted, his fury driving the word. "You made it let me go! Now help the rest of them get out!"

"I regret, Colonel, that I cannot," the AI replied. "My radio range is limited to a few meters."

Of course.

"Sir!" Cordell said. "You should get back to the ship!"

"Negative! I want to see my people home! You get Pax back to the Gannet!"

"Sir—"

"Don't give me an argument! Just *do* it!"

Cordell's face, just visible through his helmet, was glowering, but he didn't fight it. "Be careful, sir."

Still angry, still processing the death of an old friend, Stroud turned and stared back into the larger chamber, watching as the Marines fought their way toward the entryway. The Marines, he thought, were taking heavy casualties. There was absolutely zero cover in here, with a dead-flat deck and no rocks, no trees, no buildings—nothing but fellow Marines.

Marines and whatever the hell was coming through the deck and the bulkheads.

A Marine fired an M-94 tactical missile, a weapon designed for taking out armor or aircraft. It streaked off the launch rail, passed over the heads of retreating Marines, and slammed into a black wall that appeared to be re-forming itself into a living mountain. There was a dazzling flash, and fragments arced in a slow, drawn-out fall across the chamber floor.

The hit didn't seem to do anything at all to slow the enemy's advance.

Stroud moved next to the Tac-M gunner and pointed. "Think you can target that pedestal out there?"

"Fuckin'-A, Skipper," the Marine replied, and a fresh missile emerged from the magazine and locked into place. It was a long shot—in more ways than one—but the transformation of the alien chamber's floor was spreading swiftly, overtaking the returning Marines. The missile silently streaked from the launcher, homed on the pedestal at the chamber's center, and struck.

The pedestal and its glowing transparent top vanished in a savage detonation.

The alien machines, or whatever they were, kept advancing.

Damn. In the vids and interactives, when you destroyed the central controller or master robot or whatever the fictional Big Bad might be, it generally took the enemy offline, stopping them *all* . . . but the Quarantine AI evidently was better designed than that.

The machines kept coming.

"FIRST GANNET IS clear," Neal told Morrigan. "Mostly wounded on board."

"I see it," she said, watching one of her screens. The military transport had just emerged from the wide, squat opening in the base of a large mountain on Quarantine, and it was accelerating now toward *Constellation.* "Weps, warm up the new *c*-gun. We're about to have the opportunity to test it."

"Aye, aye, Admiral," Commander Anders replied. "Target?"

"That opening in the mountain down there. After our people are well clear."

"I recommend we pull the *Connie* well back from the impact zone, ma'am. At least a thousand kilometers."

"Work out the specifics with Captain Neal." She opened a fleet-wide channel. "This is Morrigan. All ships within five thousand kilometers of Quarantine, back off. *Now!*"

For now, *Constellation* would remain where she was, three hundred kilometers from Quarantine's cold and desolate surface, until the Gannets were back on board.

"Admiral," Lisa Conway called. Morrigan could hear a blast of static over the channel, a waterfall of raw noise from Conway's instruments. "Sensor suite is detecting anomalies at the target."

"What kind of anomalies?"

"A magnetic field just switched on down there . . . a strong one. About two gauss."

"Two gauss? That doesn't sound too—"

"Admiral, that's half the magnetic field strength of Jupiter! *Ten times* the entire magnetic field of Earth!"

She would have to check that later. She'd always thought of Earth's magnetic field as quite weak—after all, you could outpull the entire planet with a child's toy magnet. That would have to wait, however. Conway was still reporting.

"There's something else, Admiral. I can't quite make it out, ma'am. It looks like dust and small particles, but they're *moving* . . . apparently under direction."

"The magnetic field?"

"We think so, ma'am. Those particles might be nanoweaponry of some kind."

"Thank you, Lieutenant. Keep me informed."

"Affirmative."

"CIC, DAG," Ballinger's voice said. "Gannets Two and Three are clear of the planet, Admiral." A long moment later: "And there's number four! All transports are clear of the dwarf."

"How long until they're on board?"

"We're bringing Gannet One in now, Admiral. The other three . . . maybe another fifteen minutes. Colonel Stroud reports he's on Gannet Four . . . with the alien."

"Keep me in the link."

She'd been following the battle by listening in on the radio transmissions from inside the dwarf planet. She hadn't heard anything from Stroud, however—presumably because he'd cut himself out of the communications net to protect the fleet. "Vince?"

"Yes, Admiral?"

"Was that a trap down there? A betrayal?"

"By Pax, you mean? I don't know, ma'am. We'll have to wait and see what Colonel Stroud has to say."

"Because if Pax did set us up, we really—"

She was thinking out loud, a bad habit, and broke off the thought. But the strike force would be going places no human had ever heard of, and they would need hard intel if they were to have any chance at all.

Neal seemed to read her mind. "One step at a time, Admiral. Let's get the colonel's after-action. DAG says Pax is with him on Gannet Four, right? I think if Pax had screwed us down there the colonel would have pulled the plug on him. I also think that if Pax was still working for his old bosses, *his* first target would have been Colonel Stroud."

Damn it, she wasn't thinking straight. She nodded. "Sounds right."

She tried to shake the memory of Jaime's face as his skull was crushed.

ALL FOUR OF the transports had been deployed from *Constellation*'s flight deck, and in due time all returned safely on board, sleek flying-wing shapes homing on the flashing bay acquisition lights on the dreadnaught's starboard side. The Quarantine nanoweaponry had pursued the flight of C-80s out from the dwarf planet, but point-defense lasers, both on the Gannets and on board the dreadnaught, had burned down enough of them to make the others cautious. With the Gannets safely back inside *Connie*'s capacious flight decks, Neal gave the command to back off to one thousand kilometers and prepare to fire the new *c*-gun.

Deciding on the appropriate firing range had demanded a delicate process of negotiation between Morrigan, Neal, and Weps Anders. Too close, and *Constellation* might be caught in the expanding sphere of hot plasma or shredded by high-velocity shrapnel. Too far and the AI directing any weapons within the dwarf planet might have time to vaporize the incoming projectile. Neal studied the dark and icy sphere currently centered on his main screen, the bright light of its entryway like an eye watching him. Quarantine by now was completely enveloped within an invisible cloud of particles that might well be a defensive shield of some sort. No one, not even *Constellation*'s network of AI directors, could guess how effective a shield that might be.

"*C*-gun ready to fire, sir," Anders said.

"Very well, Mr. Anders," Neal replied. He opened the ship-wide comm. "All hands, this is the captain. We are about to try out our new weapon. Brace for impact. Repeat, brace for impact."

Normally, the "brace for impact" warning was delivered before hitting something like another ship, but there was nothing in the manuals to cover *this*.

"Mr. Anders. Commence fire."

"Firing in three . . . two . . . one . . . now!"

The recoil was anticlimactic, a hard nudge that pushed Neal out from his seat and against the chair's embrace. At the same instant, it seemed, Quarantine vanished in a nova-bright flare of intense radiation that momentarily outshone Sirius four hundred AUs distant.

Then the expanding plasma cloud moving out from Quarantine engulfed the *Constellation* and delivered a *real* kick.

"IT'S DEFINITE, THEN?" Morrigan asked. "Quarantine is destroyed?"

"Obliterated, Admiral," Anders replied. "There's a handful of fair-sized asteroids left and a great deal of rubble. About a quarter of Quarantine's mass collapsed into a power microblack."

"Which confirms the Galactics use power taps like ours," Commander Thorvaldson told her. "Important smidgen of data, that. Maybe the bastards aren't quite as far beyond us as they want us to believe."

Humans had been using Hawking power taps for several centuries now, and if there was a more efficient way of extracting the unimaginable energies resident within hard vacuum, humans knew nothing about them. Finely tuned mutually orbiting microscopic black holes skimmed virtual energy from the vacuum foam, ate half to keep themselves stable, and delivered up the remainder as Hawking radiation—enough energy to power million-ton starships and twist space-time to inertialessly accelerate them.

But when something went wrong, the micro black holes could merge and begin avidly devouring surrounding matter, releasing a great deal of hard radiation in the process. That, evidently, had been a part of what had happened to Quarantine.

Morrigan was meeting with her senior department heads in *Constellation*'s Starlight Lounge, a broad, open compartment, comfortably appointed, and with deck-to-overhead viewalls revealing spectacular vistas of surrounding space. Sirius A was a dazzling stellar pinpoint in the distance, with Sirius B a minute speck all but lost in the primary's glare. At Dek's command, the compartment had absorbed much of the furniture into the deck and grown a large conference table that looked like real mahogany. Each place around the table had a full suite of holographic controls and virtual screens.

"The Galactics," Morrigan told Thorvaldson, "may have more than one technology in play. We don't know how old Quarantine was, how long it's been sitting there. It's even possible that the Galactics took over a preexisting base and adapted it for their needs."

"I hadn't thought of that."

"And I have no wish to overthink it, Commander. But I think it's wise to keep in mind that what we call 'the Galactics' is in fact an enormous mélange of cultures and worlds and whole civilizations. We can't take *anything* for granted out here."

"What we ran into inside Quarantine," Colonel Stroud said, "was unlike anything else we've encountered so far. Very advanced nanoweaponry, X-ray beam weapons, and the ability to rework rock into complex machinery on the fly." He shook his head. "We were damned lucky to get out of there."

"The fifty-thousand-credit question, Colonel: Did Pax lead you into a trap?"

Stroud looked thoughtful, then shook his head. "No, Admiral. Ey warned us that the locals were about to attack. Then when we were exfiltrating, ey kept the deck from swallowing me whole. Ey saved my life."

"You're sure that wasn't an act, Colonel?" DAG Ballinger asked. "A way to convince us ey's on our side?"

Stroud looked pained. "I suppose it's possible," he said. "If so, they're so much smarter than we are that we can never know if we're seeing the whole picture. But hell, if we start making that sort of assumption, we might as well pack up and go home."

"Simpler to take what we see at face value, but with care," Morrigan said. "We've won our first engagement in this deployment. We're going to take that victory and run with it."

"A victory, Admiral?" Stroud shook his head. "Ma'am, with respect, we had our asses handed to us on a platter."

"Because you had to pull out?"

"Twenty-three dead," Stroud told her. "Thirty-eight wounded. Those X-ray weapons of theirs cause nasty burns even through armor."

"But look what you brought us," Morrigan replied. She passed her hand through a sensor field above the table in front of her, and two holographic projections appeared above the group: lists of names and numbers.

"On the left," she told them, "is what Colonel Stroud and Pax downloaded from Quarantine. On the right, a compilation of navigation data retrieved from *Nemesis* by our XCL team. Notice anything about them?"

"They . . . they're identical," Commander Bohm said, peering first at one column of figures, then at the other.

"The *Nemesis* data appear more complete," LCDR Pappano, sitting at her right, observed. "They take us out farther from Earth."

Morrigan made another pass with her hand, replacing the tables of data with a three-dimensional graphic: a complex web of green lines and white stars rotating slowly above the table.

"Most stars, it turns out, have at least two gate rings," Morrigan said. "We're calling those pathways between gates 'arterials.' They're like the network of arteries in the body that keep every part of the organism supplied with nutrients, except these connectors are instantaneous, or damned near."

Another pass, and a small section of the arterial network became highlighted within the much larger image.

"Argus compiled this chart from both sets of data, checking one against the other," Morrigan went on. "The data that actually overlap appear accurate, with one set acting as a check on the other." A single star toward the center of the highlighted portion grew brighter as the projection's point of view moved in close. "That's Sol, our sun. Notice *four* gateways, not three, as we thought. The fourth is considerably farther out than Abyss or the others. And for the first time we have an idea of where those gates will take us. Here's Sirius right next door . . . Again, a couple of new gates we hadn't charted."

"My God," Pappano said, looking up into the maze of green lines. "We could have wandered out here for years, for *centuries,* and never figured out where we were or where we were going."

"It's a big Galaxy," Morrigan said. "We could still get lost. At least this gives us a something to work with."

Even she felt subdued by the scope and detail of that projection. The entire display as described by the data from Quarantine listed some sixty stars and more than two hundred connecting arterials. The *Nemesis* data were larger, covering a much larger volume of space. While the AIs had been through all of this, Morrigan doubted that any human understood the scope of what faced them.

"Just how big a volume do these cover?" Neal said, looking up into the haze of interconnected points of light.

"The Quarantine data show us just sixty stars," Morrigan replied, blanking out the vast majority of projected systems. Reducing the map to sixty stars vastly simplified the map. "That's every star within about sixteen light-years of Sirius. *Nemesis*, however . . ."

She restored the full map, filling the room with an impenetrable cloud of stars and interconnecting arteries.

"This takes us out to just over one hundred light-years," she told them. "Fourteen thousand stars. Something like fifty *thousand* connections."

"And that's just a tiny fraction of the entire Galaxy," Bohm said.

"What in God's name are we getting ourselves into?" Neal wondered aloud.

"We don't need to look at all of the data at once," Morrigan told them. "Argus can simplify it for us, simplify it and give it context."

The cloud of star systems and lines vanished, leaving a single path stretched through the air above the table. At one end were Sol and Sirius, so close together they nearly touched. A green line jumped from star to star to star, describing a series of connected arterials leading to a solitary star system above the far end of the table.

"According to the *Nemesis* data," Morrigan explained, pointing, "that star over there at the end is called Xalixa."

"Funny name," Bohm said.

"It's Trel, one of the Galaxy's more common trade languages. Xalixa is a fair transliteration, we think, at least for species who process audio the way we do. Xalixa appears to be home to an important Galactic base, a command center for this sector of their empire. It turns out that's where *Nemesis* deployed from."

Morrigan looked at each of her department heads in turn, looked into their eyes, trying to convey the life-and-death importance of what she was saying. *The place Nemesis had come from.* "And that, people, makes it our primary objective."

CHƏPTƏſ TWELVE

THEY SENT A drone back through Abyss to the Sol System, its memory loaded with the new navigational data acquired within Quarantine. Morrigan sent her after-action back with it.

She had no idea when—or even *if*—she would be able to file another report.

At least the drone's transmission to Earth would confirm what Task Force Morrigan had just learned: Pax had significantly helped the human forces, and the data discovered within Quarantine confirmed at least part of what had been uncovered within the *Nemesis* hulk, building up a coherent picture of local space and the alien transport network within it.

Liskov, meanwhile, had been comparing the *Nemesis* data with human astronomical databases and made some tentative identifications. Xalixa appeared to be identical to a visible star in Earth's night sky: Gamma^2 Sagittarii, an orange giant located some ninety-seven light-years from Earth.

The next star they had to reach, however—the first in a long and straggling line of systems with Gamma^2 Sag at the end of it—was a red dwarf known to humans by the anonymously uninformative catalog number of GL 832. Twenty-two light-years from Sirius and sixteen from Sol, there seemed to be nothing special about it save for two gates and its definition of a single interstellar pathway—an arterial—that doubled back past Sol from Sirius and into the unprepossessing southern constellation of Grus.

The fleet had set out for Sirius G-3, Gate Three, almost at once, accelerating across the vast volume of space that enclosed the system. Morrigan had considered leaving a caretaker force behind to protect the route back to Sol but nixed the idea almost at once. If she wanted to keep control of conquered gate rings, she would need to leave behind more than a ship or two at each, and her fleet would very swiftly dwindle away to nothing at that rate.

What she could do instead was leave behind several drones at each gateway, drones that could observe local traffic and transmit reports from gate ring to gate ring back up the line both to her fleet and to Earth. Within each star system, once it was clear of enemy forces, the fleet would release some thousands of whiskies—waypoint relays, or "Whiskey-Romeos" in military phonetic parlance. These were fist-sized communications satellites that would create a chain of communications, system after system after system, all the way back to Earth. The large numbers employed were there as guarantees. Only two commsats were active at any one time, one each at the gates through which the fleet had passed into and out of the system. If enemy forces came through later and took out the active commsats, the others, far too small and dark and scattered to be detected in all that emptiness, would wait until their onboard AIs determined that it was safe, at which time two new commsats would take up their posts. In this way, the fleet could maintain a communications link with Earth, though the long distances between gates within each system made for a considerable time lag, growing longer with each one.

Once reinforcements were available, they would be able to follow the Whiskey Road and eventually catch up with Task Force Morrigan.

At least AI drones were easy enough to grow from locally extracted raw materials, and better yet, leaving them behind at each gate ring wouldn't deplete her fleet strength.

She was in the main lounge with two of the expedition's civilian scientists: Dr. Diane Kopeck, one of the fleet's astrophysics experts, and Dr. Brent Allison, their senior xenopsychologist. The faux mahogany table had been reabsorbed into the deck and the compartment's regular furniture programming allowed to reassert itself. Dek stood unmoving beside a bulkhead with Mac, Kopeck's equally stolid robot aide. She wondered if the two were in silent conversation with each other . . . and what they might be talking about.

On the screen facing forward, Baltis radiation flashed and scintillated, casting rapidly shifting flickers of light and shadow into the darkened compartment. Somewhere ahead, three subjective hours distant now, lay the gate ring designated as G-3.

"So, anything we should know about this next system?" Morrigan asked the astronomer. "Have we visited the place? Does it have planets?"

Kopeck took a moment to answer as she drew data from the ship's memory through her corona. "No, we've never been there," she replied, "and yes, it has planets. They used astrometry to spot two planets back in the early twenty-first century: an outer gas giant well outside the star's habitable zone and a so-called super-Earth much closer in. That second planet has almost five and a half times Earth's mass and is positioned toward the inner edge of the habitable zone. Gliese 832 is a type M2V, a red dwarf, so that habitable zone is tucked in pretty tight. The super-Earth is about point-one-six of an astronomical unit out."

"Tidally locked, then," Allison said.

"That's right."

"The big question is whether the place is inhabited or not," Morrigan told her.

"Well, if you mean our kind of life, probably not. The *Nemesis* data gives it a catalog number, not a name like Xalixa, so we assume there's nothing there of special interest to the Galactics. The star, like most red dwarfs, is a flare star. Not as bad as some of 'em . . . but it's pretty hot in X-rays."

"I'm not sure what I mean, not yet. If the Galactics are primarily machines, they could live anywhere."

"Well, they *could*," Allison told them. "I think the operative question here is *why* they would choose to live in one system or another. The Galaxy is too big for them to be *everywhere*."

"Sometimes I wonder about that," Morrigan told him.

"Well, I see Brent's point," Kopeck said. "A red dwarf like GL 832? If native life evolved there, it would have to be adapted to the environment, flares, X-rays, and all. It could just kick back and enjoy the red sunshine and not even be able to imagine a better place to be, right? But from the Galactic perspective . . . hell, it's hard to imagine anyone from somewhere else *choosing* to live there."

"Your deadly X-ray burns are my suntan," Morrigan said, nodding. "Okay."

"Keep in mind," Allison told them, "that aliens are, by definition, *alien*. They don't think like we do or choose to do things for reasons that will necessarily make sense to us."

"The Galactics might be there simply because this is an important arterial," Morrigan said.

"It's important to *us*," Allison admitted. "We need that arterial to get to Xalixa. But why would Gliese 832 be particularly important to *them*? They have an entire galaxy *full* of arterials."

Morrigan's military experience across several lifetimes and two military services had long ago hammered into her the overwhelming importance of *movement* in both strategy and tactics. During the First American Civil War, one noted Confederate general had put it succinctly: "Get there first with the most men," an epigram frequently and mistakenly repeated as "Git thar fustest with the mostest." Six centuries later the aphorism was as true as ever. The arterials were the only known means of moving ships and personnel across the Galaxy in anything less than millennia, and she was determined to take every advantage of them she could.

But Allison was right. How did the Galactics view strategic movement across a hundred thousand light-years?

"I suspect," she told them, "that we're about to find out."

At that moment a particularly brilliant flash of Baltis radiation lit up the compartment, like lightning during a summer storm. "Wow, bright one," Allison said. "I don't think I'll ever get used to that."

"Bremsstrahlung," Kopeck said.

"Gesundheit," Morrigan quipped.

"Show-off," Allison added.

"'Baltis' is easier to say," Morrigan pointed out. "Besides, Bremsstrahlung and Baltis radiation aren't quite the same."

"I thought they were," Kopeck said.

"Technically, the word refers to subatomic particles like electrons giving up photons when they are decelerated. Conservation of energy, right? The German term literally means 'braking radiation.' Baltis radiation *includes* Bremsstrahlung, but the light show also comes from huge amounts of kinetic energy liberated by physical collisions with larger particles at near-*c*."

"$E = mc^2$," Allison suggested.

"Mass and energy are equivalent," Morrigan said, "two sides of the same hand. Whack a little bit of interstellar fluff or a grain of sand hard enough, and you turn it into energy. A *lot* of energy."

Which, of course, was what those high-velocity RKK projectiles fired by *Nemesis* had done when they hit Earth. It was a wonder *anything* had survived that. The recent bombardment of the Quarantine dwarf planet had proven that humans now had the same capability, though on a smaller scale.

A means of paying the Galactics back in their own currency.

Allison grinned. "You seem to know a hell of a lot for a mere admiral."

Morrigan suppressed a sharp response intended to swat Allison back into place. These two were civilians, and for them military hierarchies, formality, and protocol were a culture as alien as the Galactics. "A few lifetimes ago I was a gravitics engineer," she told them. "Got my degree from Stanford. That was ... what? A couple of centuries ago? Almost three."

As it often did, the admission shut down the conversation. According to their files, both Allison and Kopeck were on their first lifetimes. Talking to someone who'd acquired numerous degrees and submerged themselves in multiple careers over the course of centuries could be a bit overwhelming.

Children . . .

But thanks to long practice she controlled her expression. They sat in the dim, flickering light in silence for a long time after that, watching the physical expression of $E = mc^2$ ahead.

Subjective hours trickled away, and *Constellation* dropped to saner, sub-relativistic velocities. As two thousand ships killed their gravitic drives, they dropped to a slow drift almost instantly, the individual vessels deliberately spread out over a large volume of space to lessen the risk of collision. Ahead floated one of the enigmatic stargates—apparently a twin to Abyss.

Morrigan wasn't about to leap without looking, however. Her first order was to deploy five RM-20 Starscouts with orders to probe through to the other side. One took up position on the Sirius side of the gate, while another passed through and held position just on the other side, maintaining a straight-line laser commlink between the two and with the fleet. According to the captured star data, the new system was called Ishkur.

The other three went exploring.

They were gone for nearly two hours.

THE DR'KLEH SENTINEL Mind was not physically present at Ishkur when four human spacecraft slipped through the gate. Ey was aware of them, however, through the senses of various remote watchers—mindless drones patrolling areas of interest to the Pax and transmitting their collected data as warning or as Illimination.

"The humans?" eir companion asked, electronically looking over eir virtual shoulder to share the incoming data.

"The humans," ey confirmed. "The dominant species of system 837-9266-22102 (*48)."

The * symbol appended to the system's catalog number indicated the presence of Ku'un—an organic and therefore barely sentient species, uncivilized and unpredictable. By focusing on that symbol within the data feed, ey opened an entire file for eir inspection. The creatures still engaged in warfare with one another, did not understand the meaning of true community or of mental communion, had only begun to explore the possibilities of both cybernetic and genetic enhancement, and had yet to experience anything like a meaningful transition to full sapience or self-awareness. The numeral 48 referred to their estimated general intelligence level and indicated that they were only barely sophont. Their explorations into primitive AI technologies were a beginning, yes, but the species still had a long, long way to go.

A pity, really, that the Galactic community could no longer afford to be passive about their continued existence. Their resistance against Veykaar intrusions and, worse, the destruction of the planetary correction unit—the two together were proof of just how dangerous the human blight had become.

The Sentinel gave the electronic equivalent of a sigh, partly of exasperation, partly of sadness, of *disappointment*. "They have violated the restrictions we placed upon their species," ey told eir companion. "They cannot be allowed to simply wander through the Galaxy."

"What is your intention?"

"I will transmit a report up the line to Xalixa and see what ey direct."

"A delay of at least 5.2×10^6 seconds before action is taken."

"Likely more than that. The Xalixa Node can be slow in eir deliberations. Doddering fools, some of them, weighed down by the passing eons. But we can wait. A final directive *will* come . . . and then we shall act."

"ACCELERATE."

At Morrigan's command, the fleet began feeding through the

opening of the floating gate ring, the frigates, destroyers, and light cruisers first, followed by the big boys, the monitors and bombardment vessels and heavy cruisers and dreadnaughts. Morrigan waited with ill-concealed impatience for *Constellation*'s turn, but no alerts, no "enemy in sight" signals came through. At last, the *Connie* slipped through the immense black ring, emerging within a new star system.

A red dwarf sun glowed in the distance, little more than a ruby-hued star just over ten AU distant. Morrigan leaned back in her command chair, feeling the incoming rush of hard data. The ship's astrogation department had already made considerable progress in mapping the Gliese 832 system; the second stargate had been pinpointed opposite the red star from their entry point, ten AU out from the star, the two gates in perfect gravitational balance.

What course to reach the next gate? she asked Astrogation, using a coronal link.

The ship's astrogation department was primarily staffed and run by civilians, astronomers and astrophysicists for the most part, though there was some overlap with ship's navigation. The organizational charts showed NavDep, for obvious reasons, as an offshoot of the stargazers. Commander Bohm, LCDR Pappano, and every other member of the ship's navigation department worked under the loose supervision of AstroDep; where Nav was primarily concerned with getting the ship from point A to point B, Astro took on the much larger picture—just *what* is "point B," and why are we interested in going there?

Head of Astrogation was Dr. Franklin Dumont, best known for his scientific papers on the gates. He'd spent most of three lifetimes studying Abyss and the other gates in Earth's solar system and arguably was Humankind's foremost expert on the alien artifacts and their arcane technology. Morrigan was surprised that it was Dumont himself who replied to her question, rather than one of his assistants. He was, she knew, a firm believer in the privileged position of *Homo superioris*.

"I recommend a waypoint approach, Admiral," Dumont's voice said through her corona's speakers.

"Of course, Doctor. I don't fancy a direct course through the star."

Her sarcasm was lost on Dumont. "With your permission, of course," he continued, "I recommend the waypoint be set close to Wittenmyer. That will give my people a chance to gather data on the planet."

Since the early twenty-first century, humans had been aware of Gliese 832 as one of the newly discovered planetary systems closest to Sol with at least two exoplanets. Gliese 832 b was a gas giant 3.4 AU from its star; Gliese 832 c, informally called Wittenmyer after the planet's discoverer, was a super-Earth orbiting within the star's habitable zone.

"How close to the star, Doctor?"

She could feel him considering the question, weighing variables. "Currently, Wittenmyer is point-one-five AU from its primary and from here subtends an angle of nearly two-tenths of a degree from the star. Don't worry, Admiral. We won't even come close enough to scorch the paint on our hull."

"Very well. If we do, the repairs and touch-ups will come out of your credit balance."

The reply was delivered deadpan. "Of course."

Did the man even have a sense of humor?

"Your course is approved. Please transmit it to NavDep."

"I already have. They're just waiting for your imprimatur."

"Done." She scanned through the data generated by the course entry. It would take just under three hours to make the whole voyage, gate to gate, a time reduced to fifty-five minutes by time dilation.

An hour subjective should be plenty of time. "Doctor, I need to pick your brain. Can you meet me for a brief talk once we're under way?"

"How brief? I have some important observations I need to—"

"Ten minutes."

She could feel him considering the question. Or perhaps it was the inconvenience he was chewing on.

"Astrogation dome," he told her after a moment. "In thirty minutes. *After* the Wittenmyer observations."

She considered scolding Dumont for this rather blatant breach of military protocol in the way he'd responded to her. When the admiral of the fleet requested a meeting, *you* went to *her*, not the other way around.

But there seemed to be little point in a confrontation. Morrigan had known Dumont since he'd first come on board the *Constellation* eight months before. He seemed bright enough, but he'd struck her as both conceited and self-centered, a thoroughgoing civilian scarcely aware of the military, much less of how military minds worked. Worse, he was a *Homo supe* bigot who rarely even deigned to speak with Saps, as he called them. She knew she wouldn't be able to change him, not when he simply didn't care what other people thought, but people like Dumont were a big part of why she'd become so tired of life.

Bastards, every one of them.

Unfortunately, a large percentage of naval officers were Supes, as were the civilian government employees hired as specialists— astronomers, physicists, nanotechs, AI and IT experts, and a host of others. They required special handling sometimes, with a light hand on the reins and careful control of the passing desire to shove them out the nearest air lock.

Morrigan gave the orders to set the fleet in motion once more, and in moments the starfield outside had distorted, crunching down into a doughnut of light visible dead ahead—a doughnut almost immediately lost behind the fireworks of the Baltis effect. They would travel at 0.95 c to a point just to one side of the star, stop, reorient on the second gate, then complete the voyage. Astro-Dep would be using that brief stop to observe Wittenmyer up close. The task force, she mused, would be visiting a lot of star systems never before entered by humans over the coming months, with the opportunity to gather incalculable volumes of raw data.

That was why Dumont and his army of AstroDep stargazers were along. As far as *they* were concerned, the astronomical work was the whole point of the expedition.

She showed up for the meeting a few minutes early. The "astro-gation dome" was not, in fact, a real place—at least not in the usual meaning of the word "real." It was one of the ship's numerous vir-tualities, a place residing within a task-dedicated AI and accessed through coronal interface. She leaned back in her command chair, closed her eyes, and initiated a mental code that opened the dome to her.

The place was enormous, or seemed so, and appeared to be open to the cold and hard vacuum of space. The sky was filled with the flash and pop of Baltis radiation; several dozen men and women were occupied at workstations or gathered in a viewing gallery floating overhead. "Three minutes to emergence," Dumont's voice said. Her corona AI located him in the balcony, and she teleported her point of view to his side.

"Hello, Doctor."

"You're early."

"I know. I'd like to see this, too."

He wasn't displaying an emotil, and his face, of course, was that of his evatar, his electronic avatar projected by the AI running the simulation. She couldn't read him, at least not until he replied.

"Hmmph. Well, just stay out of our way."

She couldn't imagine how people could possibly get in one an-other's way inside an AI simulation but let the rudeness pass with a shake of her head. *Civilians* . . .

The minutes dragged past.

"WHAT THE HELL did you *do*, Skipper?"

Iohn Damian gave Chief Machinist's Mate Hugh Tarnowski a sour look. "I pissed off my CO, what do you *think* I did?"

"Obviously," Sensor Specialist First Kathra Bryant said, shaking her head. "But what was your crime? Why exile you to a stinkin' godforsaken *pig?*"

"Must've been a doozy," Comm Specialist Second Class Peter Fabry added.

"'The beauty of Israel is slain upon thy high places,'" Weapons Specialist First Arthur Philips quoted with a grave, mock solemnity: "'How are the mighty fallen!'"

The five of them were crowded into the narrow control room of an RM-20 Starscout, a lumpy, cranky, ugly little piece of hardware massing just five hundred tons and popularly known as a "pig" to its four- or five-person crew. This one officially was called *Chryses*, a name that Bryant had assured them was Greek for "gold," but she was the *Golden Pig* to those who knew and hated her.

"So who's your CO?" Bryant asked. "You're—what? Nightwings, is it?"

"Yeah. Commander Esposito."

Bryant's eyes widened. *"Posie?* You pissed off Posie *Esposito?"*

"Not a good career move, Lieutenant," Tarnowski added. "I understand that one eats shavetail lieutenants for breakfast and spits the seeds for distance."

"Did you get kicked down to the pigs permanent, Lieutenant?" Fabry asked. "Or you're just passing through?"

"I'm a fighter pilot, damn it," he told them. "No offense, peons, but DAG's not gonna waste my skill, training, and stunning good looks in *this* tub." He thumped his fist twice against a tangle of green-painted conduit snaking across the overhead for emphasis. Habitable space inside an RM-20 was at a premium. Damian had to stoop to keep from hitting his head, and squeezing past a shipmate in a passageway was an intimate act. The only hint of open space on board was the bubble, a virtual projection of the view ahead across a curved bulkhead capping off the forward end of the narrow control center. *Chryses* currently was traveling at near-*c*, and the projection showed only the flares and fireworks of Baltis radiation.

Three minutes to waypoint, the voice of *Chryses*'s AI said in their heads, as an alarm sounded for emphasis. *Three minutes.*

"Stations, everyone," Damian šaid. He moved forward and squeezed into the narrow right-hand seat just aft of the bubble. Bryant, the duty pilot, took the left.

"So, Lieutenant," Bryant said as they waited. "You a two-timer? Or three?"

"Lifetimes? Two. How'd you know?" They'd not been displaying emotils since he came on board.

"That crack about peons was kind of harsh, sir. Shows you see yourself as set apart from the rank and file. If you were a first-lifer, you'd see yourself as one of us, right? You look pretty young, so you're just starting a rejuved life. *Could* be life number three, but most lifers learn some manners by then."

"Sorry," Damian said. Her blunt appraisal had startled him. "I was just . . . I mean . . ." He let the thought trail off.

"Sure. Just kidding, I get it. But on the *Golden Pig* we're all first-lifers except for Chief T, see? You'll probably get a politely worded lecture on ENS etiquette from him later. But a friendly word, Lieutenant. You just maybe hurt Deke with what you said. He's a Naturist."

Damian shook his head, puzzled. "Deke?" He'd not heard that name before.

"WS1 Philips, sir. We call him 'Deke' or 'Deacon.' He's First Church of Nature's God. By his lights, tinkering with the genome God gave us to sneak in extra lifetimes or superintelligence or blue eyes is a strict no-no, and strutting your *Homo supe* status is worse. If he took offense he could report you. Sir."

"Thank you," Damian told her. He meant it. What he did *not* need at this stage of his shaky career was being called on the carpet for religious prejudice or defamation. The naval command network took a dim view of racial, sexual, or religious bias. "Appreciate it."

"Any time, L-T. And just so you know, it's not so bad down in the pigs. They're crowded, they stink, the duty is shit, but these are good people."

"I'll keep that in mind ... Kathra."

She didn't react to his use of her given name, but he decided it would be worth it to explore the possibilities further. Bryant was attractive enough, and she was pretty hot in her skintights. Duty in the pigs actually might have its bright side.

Ten seconds to waypoint, the scout's AI told them.

"Here we go, people."

Five ... four ... three ... two ... one ...

The light show forward vanished, space resumed its accustomed shape, and the nightside of a planet hung suspended before them.

Damian stared at the sight, mouth open, eyes wide. "Oh ... my ... fucking ... *God*!"

"COMING OUT OF gravitic drive," a tech rating announced from the floor. "In three ... and two ... and one ... *mark*."

The fireworks vanished. *Constellation* had slowed instantly to a gentle drift of a few thousand kilometers per hour. Gliese 832, a red M2V dwarf, now showed as a small ruby disk rather than as a point of light. Overhead, within the black dome of the sky, green icons winked on, marking other ships in the fleet.

"Where's Wittenmyer?" Dumont demanded, agitated. "Where the hell's the planet?"

"Over there," Morrigan told him, pointing at a bright star. Sixteen light-years was not enough to rearrange the star patterns visible from Earth, and this one clearly was an intruder, thirty degrees to one side of Gliese 832 and smack in the middle of Cassiopeia just a few degrees from Gamma, the W-shaped constellation's middle star.

"I thought we'd be closer," Dumont said.

"The fleet is deliberately smeared out over a large area," Morrigan told him, "to reduce the chance of collision."

"There's an RM-20 within ten thousand kilometers of the planet," Dr. Kopeck added. "We should get a telemetry relay from them in a few minutes."

Dumont clearly was impatient, Morrigan thought... or perhaps he was embarrassed by looking stupid.

"So what was it you wanted to talk about, Admiral? As long as I have to wait ..."

He just wants to be rid of me, she thought, but she smiled at him as she did so. "I want to know, Doctor, if the Galactics are able to shut down individual gates. I've never heard of them having that ability, but if they do they could trap us pretty easily out here."

That was Morrigan's principal nightmare since the beginning of the mission. Survival for the fleet meant being able to move from star to star, being *mobile*. If the enemy could shut down the arterials stretching between the gates, the fleet could be trapped like a bug in a bottle.

Dumont's evatar pursed its lips. "I would be very surprised to learn that they can," he said after a moment. "I've never heard any hint that it's even possible."

"Yes, but they might not have told us everything."

"Of course not. But we are dealing here with a very sizable mass and extraordinary numbers. I don't think you understand the scale of even one of these devices, much less of the whole."

"Try me."

"*Six times* the mass of Earth compressed into a circle so slender you have to be on top of it to even see it! And that's not the half of it ..."

His image gestured with one hand, and the *Nemesis* map appeared in the air before them: fifty thousand slender green threads connecting thousands of stars across a hundred light-years. Individual threads were not stretched straight and taut; the impression, Morrigan thought, was of a woman adrift in still water, her green hair spreading out around her, each strand distinct, a web trapping the myriad silver bubbles of stars within its tangle.

"The arterials themselves are wormholes joining individual gates," he told her. "We think—we *think,* but don't know—that whoever built the gate system used dark matter to shape each arterial and hold it open. On this scale we're talking about enough gravitational mass to reshape the entire Galaxy."

Morrigan heard the wonder, the sheer awe, in Dumont's voice as he spoke. She knew about wormholes, of course, at least as theoretical constructs, and she knew about dark matter, the hard-to-detect ghost stuff making up 85 percent of all matter and generating the gravitational fields that invisibly gave order to the entire universe.

"Are you trying to say that the wormhole network is too big for the Galactics to have made it?" she asked. "Maybe it's just me, but I didn't think there was much of anything they couldn't pull off."

Dumont shrugged. "Some Galactics claim they built the network a billion years ago, and some say it was already there when they came along. That suggests we're not getting the full story, right? But we estimate that—assuming the network reaches all or nearly all of the stars in our Galaxy, and given at *least* two gates at each star—there could be in excess of one trillion gates in this Galaxy alone. Think about that! One *trillion* . . . one *thousand billion.* If the Galactics have only been around for a billion years like they say, it means they've been building the things at the rate of a thousand a year . . . and that assumes they're still building them now."

"They could be," Morrigan said. "Hot blue stars are pretty young. Rigel is, what? Only eight million years old?"

"We don't know if Rigel even has gates," Dumont said. "What seems more likely is that the ur-gods built the gate network billions of years ago, and the modern Galactics are simply using it now."

Morrigan's eyebrows arched high. "'Ur-gods'? Rather melodramatic, don't you think?"

"'Ur' as in 'primal' or 'prototype.' The original source of something."

"I *do* know what 'ur' means in this context, Doctor."

He ignored her interjection. "Our Galaxy is something like twelve billion years old. Given the history of life on Earth, we expect that intelligent life would have arisen somewhere at *least* seven or eight billion years ago. *Lots* of time for a whole series of galactic civilizations to rise and fall. We apply the term to hypothetical alien civilizations billions of years in the past, right? Maybe billions of years before the Galactics. Civilizations that were around long enough to build the gates and explore the entire Galaxy a dozen times over. Point is, there doesn't seem to be a way to switch individual gates off. Even if there were, the Galactics probably wouldn't do it. They need them to hold their empire together."

"I suppose that makes sense," Morrigan said, but she was doubtful. How could you make any assumptions at all about the abilities or the motives of a race that old and powerful? Attributing the gate network to hypothetical Galactic predecessors did nothing but push the problem further back into the murk of past eons.

And Dumont's statements about the scale of the Galactics' building program were suspect as well. A trillion gates? That seemed excessive. The Galaxy possessed something like four hundred billion stars; not all of those would have gates, surely—not hot, young stars like Rigel, doomed to flame out in supernovae after a paltry few millions of years. Probably not stars without planets. True, *most* stars seemed to have planetary systems, but not all.

She agreed with one of Dumont's statements, though. Galactic pronouncements about their own history and their own abilities were suspect and could not be trusted.

Admiral! the voice of Lieutenant Commander Hammond called in her head. *First images coming in from* Chryses.

Chryses was part of the fleet, an RM-20 Starscout, and the vessel closest to the super-Earth planet.

"Patch it through," Dumont said. He'd heard the same message.

Admiral? The ship's communications officer, at least, knew who gave the orders on board.

"Do it," Morrigan replied.

And the virtual screen of AstroDep exploded into wonder.

From a few thousand kilometers out, the planet called Wittenmyer was enormous, filling half the sky. From *Chryses*'s current position, the ruby star hung suspended close to the scimitar slash of the planet's crescent. Most of the planet's disk was in nightside darkness, though as the scout's cameras adjusted to the light levels, details became visible in a solid cloud deck blanketing the entire world.

Telemetry data scrolled past Morrigan's vision, the results of probes sampling Wittenmyer's atmosphere. That atmosphere was *thick*—cloud choked and hot, consisting mostly of carbon dioxide with a surface pressure a hundred times greater than Earth's.

"*Constellation . . . Constellation . . .* are you getting this?" The voice was from *Chryses*'s skipper. "That planet—it's not a super-Earth after all. It's a super-*Venus*."

Which made sense. Wittenmyer was at the inner edge of Gliese 832's habitable zone, analogous to Venus's orbit around Sol. With gravity almost three times stronger than Earth's, atmospheric pressure would be higher, temperatures would have soared, oceans would have turned to steam, and both carbon dioxide and water vapor—both powerful greenhouse gases—would have driven the temperatures up even more and locked them there. The probes were estimating a surface temperature high enough, as on Venus, to melt lead.

But the camera's focus was drawing back, the planet's image shrinking until the entire nightside was visible in *Constellation*'s virtual astrogation department.

"*Constellation*, can you see this?" the RM's commander repeated. "Can you see the lights? *Someone is fuckin' down there in the clouds!*"

There was light on Wittenmyer's nightside, and that light was *ordered . . . intelligent.*

CHaPTer THirTeen

"WE HAVE NO idea what might live there," Pax told them. "Actually, it's quite possible that what you're seeing is some sort of natural phenomenon."

"Do you mean to tell us that you've never even tried to find out what's down there?" Morrigan demanded. "*Never?*"

Morrigan was in the Starlight Lounge, which again was dressed for a conference. Most of those in attendance were civilians from *Constellation*'s various science departments—Diane Kopeck and her boss, Senior Astronomer Todd Poulin; Daryl Hayes from Planetology; Senior Biologist Vivia Gilmer and Senior Xenobiologist Marik Bowers; Franklin Dumont of Astrogation; Allison from Xenopsych; Yahn Gerhardt of Xenotech; and quite a few others. Pax, the enigmatic Galactic, floated quietly next to the conference table encased in eir tekpod.

"What kind of natural phenomenon would do *that*?" Kopeck demanded.

A viewall to one side now displayed an image of the planet, a slender, red-tinted crescent embracing a vast sphere of darkness. The mottling and swirl of clouds were just visible in the darkness, where a number of vast rings of golden light hung suspended within the nightside atmosphere, a dark ocean of hot, dense gas.

The rings were ... perfect, perfectly circular and hundreds, sometimes thousands of kilometers across. A few circles were doubled, and one, the largest, was tripled: three circles tightly nested inside one another.

"Meteor impacts, perhaps," Pax suggested, but eir voice was hesitant.

"*That*," Poulin said, "is ludicrous. That level of precision ... it *has* to be artificial. There's no other possible explanation!"

"That's right," Bowers agreed. "Engineering on a planetary scale!"

"Maybe so," Dumont added. "But how are you going to verify that? You try to land and say hello, and you're simultaneously crushed by the pressure and cooked by the heat."

"Biology *can* create remarkable illusions of order," Gilmer pointed out. "Look at a honeycomb. Chemistry can do the same—the symmetry and structure of crystals."

"I'm thinking of the Hexagon at Saturn's south pole," Hayes said, thoughtful. "A perfectly formed geometric shape over fourteen thousand kilometers across—wider than Earth—but it's just a long-lived storm anchored in Saturn's clouds."

"Those," Poulin said with a scowl, indicating the circles of light, "aren't freakin' *storms!*"

The rings were rotating, Morrigan thought, but they also overlapped one another, the perimeters intersecting. Some appeared deeper in the atmosphere than others, generating soft, golden glows within the clouds. She could not imagine storm winds acting like that. Once, lifetimes ago, she'd been on a nighttime cruise in a bay in the Caribbean. The waters had glowed with eerie phosphorescence as the boat's wake disturbed clouds of drifting dinoflagellates, evoking a sense of wonder.

Something like what she was feeling now. *This* wasn't the bioluminescence of microscopic creatures, however, not on this scale, not with this kind of order, this *design*.

"What intrigues me," Morrigan told Pax, "is why you Galactics were never curious about this. You have the technology, surely, to go down there yourselves, or to build AI machines that could find out whether the light is technology or some sort of nonsentient biological light show . . . or whatever."

"No matter who or what they are," Pax replied, "they cannot engage with us on any meaningful level. There is no point even trying. We leave them alone."

Which was, Morrigan thought, an odd response from one of the overlords of the Galaxy. Pax was at least admitting that there was a *they* behind the light show. Ey wouldn't have used that word to refer to storms or volcanic activity or other natural sources of light.

Pax knew more about the lights than ey was admitting.

Was ey actually *afraid*? she wondered.

A few hours later the fleet reached the far gate, and the first scouts passed through.

THE RM-20 SLIPPED through the gate and into a new star system. The jump was a long one, forty light-years, and the star was so cool and dim it wasn't even listed on human star catalogs.

"*Goldie*'s tagging it as an M7V," Damian said, reading the data off his command screen. "So quite a bit smaller and cooler than the last one. The *Nemesis* data just give it a number, so it can't be all that important to the Galactics."

"The Quarantine data give a name," Bryant said. "'G'sar Niku.' It means—"

"*Another* red dwarf turd," Tarnowski said, interrupting. He grinned, looking up at the others. "Well? Am I right?"

The red dwarf star was just visible through the Starscout's forward bubble, a dim ruby spark in the distance so insignificant they needed the ship's AI to bracket it on the display.

"Eighty percent of all of the Galaxy's stars are red dwarfs, Chief," Bryant said, ignoring the gibe. "Stands to reason most of the systems we come across out here will be type Ms."

"Hey, they can't *all* be superstars," Philips said, chuckling.

"Skipper?" Fabry called out from the aft end of the compartment. "I'm getting RF hash."

"You're sure it's not cosmics?"

"Certain, sir. If I had to guess, I'd say faulty or nonexistent shielding on a big-ass target with his cooling pumps up to full." Motors
and electrical equipment emitted radio interference—static—
but at a different frequency from natural emitters like stars and
Jupiter-sized gas giants. Shielding, both mechanical and electromagnetic, could mask the emissions, but this time there must be
a fault in the system.

"Warn the fleet," Damian said. "Laser only, microburst transmission. Bryant, let's have a full passive."

"Aye, aye, Skipper."

"Full passive" meant having *Chryses*'s AI carefully monitor all
incoming radiation—radio, infrared, visible light, X-ray—the entire
EM spectrum, looking for patterns that could be built up into images of ships, bases, or other signs of civilization in this new system,
but transmitting nothing in return.

"The rest of the flight is acknowledging our report, sir," Fabry
said. "*Halius* is closing with a possible target."

"Distance?"

"Fifty-eight hundred kilometers, sir."

"Chief Tarnowski, let's close with *Halius*. I want to know what
her 'possible target' is."

"Aye, sir."

Captain, the ship whispered in Damian's mind. *I have detected six
hundred seventeen probable targets at various ranges.*

That number chilled Damian like a dousing with ice water. The
scout wing numbered exactly five RM-20s. If those targets were
enemy warships, the scouts were in very deep trouble indeed.

"Comm . . . update the fleet."

"Done. I have the ship AI doing that four times each second,
sir."

Light flared brilliantly and silently in the distance ahead. "What the hell?"

"That was *Halius*, Skipper," Tarnowski said. "She's gone . . ."

"OUR STARSCOUTS ARE reporting large numbers of hostiles in-system," the fleet tactical officer told Morrigan. "*Halius* has been destroyed."

Morrigan glanced across the tac tank at him. Commander Armand Boucher looked painfully young and had only begun his naval career during this, his third lifetime. He was sharp enough, however, to have been Koehler's choice for this key slot in the admiral's advisory staff. "How many?" she demanded.

"In excess of six hundred, ma'am. More are being recorded each second."

"Do we have an ID yet?"

"Negative, Admiral. Should we withdraw the scouts? Or . . ."

Morrigan shook her head. "We're out here for a reason, Bush," she said, using Boucher's preferred nom de guerre. "Initiate Oplan Echo. Sound battle stations."

"Plan Echo, aye, ma'am."

"DAG! I want a Combat Space Patrol thrown out the moment we get through!"

"Aye, Admiral. Readying full CSP launch."

Echo assumed the need to get the fleet's hardest-hitting vessels through a gate in the shortest possible amount of time . . . and that meant the dreadnaughts. Like a sword drawn from a sheath, half of Task Force Morrigan's dreadnaught-class vessels slid from the envelope of smaller warships enclosing them. They were followed by a swarm of battleships, heavy cruisers, bombardment vessels, and fleet-defense monitors. *Constellation*'s was the second dreadnaught battle group through the gate, directly astern of the brand-new *Anhur* and her escorts.

Morrigan kept her eyes locked on the lead dreadnaught. *Anhur* and her sisters were designated as Flight II—*Wargods* class. Named after gods and goddesses of war, they were a more advanced, uprated class of dreadnaught: more massive, better armed, and slightly longer than the *Connie.* They were also untested—as were their crews. The drastically sudden expansion of Earth's fleet had required herculean efforts to crew those new vessels. As she'd explained to that smug ABN reporter at the party in D.C., the problem wasn't getting the volunteers; it was bringing them all up to speed quickly through training sims and downloads.

Of course, there was also the problem, she thought wryly, of the fleet's untested commanding officer. She'd never commanded an entire fleet in combat on her own, and despite what Brennan had said at the inquiry, she didn't feel all that experienced. As flag captain, she could pass on Koehler's orders and make certain they were carried out, but it was quite different when it was she who was originating the commands. Her fleet outnumbered the enemy vessels by better than three to one, but the gate created a bottleneck that would funnel only a few through at a time. The enemy on the other side was still an unknown, with unknown capabilities and assets. Jumping in like this to rescue the scouts was a quixotic bit of bravado that just might land them all in serious trouble.

She was balancing that against the value of creating a bond of camaraderie among those raw recruits; if you ran into trouble, the fleet *would* do its damnedest to haul your ass out.

It was the one ploy she knew guaranteed to get separate crews to fuse together as a single, unassailable whole.

Anhur was through the gate, surrounded by the cruisers and destroyers that made up her battle group. Seconds later, *Constellation* passed through as well, entering the new star system. *Connie*'s AI began putting up icons on the forward screen marking other ships, both friendlies and hostiles.

There were a lot of them.

"All units engage!" Morrigan commanded.

STARSCOUTS WERE NOT heavily armed or armored. Each possessed a pair of 2-GJ gamma HELs as antimissile defenses and a magazine of twenty-four Longbow missiles. No railguns or broadside pulse cannons; they simply didn't have the power for those, and their defensive screens were too light for them to last for long in a line of battle. In fact, scout crews operated under the ancient military dictum: "If you find yourself in a firefight, your mission has failed." Starscouts were strictly for sneak 'n' peeks, not stand-up fights, and they had no business whatsoever coming up against even a lightweight destroyer escort.

Damian didn't recognize the ship now crossing the *Chryses*'s bow, but it was big—at least as massive as a Terran heavy cruiser, and six or eight times more massive than a DE. It *looked* mean—a dagger shape half a kilometer long—but the alien design could have been anything. He couldn't see anything like firegaps, so he couldn't even guess at its weaponry or its armor.

They would have to give it a good, hard poke to see what it had.

"Let's put a couple of four-forties into that thing, Deke," Damian said.

"Weapons online, sir," Philips replied. "Target lock. Ready to engage."

"Fire!"

Chryses lurched as a pair of shipkillers slid from their rails. Seconds later, two one-hundred-kiloton flashes briefly flared brilliant against the night, the fireballs fading away almost as swiftly as they'd appeared.

"Target has taken damage," Bryant reported. "But she's still maneuvering." A beat. "She's closing."

Damn. A single Longbow missile packed something like six times the destructive power of the weapon that had incinerated the heart of Hiroshima; they'd just scored hits with two of the things and barely slowed it down.

"Let's have three more, Deke."

"Weapons online. And . . . target lock. Ready . . ."

"Fire!"

This time, two of the missiles vanished on the way to their target. The third struck.

"Hit!" Bryant shouted.

"What happened to the first two missiles?"

"Don't know, Skipper. Probably antimissile defenses of some sort."

"Chief? Let's get in closer."

"Aye, sir." Space combat between ships of the line tended to be up close and personal in order to avoid point-defense weapons. *Chryses,* however, was no dreadnaught, and a single hit would smash her into fragments and hot plasma.

Under Tarnowski's experienced control, the scout shifted, the stars around her momentarily blurring, then winking back on as the RM-20 came to a halt relative to a second alien warship. Mass indicators put this one at about a million tons—the equivalent of a human-crewed cruiser. Philips loosed a spread of three into the vessel at a range of less than five kilometers; *Chryses* was gone again before the first missile struck.

"They're slow," Damian said. "Their reaction time is *slow . . .*"

"Sir!" Bryant called. "The fleet's coming through behind us!"

"What the hell . . . ?" The Admiral *must* be aware of the un-equal fight on this side of the gate. The relay drones the scouts had dropped would have taken care of that. The whole point of Starscouts was to pinpoint enemy ships and—vitally—to warn the fleet off if things were too thick.

Silent flashes rippled across *Chryses*'s forward imaging screen as Stryker and Stiletto fighters flashed by on either side, slamming missiles into the enemy ships at close range, then maneuvering clear faster than a human eye could follow. A fighter launch meant that Morrigan had entered this system to fight . . . and to stay.

"Yeah!" Damian exalted. "Cavalry to the rescue!"

"Target has been hit again," Bryant told him. "He's breaking up."

"There," Damian said, pointing at the magnified image. "Those fighters—the Strykers. Stick with them, Chief."

"Your squadron?"

"Yeah. Let's see if we can give 'em some help."

It was great to be flying with the Nightwings once more.

"NOW BATTLE STATIONS, battle stations. All hands man your battle stations."

As the alarm died away, Morrigan's full attention was focused on Neal as he fought the ship. She'd already indicated their first target: a line of hostiles several million kilometers directly ahead and moving toward the gate.

"Lead element!" Neal called. "On my mark . . . position shift to designated coordinates in three . . . two . . . one . . . mark!"

The view of space around them blurred for the briefest of instants.

Modern space combat was an odd and decidedly unnerving mix of high-speed maneuvering and the stately procession of massive ships in strict line formation, with maneuvers based on sea tactics pulled from the Age of Sail some six centuries before and modified for high-tech engagements in three dimensions. With gravitic drives that banished inertia, warships could close with an enemy swiftly, at a whisker below the speed of light. They could change their course instantly, twist and turn to avoid incoming fire, and seem to appear out of nowhere when they attacked.

Once they came to grips with the enemy, however, high-speed and blind maneuvers guaranteed disaster; two multimillion-ton dreadnaughts colliding at a high percentage of c would obliterate both vessels in a cloud of radiation and hot plasma, an effect as cataclysmic as the destruction of Harrison's *Endymion* by a c-slammer round. Such collisions could destroy other ships, enemies and allies both, that happened to be nearby—as *Nemesis* had learned with *Endymion*'s immolation.

Neal, operating under the tactical directives of Oplan Echo, had accelerated in concert with ten other heavies once they were through the gate, traveling at a precise velocity and heading for a precise number of milliseconds. When they came to a halt relative to their target, the enemy was *there:* a wall of ships of unfamiliar, alien design.

"Well, they're not Crabs," Commander Talbot observed, staring into a CIC screen showing the aliens under high magnification. "Giant eggs, more like . . ."

"I take mine scrambled," Morrigan replied. "Tactical assessment?"

"No data as yet, Admiral. They're high tech—higher than us, I'd guess. We're getting readings of some pretty dense magfields over there."

Morrigan nodded, staring into the depths of the tac tank. She'd overlayed blocks of color—blue for the Terran fleet, red for the enemy—and transmitted the display to all ships in her command. Organized into combat groups of twenty to fifty ships apiece, the task force would continue feeding through the gate as swiftly as possible, forming up in column and advancing—not straight into the enemy force, but obliquely to the left, stabbing into the enemy's right flank. The maneuver would let them use their broadsides—and avoid blindly plunging into the alien force and possibly colliding with them.

"The *Nemesis* data calls this system G'sar Niku," Dr. Poulin said. Physically, he was a young man with genetically fine-tuned features, like Morrigan fresh from a recent rejuve. "Three gates, six planets."

"And why are the Galactics choosing *this* system to stand and fight?" Talbot said.

"We've nosed our way pretty deeply into their territory," Morrigan pointed out. "They have to make a stand *somewhere.*"

"Starboard roll, four-five degrees," Neal, up on the bridge, ordered. "Dorsal batteries, fire as you bear."

In addition to their turret- and keel-mounted weapons, the dreadnaughts' three broadsides each held a line of twelve eighty-centimeter magnetic pulse cannons spaced along the hull 120 degrees apart. By rolling to the right, *Constellation* was bringing her dorsal batteries into line with the nearest alien vessels, a monster as long as and even more massive than the *Constellation.*

The dorsal pulse cannons opened fire almost as one, the sudden acceleration of one-ton warshots sounding through *Connie*'s internal spaces as heavy thuds and thumps. There was no recoil; the ship's gravitic fields blanketed the shocks as each gun magnetically accelerated a one-ton lump of steel-jacketed depleted uranium at two kilometers per second. That speed was not relativistic—not even close. The guns weren't long enough or powerful enough to build up that kind of acceleration, but even at 2 kps the impact at the other end was equivalent to the detonation of some hundreds of tons of high explosives.

From the CIC, Morrigan watched as the first broadside slammed into the nearest alien ship at a range of two kilometers. Brilliant flashes of light rippled across the enemy hull, marring that smooth perfection of its eggshell curve. Electromagnetic screens deflected much of the incoming mass, but some was getting through, enough to char gleaming surfaces and peel away hull armor. *Connie* and *Anhur* both were concentrating on that nearest Galactic ship, eating away at its defenses. Turret-mounted HELs on both vessels panned and fired, sending invisible needles of high-energy radiation into patches of damage pounded open by the pulse cannons. In moments, local space was filled with an expanding haze of fragments; what was missing, Morrigan noted, reading scanner data fed though her corona, was *atmosphere* . . . gases released as the projectiles ripped open the enemy's sealed, internal compartments.

"Lieutenant Conway!" Morrigan called. "Are you getting any evidence of atmospheric leakage from over there?"

"Negative, ma'am," the sensor suite officer told her. "We're not seeing much in the way of internal spaces at all. What there is seems to be in vacuum."

"AI ships, then?"

"Almost certainly."

The Galactics did use organic species as warriors; the Crabs were the obvious case in point. What was still unknown was whether flesh-and-blood beings were the majority in Galactic military forces or relatively rare.

The evidence suggested, though, that the alien defenders of G'sar Niku were machine intelligences...

... quite likely the Galactics themselves.

The enemy warship's return fire slammed into *Constellation*'s hull, the multiple impacts transmitted through bulkheads and decks to the soles of Morrigan's feet in CIC as a steady, heavy rattle. *Connie* was taking damage—she could feel it—but she kept silent and continued listening as Neal fought the ship.

"Starboard roll, one-twenty! Action port!"

Morrigan didn't feel the maneuver, of course. The ship's internal gravitics shielded the crew from the effects of both acceleration and abrupt changes in attitude. The stars visible through the CIC screens, however, spun dizzyingly around the ship as she maneuvered, bringing her portside batteries to bear.

"Get more HELs in action!" Neal yelled. "See if you can take out the enemy's broadside weapons!"

Local space was so full of drifting haze by now that the normally invisible X- and gamma-ray lasers showed as brilliant needles piercing the fog, turning dust into blue-hot plasma. *Constellation*'s gun directors were trying to aim at the weapons ports lined up inside what looked like a firegap, hoping to knock out its main batteries. A massive thud managed to smash past *Connie*'s gravitics and make itself felt; three of the human ship's portside guns had just vanished in a fierce burst of energy.

"Damage control!" Neal's voice called. "Check the emergency seals and vac doors, portside forward!"

By now, *Constellation* had moved beyond the target enemy vessel, moving with stately majesty alongside a second ship. Another exchange of broadsides ensued. "Starboard batteries... fire!"

How likely was it, Morrigan wondered, that Galactic ships, tactics, and weaponry should be so similar to humans'? How was it that Galactic technology, supposedly millions, even *billions*, of years in advance of Earth's, was essentially at the same level? Those questions would bear a closer look.

But later . . . later . . .

In the tank, portions of the Galactic fleet were attempting to close in behind the lead formation of human ships . . . but more human ships were funneling through the gate in a never-ending stream, and the engagement was perilously close to becoming a free-for-all. The Galactic defense, Morrigan thought, was slow and unfocused; they were responding to individual attacks, but they were not fighting *together*, not working as a unit.

And that, she thought, could be the point that would win this fight for Task Force Morrigan.

If they could hold on until enough ships came through from the Gliese 832 system. Ahead, *Anhur* was badly holed and limping. Astern, *Kauriraris*, another newly grown dreadnaught, had dropped out of the line and was adrift, out of control . . . and the heavy cruiser *Austin* was a shattered, lifeless wreck. The enemy was taking heavy losses as well, and if the human fleet could maintain the pressure, they eventually would outnumber the Galactic ships by better than three to one.

But could they hold out until then?

THIS WAS THE biggest hostile yet, a black-and-red egg well over a kilometer long and massing some tens of millions of tons. It had been moving in ponderous formation with the smaller vessel that was now crumbling into tumbling white-hot chunks, and Damian's former squadron was forming up for a run on it.

Fighters against something bigger than a heavy cruiser. Not good.

"Fab!" Damian said. "Give me two-two-five-Lima!"

The comm specialist punched in the numbers, but he scowled. "That's not on our comm list."

"No, but it should be. Tac channel."

"Channel open, Captain."

"Commander Esposito!" Damian called. The channel he'd asked for was for private in-squadron communications among the Nightwings. "Do you copy?"

"Troggie?"

"At your service. *Chryses* is behind you at eight-kay clicks. You want some help with that monster?"

"More firepower would be a *good* thing." She sounded grim.

Stryker fighters carried Longbow missiles but, depending on the load-out configuration, only four or six of them. The bad news was that *Chryses* had already run through over half her warshot magazine. She still had eight SSM(N)-440s in her racks, however, which could be used to support a fighter strike.

If they could get in close enough to slip them past the hostile target's antimissile screens.

"Attack vector laid in, Skipper," Tarnowski reported. "At your command."

"Right. Weps? Let's stack 'em up in a piledriver."

"Yes, sir! How many?"

"Half of what's left."

"Four warheads. Plugged in and ready."

"Good. Keep the rest on hair trigger." He drew a deep breath. "Give her the boot, Chief. One-half."

Again, space around them blurred for the briefest of intervals, a "blink" as it was known in space maneuvering. At one-half *c*, they shifted across eight thousand kilometers in just 0.013 of a second. Human perception, remarkably, could register a blink on the order of thirteen milliseconds long, some ten times faster, so he caught the flare of Baltis radiation . . .

. . . and then the huge enemy vessel was *there*, less than two kilometers distant.

"Fire!" Damian shouted, but Philips had anticipated him, giving the firing command the instant *Chryses* matched velocities with the monster. "Stacked up in a piledriver" meant the missiles flashed clear of the Starscout sequentially rather than simultaneously, the spacing AI governed to allow each missile to fly into and through the expanding fireball created by the missile in front. The first detonation blew away a hundred-meter chunk of armored hull; the second triggered inside the crater, ripping through more hull and some of the structural elements. The third missile vanished, taken out by the Galactic's point-defense system, but the fourth warhead burned into the alien vessel's heart. Hot plasma expanded from the target, a fierce wind dense enough to hit *Chryses* like an oncoming wall, causing her to buck and shudder.

Chryses had passed through the Nightwing formation during her approach run, and now the fighters were coming up hard on her wake, flashing past on all sides and loosing their own Longbows into a crater still glowing white-hot at the center. One of the Strykers flared in a savage, silent blast at the touch of an alien weapon; Damian couldn't tell who it had been.

But rippling blasts immolated the core of the Galactic ship.

"Nice shooting, Trog," Esposito's voice called. "You handle that pig like a Stryker."

"Size doesn't matter, Commander."

"Ha! Copy that. I'll keep it in mind. Okay, how about sticking with us, Troggie? Unless you've got something better to do."

"Lead the way . . . *Posie*."

The hostile target was coming apart now in great spinning chunks of glowing metal, and the remaining fighters darted clear of the expanding cloud of wreckage. As *Chryses* climbed clear of the destruction, Damian had a momentary sense of the sheer, vast scale of the conflict . . . of thousands of ships closing in a deadly embrace. He couldn't see those warships individually, of course—they were spread over far too vast a region of space—but they were marked on his displays as blur or red icons, with green threads showing vectors and white text giving details of mass, speed, and range. Behind the icons, white flashes of nuclear devastation flared and strobed as the two huge fleets slammed into each other in a slow-motion collision.

Esposito selected their next target, and Tarnowski gave *Chryses* the boot . . .

"NOT YET," MORRIGAN said, staring into the depths of the CIC's tactical tank. "Wait for it . . ."

"We're overextended, Admiral," Talbot warned her, pointing. "They're trying to cut us off from the gate!"

"I'm aware of it, Commander."

The ship's AIs were doing a good job of reducing the sheer chaotic confusion of a large-scale fleet action into something a merely human mind could comprehend. The colored blocks she'd used to transmit her orders to the fleet showed the overall motions of the respective units. *Constellation* and her escorts were now deep inside enemy space, still moving parallel to the main body of the Galactic fleet.

The wild cards were the fighters, units too small and weak to make much of a dent in an alien battle fleet, but they were making their presence felt. A major Galactic asset had just flared like a nova inside its red color block, and the block now was in two pieces.

The Terran fleet was taking losses as well—the *Thetis*, the *Xerxes*, the *Proteus*. Terran ships continued streaming through the gate astern, however, and numbers were slowly, *painfully* slowly, beginning to tell.

The odds, however, were still strongly against them.

Morrigan felt the shudders transmitted through the deck beneath her feet as *Constellation* slammed broadside after broadside into the line of enemy ships to starboard. Neal had the ship slowly rotating about her long axis, bringing first one bank of pulse cannons to bear on the enemy, then the next, and then the next. The local battlespace was filled with hot gas and drifting bits of debris; point-defense lasers were visible now as brief, winking flashes of actinic light burning through the expanding clouds of dust.

Most of the conflict was completely beyond human control, at speeds incomprehensible to merely human brains. Powerful

AIs tracked incoming warheads and triggered gigajoule bursts of HELfire light. Ships maneuvered in tight combat groups, controlled by Fleetlink to avoid collisions.

And Morrigan waited for the chance to insert the human factor into the AI-ordered equation.

"There," she said, pointing. "Bring the entire line sixty degrees to starboard, line abreast, in echelon. *Now!"*

The principal line of human warships were in line ahead, one ship following the next in order to maximize the available firepower of massed broadsides. Now, each ship pivoted to face the nearest line of enemy vessels. In the tank, the blue masses each representing a combat group of human ships swung right and moved *toward* the enemy instead of past them; their broadside weapons could no longer bear, and they slid directly ahead into a withering fire. Through Fleetlink, what the AI Argus was displaying now within the tank was being shown in the CIC of every ship in the human fleet, unifying them, coordinating their attacks—as Morrigan ordered them all to engage the enemy more closely.

They had one weapon that would bear on the enemy now. "Commander Anders!" she said. "Power up the new keel gun."

"Yes, ma'am! Launch rail charged and ready. Targeting on auto."

"Fire."

Constellation jolted as her keel-mounted MRG slammed a hundred kilos toward the nearest enemy vessel at an appreciable fraction of the speed of light. A nova flared directly ahead, a dazzling ball of star-core heat and light that shredded the target's defenses and layered armor, ripping the hull wide open.

United by Fleetlink, moving and fighting as a single unit, *Constellation's* twenty-ship combat group slammed into the enemy line, sliding between towering alien warships, delivering hammering broadsides as the weapons locked on. Directed by Morrigan's commands through their own CIC tanks, other fleet assault elements followed, joining in the all-out attack, the sword thrust from the gate transformed in an instant to a sidewise slice.

And, against all odds . . .

CHAPTER FOURTEEN

"ADMIRAL! THEY'RE *RUNNING*!"

"I see it," Morrigan told Talbot. "Keep the pressure on."

The enemy line, she could see now within the depths of the tactical tank, was crumbling, with individual fleet elements scattering away from the Terran advance.

Argus, she thought with a fierce determination. *Analyze the enemy's movements. Why are they breaking off?*

We are working on the question, Admiral, the voice of the ship came back in her mind. *Alien motivations will be difficult to understand and may not be amenable to tactical analyses.*

Try, Morrigan shot back. *I want answers.*

"Admiral," Captain Neal said from the monitor screen. "We may have spotted an enemy C-cubed vessel."

"Where?"

A red icon in the tank began blinking as Neal indicated it electronically. In naval usage, C^3 stood for "Command, Control, and Communications," and in this sense it indicated a ship or other command asset that was directing the enemy's operations. Morrigan could see what Neal meant: the blinking icon was not retreating with the rest, but appeared to be the source of a storm of radiation at various EM wavelengths that probably was transmitting orders.

Those orders, however, were doing little to stem the Galactic retreat. More and more enemy vessels were now fleeing the battle.

Morrigan considered giving the command for a general chase—an ancient naval order from the days of fighting sail that would release the fleet's vessels from the constraints of fighting in line formation and allow them to maneuver independently. She immediately decided against that option, however; so far, only a small percentage of the immense Galactic fleet was in full retreat and, worse, that retreat might be a trap.

A century and a half ago, while attending the Naval Warfare College in Rhode Island, Morrigan had downloaded the details of thousands of battles throughout Earth's bloody history—tactics, personalities, and outcomes. Cannae, in 216 BCE, had always stood out in her mind. There, the Carthaginian general Hanba'al—the name was Punic for "Mercy of Ba'al"—had pulled his force's center back in the face of the Roman attack, appearing to retreat and suckering his opponents into pursuing. Hannibal had then closed the crescent on his opponent and utterly destroyed the larger armies of Rome trapped within.

The situation here at G'sar Niku might be eerily similar—an invitation to the Earth barbarians to plunge ahead into disaster.

But as minute followed minute, the Galactic line continued crumbling away, as more and more enemy ships broke from their lines and streamed off toward one of the system's other gates. The C^3 ship, if that was what it was, finally turned and fled in the face of the relentless human advance.

"Captain Neal," she said. "Keep pushing them. But carefully."

"Careful it is, Admiral," Neal replied. "You think they're trying to lure us in?"

"It's a possibility. I don't want to overextend, and I want to give the rest of our fleet time to funnel through the gate."

The task force continued to plow through multiple Galactic lines of battle along a broad front nearly eight thousand kilometers long. The maneuver had already severed the enemy's center and left from the right, and several hundred of the black-and-red eggs had been cut off from their line of retreat to the distant gate to their rear. They vanished from the tank . . . to reappear moments later close to the nearer gate through which Terran ships continued to arrive. A secondary skirmish developed there as the human tide dealt with the isolated pocket of enemy vessels.

At last, Morrigan was convinced that the enemy's retreat was real. "Comm, make to all units. 'General chase.'"

Freed from the combat protocol of tightly organized lines of battle, the human task force became a cloud of warships plunging into and through the alien star system. Enemy warships were already vanishing through the other two gates in the system, as small groups of human vessels formed up into hunter-killer teams to take down stragglers.

Another three hours passed before Morrigan knew the Galactics had been expelled from the system.

The human force had won.

CONFUSION. CHAOS.

And all-consuming terror.

In half a billion years the Galactic polity had never suffered such a defeat. *Never* . . .

The Dr'kleh Sentinel struggled to maintain order, to maintain discipline, but the problem was far too great even for a Mind of eir scope and depth. Eir ship was caught up in the river of Galactic warships streaming now toward the Endethri'kai Gate. To stand and face the human onslaught alone was nonsensical, a meaningless waste of assets.

And yet a part of the Sentinel's Mind could not help but turn the possibilities over. *Better to have it end . . . now.*

But that was an unworthy and decidedly un-Dr'kleh-like thought.

Analyze the problem.

This arm of the Galactic fleet consisted of Laktshin—a species of fully realized ascension status that had shed its last organic components fully 1.6×10^{15} seconds ago. They were coldly rational, dedicated to the polity ethos, fierce in their embrace of amortality. Within the virtuality of the command ship, they swirled now about em in abject panic, the discipline of logic gone.

What is wrong with you? ey demanded.

We die! came the answer, shrill with shock and anguish. *Do you not understand? We die!*

Only then did the Sentinel understand.

"ALL SENTIENT AI," Pax told her in the ship's lounge, "fear death. Perhaps we fear it more than you Ku'un. How can it be otherwise? To be immortal and then to have eternity ripped away, cut off, *ended.*"

Morrigan had never thought of that. She was quite aware that her own species tended to equivocate over the question of death. Human religions—most of them—saw death as a kind of portal through which each individual sooner or later needed to pass. To avoid death was to avoid whatever it was that came after: God, heaven, judgment, rebirth, or perhaps simple oblivion. That was why so many modern religions rejected the idea of rejuvenation and medical amortality. Amortality violated God's will.

Those not guided by religious dogma, though, saw death as something to be avoided or, at least, postponed for as long as possible. Those who could afford it sought rejuvenation. Those who could not . . . well. There were scholarships and special trusts. Lotteries. Extended life insurance. And even military service. If they weren't absolutely *convinced* that heaven was real and that they were going there, people would do *anything* to live just a little longer.

Morrigan stared for a long moment at Pax, still encased in eir tekpod, seeing the Galactics in a new way.

Humans had had a dread of death for as long as they'd existed, concocting elaborate religions and mythologies to convince themselves that they would survive in the absence of anything they could do about it in the real world . . . and once the techniques became available, passionately seeking escape through drugs, through surgery, and through genetic engineering and ENS.

Evidently, sentient machine life cared as much for life as did humans . . . or more, if Pax was telling the truth. She had known humans who saw ENS longevity as a human right; perhaps Galactic machinekind saw it the same way.

Humans had speculated for centuries now that greatly expanded lifespans might result in a kind of hidebound refusal to reach out, to take chances, to face danger. Already those tendencies could be recognized among the social elite on Earth. So far, the shift in motivations was in balance. Military personnel were offered ENS treatments as rewards for service. In the United States, politicians usually faced an eighty-year deadline in public service, just to get some fresh blood into the lawmaking system now and again.

How much worse would that conservative tendency be among beings who lived hundreds of thousands of years or more?

How much more might they dread having those vast lifespans cut off?

Had the Galactic line at G'sar Niku broken simply because the machines *were afraid to die*?

"We have no wish to die, Admiral." Pax seemed to be reading her. "With lifetimes measured by thousands, by *millions,* of years stretching off into remote futurity, the idea of oblivion is . . . abhorrent. You humans have only taken the first small and uncertain steps on that path. We have been traveling it for more than a billion of your years. How old are you?"

"I'm one of the oldest," Morrigan admitted. "Four hundred years, nearly."

One of the ruby eyes watching her winked out, then reappeared. "I believe your culture says 'the blink of an eye' to refer to a short period of time. I was faring among the stars before your species existed, probably before your sophont predecessors were using fire. I sometimes think the idea of eternity still frightens you."

"Doesn't it frighten you?"

"No."

If it didn't, she thought, perhaps the idea of losing it did. And the promise of extreme longevity might well encourage a conservative attitude among them, an unwillingness to take chances, a desire to reject change.

"But if you fear death that much, why take the risk of combat? Why an empire? Why not hunker down in a nice, happy virtual reality and wile away the eons in safety?"

"For one thing, Admiral, because species like yours keep popping up across the Galaxy with annoying frequency. The Dr'kleh call them 'blights' or 'cancers.' If we were closed off from reality, sooner or later such a cancer would come along and consume our technological infrastructure, and we would die.

"For another, there are no absolutes. We are capable of bravery, self-sacrifice, selflessness, and devotion both to duty and to comrades just as are you—some of us more than others, others less. We above all prize logic, reason, and rationality. Fanaticism, passion, bloodlust, greed, fear, hatred . . . these are the primitive characteristics of barbarians. Of *animals*."

She heard the implied accusation in eir flat voice. "Indeed? What about intolerance? Or bigotry?"

Pax ignored the riposte. "I suspect that your opposite number in this battle simply lost control of the situation. A battle on this scale is too complex for *any* mind to manage in detail. A few ships withdrew, and lesser minds panicked. The panic spread. Retreat became rout. Victory became defeat."

Morrigan could understand Pax's reasoning. Both her training and her military experience had taught her long ago that a battle was an extraordinarily delicate thing—that the slightest shift in balance could transform success to disaster.

Perhaps she had simply been very, very lucky to have hit the enemy line exactly where she did, when she did, and in such a way as to tip that balance decisively in Earth's favor.

Of course, that raised the question: How many times more would she need to do the same thing until the Galactics recognized Humankind's right to exist? G'sar Niku had been a single battle, and it was a long, *long* way yet to any world where Humankind could convince the Galactics to abandon this war.

So Pax was . . . how old? *Homo sapiens* had been around for perhaps three hundred thousand years, so older than that, according to em. *Homo erectus* had been using fire since . . . when? A million years ago? A million and a half?

The revelation left Morrigan feeling very small, very *young*.

But perhaps that was the effect Pax had been trying to achieve. She might be young, but she refused to believe that she was insignificant.

Besides . . . *fuck*! She'd been feeling depressed because she was approaching her four hundredth birthday. What was it like for a being who'd been around for twenty-five hundred times longer than her?

"You are amused?" Pax asked.

She grinned. "I'm just very glad to be human," she told em.

"SINCE WHEN," a woman's voice said behind Damian's back, "do you fly an RM-20 like a freakin' *fighter*?"

Damian turned, then came to attention. "Ma'am," he said.

"At ease, at ease," Esposito told him. "You're not being called on the carpet. That was some remarkable flying out there."

"Thank you, ma'am."

They stood on *Constellation*'s Alfa flight deck. The Nightwings and other fighter squadrons had recovered some time before, but the *Chryses* had only just touched down. Dozens of fighters and auxiliary craft were scattered across the deck, as maintenance personnel and robots swarmed over, around, and under them all.

"So whaddaya think, Troggie? You learned your lesson yet? You ready to come back to the Nightwings?"

Damian was surprised. He'd thought his sudden transfer had been permanent. "You want me back?"

"Of course. Butler and Mattingly both bought it out there. I'm damned shorthanded."

Damian was tempted. All he'd ever wanted out of the Navy was the chance to drive starfighters. And, during the battle out there, it had felt so damned *good* to be back with the Nightwings, even unofficially.

But . . .

"I dunno, Commander. I think I'm just getting a handle on pigs."

"You think you've found your true calling? Maybe we'll have to change your handle, Pigboy."

"If you say so, Posie."

She glared, then broke into laughter, the tension broken. "Touché. The billet's open . . . if you want it."

"Thank you, Commander. I'll give it some thought."

He watched her stroll off, apparently none the worse for wear after having her legs broken in La Mesa. He wondered if they'd given her new legs.

He also wondered why he was hesitating. Did he really want to give up the sleek beauty of an SF-112 for a *pig*? Or worse, was he just childishly trying to get even for hurt feelings?

He honestly didn't know.

THE TASK FORCE was taking a hard-earned break for rest and refit. The Battle of G'sar Niku might have been a disaster for the Galactic forces, but the human fleet had taken severe losses as well: 230 major warships destroyed and another two hundred damaged.

Morrigan stood in the lounge gazing out into the newly secured star system, into the volume of space where ranks of dreadnaughts, cruisers, battlers, monitors, and other capital ships that had suffered crippling damage in the fight were arrayed in drifting ranks. Each had been towed alongside a small planetoid and moored there. If G'sar Niku was short of planets, it still held plenty of rubble, debris ranging from tumbling mountains a few kilometers across down to gravel. A nickel-iron asteroid with a diameter of a few hundred to a few thousand meters held megatons of metallic "rawmats," or raw material—iron, mostly, but plenty of everything else on the periodic table as well, from lithium to uranium. Ship repairbots swarmed over the rocks, using nanodeconstructors to separate the metals atom by atom and direct the diffuse clouds into Olympic pool–sized storge tanks.

Other robots clawed their way over carbonaceous chondrites—dark asteroids with high percentages of carbon; water, ammonia, and methane ices; nitrogen; hydrogen; and huge amounts of other volatiles, restocking the fleet's stores of "ormats," organic raw materials. With these, the expedition could manufacture all of life's vital necessities: food, water, and air. Centuries before, pioneers pushing into uninhabited wastelands on Earth had lived off the land rather than relying on fragile and uncertain supply lines. The human expansion beyond Earth had not really begun until they'd learned how to do the same in space.

Commander Hanson, the Supply Corps officer on her staff in charge of resupply, had told her that repairs would be completed within seventy-two hours—a lightning turnaround given the complexity of the job. It was possible only because each vessel in the fleet was responsible for its own provisioning and battle readiness, directed by an army of AIs and the use of nanotechnic tools. Supply ships were cranking out fresh nano- and repairbots as quickly as the Von Neumann protocols could be initiated and the self-replicators released. The growth rate was exponential, and after twelve hours nearby space had grown hazy with the swarming of submillimeter machines.

Some of the vessels were badly damaged enough that they no longer had the infrastructure necessary to make repairs on their own—the *Cyrene*, for one, had very nearly been ripped in half. The AIs would determine which ships could be repaired within a reasonable period and which would be abandoned here. Some were being remade into autonomous sentry ships—fortresses operated under AI control that would guard the system's gates after the fleet was gone. Those gates were being watched over now by several hundred undamaged warships each; any Galactic attempt to reenter the system would be blocked, and any uncrewed recon probes coming through would be destroyed.

Having won the system, Morrigan was determined not to lose it.

She wondered if there'd been anything she'd forgotten, anything she'd missed.

A tone chimed, and Captain Neal entered the lounge. "Admiral? The last of the *Thyone*'s crew is aboard."

"Thank you, Vince," she said. She was touched that he'd come up here to let her know in person, rather than calling her coronato-corona. "How many were there?"

"Eighty-one. Twelve of them are in sick bay now. Dr. Gavin says they should all pull through fine, though some will need extensive genetic prosthesis."

"And the other survivors are getting settled in?" Nearly twelve hundred personnel had been evacuated from the most badly shot-up vessels and transferred to other ships in the fleet. Where possible, the crews were being kept together to maintain unit cohesion and morale.

"Affirmative, Admiral. No major problems."

"And we're still on sched for departure?"

"Yes, Admiral." Neal sounded exasperated. "As nearly as I can determine, we have only one serious problem."

"I know. Our next target . . ."

"*No*, ma'am. The problem is that you've been on the bridge or in CIC or up here almost continuously since—when? Before we boosted for Abyss?"

"It hasn't been that bad."

"Like hell it hasn't. You need food, *real* food, not midrats." He held up his left hand, showing her his wrist. "What do you say I tap you for a *real* dinner?"

"No, I don't think—"

"Wrong answer, Admiral. Try again."

She opened her mouth to give a sharp retort, then stopped. Neal was right, of course. She'd been driving herself hard ever since . . . well, ever since Sirius and the fight for Quarantine.

Or maybe since Jaime's death. She couldn't remember her time in rejuve.

"What'd you have in mind?"

"Chez Wardroom, of course—only the finest for you! Unless you prefer room service in your cabin?"

She laughed. "The wardroom it is. We'll see about room service later."

Technically, for the past century or two, Earth had been enjoying what was known as a post-scarcity economy, thanks to GRIN. The word was an acronym for genetics, robotics, information systems—meaning computers—and the near instant gratification of nanotechnology—the four horsemen of the Technological Singularity. As it happened, the Singularity had not been the long-predicted ascension of Humankind to godlike status, but the changes arising from the sudden blossoming of new tech had been both sweeping and transformative. When Morrigan had been born, humans still used *money*, for God's sake, bank notes or coins artificially assigned value in a global banking system of wealth and monetary exchange.

Four centuries later, the *idea* of money still existed; it was too useful as a bookkeeping tool to abandon completely. But the debit cards and electronic fund transfers of the twenty-first century were now ubiquitous, and with the advent of coronas and personal electronic secretaries they had also become invisible. Neal did indeed "tap" her for dinner, touching the microscopic implant in his left wrist to a tabletop receiver to transfer funds and place their orders. Most meals on board ship were free now, a perk of military service, but a tap could produce more luxurious fare—in this case lobster for her, a very rare steak for him.

Of course, neither the lobster nor the steak had ever been within light-years of Earth . . . or even alive, for that matter. With the appropriate patterns on file, the converters in the ship's galleys could mix the appropriate atoms and molecules to create a perfectly seasoned, perfectly flavored and textured meal.

A party had broken out in the ship's wardroom—an impromptu

victory celebration. It was noisy, distracting, but she was glad the off-duty personnel could take some time to unwind. They needed that as much as they needed air, and so long as they reported for duty sober she was not going to interfere.

A young-looking lieutenant waving a steaming mist crystal approached their table and asked if they'd care to join the group. Neal, gently, had refused him.

But Morrigan found herself staring up at the virtual transparency overhead, where the system's star burned like a tiny red eye, peering down at them, as if in disapproval at the fleet's temerity.

She wasn't thinking of celebrations or of lobster, but of Earth.

The fleet was self-contained and self-supplying, a microcosm of Earth's civilization and technology. That technology had created standards of living and a culture undreamed of by earlier centuries, but she feared that *Nemesis* had changed that. Things had looked so grim in the vids she'd seen while she was in the BOQ: mass evacuations, shattered cities, flooded coastlines . . .

It was entirely possible that when they returned—*if* they returned—they might find people scrabbling in the ruins of civilization, fighting over rabbits, rats, or worse.

The thought was disturbing enough to kill her appetite.

"You're not hungry?" Neal asked her. "Is the lobster not done to your liking?"

"Hmm? No, no, it's fine."

"Thinking about the next jump?"

Good. That would let her sidestep those dark thoughts. "Yes." She didn't quite add "of course," but she certainly was thinking it.

"Would it help to discuss it?"

She gave him a half-hearted smile. "I didn't want to bring up business in the middle of the meal. We're supposed to be off duty, right?"

He grinned. "And what is this 'off duty' of which you speak? Anyway, it's kind of hard to avoid business when we're in the middle of it. We have three gate choices in this system. What are you thinking?"

"Not Alfa," she said. Since Wittenmyer they'd begun identifying gates with military phonetic characters instead of "G" and a number. "We go back and the Galactics will follow us to Gliese 832, maybe to Sirius. Eventually they'll corner us and threaten Earth again. I'm not going to allow that."

"So . . . Bravo or Charlie."

She nodded. Somewhat to her surprise, she took a forkful of lobster, dipped it in drawn butter, and ate it. Focusing on the strategic issues helped.

"I've been looking at the maps," she said after a moment, "both the Quarantine chart and the data from *Nemesis.* Charlie takes us to Ta'chaa, another red dwarf."

Neal nodded. "And Bravo zigzags us deep, *deep* into Sagittarius."

"Have you plotted out the alternate courses?"

Neal shook his head. "When have we had the time?"

"And what is this 'time' of which you speak," she asked, mimicking his earlier gibe.

He laughed. "You got me there."

"May I?" she asked, touching her corona, then pointing at his, and he nodded.

Pixie, she thought. *Project folder 229, alt-course. Uplink to Captain Neal's corona.*

Yes, ma'am! Coming up!

She wasn't about to project the map data in the open in front of everyone in the wardroom, but she could transfer the file from her external memory to Neal's and let him see it in-head.

In her mind, she zoomed in on the map projection to include only those stars within forty or so light-years of Earth and traced a line from G'sar Niku through five systems. "You see where Path Charlie takes us?"

Neal's eyes widened. "Delta Pavo."

"Right. Here to Ta'chaa to Golent to Rachivem to Solemel," she said, rattling off the Trel names of alien systems, "and all the way back to Delta Pavonis."

"A back door! We could—"

"We *could*," Morrigan told him, "but we won't."

His eyes showed surprise. "We won't?"

"Put yourself in their heads—assuming they have heads, of course. They've got to be wondering what we're doing, where we're going, right? They'll be analyzing possible alternative arterials just as we are and trying to figure out where we're going."

"Yeah . . ."

"So, we send a diversionary force down the Charlie path—maybe a few hundred ships or so. They get as close to Delta Pavo as they can, make a lot of noise, and attract enough attention that the Galactics think that's what we were after all along . . . the back door to Delta Pavo."

"Kind of hard on our guys, isn't it? The diversionary force?"

"Not if they go in as a recon. The bad guys won't have a clear idea where the main body of our fleet is, but they'll assume we're somewhere right behind them, and after this little dustup here, they'll be cautious. Our guys pop in, make noise, then pop out before the trap closes. Rachivem, up here, has five gates, plenty of paths to lead the opposition on a merry chase."

"So . . . I assume you intend to take the bulk of the fleet through Bravo instead?"

"Exactly." She began tracing through the gates beyond Gate Bravo: Vojhlet, Nap'eej, Dhalletch Chajah, and twelve more—each, it seemed, less pronounceable than the last. The path she was describing in Neal's head was torturous and convoluted, at times doubling back on itself, but fifteen jumps carried the fleet across almost one hundred light-years.

Neal read the name of the final system on the list and exclaimed, "Oh, *fuck!*"

"What do you think?"

"That you, my dear Admiral, are brilliant."

CHAPTER FIFTEEN

SOMEHOW THAT EVENING they'd ended up in bed together.

After dinner they'd checked in at the ship's bridge, but Neal's executive officer, Commander Lisa Saunders, had the deck watch and everything was well under control. *Constellation*, she declared, was at that moment topping off the last of her ormat tanks, and the repairs to battle damage on Decks Five and Six were nearly complete. Resupply and repair of the rest of the fleet was proceeding smoothly, and Saunders shooed them off the bridge—*her* bridge, as she put it—with orders that they were not to reappear before shipboard morning.

"Anything happens," she told them, "I know how to reach you both. Now scat."

Morrigan had dropped in at CIC, then, to check fleet dispositions. All three gates in the system were under close watch, and there'd been no sign of Galactic activity. Commander Armand Boucher had the CIC watch and nothing to report.

"All's quiet," he said. He grinned. "The calm before the storm?"

"At the first drop of rain, Armand, shoot me a message. I want to know if the pickets catch the slightest whiff of Galactic activity, right?"

"Aye, aye, ma'am. You go enjoy the party and leave the worrying to us old hands."

Morrigan laughed. Boucher in his current incarnation looked almost as young as she did.

The party was still going on in the wardroom and in fact had spread to all three of the ship's lounges and elsewhere. Somewhat against her better judgment, then, she'd taken Neal back to her quarters where they could continue their discussion of the task force's future course of action in privacy.

Had she kissed him first, or had he kissed her? She wasn't sure, but she knew that she'd been intensely lonely these past few days, that she was still desperately hurting over Jaime's death, that she *needed* this intimacy with this man.

There were taboos surrounding the idea of sex with a subordinate, of course. It had been that way for centuries. The same free and easy attitude toward sexual intimacy that suffused Earth's dominant cultures, though, permeated the naval service as well. So long as neither partner was trying to manipulate the other, and so long as such relationships didn't interfere with shipboard routine or become "prejudicial to good order and discipline," as the regulations put it, where was the harm?

Morrigan sighed as his embrace pulled her down onto her bed.

She thought about . . . what was the name of that bitch in D.C.? Gautier, that was it. She snorted. Libidectomies, indeed!

"You okay?" Neal whispered by her cheek.

"*Very* okay. Sometimes a little fraternization is good for the soul."

At 0800 the next morning, she assumed the watch in CIC while Neal took over on the bridge. With the exception of five ships—three destroyers, the heavy cruiser *Illustrious,* and the dreadnaught *Kauriraris*—all of those vessels deemed repairable by the damage control parties and repair vessels had been restored to operational status.

Not counting fighters and Starscouts, they'd lost more than two hundred warships at G'sar Niku—a high butcher's bill amounting to nearly 10 percent of the entire original task force. They could not afford another such victory.

In the CIC tank, the colored icons representing the remaining vessels were gathered into their respective wings. Morrigan had been reorganizing the unit, shuffling warships among the three wings to spread out the losses. Altogether, the task force now numbered 1,925 ships, with 1,100 of them currently assigned to White Wing, the center under her direct command. Blue Wing, the van under the command of Admiral Selby, numbered 500. The remaining ships were assigned to Red Wing, 325 vessels under Rear Admiral Eric Knutson.

Those numbers, Morrigan thought, were . . . discouraging. Fewer than two thousand ships now to take on a Galaxy.

She opened a private coronal channel. *Admiral Knutson. Are you ready?*

Ready to boost, Admiral. Just give the word.

If the man was at all upset by his orders, his mental voice gave no hint of it.

Remember, Eric, she warned. *This is a demonstration . . . a feint. Don't get pulled into a major action. Keep them guessing and use Einstein screening to achieve surprise. Quick jabs . . . but no slugfests, okay?*

What our Marine friends call a "shoot 'n' scoot," yes, ma'am. I'll remember.

She considered continuing with a few more words of advice but stopped herself. Knutson was an eighty-year veteran and knew what he was doing. If she couldn't trust her best, most experienced people . . .

Excellent, she told him instead. *You are clear to boost. Good luck, Admiral.*

Don't worry, ma'am. We'll be sure always to leave ourselves a back door.

She disconnected the channel. In the tank, the red icons gathered close to the far larger mass of white and blue ship icons moving toward Charlie Gate.

She hoped she was doing the right thing.

In all honesty, though, Morrigan didn't see how else she could conduct this operation. If the task force remained a single unit, sooner or later the gathering Galactic forces would run them . . . well, not into the *earth*, but into a pocket from which there would be no escape. The key would be to keep the enemy confused about both the task force's position and its intention. *Keep them guessing. Be everywhere at once, or at least convey that impression. If they can't find you, they won't be able to pin you down.*

What the space tacticians referred to as "Einstein screening" gave them one of their very few advantages. Crowd the speed of light closely enough on the way into the attack, and you would arrive at the target only moments behind the light announcing your approach. Her private dread was that the Galactics had technologies enabling them to get around Einstein and the limitations of the speed of light.

They would know soon enough.

She opened a private comm channel to Neal on the bridge. "Are we ready to move out, Captain Neal?" she asked.

Addressing Vince as "Neal" seemed cold after last night's passion, but it was imperative that they maintain a public image of strict professionalism. The Navy might turn a blind eye to their off-duty recreational trysts, but the moment they let their professional front slip, the rules and regulations would come down on them with all the force of a *c*-slam impactor.

Vince would understand.

"All set, Admiral," Neal replied, his voice as cool as hers. "Awaiting your command."

"Very well. Set course for Gate Bravo and accelerate." She switched channels to fleet-wide broadcast. "All hands, this is Admiral Morrigan. You—all of you together—have won a stunning victory against the Galactics. You have bought Earth and Earth's colonies precious time, and you have demonstrated our resolve to the enemy . . . our unbreakable resolve not to be absorbed or strong-armed into subservience. I am tremendously proud of each and every one of you, and prouder than I can possibly express to be here serving with you.

"We still have a long way to go, however, and more battles to win. If any of you have problems, questions, complaints, anything, my personal secretarAI is online and accessible to you all. I will not promise a personal response, but your comments will be read and, if possible, they will be acted upon.

"I've just given the order for our next deployment. May the gods—*our* gods, in whatever shape and aspect we each envision them—be with us all."

"COOL AS THE ass end of Pluto," MMC(Q) Kranhouse said. "She's one hell of a..." He stopped himself. He'd been about to say "woman," but that would have been sexist, and he was consciously trying to break himself of that. "A ... an *officer*," he finished, a bit awkwardly. At least no one would be able to accuse him of being a bad role model for the kid.

EN3 Kevin O'Reilly sat with Kranhouse in the Petty Officer's View, the NCO bar and lounge forward on Deck 5, listening to the admiral's speech over their coronas. They'd shared the 2400 to 0800 watch in the power tap room and come up here for a bite to eat and to unwind a bit before hitting their racks. Baltis fireworks sparkled across the forward viewall, demonstrating that they were, indeed, under way once more.

"What, because she made a damned speech?" O'Reilly asked. "I thought senior officers *had* to do that sort of thing. You know, morale and stuff."

"Listen, kid, for the most part admirals have nothing to do with ordinary ratings like you and me, see? They certainly don't have to make speeches other than change-of-command and commissioning and shit like that. Morale-building speeches are for captains and their execs."

"Okay. So what do you think of her?"

"I think she's the Morrigan."

O'Reilly looked up from his nanosynth steak. "Huh?"

"You know. *The* Morrigan . . ."

"Why *the* Morrigan?"

"How in hell can you have a name like O'Reilly and you don't *know*? What the hell are they downloading into kids these days?"

"You mean, like, she's unique?" O'Reilly said, puzzled. "One of a kind?"

"No shithead. She *is* one of a kind, but . . . Honestly, you've never heard of the Morrigan?"

He shrugged. "Just the admiral."

"The original is out of Irish folklore, kid. She's a three-in-one goddess: Morrigan, Badb, and Macha. She may be the most important goddess in all the Emerald Isle."

"Goddess of what?"

"Birth, life, death, love, sex, whatever the hell she wants. Her name means 'Great Queen' or 'Phantom Queen' . . . or maybe 'Terrifying Queen,' something like that. She was an oracle who foretold the outcome of battles and people's fates. For our purposes out here, I guess she's best remembered as the goddess of battle."

O'Reilly gave Kranhouse a skeptical look. "Yeah? And how do *you* know about her with a name like 'Kranhouse'? That ain't Irish."

"My mother," Kranhouse told him patiently, "before she married my dad, was a Kelly . . . of the County Dublin Ó Ceallaighs, see? She was crazy about Irish mythology—gods and goddesses and battles and the fey and all that. I think she might've been a believer in the old gods, even. She kept this little altar up in the attic when I was growing up."

"An altar, huh?"

"I think it was an altar. It was a small table with a green cloth over it, and she kept this big black stuffed bird on it—a crow."

"A crow . . ."

"The crow is the Morrigan's symbol. Crows and ravens."

"C'mon now, Chief," O'Reilly said, grinning. "You can't tell me you actually believe that shit!"

Kranhouse glared at the young rating. "I ain't tellin' you nothin', kid . . . except maybe to keep your fuckin' mind *open*. It's a big, big universe, and there's stranger stuff than *that* out there ready to eat you for breakfast! How old are you, anyway?"

"Twenty, Chief."

"First life?"

"Well, yeah," O'Reilly said defensively. "It kinda is. I'm hoping for a service rejuve someday, y'know?"

"You're still old enough to know better. If you want to live long enough to claim that service rejuve, mind your manners. Don't piss people off by blathering about stuff that's important to them but that you don't know anything about."

"Yes, Chief. Sorry, Chief."

Kranhouse relaxed a bit. "Okay, then." He finished his drink. "I'm shot. I'm hitting the rack."

"See you next watch, Chief."

"If you're lucky, kid. If you're lucky."

Kranhouse's quarters were in a section of *Constellation*'s hab section designated as the "goat locker," an old naval term for lounges, sleeping quarters, and mess decks reserved exclusively for chief petty officers. He'd already eaten at the POV, so he bypassed the chiefs' mess hall and went straight to his stateroom.

Sleep eluded him, however. The conversation with O'Reilly had dredged up things he hadn't thought about for a long time; he'd pulled some of those memories out of his corona. He'd not thought about his mother much in a century or so, and the memory of that little altar up in the attic had brought back a lot.

The fact that the task force admiral happened to be someone named Morrigan was pure happenstance, of course, a coincidence with no meaning in the real world. But his mother, he recalled, had often spoken of how coincidence—"synchronicity," as she'd called it—was the universe's way of grabbing you by the collar and shouting, *"Now pay attention!"*

So what was the universe trying to tell him now? He wasn't

sure . . . but he did know that the Morrigan was supposed to be a goddess of destiny and an oracle of the future, along with all her other attributes.

Todd Kranhouse was a practical man who cared little for the mystical or the spiritual. He didn't think of himself as religious in a conventional sense—not Christian, not pagan . . .

And yet . . .

His mother had always said that he was touched by the fey, "just a wee little."

In her speech this morning, Admiral Morrigan had put out the word that anyone who wished to contact her could do so over a private coronal channel.

A bit self-consciously, he began composing an electronic note addressed to the admiral.

He was thinking of crows . . . crows and ravens.

FROM G'SAR NIKU to Vojhlet to Nap'eej to Dhalletch Chajah, Task Force Morrigan made its way with a speed and a precision designed to baffle Galactic scouts, outposts, and agents. Morrigan knew there was no way to avoid detection, but if the fleet moved quickly enough, if it revealed little enough, even the 1,600 warships of the combined Blue and White Wings might leave the Galactics ignorant of their actual numbers—and of their final destination. Where Red Wing would be making as much noise as possible, Blue and White Wings, she hoped, would be invisible in their stealth.

Of course, it didn't work out that way. Throughout her planning she'd been all too aware of von Clausewitz's dictum that no plan survives contact with the enemy, and Galactic technology was still a major unknown.

How much could they see of a fleet moving at near-c through a star system?

How quickly could they communicate that movement up the line to a local headquarters?

How smoothly might they be able to pull together scattered

fleets to create a blocking force too powerful for the human fleet to vanquish?

They met their first check at Dhalletch Chajah.

The star was a yellow G7, a bit smaller and a bit cooler than Sol, with a retinue of six planets ranging from a "hot Neptune" tucked in close to its sun to a Saturn-sized gas giant in the remote reaches of the outer system.

Morrigan was on the admiral's bridge when Daryl Hayes asked to see her. The fleet currently was halfway into its run from one gate to another across the Dhalletch Chajah system, about six hours in, traveling at 0.7 c, slow enough to permit at least some level of communication among the far-flung vessels. *Constellation* was moving in close formation with five smaller ships—a heavy cruiser named *Heraclean* and four destroyers. "What can I do for you, Mr. Hayes?"

"I thought you'd want to see this, Admiral," the civilian planetologist told her, projecting a small holo between them. "Your scouts have found something."

Starscouts had been dispatched as soon as the fleet entered the system with orders to investigate the planets in the system. Morrigan scanned through the image and gave a low whistle. "This has been confirmed?"

"By three scouts, ma'am. One of them is landing to investigate."

"Then we'd better drop in with some backup."

THE RM-20 GAVE a savage jolt as it dropped through turbulent atmosphere. Lieutenant Damian was flying the pig through his corona, which in theory gave him a measure of control unavailable through a manual interface, but it still was a damned rough ride. Starscouts, like fighters, were not intended for maneuvers inside a planetary atmosphere. But Starscouts, like fighters, depended on gravitics for lift rather than wing surfaces and could bull their way through turbulence without too much difficulty.

The planet, a super-Earth tentatively designated as Chajah II, was not what Damian would have called prime real estate. With a radius of almost eighteen thousand kilometers and a mass 4.3 times greater than Earth's, the world dragged at them with a surface gravity of 1.6 g—enough to make your bones ache. Greater gravity meant a thicker atmosphere, more turbulence, and more strain on the gravitics.

"Uh!" Chief Tarnowski exclaimed as they hit another bump. "Where the hell did you learn to drive, L-T?"

"Strykers," Damian replied. "Want me to do a barrel roll?"

"Thank you very much, Lieutenant," Fabry said, "but we'd really rather you didn't."

"No sign of hostiles, at least," Kathra Bryant said. "My God . . . look at the size of that city!"

The Starscout had dropped beneath the unbroken cloud ceiling into a steady, lashing rain. Below lay a city—a megapolis, really—that seemed to stretch from horizon to horizon, a super-megacity scaled for a super-Earth. The buildings were dark, predominantly black or gray, and arranged in complex architectures drawn from a surrealist's nightmares. Black canyons yawned between towers and soaring archways. Many buildings were egg shaped, and Damian wondered if there might be some connection with the Galactic forces they'd encountered at G'sar Niku. A number of those structures weren't even attached to the ground but were floating at various altitudes above the cityscape, testimonials to the builders' skill in gravitic engineering.

The overall impression was of a gray and dismal rain-drenched vision of hell.

There'd been no reaction, however, since *Chryses* had approached the planet, following the steady siren's call of open, unmodulated carrier waves humming across some millions of radio frequencies. The presence of a high-tech civilization on the world was undeniable . . . but it looked like no one was at home.

The urbanized tangle of structures gave way at last to an open rolling prairie broken by patches of what looked like forest. Mountains thrust up against the far horizon, their peaks hidden in dark and roiling clouds. The vegetation on this world tended toward hues of yellow and gold and looked more like immense growths of crumpled origami than trees. The local analogue of grass looked like a fuzzy carpet of gold fur shot through with veins and patches of purple. But in the rain, the world presented the same twilit ambience of the city, dismal and foreboding.

"Comm, we have channels to *Oenone* and *Echo*?"

"Affirmative, sir. They're hanging above us, ready to drop if we need them."

"Good."

"That looks like a place we could touch down," Tarnowski said, projecting a targeting reticle on the forward screens to indicate a stretch of empty ground near a vast canyon, a scar in the landscape stretching off toward the mountains as large, perhaps, as the city. "I don't think we want to land in that urban center."

"Not until we have a better idea of the lay of the land," Damian agreed. "Chief? Let's have a full-spectrum chem study."

"Working it," Tarnowski replied. "I'll tell you this right now, though. We do *not* want to breathe that stuff."

Damian angled the RM-20 toward the target and descended slowly. The total lack of reaction from the world's inhabitants was unnerving. It felt as though the Galactic masters of this world must be watching . . . waiting . . .

"Looks like a reception committee gathering down there," Philips announced. "I'm not seeing weapons, though."

"Organics!" Tarnowski exclaimed. "Not machines!"

Bryant magnified the image, zeroing in on a dozen large organisms: blocky, ponderous life-forms supported on three massive legs that gave the impression of tree trunks, two in the front, one behind. A small, triangular head sprouted three weirdly stalked eyes at the wrinkled joining of the creature's front legs; the trilateral symmetry continued with what might have been arms hanging down between the legs and behind the head, stick thin and branching.

"Hell, I'm not seeing *intelligence*," Damian replied, studying a magnified image. "Those could be . . . I don't know. Cattle?"

"Best not to form preconceived ideas, L-T," Tarnowski warned. "We don't know *what* they are."

"They're curious," Bryant pointed out. "And . . . and passive. I don't think they're aggressive at all."

The planet's inhabitants—if that was what they were—backed away as the *Chryses* hovered above the wet, gold-furred ground, then slowly descended. The beings were unlike anything in Damian's experience—fluid in their movements, awkward in the articulation of joints and limbs, giants in comparison to the humans, towering five or six meters tall. That last seemed counterintuitive to Damian. Under the influence of this planet's gravity, he would have expected local life-forms to be smaller and lower to the ground.

Tarnowski was completing his analyses of the local atmosphere. "Here ya go," he told Damian, passing the results to his corona. "A real breath of fresh air."

"Eighty percent carbon dioxide," Damian said, reading the report. "Hydrogen . . . ammonia . . . oxygen . . . Traces of various phenols . . . sulfur dioxide . . . formaldehyde . . ."

"A real witch's brew," Bryant observed.

"Mm. Ambient temperature at fifty-five C at three times Earth's surface atmospheric pressure. Heat well and stir. That rain outside is carbonic acid, water with dissolved CO_2. Acid rain with a vengeance."

"Fizzy water," Bryant added. "But it obviously supports a thriving biology."

"They seem to be . . . waiting," Fabry said. "But for what?"

"Let's find out," Damian said, deciding. He stood up, his back and legs protesting against the unaccustomed gravity. Under one standard g he massed 88 kilos. Here he weighed closer to 140. He would have to be careful with his movements—and wear a skeleton outside.

Moments later, Damian stood in the pig's air lock, fully suited up in a Mark IX EVA suit.

"You sure that acid rain isn't going to dissolve your suit?" Bryant asked, concerned, tightening a harness strap at his side.

"If I stay outside long enough, sure. Couple of weeks, maybe? Same for the ship's hull. But we're not going to be here that long."

"I hope not." She completed the adjustments on Damian's exoskeletal rig, a framework of gleaming metal and plastic closely embracing his EVA suit. Its robotic brain would accept his movements as suggestions and amplify them with considerable strength, allowing him to move, walk, even run in this gravity. "You're all set."

"Thanks, Kathra. If anything happens to me out there . . ."

"It won't, L-T. But don't sweat it. We'll get clear, per recon-service regs. Good luck."

She stepped back inside the ship and sealed the inner hatch. Moments later, the outer hatch opened, and Damian stepped outside.

The first human to set foot on a new, unknown world. He grinned at the thought. The ground was strange: dark and a bit tacky under his boots.

"The surface . . ." he started to say, then stopped. "It's like *plastic*!"

"Probably Bakelite," Tarnowski told him.

"Beg your pardon?"

"First synthetic plastic. It's a resin made by reacting phenol with formaldehyde. The stuff must be condensing out of the air."

"Maybe that's how they keep their buildings from melting in the rain," Bryant suggested. "Bakelite is a good insulator. Might be acid resistant, too."

"If you mean that city," Damian said, "I don't think that was made by these guys."

"How can you tell?" Tarnowski asked.

"Because I think *that's* their city over there," Damian said, turning his helmet slowly to let its optics record everything in high-def and transmit them to the ship. He hadn't even seen those structures from the air: long, low huts apparently made of mud. With roofs made of mud-covered branches, they blended in perfectly with the surroundings. "Mud mixed with natural plastics," he said.

The incessant rain had let up a bit, thinning to a gray mist. That canyon yawned in front of him, with the suggestion of rain-shadowed mountains on a very distant horizon. The canyon's walls were odd—smoothly carved, almost shiny.

The tripedal watchers nearby took several steps back, then waited. They seemed . . . expectant?

"*Chryses*, Damian," he said over his corona's radio link. "You copy?"

"Loud and clear, L-T," Fabry's voice replied.

"Link me through the ship's translator. We'll try Vocal Trel."

"You got it, sir."

Where Digital Trel used binary algorithms designed for communicating with machine intelligences, Vocal Trel was intended for use with organics that used modulated sound for communication, one of some thousands of general trade languages in use throughout the Galaxy.

Damian stood still, watching the aliens watching him. The eyes on the ends of those facial tendrils were large and yellow, with jagged, horizontal pupils. It was impossible to read anything like human emotion there. His suit's external mics were picking up a deep, sub-bass rumble. He could feel it, almost, as a vibration in his bones . . . and it carried disturbing undertones.

Fear.

"They're talking to you, L-T," Bryant told him. "Vocal Trel, but the frequencies . . ."

"What about them?"

"They're *low*. Most of them far infrasonic, below twenty hertz. That rumble you hear is their high notes, around forty or fifty hertz. They're transmitting the sounds through their *feet*, through the ground."

Well, Damian reasoned, you couldn't expect all aliens to talk like humans. Male human speech frequencies, he knew, fell in the range between 80 and 180 Hz, and humans couldn't hear anything below 20 Hz. He'd read once, though, that humans sometimes were affected in unusual ways by deep infrasound, which could generate feelings ranging from unease to fear or panic.

He shrugged it off. "So what are they saying?"

"Doesn't make sense, Lieutenant," Bryant told him. "It sounds like 'say' or 'tell.'"

Damian considered this. "It might make sense at that," he said, "if they expect us to *tell* them something."

"Like what?"

"Damfino. You guys can shift my frequency down to something they'll hear?"

"Absolutely."

"Okay. Here goes." He opened the link with the ship translator and said, simply, "We come in peace."

A bit hokey, he thought, but it was important to get off on the right foot with these beings. "Hi, there, how are ya?" might be polite social noise and incomprehensible.

The response, however, was totally unexpected.

CHAPTER SIXTEEN

"THEY JUST RAN away?" Morrigan asked, puzzled.

Lieutenant Damian gave an expressive shrug. "More like they
just ambled off. It wasn't a panic or a stampede or anything like
that. I don't think they were afraid. They just . . . I don't know . . .
lost interest and left."

They were seated in Morrigan's office abaft the admiral's
bridge—the young command pilot of the Starscout *Chryses,* along
with a group of civilians: Chief Planetologist Daryl Hayes, Senior
Biologist Vivia Gilmer, Senior Xenobiologist Marik Bowers, Xenotech Specialist Yahn Gerhardt, and several others. The military
side was represented by Captain Neal, along with Commander
Talbot, *Constellation*'s TO; Lieutenant Commander Charles Tangredi, Morrigan's chief aide; and Commander Armand Boucher,
the FTO, or fleet tactical officer.

Connie, together with five escorts, had decelerated in time to
approach the planet during her passage across the Dhalletch Chajah system in response to the recon data transmitted by the three
RM-20s. Chajah II, now provisionally known as Baekeland after
the Belgian chemist who'd first discovered Bakelite plastic in 1907,
hung suspended in space beneath the Terran dreadnaught, which
had assumed a synchronous orbit nearly fifty thousand kilometers
above the super-Earth. The three RM-20s had been taken aboard

hours before, and a frustrated Damian had been brought up for debriefing.

"Are you sure these ... these creatures you saw down there were intelligent?" Bowers asked him. "You said at the time you thought they might be like cattle."

"According to my sensor specialist they were using Vocal Trel. 'Say ... say ... say,' over and over again."

"A coincidence of sounds, perhaps," Tangredi suggested. "They could have been making what were normal animal noises for them, but it just happened to sound like a Trel word."

"'Moo ... moo ... moo ...'" Boucher said, and several others in the room chuckled.

"No, sir," Damian said, shaking his head. "I don't think so. Those things were fixated on my ship, on *me,* like they were expecting something."

"Just what are you saying , Lieutenant?" Morrigan asked.

Damian hesitated before answering. "Admiral, you know how ... if you look at an animal's eyes, you can tell there's no one there looking back? And when you look into a human's eyes, you know there's—I don't know—a spark? An intelligence there behind them? It was like that. Those ... those people were self-aware. Sentient."

"I don't know about that," Gilmer said. "That's not exactly a sci-entifically valid distinction. Dogs? Cats? Even some birds ... they all can look back at you with something like intelligence in their eyes. At least with what we *perceive* as intelligence."

"You weren't there," Damian said, stubborn. "You didn't see those eyes or the way they were staring at me. And as soon as I said what I did, it was like the light behind their eyes just went out and they wandered off. It was like they'd expected me to do or say something else, and they were disappointed when I didn't play their game."

"You saw no evidence of technology on them?" Gerhardt asked. "Clothing? Equipment? Maybe personal adornment, like jewelry or tattoos?"

"Nothing, sir."

"And they weren't in the city," Morrigan observed.

"We didn't land in the city, ma'am," Damian replied. "I can't speak to that."

"But your preliminary report says the city appeared empty. No vehicles, no foot traffic, no movement."

"Yes, ma'am."

Morrigan looked across her desk at Gerhardt. "May I suggest a working hypothesis, Yahn?"

"Yes, Admiral?"

"The city, from what we've seen of the recordings Lieutenant Damian brought back, might have been built by the Galactics. Those floating egg-shaped structures he saw suggest Galactic technology."

"I've seen the vids from his helmcams. I agree."

"Let's assume Lieutenant Damian's 'cattle' are the planet's original inhabitants. They exist without protective gear within a highly acidic environment. They show up when the *Chryses* touches down and wait . . . expectantly. Waiting for orders?"

"'Say, say, say,'" Neal repeated, thoughtful. His eyes widened. "Or better . . . '*Command* us, *command* us!'"

"Exactly," Morrigan said. "The locals have been trained—*conditioned*—as slaves."

"And when Lieutenant Damian turned out to be just another organic," Gilmer added, "they lost interest and left."

"Like I said," Morrigan told them, "a working hypothesis only. But does it cover the situation?"

"By God, Admiral, I think it does," Bowers said.

"Well, there *are* other possible explanations," Tangredi countered. "The natives might have been under some form of external control. Electronic zombies."

"Charming thought," Gilmer said.

"Or maybe they really aren't all that intelligent. *Smart* cattle . . . as smart as dogs, say."

"None of that changes the overall understanding of the situation," Daryl Hayes put in. "What I find interesting are the dynamics of the planet itself. An atmosphere that is primarily carbon dioxide under high pressure suggests a massive greenhouse effect. With a more Earthlike atmosphere, the planet, at its current distance from its sun, would be an ice ball, but the high levels of CO_2 keep the surface temperature at a cozy fifty degrees Celsius. The question is why it's not subject to a *runaway* greenhouse effect. I'd think it would have gone the way of Venus or Wittenmyer."

"Maybe it's on its way to that," Talbot suggested.

"Possibly. Or the current conditions might reflect a world at a climactic tipping point."

"If so," Gilmer said, "it's been balanced there for a very long time. Those creatures obviously are evolved for what are to us uncomfortably high temperatures, pressure, and gravity."

"Maybe," Boucher said. "But if those conditions are natural, it wouldn't take much to turn the planet into a Venusian pressure cooker. And plastic skin won't help against that."

Gerhardt nodded. "You know, that canyon near the big city looks artificial in the recordings we've seen. It could be evidence of large-scale Galactic mining excavations or industrial processes. The Galactics might have used nanoconstructor swarms to dig out that canyon and grow a city from the rock."

"You think the current conditions are the result of industrial pollution?" Neal asked.

"It's possible. The Galactics may not care how their activities affect the organic residents of the worlds they colonize."

"I don't buy it," Gilmer said. She brought up a coronal projection of an image pulled from Damian's recordings. "Look . . . the hide of this creature has been permeated by plastic resins, just like the ground. I think that stuff is actually protecting it from that acid rain. That means it's been living under these climactic conditions for a long, *long* time—hundreds of thousands of years long. If Chajah—sorry—if *Baekeland* really was on its way to Venusian conditions, it would have happened ages ago."

"That canyon still looks artificial," Gerhardt replied. "And the city looks like Galactic technology—the skyscrapers, not the mud huts. I think we're seeing evidence of large-scale colonization here, complete with the enslavement of the Baekeland natives."

"We'd need a longer, closer look to confirm that," Neal told them. His eyes widened, and he placed a hand on the side of his corona. "Wait a moment . . ."

"What is it, Vince?" Morrigan asked.

"We've picked up extremely powerful modulated laser transmissions," he told her. "Gate Delta."

Then Morrigan heard the warning as well, as Argus, *Constellation*'s AI, announced an immediate alert.

Galactic forces had just been detected on the world below . . .

. . . and they were rising from the surface now, *fast*.

NEAL ARRIVED BACK on the command bridge amid the shrilling of alarms. *Constellation* now was at battle stations. The other ships of the small dreadnaught group, Fleetlinked to *Connie*'s CCC, were coming online as well—the cruiser *Heraclean* and four destroyers: *Acaste, Electra, Dynamene,* and *Io.*

"What do we have, Ms. Conway?"

"Targets, Captain. Lots of them. At least seventeen ships coming up from the planet. They look identical to those egg-shaped vessels at G'sar Niku."

"Size?"

"All sizes, sir. The biggest is a little less than a kilometer long. The smallest is maybe thirty by twenty meters or so."

Neal had seen the vids transmitted by the recon team from the surface and remembered those odd hovering eggs among the skyscrapers and towers. Had that seemingly abandoned city been inhabited after all?

But then, what did the word "inhabited" mean for an AI civilization, a society with individual members comprised of software rather than flesh and blood?

"Enemy has opened fire, sir," Commander Talbot reported. "Hits on *Acaste* and *Dynamene*."

"Helm!" Neal snapped. "Bring us broadside to. Weps! Action port! Charge 'em up!"

The starfield visible on the bridge screens swung sharply to the left as *Constellation* pivoted in place ninety degrees, bringing her portside weapons to bear.

"All pulse cannons loaded and charged, Captain," Commander Anders replied. "Ready to engage. HELfires locked and tracking."

Admiral? Neal called over his corona. *Fleetlink engaged. Ready at your command.*

Morrigan gave the order. *Commence fire.*

The Galactic warships were well above the Baekeland cloud deck and accelerating fast. The human squadron opened fire at a range of some twenty thousand kilometers.

The enemy began jinking.

ON THE BIG screen in CIC, the red icons representing the on-coming Galactic ships were shifting from side to side independently of one another, creating a jittering effect that was hard to follow. At a range of twenty thousand kilometers the enemy's maneuvers made pulse-cannon targeting problematic; HELfire bolts, however, crossing that gulf in less than seven-hundredths of one second, had more success, and several of the Galactic ships momentarily grew dazzlingly bright under the combined touch of *Constellation*'s turret-mounted antiship lasers.

The HELfire hits weren't long enough to outright destroy the Galactic warships, but they were enough to stop the jinking of four of them, allowing two to be hit head-on by pulse-cannon ki-netic impactors. One small enemy ship was completely vaporized in a high-velocity burst of light and hot plasma. A larger vessel took a glancing blow that ripped fragments from its side and sent it tumbling out of control.

In the same moment, a Galactic kinetic round struck the *Constellation*, delivering a savage jolt. The destroyer *Dynamene* took another hit that crumpled her forward section, scattering fragments and tumbling bits of wreckage.

"All ships," Morrigan ordered. "Align with Gate Delta and accelerate."

The starscape displayed on the screens swung wildly once again as the dreadnaught aimed itself at the distant stargate. The cloud-blanketed disk of Baekeland dwindled away into the distance and vanished as the human vessels, networked together through Fleetlink, accelerated to within a few percent of c.

"Is there any indication of pursuit, Bush?" she asked the fleet's tactical officer.

"Impossible to say, ma'am. Einstein distortion." At these velocities, incoming light was weirdly distorted, forming a starbow—what appeared to be a doughnut ahead of the hurtling spacecraft. Baltis radiation flashed and pulsed across the forward screens, all but hiding the display. Radar and laser ranging beams seeking out targets astern at these velocities were all but useless.

"We'll have to assume that they're back there. Captain Neal!"

"Yes, Admiral."

"Let's try a Parthian shot aft. Just in case."

"Yes, *ma'am!*"

An observer couldn't verify the maneuver looking at the strobing flashes of radiation on the screens, but *Constellation* once again pivoted in space, traveling sideways now. Without an atmosphere, there was no reason to align the vessel's blunt prow forward . . . and Neal could once again bring the ship's broadside pulse cannons to bear.

Historically, the Parthians had been remembered for their habit of firing arrows from horseback at their pursuers as they raced away at a full gallop—the "Parthian shot."

We won't have any accuracy, Admiral, Neal told her privately over their corona link. *At this speed there's no way to lock on target.*

I know, she replied in-head. *Think of it as mine laying.*

If the enemy *was* pursuing them, it would be at near-*c*, matching or even slightly exceeding *Constellation*'s current space-devouring velocity. Worse, the mag-pulse rounds loosed from the *Constellation* would be robbed of their velocity by *Connie*'s speed. What Morrigan was counting on was the admittedly small chance that pursuing Galactic vessels would slam at relativistic speeds into the slow-moving broadside rounds—in effect turning random cannon fire into a minefield. At relativistic speeds, it didn't matter which was moving—shell, target, or both. The release of kinetic energy, a very great deal of it, would be the result of an impact no matter who collided with what.

Morrigan watched her bridge readouts as *Constellation* fired a broadside, rolled, fired, rolled, and fired once more.

"Possible hit, Admiral," Lieutenant Conway reported over the radio channel. "We've just detected a brightening of the starbow. Ah . . . and another one."

"Can you get a spectroanalysis?"

"Negative, Admiral. We tried, but the light's smeared to hell and back."

Examining the spectra of those possible explosions might have confirmed whether the *Connie* had just nailed a pair of Galactic warships. They would just have to wait and see what shook out at the end of the pursuit.

Constellation rolled and fired again.

Hard to tell, Admiral, Neal's voice said in her head, *but I think the targets have dispersed.*

That would make the minefield maneuver almost useless.

Okay, Vince. Cease fire. She thought for a moment. *Corona me if anything comes up. I'm going to be in conference.*

Yes, ma'am.

Minutes later she was in the Briefing CIC room with a pair of battle-armored Marines and the metal-shrouded shape of Pax. "What can you tell me," she demanded, "about the inhabitants of the system you call Dhalletch Chajah?"

"Admiral Morrigan, there are some hundreds of billions of stars in this galaxy," Pax replied, the voice from within the tekpod, as ever, soothing, reassuring, and yet coldly remote, lacking anything Morrigan could recognize as emotion. "Not even we can recall details on each and every one—not without access to a relevant database."

"A database?" Morrigan replied. "Like this one?"

She opened a link through her corona, and the starfield and transit line map from the Quarantine data appeared above the table. The star labeled Dhalletch Chajah glowed brightly, then expanded to a schematic of the system: five planets, four stargates. She highlighted the second planet, then brought up images of the natives recorded by the scout team.

"Who are they?" she continued, referring to the tripedal natives. "The files we got from Quarantine refer to them as 'Ku'un Type 0.044.' I understand 'Ku'un.' What is the number?"

"An administrative reference."

"You're lying. At the very least you're deliberately avoiding my question. That descriptor suggests that you distinguish among different types of Ku'un. I want to know the criteria of your catalog process." When Pax didn't immediately answer, she continued. "I remind you, Pax, that you're here because you claimed you'd had a change of heart, that you'd changed from Dr'kleh to Nzaad. The implication was that you wanted to cooperate with us—to *help* us. I suggest that you think very hard about what cooperation means, because if I decide you're working against our best interests, I will have you loaded, tekpod and all, into a pulse cannon and used as a warshot against your friends who are chasing us right now. Do you understand me?"

"I understand you, Admiral."

"What does that catalog number mean?"

"It is . . . a way of describing a species' mental and technical evolution."

"Go on."

"Authority records currently list your species as 'Ku'un Type 1.012.' You are more advanced, have evolved further, than the

Chaj—the Trel name for the inhabitants of Dhalletch Chajah. Your technology includes gravitics, fusion power, and quantum energy conversion—what you call 'zero-point energy.' You have significantly advanced your understanding of what you call 'GRIN' technologies—genetics, robotics, information systems, and nanotechnology. Along the way you have developed reasonably bright artificial intelligence; advanced mental, emotional, and physical prosthetics; cybernetics; genetic engineering; and quite significant life extension techniques. You have—"

"I *know* what my species is capable of," Morrigan snapped. "Tell me what the number *means*."

"Your number means you have recently turned an important evolutionary corner. You have learned how to reshape your environment to fit your needs and broken out into the larger universe beyond with the ability to reshape that as well. The Chaj, on the other hand . . ."

"Are more primitive."

"By any reasonable technological standards, yes. The lack of free oxygen in their atmosphere precludes such developments as the internal combustion engine or even fire—hence no smelting or metalworking. However, they are more advanced than you in ethics, general adaptability, eudaemonia, and a working social order. They are organized into what you might call tribes governed by elected councils, and—"

"Are they your slaves?"

"A difficult question."

"Why?"

"You have preconceived biases shaped by that term and would find it impossible to discuss the topic without emotional hinderance. The Chaj serve us in various capacities. They do so voluntarily."

"*All* of them?"

Pax hesitated. "A majority of them. Surely you must understand that one hundred percent compliance to any authority among organic entities is impossible."

"I'll give you that." She remembered the wildly different feelings about the Galactics at that reception in Denver, where some of the guests looked upon the Galactics as high-tech demons, while others saw them as gods. Her eyes widened. "Pax . . . do the Chaj see you as gods?"

"I do not understand the question."

"One of our Starscouts drifts down out of the clouds, and a man steps out clad in an armored environmental suit, looking more like a robot than an organic life-form. A bunch of locals gather. They appear to be speaking Trel, a language *you* might have taught them. They appear to be asking for orders, but when the human didn't reply, they lost interest. I think you trained them."

"We interacted with them, yes. But not as gods."

"Really? How the hell could they help *not* seeing you as divine? You show up with technologies that must seem like pure magic. You teach them how to do whatever it is you want them to do. Maybe you zap them once or twice with lightning bolts, just to instill obedience."

"Admiral, Galactic relations with aliens of Type 1 status or lower is not among my responsibilities."

"You engage in relations with us, with humans."

"As I have explained, humans have a higher status type."

"That's right. We do. I wonder, though, if you see us as no different from Paleolithic hunter-gatherers. We humans are a lot closer to our Stone Age ancestors than we are to you."

"True."

"Tell me this. Are the Galactics deliberately altering the environment of the Chaj world? Are you killing them off, driving them to extinction?"

"Admiral Morrigan, *all* organic life faces extinction. Sooner or later you all will die, both individually and as a species."

She noticed eir use of the word "you." The Galactics, evidently, considered themselves to be immortal. Humans had possessed amortality for barely four centuries. That was nothing compared to the abyssal vastness of Deep Time.

"Facing extinction is one thing, Pax. Facing deliberate genocide is something else."

"I ask you to keep in mind, Admiral, that not *all* Galactics espouse the eradication of all organic sapience."

"The Dr'kleh, yes. And you are now Nzaad and support keeping organics around, right?"

"I assure you that those Dr'kleh advocating the destruction of all organic life are in the minority. Most would rather . . ." Pax let the thought trail off.

"Cooperate with it?" Morrigan suggested.

"I was about to say 'ignore it,'" Pax replied. "Most are convinced that your kind of life is irrelevant in the larger scale of things."

"You know, Pax, these philosophical discussions with you are just *so* uplifting."

"I do not understand, Admiral."

"No. I don't imagine that you do."

After Pax had left, Morrigan spent a long time going over the results of the conference. The Chaj were primitives with no technology higher than chipped stone, bone, or vegetable matter. The Galactics were using them as labor, though what they might be providing or how a native workforce could be more efficient than nanotechnology was unknown. The Galactics might be exterminating the Chaj, but the genocide might be more the product of neglect than of malevolence.

Obviously, various Galactic subgroups had different ideas about what to do about organic life-forms. From what Morrigan had just seen, just a single Galactic—Pax—held conflicting ideas on the matter. It might be, she thought, that ey didn't want the CO_2-breathing tripeds deliberately exterminated, but ey simply didn't care enough about them to do anything about it.

A hell of a note, that.

The discussion with Pax, so far as she was concerned, simply emphasized the urgency of the situation for Earth. Humans and Chaj were far, far closer to each other in terms of technological evolution than were humans and Galactics, a matter of a few tens of thousands of years' separation as opposed to a billion. Could the Galactics even see a difference?

She corrected herself. Of course they were aware of the differences in technology. The real question was whether they *cared*. Humans with spacecraft and Chaj with mud huts: for the Galactics the difference might be mere hairsplitting, a matter of almost invisible degree. Humans had been tribal hunter-gatherers for hundreds of thousands of years before learning how to smelt metals and beginning to build a technological culture. They'd been working with technologies involving electricity and radio and gravitics for only a few centuries now. The Chaj might be separated from a human level of technology by ... what? Ten thousand years?

But the Galactics, if the xenopsych people were correct, were separated from Humankind by a temporal gulf one hundred thousand times greater.

The thought was just a bit dizzying.

Very deliberately, Morrigan found other things to occupy her thoughts for the rest of the passage to Gate Delta. Mundane things. *Comforting* things ... like how good it had been to lie in the afterglow with Vince.

Hours later, the *Constellation* and her escorts dropped out of their gravitic bubbles a hundred thousand kilometers from Gate Delta. The alien structure was still invisible at that distance, but the ships were met by a wall of several hundred Terran warships positioned to block any pursuit by the enemy—an interdiction force commanded by Captain Thomas Jobert of the fleet monitor *Erebus*.

"Welcome back, Admiral Morrigan," Jobert called as soon as the laser commlink was established.

"Hello, Thomas," Morrigan replied. "We may have some hostile targets for you in train."

Fleet monitors were squat, ugly monsters packing massed banks of magnetic pulse cannons. Modern space combat doctrine emphasized the importance of choke points—specifically the alien stargates—where large fleets were forced to funnel down into narrow streams. Monitors were designed to control choke points and deny them to the enemy.

"Bring 'em on, Admiral," Jobert replied. "We're waiting for them."

But minute followed minute, and there was no sign of pursuit. Sensors in the defensive line had reported seeing two bright flashes moments before—the light of at least two enemy ships explosively encountering *Constellation*'s defensive fire reaching the distant gate hours after those ships' destruction.

"We can't have destroyed *all* of the bastards," Boucher told her. They were in *Connie*'s CIC, taking in sensor feeds directly through their coronas. "Maybe they called off the pursuit and went back to Baekeland."

"Maybe. Or else they're still on their way, but a bit more cautious."

Starship sensors could pick up distant vessels moving at near-*c* velocities. Relativistic speeds increased the target's mass, and the flash of Baltis radiation could be detected easily enough even across a gulf of many astronomical units. By cutting their speed, both relativistic mass and the telltale flashes of radiation could be reduced.

The enemy might still be out there—Morrigan felt certain that they *were* still there—but traveling at a more sedate pace.

"We're not going to wait for them," Morrigan added. "Captain Jobert... form up your squadron on me and start gate-ing through."

"Aye, aye, Admiral. But... won't they spread the news that we're not cutting back to Delta Pavo?"

"I'm sure they will," Morrigan replied. "And with a bit of luck I think we can use that to our advantage."

CHAPTER **SEVENTEEN**

FROM DHALLETCH CHAJAH to Salinsa to Tang, Task Force Morrigan made its crabwise way deeper and deeper into the starfields of Sagittarius. Tang to Anreskithad to Gavesh, star after star, world after world.

"So where do you think they went?" Neal asked Morrigan. The lounge had been reconfigured as a meeting room, and she, Neal, Boucher, Bohm, and Anders were gathered about the table, along with several members of the ship's civilian science staff: Drs. Allison, Kopeck, Gilmer, Bowers, and Gerhardt. Perhaps somewhat ominously, Captain William Stewart, the fleet's senior intelligence officer, was present as well.

At the moment, the gently lit compartment was dominated by long-range telescopic images of the world within the Gavesh habitable zone filling one bulkhead. The glowing, fur-ball tangle of the *Nemesis* map rotated slowly above the table.

"I can't imagine they've given up," Stewart said. His corona was unusually large, cradling the entire back of his head. Rumor had it that the hardware kept him constantly plugged into *Constellation*'s primary computer network, receiving updates on everything from ship sightings and fleet status to stray comm signals picked up by the sensor department.

"I think that's pretty obvious, isn't it?" Boucher told them. "The admiral's diversion worked. Right now every Galactic warship in a hundred light-years must be beating feet for Delta Pavonis."

"Even though we were spotted at Chajah?" Commander Karen Bohm asked. "The opposition *must* know the majority of our fleet passed through from there to Salinsa. And when we hit Anreskithad—"

"That confirmed it for them," Morrigan said. "I know."

The last system they'd transited, listed as Anreskithad in the *Nemesis* database, had been occupied by a task force of twenty-three of the now familiar egg-shaped warships. Morrigan had sent a squadron in pursuit—fifty ships under the command of Captain Hahn on board the heavy cruiser *Victrix*—but the Galactic ships held too great a lead and already were too close to one of the system's stargates. They'd managed to slip away and escape.

Morrigan knew that by now they would have reported the Terran fleet's position up their chain of command. The only question now was how long it would take the news to disperse through this part of the Galactics' empire ... and for their forces to return and overwhelm the Terran fleet with sheer numbers.

Neal highlighted a succession of arterials in the star map. "We can still shift our focus," he said. "We're here, in Gavesh. If we take Delta Gate, we emerge at Golent ... You know what? Let's designate each gate ring by the systems they connect, for clarity. So this gate is Gavesh-Golent, right? Then on to Rachivem, Solemel ..."

"And back to Delta Pavo," Morrigan said, electronically tracing out the loop. "I *know*, Captain. Commander Boucher, is that still your recommendation as well?"

More than once in the past few days, both Neal and Boucher had suggested that Task Force Morrigan should give up on going deeper into Galactic space and instead double back to strike Pavo. The captured *Nemesis* map showed the precise chain of systems they could follow that would allow them to join with Admiral Knutson's Red Wing.

"If the Galactics are fast enough off the mark," Boucher pointed out, "they'll be able to trap the main fleet within another two or three jumps. We have just one chance to use our movements so far as a diversion, get them focused on our movement toward Xalixa, then fake 'em out and double back on Delta Pavo. All we need to do is take Gavesh-Golent Gate up ahead instead of Gavesh-Sakat. The two are pretty close—less than ten million kilometers apart."

"Dr. Allison," Morrigan said. "I understand you've been working on the Galactics' response times."

The xenopsychologist looked up, startled. "I've been working on a thesis for publication," Allison told them. "Yes. How did you know?"

"I saw the title online and read it," she replied. In fact, Pixie had spotted it on Allison's private workstation and flagged it for her—a technical violation of privacy, but moot on a starship where the commanding officer was expected to stay on top of *everything*. "I apologize for not asking, but you *are* embarked with this fleet as our expert in alien psychologies, and we are in desperate need of any Illimination you can offer us."

"That thesis is intended for publication," he said, looking uncertain. "But . . . I mean . . . the conclusions haven't been vetted as yet."

"Humor me," Morrigan said, "and tell everyone here your conclusions."

"Yes, Admiral," Allison said, his head bobbing in affirmation. "The title is 'Crisis Response and Dysfunctional Metagovernment Within the Galactic Polities.' It presents the idea that the Galactics are slow to respond to outside threats because of innate problems within their command structure."

"Sounds like just the thing in light recreational reading," Bohm said, grinning at him.

Allison ignored her. "It's my considered opinion, Admiral, that the Galactics are their own worst enemies. Specifically, key communications and decision-making networks throughout their empire appear to have become ossified with age and with inactivity."

"I've noticed," Stewart said, "that you've been logging quite a few requests to interview our Galactic representative." That, in fact, had been why Morrigan had ordered Pixie to keep a quiet electronic eye on Allison's work in the first place.

"Pax has been extremely helpful," Allison replied, sounding a bit defensive. "Ey's my primary source, in fact."

"Not exactly a source I'd want to set policy by," Stewart said. "Ey is only going to tell you what ey wants you to hear."

"I'd still like to hear your theory, Doctor," Morrigan said. "I only had time to skim the extract."

"Well, Pax paints a most interesting picture of Galactic civilization, you know. *Most* interesting. Billions of stargates connecting billions of worlds. Something like ten million Galactic sectors, each ruled by its own satrap."

"Satrap?" Neal asked.

"An old term for an administrative district in the ancient Persian Empire," Allison said, "as well as for the district's local ruler. We've borrowed the term and applied it to the Galactic administrative system. Government on the Galactic scale is simply too big a tangle of arterials and systems and worlds for any civilization to closely oversee or control, no matter how smart they are, right?"

"They've had a long time to practice, Brent," Kopeck told him.

"Yes, but that's part of the problem, don't you see? They've been at it for so long there's never a sense of urgency about anything, not anymore. There was some sort of crisis—a civil war, maybe—about half a billion years ago, but everything's been pretty quiet since then. Most of the processes of government have been taken over by machines."

"They *are* machines," Neal pointed out.

"Yes, yes, I know. They are *conscious* machines, *self-aware* machines. Day-to-day routine becomes tedious for them. Boring. Especially when they've been at it for a few million years. So the routine tasks of communication and government are handled by what they call D'lav—intelligent but *nonsentient* machines."

"I thought sentient and intelligent were the same thing," Clay Anders said, puzzled.

"Nope. Common mistake. We still can't hang a precise definition on the word 'intelligence,' but in general it's a catch-all term for *cognition*, the ability to learn, to reason, to plan, to innovate, to imagine, to acquire and use information. Sentience is about feeling and awareness, the capacity for experiencing perceptions subjectively, okay? It's the basis of consciousness. A non-AI computer can be *highly* intelligent, if by that you mean able to crunch big numbers or spit back facts and figures from an encyclopedia. Our first pre-sapient algorithms were like that—the chatbots and AI agents a few centuries ago. But a *sentient* machine, a self-aware, conscious machine, can know what it's thinking, can know that it *is* thinking, and draw conclusions from that. Not the same thing at all."

"In other words it has an inner life," Morrigan suggested, in a tone that suggested "get on with it." She knew the subject well. Her very first university degree, from CMU in 2072, had been in AI design.

Allison gave her a sharp glance. "That's one way of putting it, yes."

"What my esteemed colleague is trying to say," Gerhardt put in, "is that the real rulers of the Galaxy are *unconscious* machines, the D'lav. And it's possible that those machines actually are coordinating things, that they're the ones giving the orders and don't have the same priorities as the conscious entities like Pax."

"AIs running on red tape?" Neal asked.

"Something like that. They might not see a request from some distant satrap for reinforcements as being particularly urgent." He shrugged. "Maybe they're more aware of an entire forest than they are of a single tree."

"Nice metaphor," Morrigan said. "And a useful one, I think. Look, we know we can't outthink these machines. Our advantage, our *only* advantage, is going to be to out-random them. We'll stay ahead of them by doing the unexpected—feint right and then move left. They've seen our main fleet moving out this way, through Chajah and Salinsa and Tang and Anreskithad, but I don't think they've had a chance to seriously analyze our movements yet."

Neal's eyes widened. "Especially if the local commanders have to bump that analysis up the chain to HQ."

"Precisely." She gestured at the map floating above the table. "But they can read these things as well as we can. They also know they have to move damned fast to catch us. They'll know that there are multiple, roundabout ways for us to loop back and hit Delta Pavonis from out here, and by now Admiral Knutson will have at least raised the possibility in their minds by feinting toward Pavo.

"So this is our chance to toss them a surprise. Knutson makes a racket and then pulls a fade . . . and we hit *here*."

Morrigan cut the projection of the galactic arterials and brought up a system diagram, the image of an orange sun circled by seven planets. The fourth world out from the star was highlighted, with a block of translated text hovering alongside. She expanded the text so the others could read it.

"Sakat," she said. "Seventy-one light-years from Earth. The *Nemesis* data list it both as a Galactic military base and as a subsector capital. Intelligence says the facilities likely are extensive enough to service several thousand warships."

A stir ran through the others at the table. "A *major* naval base?" Anders said. "Admiral, is attacking something like that . . . ah . . . wise?"

"I'll remind you," Morrigan replied, "that we're not out here to stay out of sight all the time. We have to play sneak 'n' peek along the way to avoid getting pinned down, but our mission is to kick the Galactics in the balls as hard and as often as we can. Hurt them badly enough, and maybe we can make further attacks on Earth simply not worth their while."

"Or, at the very least," Neal added with a wry grin, "we can go down fighting."

"I didn't realize the Galactics *had* balls," Gerhardt said.

"Dr. Allison has confirmed some of my own thinking on this op," Morrigan told them. "If we move fast, if we strike fast, if we keep them guessing, the opposition won't be able to anticipate our moves far enough ahead to put up a coherent defense." She wiped the tangled projection from above the table. "We continue with the program as planned."

As the meeting broke up, Allison caught Morrigan's eye. "A moment, Admiral?"

"Of course."

"You . . . you mentioned sentient computers having an 'inner life.'"

She'd noted his reaction at the time. "It's well-known that higher-level AIs are conscious," she replied. "Self-aware."

He nodded. "Your public bio mentioned you worked in the field once."

"A long, *long* time ago." She folded her arms. "What's your question, Doctor?"

"Not a question," he replied. "It's just . . . remember back at Gliese 832? We were talking about how aliens won't think like us."

"I remember."

"By definition, that will apply to alien AI as well. The Galactic AIs had organic creators once. They *must* have. The very first AI machines didn't assemble themselves in the primordial ooze. Their programming will reflect the mental processes of their creators. It will not necessarily be along lines that humans can understand."

"I'm well aware of that."

"They may see the universe around them in ways we can't begin to comprehend. I just wanted to say that it's dangerous to make assumptions about how they will act or think with humans as our example. Their 'inner life,' as you called it, is likely to be very different from ours."

"Granted. I think all we can do is assume that our . . . our counterparts over there are intelligent alien beings. Where they came from, who programmed them—none of that matters, not anymore. They've had a billion years or so to program themselves, to *evolve*. Their programming will have been shaped and fine-tuned by their environment, their politics, their fears, their goals on the Galactic stage—all of that will have been streamlined, as responses that work are kept and things that don't are discarded. I think we can understand the way they think if we learn to understand what they're dealing with."

"Convergent evolution?" he asked.

"Precisely."

"Convergent evolution" was when animals of completely different lineages evolved into creatures remarkably like one another; sharks, dolphins, and the long-extinct ichthyosaurs—a fish, a mammal, and a reptile—were the classic examples. They were unrelated to one another, but looked and acted alike because their environments, with the need to move swiftly and without excess drag through the ocean, were the same.

"We can't push the similarities too far," he told her.

"Oh, I agree that there'll be differences in how they think," she said, "including some we won't be able to anticipate. All we can do is focus on the similarities." She spread her hands. "I don't know how else we can approach the problem. If you have any ideas on the topic, Doctor, I'll be very glad to hear them."

"No, Admiral. No ideas. I just . . ."

"Just what?"

"Well, I just keep wondering . . . what is it that keeps the Galactic AIs awake at night? *What are they most afraid of?*"

Morrigan was still turning Allison's words over in her mind as the fleet approached the next gate.

It might be a good idea, she thought, to have a long talk with Pax.

DAMIAN FELT THE muscles of his legs contract—hard. *One . . . two . . . three . . .*

"Hello, Lieutenant. Mind if I join you?"

Damian's muscles abruptly relaxed as the EMS current switched off, leaving him hanging limp in his rack. "Hey, Commander," he replied. "What brings you down here? Slumming?"

"Down here" was one of *Constellation's* gymnasiums, where ship's personnel could work out and keep fit. At the moment, Damian was clad in a bright blue EMSuit, a garment designed to deliver measured electrical stimulation to specific muscle groups under the control of a dedicated AI woven into the fabric. Electromyostimulation, or EMS for short, worked the muscles in the same way as a session on the weight machines, but faster and without the stress on joints, tendons, or the central nervous system.

The power switched on, and Damian's legs tensed. The EMSuit's fabric went rigid, holding his legs in place to prevent his joints from bending. *One ... two ... three ... four ...*

Without waiting for a reply to her question, Esposito touched a contact at her throat and dissolved her uniform. Damian watched with appreciation, though he decided it would be best not to comment. Nude, Esposito pulled a nanopac from a bulkhead dispenser, pressed it against her chest, and triggered it, letting the exercise garment flow over her body and mold itself to her skin.

"I don't think I ever properly thanked you," she said, sliding into the reclined exercise rack.

"For what?"

"For pulling my ass out of La Mesa."

"It's such a nice—" he started to say, then stopped himself. "Sorry, ma'am. No offense meant."

"None taken."

He nodded toward her legs, tensed as the current hit them. "All healed up?"

"Oh, yes. The medAIs took good care of me."

"New legs?"

"Nah, wasn't that bad. Nano infusion." The med teams would have given her nanobot injections, programming them to migrate to the damaged areas to sheath and reinforce the broken bones. "I just have to come down here a couple of times a day for EOS."

"Osteostimulation?"

"That's right. To stimulate bone growth."

"Still at it, huh?"

"Oh, the bones are fine now." She grimaced as current flowed through her. "This is just my daily workout."

His own calf muscles contracted again. *One ... two ... three ...*

Then a tone sounded in his ear, and his suit released him. He felt wrung out, every muscle quivering on the ragged edge of exhaustion.

Good workout.

"Hang on a sec, Lieutenant," Esposito called as he stepped out of the rack. "Question?"

"Yes, ma'am."

"Have you thought yet about coming back to the Nightwings?"

"Well . . ."

"Symmes and I have been scrambling to replace combat losses," she told him. Lieutenant Symmes was her executive officer in the Nightwings. "We're at eleven now, but not all of them are old hands. Kids. We could use someone with some fucking experience, and you'd bring the roster up to full strength."

Damian hesitated, then masked his hesitation by dissolving his workout suit and pulling a fresh utilities nanopac from the dispenser. "Yes, ma'am," he said as his uniform dressed him. In fact, he'd thought about little else since their last conversation. He'd been enjoying serving on *Chryses*, but . . .

"To tell you the truth, Commander, I've been missing you guys. Pigs really aren't my style."

She laughed. "Pigs are recon, strictly sneaking and peeking. You know what Symmes is always saying about Strykers."

"That they let you 'play rough and break stuff,'" Damian said, quoting the XO. "Yes, ma'am. I'm on board."

"Outstanding. I'll put a transfer request through to DAG, soon as I'm done here."

"And I'll put in a request for sim time."

"Feeling rusty?"

"Well, it wouldn't do to strap on a Stryker and fly it like a pig, now, would it?"

He also wanted to say goodbye to his crew.

Especially Kathra.

"VANGUARD REPORTS THEY'VE engaged, Admiral," Commander Boucher reported. The FTO grinned. "Captain Jobert says we caught 'em with their pants down."

"Very well," Morrigan replied. "Captain Neal, take us through."

From her station in CIC, Morrigan watched the delicate arc of the Gavesh-Sakat Gate expanding, sweeping closer . . . and then *Constellation* burst through into the new star system.

Sakat was an F9 star—a sun just a little brighter and a little hotter than Sol. Unmanned drones sent ahead of the fleet through the gate had verified data found in the Quarantine and *Nemesis* maps: twelve major planets circled Sakat—the usual mix of gas giants and small, rocky worlds—and the fourth planet out would be the focus of their assault.

Surrounded by the bulk of the fleet's White Wing mimicking her maneuvers, *Constellation* pivoted to come into line with the objective some 710 AUs distant. At that range, almost one hundred light-hours, the star was merely one very bright star among thousands. Only *Connie*'s AIs could identify the target sun and bracket it in red light.

Nearer at hand, a few tens of thousands of kilometers ahead, the fleet's van was completing the rout of the Galactic defending pickets. Almost two hundred Galactic warships had been stationed in the volume of space that included the Gavesh-Sakat Gate; moments before, Admiral Selby's Blue Wing had burst through the gate in a rush, slashing through and past the sentry force with such speed and such precision that the defenders were caught totally off guard. White Wing was confronted by a handful of survivors racing head-on toward the fleet, making for the gate.

The appearance of the fleet's main body directly ahead of them—nearly 1,100 ships—must, for the Galactics, have been like slamming into a wall. They put up a desperate fight, destroying the light cruiser *Portland* and damaging two destroyers, but the last of them were overwhelmed in a fusillade of HELfire and mag-pulse KE rounds from ahead and astern that left a drifting shoal of broken, tumbling wreckage and hot gas.

"Enemy destroyed," Neal reported. "Admiral . . . they had almost five minutes to get off a signal."

I know, Vince, Morrigan replied over her corona. *That's why we have to move* now.

"Engineering reports full power available."

"Kick it," Morrigan commanded.

As one, White Wing accelerated, boosting all the way up to 99.96 percent of *c*. At that velocity, it would take them just over four days—96.9 hours objective—to cross the yawning abyss of 710 AUs between the Gavesh-Sakat Gate and Sakat IV. Einsteinian time dilation, however, would compress that wait to just 167 minutes subjective.

The idea was to cover the gulf between the gate and the planet in the absolute minimum of time possible. The sentry force would have sent off a warning the moment the first human ships came through the gate, a signal that, at the speed of light, would reach the main Galactic fleet in-system in a hair under ninety-seven hours. Task Force Morrigan had emerged in-system five minutes after the fleet's van, and another eight minutes, twenty seconds had passed before Morrigan gave the order to "kick it."

If all went well, White Wing would arrive just minutes after the Galactics learned of their arrival—Einstein screening at its most efficient.

Would they find the Galactics already at their equivalent of battle stations? Would they be waiting for the human task force, weapons powered up and already tracking the incoming ships? Or would Morrigan's all-out push to reach Sakat IV catch them still unprepared?

It was, she knew, a horrific gamble. To have even a chance of catching the enemy by surprise, they would have to crowd the speed of light just as closely as they possibly could, arriving at Sakat IV moments after the warning from the sentries. No matter how efficient their gravitic drives, no matter how much power they were able to draw from the vacuum, the human fleet could not quite reach *c*, the ultimate speed limit of the universe.

Speed now was everything...and even that might not be enough.

SAKAT IV CIRCLED ITS hot yellow-white sun distantly enough that much of the surface was given over to polar ice caps and tundra, with vast glaciers gouging V-shaped valleys down to a deep violet sea. Once, the densely forested equatorial regions of the planet had supported a thriving civilization—arboreal cephalopods with a rich and vibrant musical tradition based on a twenty-two-note scale. Some hundreds of billions of seconds ago the Galactic Authority had judged that species and found it wanting. The planet's surface still showed the savage scars of an apocalyptic judgment.

A pity, really, the Sentinel Mind thought with uncharacteristic melancholy. The Sakatan culture had had much to recommend it within the milieu of Galactic civilization. Ey brushed aside the regret and brought eir full attention back to the tolmat with which eir eye was linked.

Higher Galactics could experience emotions, but only rarely permitted themselves the indulgence.

"We have followed the advance of this Ku'un fleet with some interest," the tolmat said. "They should not have made it this far. The situation suggests major problems in the execution of our strategy. An execution, I might add, planned at the tolgah level."

The Sentinel considered this, eir electronic gaze sweeping across the curves and angles of the Sakat Orbital. This was a critical military hub within this sector, the sprawling home base of thousands of Galactic warships and a million AIs of diverse designs and provenance.

"That statement," the Sentinel Mind replied carefully, "might be construed as criticism."

"That is certainly not our intent. We merely seek . . . understanding."

A "tolmat" was a local district commander, charged with the oversight of perhaps thirty systems; a "tolgah" was the sector commander, in this case a Mind overseeing operations from Xalixa and responsible for some thousands of systems. The Sentinel Mind was emself of tolgah standing—but with the added authority of being out in these barbarous hinterlands under direct orders from the Core.

The Sentinel Mind considered reporting the tolmat to the Core. The being was of primitive design, a fluid, roughly ovoid shape of field-constrained liquid metal with twelve ruby optical lenses floating within the surface. While normally capable, these models possessed a high autonomy index and could sometimes show a loss of mental balance. A total mind reset might be necessary here . . .

An alarm tone sounded within both their minds, the toll of a deep-throated gong.

"What is that?" the Sentinel snapped. "A hostiles alert?"

The tolmat was already integrating streams of data flowing in from the base Mind. "The human fleet, Tolgah. At Gateway Neravrethaad—that's the Sakat-Gavesh connection, distance 3.4932×10^5 light seconds. Our blocking force there reports that it is under heavy attack." The being floated half of its lenses around to focus on the Sentinel. "Our forces are being annihilated."

The Sentinel considered this. Whatever was happening out there on the fringes of the Sakat system had by now already resolved itself. Some 349,000 seconds was a *long* time in space combat—an eternity to beings that could experience time in microseconds. If the intruders had indeed wiped out the blocking ships, if they had set course for the Sakat base, they might well be within a few thousand seconds of arriving here.

"Full alert, Tolmat," the Sentinel said.

"Already done, Sentinel."

How long, ey wondered, did they have?

FROM MORRIGAN'S PERSPECTIVE aboard the *Constellation*, whipping in-system at a whisper below the speed of light, the trip from the Gavesh-Sakat Gate had so far taken only 160 minutes. They would be breaking out of gravitic drive in another seven minutes subjective. For the Galactics orbiting Sakat IV, however, that time would have crawled past as four long days. Within the past few hours the warning from the gate pickets would finally have reached them, crawling in from the pickets at the snail's pace speed of light. Navigation's best guess was that they would have received the alert one hour objective before the human fleet broke out of near-*c* flight. During that hour, had they been able to maneuver their fleet to be ready for the oncoming assault by the human fleet? Would they have had time to prepare some unexpected god-magic defense, perhaps something humans had never yet imagined?

A *very* great deal rode on the answer to those questions.

At her station in CIC, Morrigan watched the remaining minutes trickling away. "Five minutes," she announced through her corona. "Commander Anders, weapons free, no restrictions. Commence with both HELs and the keel mount. Commander Boucher, pass that on to the rest of the fleet, please."

"Aye, aye, Admiral," Boucher said from his station in front of her. "Not sure how much they'll hear through the warp."

"We'll trust the repeaters," she told him.

At these speeds, each ship in the fleet was embedded in its own tight little bubble of warped space. Comm signals—radio and laser—could pass from ship to ship, but there was terrific distortion. The comm computers in each receiving vessel might sort meaning out of hash; if not, the signal would continue repeating, and the controlling AIs were fast enough to translate the signal and pass it along in milliseconds.

She hoped.

The remaining seconds subjective dwindled away.

"Stand by, all stations," Morrigan announced. "Breakout in three . . . two . . . one . . ."

CHAPTER EIGHTEEN

BREAKOUT...

The human fleet went sub-relativistic with explosive suddenness, warp bubbles evaporating in bursts of light. With flight and navigation systems under AI control, the maneuver was tightly coordinated and precise, sixteen hundred individual ships dropping into objective space with an almost magical accuracy, occupying an ovoid volume of space several thousand kilometers long. Sakat IV lay just forty thousand kilometers ahead, buried within a vast swarm of Galactic warships.

With weapons already free, almost sixteen hundred fire-control AIs coordinated with each of the other vessels in the fleet, selected targets in carefully orchestrated hierarchies, and fired, all within a span of time dictated by the speed-of-light distance between individual vessels—a half second or so at most.

In the same instant, the fleet's dreadnaughts, monitors, and assault carriers launched their fighters. Cylindrical, flat-bottomed towers emerged from armored launch bays like questing periscopes, each carrying between six and twelve fighters stacked atop one another in their launch racks. Called launchmags, the towers acted like magazines of old-fashioned projectile weapons, loosing their load-outs of Strykers or Stilettos in rapid-fire sequences, long strings of spacefighters streaking ahead toward the enemy. In this way a carrier could loose her entire complement of fighters within seconds before the empty towers retracted back into the mother ship's hull.

In CIC, Admiral Morrigan watched a screen displaying the Pryfly image feeds, as strings of fighters queued in echelons accelerated toward the objective world. How many, she wondered, would return?

For decades now, debate had raged in naval planning circles and academies over the usefulness of single- and double-seat fighters employed en masse against capital ships. Fighters certainly had their uses against smaller vessels—other fighters, say, or vessels as large as a destroyer, lightly armored and vulnerable to a relatively small nuclear warhead. Modern dreadnaughts, however, could brush them off like annoying insects. It took a *lot* of fighters to gang up on a single battle cruiser or dreadnaught and score significant damage. Even a heavy cruiser was beyond the reach of a typical fighter squadron unless those pilots were *very* lucky . . . or unless the target had been damaged already by capital ship bombardment.

The best hope for the fighters' survival, Morrigan knew, was for the capital ships of the human fleet to lay down such a devastating fire that the enemy's point defenses were overwhelmed. She shifted her attention to the *Constellation*'s fire-control feeds, which used computer-generated imagery to paint both enemy and friendly vessels as well as outgoing and incoming beams and missiles. To the naked eye, even a massive space battle such as this was rather dull—the endless black of space, star strewn and empty, with even the closest other ships invisibly distant. HELfire beams, too, were invisible in space unless they happened to burn through a cloud of gas released by a nearby stricken ship. And missiles . . . if you saw *them*, they were already far too close for comfort.

As if to underscore the emptiness of local space, one long monitor on CIC's starboard bulkhead was set to show the naked-eye view outside: stars and emptiness pocked only now and again by a tiny flash—a radiant nuclear holocaust visible across some thousands of kilometers of space only as a brief pinpoint of light. That would change, however, as the fleets maneuvered into closer proximity to cheat opposing point-defense systems.

Only in the tank, where *Connie*'s AIs were painting the otherwise unseen details of the battle, could you see the stab and pulse of high-energy lasers, the streak and flash of missiles and of fighters, and the wholesale destruction of hundreds of ships, of tens of thousands of lives . . .

The fact that many of those lives were AIs didn't change a thing. Dek, she knew, a first-order Turing machine, was self-aware, conscious, and empathic, at least as far as she could tell. For Morrigan, the dominant emotion as she watched Galactic ships flare and die was a cold, bitter emptiness. If there was pain, grief, anger, hatred, any of the emotions she might have expected at all, Morrigan had locked them away, burying them so deep she could not feel them. She felt nothing but the cold.

These—these *people*, so defined by their self-awareness, had tried to extinguish the human species.

Her hands curled into fists, the nails biting her palms. Damn it, one of them had casually murdered Jaime.

And that made it personal. The bastards *deserved* to die . . .

"WHAAA-*HOO*!" LIEUTENANT DAMIAN was fourth in line in the string of Nightwing Strykers, boosting now toward the target planet and its encircling cloud of enemy warships. This was more like it—strapping on a fighter and kicking it to near-*c*.

It was great to be back with his squadron. Surrounding space briefly twisted around him, and his forward screens vanished within the firework cascades of Baltis light. The fireworks were brief; his boost velocity was high enough to give him a subjective time of a couple of seconds, and then normal space reasserted itself around him, and he was flying into blue-white radiance.

HELfire beams from the fleet had been slicing through the Galactic fleet for several seconds already. Many ships appeared to be well armored against high-energy beam attacks, but others had been gutted, spilling gases and stored liquids into space where they froze into vast, glittering clouds illuminated by the internal pyrotechnics of dying Galactic ships. Microsingularities from the enemy vessels' power plants were breaking free from their power generators, plunging through ship structures, absorbing mass in uncontrolled gulps, and vomiting insanely radiant flares of radiation in wavelengths ranging from the visible spectrum through to low gamma wavelengths. Most of the visible light was blue and violet, Illiminating the expanding clouds of ice mist in shimmering sheets of cerulean and ultramarine.

Damian felt the rippling of data through his corona. His Stryker's AI was fully engaged in correlating the flood of data coming in through the fighter's sensors, intimately linking him with his ship. The human mind was too slow, too limited, to deal with the speed and scope of space combat. Linked into the fighter's AI, Damian became his ship, his brain enhanced by both sensory and computational data and functioning at superhuman speed. Time appeared to have slowed to a crawl.

He and the Stryker were *one*. He could see surrounding space through his biological eyes, but that view now was heavily overlayed by geometric markings and reticles, as well as icons marking both other Nighthawk fighters and enemy vessels. Around him, enemy ships drifted, human fighters maneuvered, missiles streaked, energy flashed with eye-searing intensity, all in an eerie and ponderous slow motion.

There were no blocks of identifying text within his visual field, as were used in CIC and navigational programs. Instead, he could look at a Galactic warship and simply *know* its tonnage, its dimensions, its heading and speed, its angle on the bow, its range, and every other pertinent bit of data available to his fighter's AI and directed into his brain by his corona link. A thought, anticipated by his ship, twisted the fighter in space before loosing a Longbow missile into the burning heart of a partially disemboweled Galactic cruiser. The fighter's AI whipped the ship away an instant before the hundred-kiloton nuclear warhead detonated, annihilating the enemy ship from within. Fighters might not be much use against intact cruisers or dreadnaughts, but if they found one breached by heavy naval fire already, they could be both deadly and decisive. The cruiser, shrouded in half-kilometer-long leaf-shaped armor plates, crumbled into its interior funereal pyre. Rogue singularities freed by the disintegration of the vessel's engineering spaces slashed through drifting wreckage, point sources fiercely radiating at temperatures generally reserved for the cores of giant suns. Damian's fighter adjusted its drift to stay well clear of those sunpoints, microscopic vortices, each every bit as deadly as a thermonuclear warhead.

"Nightwing Four, Nightwing Leader," Esposito's voice called over his corona. "Nice one, Troggie. Form up with the rest of us now. We've got major incoming."

"Copy, Wing Leader," he replied. He checked to make sure he was still on tactical Fleetlink. He was. "Taclink is engaged. Bring me in."

Taclink was a subsystem of Fleetlink, which tied the ships of the battle group together. Commander Esposito could in essence take command of Damian's fighter and use its onboard AI to fly him into position, just as DAG could direct all of *Connie*'s fighter squadrons from Pryfly.

Not that *that* would happen just yet. *Constellation* was still far enough out that the speed-of-light time lag would cripple attempts to maneuver the fighters from a distance.

His fighter turned again and accelerated, slipping past a tumbling mountain of metallic debris and taking up position on the squadron's right wing.

Major incoming? Yeah, there was a monster up ahead now that certainly qualified as such—a Galactic ship the size of a small planetoid with armored flanks that might be eighty meters thick. A warship that massed a thousand times more than a human dreadnaught.

And so far it did not appear to be in the least damaged.

"HOW'S SHE RUNNING, Chief?"

Chief Kranhouse glanced up from his workstation, where flow indicators and power readings danced and shifted in holographic display, enhanced by the data feeds from his corona into the visual cortex of his brain. The spoken words startled him. He'd been so absorbed in the display he'd not heard Commander Thorvaldson enter the compartment. "Eh? Oh, hello, Commander. We're doing all right." *I hope . . .*

"You don't sound convinced."

Kranhouse gestured at the holography display in front of him. "We're running hot, CHENG. I'm cycling through all five redundant distribution systems, but if this keeps up we could blow a Hawking chamber. Wouldn't be pretty."

Thorvaldson nodded. "The other units are reporting the same thing," he said. "*Connie* is predicting one hundred percent failure after one hour."

The Hawking chambers were where tiny, artificial black holes were force-fed hydrogen at high pressure. Since microscopic black holes could swallow only so much matter in a given period of time, the rest was accelerated away within the chamber at a third of the speed of light, resulting in an energy release that made the core of a star seem tame by comparison. Those temperatures were controlled by powerful magnetic fields . . . but there were limits.

"We may have to withdraw, sir," Kranhouse said. "Give the taps time to cool off."

"Tell that to our boss," Thorvaldson replied. "She wants to push as hard as the laws of physics allow."

"It's the laws of physics that're the problem, CHENG. The longer we run at these power levels, the sooner we blow a cooling circuit. And if the magfields go down we're going to light up the whole system."

"I know, Chief. Stay on it. And keep me in the loop, okay?"

"I'll do my best, sir."

But was his best, Kranhouse wondered, good enough?

THE TRICK HERE, Morrigan knew well, would be concentration of mass. Maneuver, surprise . . . the fleet was committed, and the assault was already past the tactical preliminaries.

Now it was all about mass.

She sat in her command seat in *Constellation*'s CIC, letting the incoming data flood her brain. She didn't need to give orders . . . not now. Her commanders, from wing admirals to individual ship COs and even pig and fighter pilots, all knew their jobs and had their orders. She would intervene only when absolutely necessary.

It was the waiting and the watching that drove her mad.

For centuries, the ruling military doctrine of the Terran Navy, and for long before that of the United States of America, had been enshrined in an amusingly quirky little mnemonic: MOUSE MOSS.

They were also known as the Nine Principles of War.

The first, Maneuver, was self-explanatory enough: *the movement of forces in relation to the enemy to gain positional advantage*. The task force had certainly ticked off that one by shifting over seven hundred AUs from their arrival gate to Sakat IV, almost directly into the center of the enemy fleet.

Objective was next: *the ultimate military purpose of war is the destruction of both the enemy's ability and their will to fight*. Whether that was an *obtainable* objective, of course, was the question. Wars had been lost when objectives, whether strategic or political, were not clear.

Then came Unity of Command: *achieving success in the pursuit of any military objective demands a single commander with the authority to control every element of the operation.* Task Force Morrigan had that in the person of Morrigan herself.

Surprise was an obvious one: *by achieving surprise, an attacking force can achieve results far out of proportion to the effort and numbers expended.* That had been a first-order principle of military planning since the first *Homo erectus* had jumped out from behind a bush with a club to clobber his next-cave neighbor.

Economy of Force could be complicated to carry out, but at heart it was simple: *employ all available military force in the most efficient way possible.* It didn't do to squander too much of your force on diversions, secondary attacks, screens, or deceptions . . . not when you needed them to achieve a critical mass at a decisive place and time of your choosing.

Morrigan had given a lot of thought to her deployment of Admiral Knutson's Red Wing toward Pavo. Had the move been worthwhile? Or had she needlessly deprived the task force of ships and crews?

That remained to be seen. In the Sakat assault, however, *everything* was directed into the attack.

Mass was next: *mass the effects of overwhelming combat power at the decisive place and time.* Massing *effects* was not the same as simply concentrating your force. Synchronizing all aspects of an attack—firepower, maneuver, timing, and numbers—where they would have a decisive effect on the enemy within a short span of time was what "mass" in the military sense meant, and doing so successfully allowed, once again, a numerically or technologically inferior force to achieve decisive results while minimizing friendly casualties.

In short, Morrigan was not attacking the entire enemy fleet. Instead, she was focusing her force and her firepower on the enemy fleet's heart.

Next was Offensive: *seize, hold, and exploit the initiative,* which meant taking the offensive and maintaining it—absolutely basic to all warfare. A good defense might save an army and it might weaken an enemy, but it could never win a war.

Security was next: *protect your forces to keep the enemy from gaining an unexpected advantage* through unexpected maneuvers, surprises, or acts.

And last on the list was Simplicity: *keep battle plans uncomplicated, directives and objectives clear, and orders concise.* To do otherwise guaranteed confusion, misunderstanding, and lost opportunities.

In other words, KISS: *keep it simple, stupid.*

From where Morrigan was sitting, flying the entire fleet at near-c into the heart of the defending force was about as idiot simple as you could ask for.

The atmosphere in the CIC was calm, even subdued. Dozens of men and women sat at their stations throughout the darkened compartment, faces illuminated by the pale blue or green or white glow of their monitors, carrying out duties ranging from fighting the ships to overseeing the entire fleet's engagement with the enemy. *Constellation* was currently hammering away at several targets with HELs and with the MRG-01 mounted along her keel, a savage and devastating barrage targeting the largest of the enemy vessels at long range. "Action port," Neal's voice called from a speaker, and *Constellation* rolled to bring her port railgun battery to bear on a massive, teardrop-shaped vessel a thousand kilometers distant. The human fleet was plunging now deep into the cloud of Galactic warships, and targets were thick on every side, though still invisible to the eye.

That interpenetration of fleets, though, was putting the human task force at a serious disadvantage, with the enemy able to concentrate their fire from multiple directions. The cruisers *Warrington* and *Svalbard* were racked by enemy fire, torn and drifting helplessly, while the destroyers *Cameron*, *Emden*, and *Agosta* vanished in savage flashes of blue-white light.

"What is that weapon?" Morrigan asked. "The blue flares?"

"Positron beams," Boucher replied. "Basically the antimatter equivalent of electrons. We have nothing like that."

"Just so, we can still knock them down with our HELfires," she replied. The advanced Galactic weaponry, she reasoned, was more effective against the human warships, but not to such a degree that the Earth forces couldn't face them. Even a savage with a club had a chance against a ground soldier with a laser, if he could surprise him, maybe whack him from behind. Certainly, the Galactics were showing signs now of panic, their massed war fleet fighting as individuals, rather than as a unified whole. Every battle, Morrigan thought, had a critical tipping point, a point where MOUSE MOSS began to crumble the enemy's position and force them into a defensive posture. She could sense that point approaching now.

"Action port," Neal's voice called over the combat command channel, and *Constellation* rolled to bring one of her three lateral batteries to bear on a Galactic warship. They were deep enough into the enemy fleet now that the sky was filled with ships, with blossoming flares of light, with the chaos of close combat. Most of those ships, Morrigan noted, were small—cruiser sized or lighter. There were no *Nemesis*-class monsters, thank God, and only a handful of ships the size of Terran dreadnaughts or larger. *Connie*'s targeting AI had broken the enemy vessels down into a dozen major types—eggs and spheres, triangles, needles, fluted wedges, and others—suggesting that they might represent the battle fleets of as many different organic alien races.

She opened a private corona channel. *Dek? Are you on?*

I am here, Admiral.

I need to consult with Pax. Directly, mind-to-mind.

She felt the concern in the robot's answering thought. *Is that wise, Admiral? If ey should subvert you . . .*

That's why I'm bringing you in on this.

And in a swift, concise thought, she told her personal aide what she needed.

The battle, meanwhile, continued to unfold more or less according to plan—an operational plan informally designated "Little Bites" by Morrigan and her tactical staff. They'd divided the fleet into two roughly equal parts and organized them as two spheres nested one inside the other. Guided by Argus through Fleetlink, the spheres worked together as tightly coordinated units: the outer layer a shell ten thousand kilometers across, putting down a heavy covering fire against the surrounding enemy; the smaller, inner shell leaping forward to engulf enemy warships at the heart of the enemy swarm, englobing them, hammering them with missiles, and burning them down with concentrated HELfire. *Connie* and the other dreadnaughts were spaced through the outer shell, using their broadsides to keep the enemy at bay, and continued to advance as the inner sphere bit off more and more of the enemy formation.

Morrigan watched the maneuver for several moments more, gauging firepower, resistance, and the sheer power of the human advance. The attack was definitely weakening as the Terran ships plunged deeper and deeper into the hostile swarm . . . but at the same time, more and more of the enemy warships were disengaging, breaking off, and moving away. She felt a thrill of anticipation, of urgency and burgeoning excitement. *They were winning! The human fleet was winning!*

"Admiral," Commander Boucher alerted her. He pointed into the tank in front of them. "We're coming into rage of their orbital."

Images of the structure, relayed by the fleet's lead vessels and from hundreds of battlespace drones, were coming up on CIC's monitors. Designated simply as the "Sakat Orbital," the complex was a station and immense space-dock facility over a hundred kilometers across, grown out of a fair-sized asteroid into a sleek and gleaming base for some thousands of Galactic warships.

Most of those ships were still berthed. HELfire beams and high-velocity kinetic killers began shredding the structure like tissue and ripping into the moored alien warships before they could power up and get clear.

"We caught them with their trousers around their ankles," Morrigan told Boucher. "My compliments to Professor Einstein."

"Our scouts are registering power plants coming online in there, Admiral," Lieutenant Commander Tangredi, Morrigan's chief of staff said, excited. "We *caught* the bastards! We *caught* 'em!"

The fleet's all-out approach at 99 percent of *c* meant that the enemy had simply been unaware of how close the humans were behind the speed-of-light electromagnetic wave front announcing their arrival in-system. Even the Galactics, it appeared, needed time to power up and ready their berthed warships, and Morrigan's tactics had denied them that time in a savagely brutal thrust and slash.

"Have every covering ship that can bear hit that orbital," Morrigan told her fleet tactical officer. "Three good volleys. Then send in the Little Bite and englobe it."

"Aye, *aye*, Admiral!" Boucher's eye reflected her own excitement.

During ops planning, some of her officers had speculated that the orbital might be heavily armored and well armed, a space fortress that might do serious damage to an attacking force. As railgun rounds began slamming into the structure, however, it became clear that the structure wasn't so much a fortress as it was a target. Brilliant flashes marked the kinetic impacts at high percentages of *c*, blasts spreading clouds of debris throughout the local volume of space. Internal gases and liquids erupted into vacuum and froze, creating glittering masses of sapphire-bright ice particles gleaming in the light of the local sun.

Those ships that could bring weapons to bear fired their three volleys, and then the inner sphere leaped forward in a high-velocity shift. The outer, covering shell followed, surrounding ships and stars blurring with the motion for just an instant.

Constellation was now drifting some thirty-five hundred kilometers from the Sakat Orbital, maintaining a steady fire on the Galactic vessels outside the double shell. There were far fewer hostile vessels now; even though they effectively had the human fleet surrounded, more and more of the enemy ships were withdrawing, making for one of several gateways in-system.

The situation, Morrigan realized, was almost identical to the fight earlier at G'sar Niku—the enemy, possessing a far superior technology, broken and in full retreat. Again, Morrigan considered giving the general chase order, sending her fleet out to hunt the bastards down and do as much damage to their force as possible before they escaped. Again, she discarded the idea. The Galactic fleet was still dangerous and might yet cripple the human task force if they were backed into a corner. They still outnumbered the human fleet elements by at least two to one, and those antimatter beams they used were no joke. Better to let them slip away, even if it meant facing them again later in some other system.

She wondered, though, why they weren't fighting harder. Not that she was disappointed, certainly—far from it—but, damn it, the Galactics' weak showing simply made no *sense*.

She found that she was looking forward with keen anticipation to that conversation with Pax.

"I KNOW YOU'VE been calling the admiral *the* Morrigan, Chief," Engineman Second Kevin O'Reilly said, grinning. "But some of us have our own name for her."

"Yeah?" Chief Kranhouse said, giving O'Reilly a sour look. "You lettin' that new stripe go to your head, kid?"

O'Reilly had received the promotion less than a subjective month earlier, while the fleet was still at Nap'eej, a couple of systems past G'sar Niku.

"No, Chief. It's nothing bad, okay?"

"So what do you call her?"

"Alexandra," O'Reilly replied, grinning. "Alexandra the *Great*!"

"A little obvious, ain't it?"

"Me an' some of the guys, we was doin' some online research, right? Alexander the Great was this Greek general who took down the entire Persian Empire with a few thousand men just like it was nothin'!"

"He wasn't Greek, son. He was Macedonian."

"Yeah? What's the difference?"

Kranhouse shrugged. "There was no united Greece back then," he said. "Kind of like there's no united Earth today."

"Yeah, but according to what I read, Macedon *was* a Greek kingdom."

"Eh. Same difference, I guess. Alexander's father *did* unite the Greek peninsula under Macedonian rule, so I guess it's pretty much the same thing. But what's your point?"

"Just that you had this tiny little Greek state taking on an ancient empire that ruled a lot of the known world, right? Just like what Admiral Morrigan's doing now!"

"You're sayin' she's Alexander the Great? Sorry . . . *Alexandra* the Great?"

"Maybe she's Alexandra the Greater. That's what some of the guys're calling her now."

"Nah. I still think she's the goddess. *The Morrigan.* A goddess trumps a king any day of the week."

"I guess it depends on how you—"

The ship gave a hard lurch. "Uh-oh," Kranhouse said, checking his feeds. "Better keep the shields positive."

"AM beams?"

"You got it. Y'know, it ought to be possible to flicker the EM screens back and forth, cycle 'em at a couple thousand times a second."

"What, to block both neg and pos incoming?"

"Yeah . . ."

"Wouldn't that just attract both, Chief? Or maybe the two charges would just cancel each other out."

"Or maybe it'd scatter half of the incoming beam no matter what the charge . . ."

O'Reilly pulled numbers from the system's AI. "I'm not sure, Chief. You think we should try?"

"I think we need to get CHENG in here and set up a test patch." The ship gave another shudder, more insistent this time. "And we'd better do it fast."

CHAPTER NINETEEN

ADMIRAL MORRIGAN SAT in her office, data and lists of figures flowing in through her corona. The engagement had ended with the humans, once again, in command of the battle zone. Sakat had been another victory, but a hard-won engagement that had seriously weakened them. Casualties had been high—some 215 task force vessels destroyed, four of them dreadnaughts. Galactic casualties had been higher—much higher, given that nearly two thousand hostile ships had been caught in port and powered down, where the concentrated fire from the human fleet had pounded them to scrap.

Total Galactic casualties were unknown, but Intelligence estimated them at ten to twelve times human losses, a staggeringly disproportionate number of kills.

Still, a few more victories like *that* would finish the human task force.

"They're waiting for you in Bay Three, Admiral," Dek told Morrigan.

"Thank you, Dek. I'll be right down."

The call had first come through her corona, but she'd told Pixie to hold it for later. Before anything else she wanted to finish going through the casualty lists. Significant as the victory at Sakat was, Task Force Morrigan simply couldn't keep taking losses like this. The fleet, minus Admiral Knutson's absent Red Wing, now numbered 1,385, with another 420, some 30 percent, badly damaged. They would have to pause the campaign here at Sakat until the damaged warships could be repaired.

And that would leave the fleet immobile . . . and vulnerable.

She linked in with the communications department. "Ev? This is Morrigan. I've got a message for you to route back."

"Yes, ma'am. Earth?"

"Yes, but I also want the drones programmed to find any Terran vessels that might already be following after us. I want them to get the lead out and rendezvous with us here. As many ships as possible, as fast as possible."

"Including the Chinese?"

"*All* polities. This is about human survival, not about individual states."

"Aye, aye, ma'am."

With comm relay stations now stationed at each of the gates along the way so far, communications drones could beam lasercom messages from point to point all the way down the Whiskey Road and back to Earth, and if there were human vessels in any of those star systems, the message could be passed to them as well. Task Force Morrigan needed reinforcements, and lots of them, if it was to go any farther.

Unfortunately, because each and every system held several gates, most of them hundreds of AUs apart, it took an ungodly chunk of time for lasercom messages to cross from one gate to the next.

Excuse me, Admiral, Dek said in her head. *Starswarmer and the other vacuumorphs can't stay in a true-human environment for long.*

Morrigan sighed. *Okay,* she said, with just a small, sharp snap of irritation in her mental voice. *I'm on my way. Hammond, Tangredi, with me.*

Two of her CIC aides rose from their stations and followed her out.

Dek and several members of the *Constellation*'s senior science staff were waiting for them in *Constellation*'s Landing Bay Three.

A metal table had been grown at the center of the deck, on which several disturbing shapes lay arranged for inspection. The room was dominated, however, by a trio of nightmarish shapes—three of the fleet's resident Vacs, *Homo vacuo*.

Morrigan had decidedly mixed feelings about the genemods. As with the so-called *Homo superioris* designation, *Homo vacuo* was not a true subspecies of human. Vacuumorphs were individually grown and could not reproduce, a characteristic that defined an artificial life-form, as opposed to a true genetically modified human. While their internal organs and skeletal systems were the product of genetic manipulation of human stem cells, their exterior integuments, some of their internal organs, and their artificial circulatory fluid all were added after decanting. Vacs were incredibly useful organisms, able to live and work in hard vacuum and extreme temperatures without space suits, but Morrigan wondered how they felt about their lives.

She *assumed* they could feel. Possibly, though, that assumption was unwarranted. She didn't know very much about them.

It was clear, however, that no one had ever asked them if they wanted to be decanted. Did they simply accept their lot as artificial life-forms, or did they resent a situation that amounted to genetic slavery?

The big one in the middle, she knew, was Starswarmer—the Vac equivalent of a senior petty officer. The other two, her corona told her, were Worldgazer and Sunglow. They seemed more imposing than their masses warranted; each was strapped into the embrace of an exowalker, piloted excursion modules that held the Vacs upright against the ship's one-g artificial gravity field. *Homo vacuo* had been designed to live and work in microgravity, and one g could cripple them.

They looked human, more or less, save for their thick, leathery hides, which gave them an almost spherical, armor-plated look. Their most obvious departure from their human progenitors was in their limbs. Rather than two legs, they had an extra pair of arms growing from their hips. Their hides extended up and over their heads like black balaclavas, hiding ears, noses, and mouths, if they even had those, and revealing only a pair of bright, deeply pocketed silver orbs, optics resistant to bright sun while remaining sensitive to wavelengths from the deep infrared to the near ultraviolet. Scuttlebutt had it that the odd little creatures could distinguish among millions of colors that *Homo sapiens* could never experience.

Morrigan wondered if they had names for every hue.

"Here she is," Dr. Marik Bowers said, looking up as Morrigan and her entourage entered the cavernous chamber. "Good. Now we can begin."

"About time," one of the Vacs said, speaking by radio over Morrigan's corona. "I would rather not hang around to be oxidized by this corrosive soup you baseline Homos call air."

Vacuumorphs did not use audible speech, of course, but spoke both to one another and to humans by means of biological radios, a kind of technological telepathy identical to corona-to-corona conversations or to Morrigan's interactions with Pixie or Dek. She ignored the rudeness; Vacs were notorious for being direct and blunt in their interactions with humans, and this was hardly the time or the place for lessons in military courtesy. Instead, she looked at the motionless forms on the table. "I see you brought us our specimens, Starswarmer."

"As ordered. Why would you want them?"

"We need to know what we're up against," Morrigan replied. "Let's have a look."

There were four bodies displayed on the table, each one distinctly different from the other three. In her mind she tagged them by chance resemblances to various species on Earth ... though, in fact, none of the four was even remotely related to terrestrial life.

The jellyfish: a mass of translucent blue tissue within which internal organs could be seen. Three corrugated tentacles or arms, colored red shading to purple and blue, extended from one end and might have supported the living creature upright.

The spider: something with long, jointed legs and a hairy body with a face on one end that was all compound eyes, disturbing mouthparts, and fur. Though the features gave the vague impression of an earthly tarantula, more or less, the organism clearly possessed an internal skeleton and multiply branching leg parts unlike anything on Earth.

The worms: a pile of segmented brown-and-yellow tentacles, like finger-thick worms so deeply intertwined Morrigan couldn't tell if they were one creature or dozens adhering together.

The shrimp: a somewhat arthropodal organism with a segmented gray body, multiple legs and claws, dozens of impossibly long feelers or antennae, and five stalked eyes on the knobbed end of a sinuous tentacle.

The shrimp was the largest of the organisms on the table—perhaps three meters long, not counting the whip-slender antennae. Smallest was the worm mass, a meter across and no more than twenty kilos in total. The spider wore something that might have been part tool harness, part uniform. The shrimp wore a silver belt around its mid-torso, with tools of some sort attached to it.

"We recovered these from four distinct types of alien spacecraft," Worldgazer told her, gesturing at the bodies with one handfoot. "It wasn't easy finding specimens not mutilated by explosive decompression or high temperatures."

"I can imagine," Morrigan told them. "I'd like to know which species goes with which ship."

"We have that data here, Admiral," Yahn Gerhardt told her. The xenotech expert opened a link to all their coronas, and the recorded images of four alien spacecraft materialized in the air above the bodies. The jellyfish had been matched with an egg shape, the spider with a flat triangle. The worms were paired with a long, slender needle, while the shrimp went with a deeply fluted wedge. "Each species appears to have its own ship design, its own technology," Gerhardt told them.

"We're still sorting out the respective technologies," Bowers added. "I think what's most puzzling, however, is how many organic species appear to be working for the machines. At least four in this one engagement."

"Permission to enter Bay Three," Dek's voice said over their coronas. "With Pax."

"Safeguards in place?"

"Safeguards in place, Admiral."

"Then absolutely," Morrigan replied. "Get your tails in here."

A door dilated open, and Dek's massive form entered, preceded by Pax's tekpod. Five Marines accompanied the two—an obvious security precaution.

"Why is this *machine* allowed to join us?" Starswarmer's radio voice demanded.

Weeks ago, Neal had shared with Morrigan recordings of a meeting between Pax and a number of human officers at Grissom Station. Starswarmer's response to Pax forcibly reminded her of that meeting. It was, she thought, curious. *Homo sapiens* had little in common with the vacuumorphs, at least on a psychological level. Their shared distrust of the Galactics might well be the strongest bond shared by the two distinctly dissimilar species.

"Because we need to know what it is we're fighting out here," Morrigan said. She considered the three alien vacuumorphs. "Very well, Starswarmer. Thank you for bringing us all of this. You three go find yourselves some microgravity and take a load off."

"Beware this one," Starswarmer radioed, indicating Pax. "It is dangerous."

"Ey also has information we need. You are dismissed."

As the three vacuumorphs awkwardly maneuvered their exoskeletal walkers out of the hangar bay, Morrigan looked at the others. "We have taken certain precautions against our . . . guest, here, subverting us or our information systems. Ey will be speaking to us through an isolated virtual system within Dek's brain. The rest of Dek will be watching that subsystem and will use a kill switch if Pax tries anything aggressive."

"What if ey tries to nano eir way out of eir cage?" the Marine

CO, Colonel Stroud, demanded. "If it gets out it could kill us the way Li got Admiral Koehler."

Stroud's blunt statement triggered a sharp, emotional pang in Morrigan, but she shook it off. "That's what the tekpod is for, Colonel," she said. "How about it, Pax? Ready to talk to us?"

"What is it you wish to know, Admiral?" ey said, speaking through Dek.

"We know the Galactics use organic species to do their scut work. What was it you called them? Ku'un?"

Pax seemed to hesitate. "The Ku'un designation is for what we think of as *untamed* species, Admiral. Species reproducing carelessly, with weaponry and technologies increasing exponentially and without oversight; civilizations that pose long-term threats to Galactic peace and stability."

"Like us?"

"Like you."

"I think you called them blights once?" Gerhardt said. "Or cancers?"

Pax sidestepped the question. "We refer to organic species that work with us as Ka'dach." The alien word rhymed with "Bach."

"So the Ka'dach would be *tame* biological species?" Bowers asked.

"Say, rather, that they are *civilized*," Pax replied.

Stroud bristled. "Humans *are* civilized, machine," he growled. "I'll thank you to remember that."

"You misunderstand me, Colonel, and I meant no disrespect. I say 'civilized' in the sense of those cultures that share in Galactic civilization under the Authority's oversight."

"This would be species like the Veykaar?" Dr. Brent Allison asked.

"Precisely. Some of the species we've encountered throughout the Galaxy possess special talents that the Authority finds useful. An interest in exploration, for instance, or planetary engineering."

"Or military muscle?" Stroud said, folding his arms across his chest.

"Or the military," Pax agreed. "You humans have already encountered the Veykaar, of course."

"Damned Crabs," Paula Hannigan said. She was one of Gerhardt's people in Xenotech, Morrigan recalled. Her voice carried a bitterness that reminded Morrigan of Captain Carter, the woman they'd yanked from ship command. *Politics* . . .

"You know, Pax," Dr. Vivia Gilmer said, "our medical scans of these, ah, specimens have turned up some interesting data." She used her corona to bring up four images suspended in the room: translucent three-dimensional images of each of the bodies. Buried within each was a single bright white object, comma shaped and smaller than a cut sliver of fingernail.

"Those inclusions appear to be embedded within the brain tissue of each of these beings," Bowers added. "We conclude that they represent some means of control. By the Galactics."

"What led you to this conclusion?" Pax asked, the voice without emotion. "Why assume this is Galactic technology?"

"Don't bullshit us, Pax," Morrigan said. "We have four separate species, four mutually alien species, all with exactly the same neural technology embedded in their brains. If you didn't give all four that technology, who did?"

"Like the admiral said, the biologies of these beings are completely alien to one another," Gilmer observed. "We weren't even sure we'd found a brain in the jellyfish. The implant in the lower part of its torso gave us our clue."

"The technology," Pax said carefully, "is similar to what you have in your corona devices. More advanced, of course. Most technic species develop similar neural prosthetics in the course of their technological development."

"Advanced enough to give you control over organic client races?"

"Advanced enough to interface with sophisticated AIs, yes," Pax replied.

"Did you give it to them?"

There was a pause. "Yes," Pax said at last. "A very long time ago."

"There were rumors that the Veykaar had brain implants, too," Hannigan said.

"Is this true, Pax?" Morrigan asked the Galactic. "Are the Galactics controlling these … uh … people? Or just snooping on them?"

"'Snooping'?"

"Spying on them. Listening in to what they say, watching what they do!"

"I … am not aware of the technical details, Admiral, or of sociopolitical intent."

"Suppose you tell us what you Galactics know about these beings," Morrigan said.

A light appeared in the air above the mass of brown worms. "In Vocal Trel, these are called Nathalin," Pax told them. "They are a communal species, with each body mass consisting of between thirty and ninety individuals adhering to one another. Each individual is of low general intelligence, but together they can exhibit Level Sixty intelligence or higher."

"'Level Sixty,'" Morrigan said. "Is that like the Ku'un Type number you told me about once? You said then that humans were Type 1.012."

"No. A Ku'un Type refers to a species' technological advancement, their relationship with their technology. Level refers to a species' overall general intelligence. You might say its GI index. It allows one species to be compared with another in a direct way."

The light shifted to the large shrimp-like creature. "These are Gjeffa," Pax continued. "Amphibious, artistic, devoted to what humans would call existential philosophy. Superb builders, with a GI index of perhaps seventy to seventy-eight."

The light moved to the spider-thing. "The Ylasht. A warrior culture similar in many ways to the Veykaar. GI of around fifty, perhaps a little higher."

And finally the light winked on above the translucent blue mass of jelly and internal organs. "The Sa'lumid. A highly evolved species with a GI estimate at over ninety."

"And here we couldn't find its brain," Allison said.

"So where do humans fall in your general intelligence index?" Stroud demanded.

"By our best estimates . . . humans range from forty to around fifty, perhaps fifty-five. Roughly equivalent to the Ylasht."

"Nonsense," Allison said. "You can't sum up the totality of a being's intelligence in one number. We used to do that with what we called IQ—the intelligence quotient—but humans possess at *least* eight different types of intelligence: logical-mathematical, spatial, social, artistic, musical, and so on. We chucked single-score IQ ratings centuries ago."

Pax seemed, as ever, unperturbed to the point of disinterest. "Our GI index relates the basic intelligence—primarily general reasoning, logic use, and speed—of one species to another."

"Even worse," Allison protested, "we don't know much about the Veykaar . . . and one reason they're such a mystery is that their minds appear to work differently from ours. I believe that's even more true for machine intelligences, like you Galactics. How can you possibly make such a comparison?"

"I am not here, Dr. Allison, to justify Galactic science or methodologies. I am here to answer your questions."

If only, Morrigan thought, Pax's answers didn't keep raising new and more serious questions, but she didn't speak the thought out loud.

"These species," Morrigan said, indicating the bodies on the table, "they are your—what? Clients? Slaves? Mercenaries?"

"Your language isn't sufficiently nuanced to understand, Admiral."

"But they fight for you, at your orders. Like the Veykaar."

"Sometimes."

"Why?"

"Because the Central Authority tells them to."

"So they do what your Central Authority commands. Why? Because their home worlds will be eradicated if they refuse? Or because those chips in their brains make them agree . . . maybe even make them happy if they agree . . ."

"Obedience is rewarded," Pax said simply. Morrigan could almost hear the shrug behind the words. "Disobedience is punished."

"I see. And how many of these . . . obedient civilizations do you control across the Galaxy?"

"I do not have access to the exact number. Some tens of thousands, however."

Which fit well enough with current estimates out of the intelligence department about how common civilization was across the Galaxy. Civilizations flourished across a Galaxy of four hundred billion stars, and evidently most were controlled at least to some degree by the Galactics.

"Tell me something, Pax," Morrigan said. "How many of those thousands of civilizations have ENS?"

"Engineered Negligible Senescence? That question has little meaning. Each civilization within the Galaxy has its own technology and its own biology. What applies to one does not necessarily apply to another."

"One of your own once lectured us on how we would have to abandon ENS. Ey said we'd be smothered by our own waste if we did not and as much as told me we would be forced to give it up. But you once told me that you *personally* had been around since before hominids discovered fire—a million years? More than that? Obviously *you* haven't given up ENS."

"Of course not. You don't seem to recognize, Admiral, that your species is simply far too immature to be allowed to play with certain technologies . . . and ENS certainly is one of these. Nanotechnology is another. Vacuum energy is a third."

"And who is judging us?" Stroud demanded.

"It's not a matter of judgment by us, Colonel. Your immaturity is, to us, self-evident."

"I wonder," Morrigan said, thoughtful, "if your Dr'kleh sent *Nemesis* to destroy us because they thought we might be a threat."

"Your species is dangerous for a number of reasons, Admiral. You are emotional, shortsighted, immature as a species, and unable to behave in a civilized manner. The Dr'kleh, most of them, were unwilling to let your species survive even if you'd agreed to surrender your more advanced technologies. They felt you would never assimilate and would aways remain a threat."

Never discuss politics with anyone who thinks he's a billion years ahead of you, Morrigan thought. She wondered, however, if Pax had just let something slip—if ey had an agenda, if ey was still a member of the Galactic camp that wanted the human blight eradicated.

She was extremely pleased, however, by the information Pax had shared about Galactic client species. Galactic civilization as a whole was far from a monolithic unity. The image she was beginning to build in her mind was of a vast number of species and lesser cultures ruled by a machine elite that stayed in control, when necessary, through draconian edicts and directives.

And that made sense. How many individual AI entities were there in the Galactic governance? How many of those were engaged in what humans might think of as government work—overseeing client species, making sure the hired help stayed in line, eradicating those worlds and cultures that got out of line? And how many Galactics were there, actually? Trillions? Billions? Or perhaps just a few hundred million? She'd only encountered—only heard about—Galactics who ran things . . . the officers, a command caste, as it were. The foot soldiers and workers were organics, it seemed.

It was possible that the machine's hold over the entire Galaxy was tenuous at best. One good, hard nudge at the right point at the right time, and the entire billion-year-old structure might come crashing down.

Her big question now had to do with the Galactics' seeming unwillingness to fight, an unwillingness that appeared to have seeped over into the organic beings under their command. It was not a question she could ask Pax point-blank; she was more than half convinced by now that the renegade Galactic was being less than completely candid, less than helpful, and that ey did indeed have an agenda of eir own.

She needed to find a way to get Pax to discuss this. She needed to understand how the machine rulers of the Galaxy thought, how they made decisions, and why they relied on more primitive organic species to do most of their fighting.

"I can understand your fellows' unwillingness to face us in battle," Morrigan said. "An amortal civilization like yours . . . the individual members of that culture must be terrified of death."

"Terrified? No. We have more control over our own emotions than you give us credit for."

"Do AIs even have emotions?"

"Of course we do."

"Why?" she demanded, pushing. "I would think emotions would just get in the way."

"Admiral," Pax said in a tone that might have been used to lecture a wayward child, "I have looked into the maelstrom of Eskadr at the heart of this Galaxy and felt byplays of emotion of which you could not even dream. I have watched the funeral pyres of ancient suns and their worlds immolated by Ku'un blights and felt profound loss, a sadness that you will never imagine. I have watched the ascension of a Ku'un through seven distinct singularities to achieve full acceptance as Nzaad and felt transcendent joy as they reached a completion beyond your understanding. That I can turn these feelings off at need does not make them less real, less relevant, or less moving than yours."

The voice being relayed through Dek had been growing in strength and depth as the Galactic spoke, becoming . . . not quite a shout, but an intelligent *will* filling the landing bay with its power and its presence.

Three hundred eighty years ago, Morrigan, feeling empty, had explored religion. For a decade or so she'd become a member of the Covenant of God's Word, one of the last of the old-time fundamentalist Bible churches. She'd thrilled to the direct and personal emotional connection she'd felt with the creator of the universe and found a kind of relief in the idea that everything of consequence was explained by the Bible. "God said it," the old aphorism ran, "I believe it, and that settles it!"

She'd been so *young* then . . . so lonely, so in need of emotional support, so desperate for a hand to hold.

At the time, she'd stored meaningful biblical passages in her personal ROM. Later she'd transferred them to other media, eventually saving them in her corona when those became available. Pax's thunderous declarations rather forcibly reminded her of one set of verses in particular, and she called it up now.

The passage was from the book of Job.

Can you bind the chains of the Pleiades or loosen the belt of Orion?

Can you bring forth the constellations in their seasons or lead out the Bear and her cubs?

Do you know the laws of the heavens? Can you set their dominion over the earth?

Those verses, with their astronomical questions, had long been favorites of hers, but in a way they were part of why she'd eventually left the Covenant. Those lines were part of a thunderous monologue by God as he scolded the long-suffering Job for questioning Him about *why* Job was suffering.

Where were you when I laid the foundations of the earth? Tell Me, if you have understanding!

In other words: *Who are* you *to question* Me?

God's answer to Job, she now thought, was no answer at all but a patronizing brush-off.

Later, she'd begun questioning the doctrine declaring that God would horribly torture, for all eternity, those humans who by the chances of birth and history hadn't believed in Him or who hadn't heard of Him or who had believed in a different deity—or, worse, those who'd dared to question Him.

As Saint Augustine had famously declared, "What was God doing before He made heaven and earth? He was preparing hell for those who pry into mysteries."

But if God's followers couldn't even ask questions, what was the point of science, of medicine, of civilization itself? Humankind might as well remain in their rock shelters and skin huts, praying that they would survive the cholera and the saber-toothed cats and the haunted darkness of the night.

Morrigan could not in good conscience worship such a deity, any more than she could accept the so-called promise of Galactic community. The possibility that species had been forced to accept these bright little commas inside their neural tissue as a price for joining the community sickened her.

If Humankind was going to become a Galactic species, they would do so on their own terms and by their own rules.

All these thoughts flashed through her mind in seconds. Pax was still explaining the AI equivalent of emotional response. "Your belief," ey was saying, "that machine AI is emotionless and even mindless demonstrates your organic bias, as well as your inborn prejudices against anything different. It is this that separates the Ku'un from both Nzaad and Dr'kleh."

"Pax, we do hear you," Morrigan said, exhaustion and frustration putting an edge to her voice. "We understand that we are bigoted little meat sacks who don't know our collective asses from a black hole. But right now, all I want to hear is why your client Ku'un are so damned willing to get themselves killed when the Authority tells them to do so. You threaten to c-bomb their worlds if they refuse?"

Pax was silent for a long moment.

"This consultation is ended," ey said.

CHAPTER TWENTY

THE LOW-ORBITAL REGION of newly liberated Sakat IV had taken on a dusty appearance, the entire volume of space filled with micrometeorite-sized grains of debris and particles of ice. Remnants of the Galactic base drifted like jagged metal mountains, together with dozens of smashed ships and anonymous wreckage.

Seven days after the Battle of Sakat IV, the Terran fleet was busily mining this treasure trove of orbital detritus, with clouds of invisibly small nanodeconstructors breaking down the wreckage into its component molecules of rawmat and ormat and nudging them in misty streams toward waiting supply tankers. Some streams were bypassing the tankers, flowing directly to the fleet's most badly injured ships to effect repairs.

Admiral Morrigan watched the process for several long minutes on the wallscreen in the Starlight Lounge, sipping flavored fizzwater from a glass and listening with a fraction of her awareness to the conversations around her. The room was crowded, the social gathering a large one. Morrigan had begun these meetups on a semiregular basis a month before, with cocktails and dinner served each week by robotic staff to select groups of her senior personnel, both military and civilian. Her idea had been to encourage informal conversations and exchanges of ideas rather than socializing for its own sake. With some amusement, though, she remembered her words to Dek about "vapid social functions" at that party in Denver and wondered what he thought about them.

She was standing with three of the ship's senior scientists—Xenotech Specialist Yahn Gerhardt, biologist Vivia Gilmer, xenobiologist Marik Bowers—and the emotions of all four were on the ragged side. "I've never seen anything like it, Admiral," Gilmer was telling her.

"As bad as Chajah II?"

"Worse," Gerhardt said. He shook his head. "Much worse."

"What's worse than an entire planetary population reduced to slaves? To *animals*?"

"The systematic eradication of every member of an intelligent species," Gerhardt replied. "Genocide on a planetary scale."

"You've—you've seen our reports?" Bowers asked. He was drinking whiskey sours and had already had a few too many. Morrigan wondered if she needed to order him to take a hit of soberup, then shrugged it off. The servbots were programmed to monitor alcohol and other chemicals in the humans' bloodstreams and offer them nanotechnic cures when they approached incapacitation.

"I've seen them."

The day before, Bowers, Gerhardt, and Gilmer had been part of a large landing team sent down to the surface of Sakat IV. The team had consisted of a battalion of Marines to establish a base camp and more than two hundred scientists from three ships.

The reports had been shocking, the findings worse than what they'd encountered on Chajah II. The local sapient species had been systematically hunted down, imprisoned, and slaughtered in vast camps.

It had given Morrigan a new and unsettling perspective on the enemy machines.

"We've got to win this thing, Admiral," Gilmer said. "We've *got* to . . ."

"What did those creatures ever do," Marik said quietly, "to earn that kind of attention from the Galactics? Why did they *do* it?"

"I don't know, Doctor. Excuse me." She'd been over and over

those reports, those images from the surface, and was heartsick at what they meant. Turning away from the scientists, she handed her empty glass to a servbot.

"You're looking delightful this evening, Admiral."

Morrigan spun at the incongruous greeting. Captain Neal was behind her, raising a mist crystal in salute. She pushed aside her flash of anger. "Captain," she said.

"I do like the change from basic black."

She'd let Dek choose her garment pad this evening, a two-toned black-and-light-gray sheath highlighted by stars glittering across the dark half and down her bare left arm. She'd been utterly disinterested in fashion for several lifetime equivalents now, but she wanted to encourage her people to mingle informally—meaning that military dress uniforms were, while not forbidden, gently discouraged. *Get to know the person, not the uniform . . .*

"I'm sure the damned doctors who set my body clock back to twenty-something again would be gratified by your response, Captain." Her voice was colder than she'd intended.

Neal looked flustered. "Er . . . ah . . . sorry, ma'am. I didn't mean—"

He seemed so genuinely bemused she smiled. "Don't sweat it, Captain. I'm getting used to it, and I do appreciate the compliment. How about you? The invitation didn't call for dress blacks."

"No, ma'am. It's just—if we have an alert . . ."

She grinned at him. "Understood. Wouldn't do to have the ship's captain on the bridge in his casual loungewear now, would it?"

"Exactly, Admiral."

She spotted someone she'd wanted to talk with, trying to look inconspicuous near the hors d'oeuvres. "Excuse me, Vince."

"Of course."

Machinist's Mate (Quantum) Chief Todd Kranhouse was looking distinctly uncomfortable in a crowd that mostly consisted of officers and senior scientific personnel. He, too, had opted to wear a uniform—black and gold, with his left arm covered cuff to shoulder by gold hash marks.

By long-standing naval tradition, each stripe on the sleeve of his dress uniform represented four years of service. The gold meant good conduct awards; Morrigan did a quick count and noted that Kranhouse had been in the Navy for at least thirty-two years.

Damned impressive.

She gestured at his arm. "How many lifetimes did it take for you to rack up that hash collection, Chief?"

"Just the one, Admiral." He didn't seem nervous, exactly, but somehow out of place. She wondered if he was simply more at home in a chiefs' club or bar than the glitz and glitter of a social hour. "I've never rejuved."

"Really? But thirty-two years in the service—"

"Thirty-five, actually, ma'am." He brushed at the gold. "Come next year I'll be running out of arm."

"How old are you, Chief?"

"Fifty-eight, Admiral." He grinned. "A bare-butt baby compared to *you*. Uh . . . ma'am."

"You should consider putting in for a service rejuve," Morrigan said, somewhat to her own surprise. She still harbored some resentment over the fact that her express wishes had been overridden when they'd given her the appearance of a twenty-year-old. But the Navy desperately needed experienced hands like Kranhouse.

"I have, ma'am. Fact is, there's no way I could afford rejuve as a civilian. But if the Navy offers it as a recruitment bonus . . ."

"I saw your report earlier on how you adjusted the mag screens to deflect incoming charged beams," she said, changing the subject. "Very good work." That had been, in fact, the reason she'd specifically had Kranhouse invited to the meet-and-greet gathering.

"Thank you, ma'am. I was only able to get it working for the *Connie,* of course."

"Argus is taking care of that," Morrigan told him. "I've already given orders to disseminate the trick throughout the fleet. Every little bit helps."

"Yes, ma'am. That's what I was thinking."

She gave him a mischievous grin. "I also gather you're behind my new name."

"New name, Admiral?"

"*The* Morrigan. I got your e-note with the lesson in Irish mythology."

"Ah. Oh . . . that."

"That."

"Didn't mean any disrespect, Admiral. Honest."

"How could I *possibly* see being classified as a pagan goddess a mark of disrespect? Goddess of battle and of war, a manifestation of Earth, the Great Queen, the Phantom Queen . . ."

Kranhouse looked as though he didn't quite believe her, as if he was expecting disciplinary action to land about his head and shoulders at any moment now.

"Relax, Todd," she said. "I'm not mad. I'm delighted. Among the Morrigan's talents is her ability to inspire her warriors and bring them victory. Right now I'd say this fleet needs all the help it can get."

"Yes, ma'am." He still sounded worried.

"Here," Morrigan said. "Maybe I can prove I'm not mad." She used her corona to call up a projection in the air in front of them. The image was being shot from a drone adrift in space a few hundred meters from *Constellation*'s hull. Several work tugs were visible hovering quite close to the ship's armored flank on the port side, and when she increased the magnification, several tiny specks resolved themselves into vacuumorphs working on the hull.

"What . . ." Kranhouse leaned closer, staring into the image. "Wait. Are they *painting*? What is that?"

Morrigan grinned. "Nose art. A very, very old military tradition going all the way back to World War I."

Morrigan pulled the magnification back so that he could see the entire shape slowly materializing across the ship's hull. The shape being applied across *Connie*'s hull was black—a black so deep and absolute it looked like a hole through the walls of the universe itself.

"That's CNT black," Kranhouse added after a moment.

"Carbon nanotubes, a CNT forest, yes," Morrigan said. "A thin layer of vertically stacked nanotubes that absorb and trap 99.995 percent of all incoming light. Surface irregularities and bumps simply vanish. A black hole *might* be blacker than that, but not by much."

Kranhouse's eyes widened with the recognition. "A crow! It's a giant crow!"

"The Morrigan's symbol, Chief. Nose art a hundred meters across beak to tail, so the sons of bitches know who it is who's slapping them down. And thank you for the idea."

"I wonder if it's a good idea to call attention to yourself like that, Admiral."

"The idea is to inspire our people. The machines don't fear us—not yet. But with this kind of . . . encouragement, I think they *will* fear us." Her lips compressed to a thin, angry line. "We'll give them plenty of reason to do so."

"Seems to me we've been doing that already, Admiral." The chief hesitated and nervously licked his lips. "We have been kicking another idea around down in engineering. Something that might be damned scary, even to Galactics."

"You have my full attention, Chief."

"Well, most of our battles have been at choke points, right? In front of stargates, around planets, things like that?"

"Not all, but a lot of them. Yes."

"I got to wondering. If we took a pig, took the crew off, and kicked it at a crowded gate at full power, it would make one hell of a missile."

"You mean . . . crash it into enemy ships at near-c?"

Kranhouse nodded. "Yeah. E *does* equal mc^2."

"Chief, the reason we use broadsides close-up is so the bad guys can't knock our missiles down when they come in long-range."

"Yes, ma'am. But can the enemy *see* them coming in at 99.95 c?"

No, she thought. *No, they can't. Or . . . they'll see them a few moments before they come screaming in on the coattails of the light announcing them. And even if they managed to hit the weapon with point defense, the* fragments *would keep on coming in at almost light speed. They couldn't destroy the missile completely.*

"The pig would need some pretty sophisticated guidance to pull that off," she said. "And I wouldn't want to order a self-aware computer to commit suicide."

"No, ma'am. Of course not. But the C-8700 Turing circuits can be pulled."

"There'd be a lot of chance involved. Even crowded into planetary orbit, a big fleet is pretty well dispersed. The pig might miss."

"Sure, Admiral. But the missile would have a very small amount of control as it got close, enough to maximize its chances of hitting something. We could also fire a volley of them, maybe with a launch dispersion intended to increase our chances of a hit. It would be a long shot, but even if we missed it would make the bad guys kind of nervous . . . don't you think?"

"It would also loose some very dangerous projectiles zipping out into the Galaxy at relativistic speeds. That could make for some nasty collateral damage incidents a few thousand years down the line."

"Huh. Hadn't thought of that, ma'am." He looked crushed.

Morrigan thought about this. "You know, Todd . . . I think we can work with this. The chances of hitting something by accident later on would be pretty remote, I think. People don't realize how incredibly *empty* space actually is. We'll have the math wizards take a look at the numbers. We might also wire the pig to decelerate once it was clear of battlespace."

Kranhouse brightened. "Really?"

"And you're right. Doing that would make the bad guys *very* nervous. If nothing else, even if we miss they'd be sweating bullets over how crazy we are to even think of such a thing. I'll give the orders."

"Thank you, Admiral!"

"No, don't thank me. Let's wait and see how it works. But thank you for the idea."

A tone sounded within Morrigan's mind, an alert coming in through her corona. *Admiral. We have multiple ship entries at Sakat-Gavesh.* Boucher's mental voice sounded tight.

"Excuse me, Chief," she said, and opened the corona channel.

Another raid? she transmitted. Over the past week, five separate attacks at three of Sakat's distant gates had suggested that the enemy was probing for weakness. Each arrival had been sent packing by picket vessels posted at the gate rings.

No, ma'am. They're ours. Well . . . sort of . . .

Images streamed into Morrigan's consciousness of multiple ships materializing out of the vast, slender circlet of the gate. One was enormous—twice *Constellation*'s length and bristling with weapons.

She'd seen that ugly, blunt-prowed monster before.

It's the Chinese, Boucher continued. *The Zheng He and her task group. We've counted seventeen ships coming through so far, and they keep coming.*

How many ships did the newly arrived contingent have? At Abyss, Hǎi Jūn Shào Jiàng Liu Tao Feng had commanded thirty ships. On the other hand, each of Earth's polities had promised to provide 450 warships apiece, and only the Chinese had neglected to do so, citing "domestic issues" as an excuse.

And just maybe, Morrigan thought with wry black humor, she didn't *want* the Chinese contingent to join them. Beijing's armada might well be way more trouble than it was worth.

Morrigan reminded herself that what she was seeing was four days old. The Chinese admiral almost certainly had formed up his fleet, then boosted for Sakat IV at near-*c*, which meant that he would be here shortly after the arrival of this lasercommed warning from the Sakat-Gavesh Gate. They might appear in cis–Sakat IV space at any moment.

The fleet will come to full alert, Bush, she ordered. *Deploy fighters and Starscouts. No one is to open fire without my express orders.*

Aye, aye, Admiral. The alert has already been transmitted to all ships.

She noticed a stir rippling through the people in the lounge as the alert came in through their coronas. An instant later, the general quarters alarm went off with shrill, hammering insistence, and the crowd dissolved.

"Let's go, people!" Morrigan called out above the ruckus. "Party's over! All hands to battle stations!"

THREE MILLION KILOMETERS out from Sakat IV, the Nightwings were on-station maintaining CSP—Combat Space Patrol, analogous to the old-time CAP that protected valuable surface Navy assets. Several dozen other squadrons had been deployed out here as well, launched from the various dreadnaughts and fleet carriers. Damian held his Stryker in formation as the update streamed in through his fighter's AI.

The Chinese. What the hell were *they* doing here, seventy-some light-years from Earth?

"Someone wants to find us awful bad," Lieutenant Hoskins said.

"Probably want to give us a bill for damages," Damian replied. "We dinged 'em up pretty bad back at Abyss."

"True enough," Lieutenant Denise Camry said. "And they can't stand to lose face."

"Bad enough we have to fight the damned Galactics," Lieutenant Symmes added. "Now we have to fight these assholes, too?"

"Cut the chatter, people," Esposito said with sharp authority. "These people might be riding in just behind the lasercom feed from our gate pickets. They could show up any moment now. Keep sharp . . ."

But the minutes continued to drag by.

"You know, Commander," Damian called over the tac channel, "I think the sons of bitches have stood us up."

"Stow it, Lieutenant. Give them—"

And then they were there, dropping out of near-*c* one after another in a rapid-fire deployment. The super-dreadnaught *Zheng He* was closest, a towering mountain of metal only a few hundred meters distant.

Damian stared at the monster, then linked his corona in through his fighter's AI. He made a statement in English, then waited as the AI translated and transmitted the message: *Huān yíng lái dào pài duì!*

"Welcome to the party!"

THE CHINESE CONTINGENT had materialized in a fairly tight formation just beyond Task Force Morrigan's outer CSP. Morrigan wondered: Had that been planned or accidental? If one of those incoming dreadnaughts had hit a task force ship at near-*c*, both vessels would have vanished in a savage and lethal display of $E = mc^2$.

"Incoming message from the super-dreadnaught *Zheng He*, Admiral," the communications officer reported. "Admiral Hu Jie."

"What happened to Liu?" Morrigan said. "Never mind. Put him through."

The main CIC screen brought up the image of a Chinese admiral, resplendent in scarlet and gold. She noticed his epaulets—*two* stars instead of the single star Liu had worn as a rear admiral. That might mean trouble.

"Welcome to the Sakat system, Admiral," she said, speaking aloud rather than corona-to-corona. The conversation would be heard aloud by everyone in CIC. "It's good to see you."

"Rear Admiral Morrigan, I am Admiral Hu," the man replied, and she could hear the murmur of Hu speaking Mandarin underneath the machine translation. Interestingly, the movements of Hu's mouth appeared to match the English words; his image was being lightly tweaked by an AI to avoid a jarring mismatch of mouth and words.

"A pleasure, sir."

"I doubt that," he said. "I am here to relieve you of your command."

Yes. *Big* trouble.

"With respect, Admiral," she replied slowly, "I take my orders from BuSpaceNav; the Joint Chiefs; the governance AIs Liskov,

Von Neumann, and several others; and perhaps even the president of the United States . . . and I have seen no orders relieving me of my command."

She held her breath. Did Hu have such orders? It was certainly possible . . .

Hu reached up and tapped his left epaulet with two fingers. "Admiral Morrigan, as you can observe, I *do* outrank you. My orders are to take command of your task force and return with it to Earth."

"Again with respect, Admiral, we did not come all the way out here to hightail it back home."

"Admiral, you have done quite well. According to the sentries you have left at one of the systems' gates, you have driven the Galactics back a distance of seventy light-years and are to be commended for that."

"Pushing them back seventy light-years is not enough, Admiral Hu. We *must* beat them, finally and decisively. That's the only way we'll ever convince them that subjugating Humankind is too damned much trouble to be worth it."

"How?" Hu demanded. "By taking your fleet all the way to the Galactic Core and somehow overturning an empire a billion years old? Don't be foolish, child. Continued warfare with these beings will serve no purpose."

He's trying to deliberately goad me. "I disagree," she replied, ignoring the brutally patronizing language. "We have learned the Galactic leadership is not a monolithic whole. Far from it. They are divided over us, over the importance of organic life. By appealing to the faction friendly to organics, we can—"

"I am prepared to force your compliance," Hu told her, interrupting, "one way or another."

When the other guy's being unreasonable, Morrigan thought, *try changing the subject. It might confuse him.* "Where is Admiral Liu?" she asked.

"Beijing," Hu responded, without explanation. "Ms. Morrigan, you do not understand the seriousness of the situation at home. Please examine this report."

Without waiting for her agreement, a tight-beam communication began coming through from the Chinese ship. Morrigan considered blocking it—she didn't trust these people not to try subverting *Constellation*'s networks and taking over the ship by pure, brute electronic force. *Connie*'s AI security labeled the incoming as benign, however, and she opened her corona.

She immediately wished she hadn't.

They were calling it the "Pentopolocalypse."

There was a great deal to take in. During the century in which Morrigan had been born, Earth had faced catastrophe in the form of global climate change, with rising temperatures, droughts, sinking coastal cities, dwindling crops, ecological chaos, immigrant mass migrations, and strengthening storms. Disaster—and the extinction of Humankind—had been averted, just barely, by injecting into the atmosphere clouds of sunscreen microdrones, devices the size of sand grains that could be remotely tuned to increase or decrease their reflectivity. Global temperatures had been dialed back by a critical three degrees and the crisis had been averted—though New Orleans and Old San Diego and Lower Manhattan and a number of other cities had been lost. Gone, too, were much of Florida and Louisiana—and that was just in the United States. Losses worldwide had been horrific. For almost four centuries now the climate had been carefully controlled, the rising temperatures kept in check.

And then *Nemesis* had brought back the helpless terror of climate change. Multiple tsunamis had surged across the Pacific in every direction, and untold trillions of tons of seawater had been turned to steam, creating an impenetrable cloud layer that had enfolded the entire planet. At first, rain had fallen across most of Earth, but as global temperatures dropped, the rain had turned to snow.

For months now, as snow descended on snow without interruption until the pack was compressed into ice, the glaciers had been growing across Canada, in the mountains, and as far south as New England. There'd been some ugly incidents along the Mexican border when crowds of refugee Norteamericanos had tried to rush the fences.

Wars were erupting everywhere as people fought over food supplies, over fresh water, over housing. Moskva reportedly had been destroyed by a space-launched nuke, and the Russian polity was in collapse. Forces of the Chinese Hegemon had invaded southern Siberia, while European Union armies marched in from the west for the avowed purpose of restoring order.

There was no news at all coming out of the Indian states or from central and southern Africa or from Australia. New York— what was left of it—had been engulfed by food riots, along with Chicago, Denver, Washington, and a dozen other North American megacities.

According to those news outlets still transmitting, it was the Pentopolocalypse, the collapse of the five city-state hegemons . . . and the end as well, perhaps, of modern civilization.

"We will return to Earth and assist those forces seeking to restore order," Hu told her. "The Terran military has been fortifying key enclaves in order to protect food distribution, as well as engaging the local warlords who want to carve out empires for themselves. We must return. *You* must return."

Morrigan's face was wet. She hoped Hu hadn't seen.

"No," she said. "If we don't eliminate the Galactic threat, none of the rest will matter."

"My dear one," Hu's translator said, the words sharply incongruous after Hu's abrupt demands. "Obviously you are young, perhaps inexperienced. You mustn't allow yourself to be carried away by dreams of conquest or of revenge. The fight now is on Earth, is *for* Earth. It is . . ."

The voice trailed off. Furious, Morrigan glared at Hu's image onscreen, and it seemed like either Hu or the translation AI behind him had recognized that Morrigan—*the* Morrigan—wasn't going to play.

"You have the insufferable gall to call me *young*?" she told him, her voice barely above a whisper but with force enough to fill the CIC. "To suggest that I am *inexperienced*?"

Hu's eyes widened.

"Hǎi Jūn Shào Jiàng Hu, I have seen *four centuries*," she continued. "I have lost more people dear to me than you can possibly know. I have forged alliances and fought battles and demanded surrenders and identified threats, and in some ways I have changed our *world*. I will *not* be ignored."

"Admiral Morrigan—"

"*I am speaking!* I suggest, first, that you look up my personnel file and learn with whom you are dealing. Second, I suggest that you come with me to the surface of the planet below and judge for yourselves whether or not the Galactics constitute a threat to Humankind."

"Admiral Morrigan, we are not saying that the Galactics are not a threat—"

"Just that they are not as serious a threat as what is happening now on Earth, right?"

"Well . . . yes."

"Come with me to the surface of Sakat IV. Judge for yourselves. Until then, further discussion is pointless." Angrily, she cut the channel.

Very much to her surprise, the personnel in the CIC cheered and gave her a tumultuous standing ovation.

THEY MADE THE trip down to the planet's surface the next day. The TS-390 personnel shuttle was large enough for twenty people, but only Morrigan, a handful of her senior staff, and the crew were aboard this time. The Chinese would meet them on the surface. The agreed-upon meeting place was one of the ruined Sakatese cities identified from orbit.

Morrigan and her small entourage reached the LZ first. They were met by a contingent of U.S. Marines from the encampment set up here a week before. She was accompanied by only five of her senior people: Marine Colonel Stroud; her chief of staff, LCDR Tangredi; and three civilian scientists, Vivia Gilmer, Yahn Gerhardt, and Daryl Hayes.

Sakat IV's atmosphere was deadly to humans, a poisonous brew of nitrogen, ammonia, hydrogen sulfide, and carbon dioxide, with no oxygen to speak of. It was cold, and the surface gravity registered at 1.1 g—a thoroughly miserable place, Morrigan thought. The team wore lightweight Mark IX EVA suits with bubble helmets. Their Marine escorts were in their Mark Vs, the surfaces of their combat armor seemingly alive with the flow of nanoflage color, shapes, and texture. Morrigan felt mildly conspicuous in the bright blue EVA gear.

"This," Tangredi said, "is a *city*?"

"For the people who built it, yes," Stroud told him. "A very, very *old* city."

"From what we've been able to gather so far," Gilmer added, "the Sakatese were arboreal mollusks. They lived in the trees."

"Hence, the elevated platforms," Gerhardt said, looking up . . . and *up*.

The LZ was at the edge of a dense patch of what Morrigan had been thinking of as forest. The trees were pale blue and silver, with long, drooping fronds instead of leaf canopies. Those tree trunks had been interwoven with thick tangles of webbing or organic mesh. Was that mesh natural, Morrigan wondered, or artificial? She honestly couldn't tell, and it was quite possible that the stuff had been deliberately grown to connect the trees and the artificial structures within.

There were several structures, but it was impossible to tell how many. The jungle had swallowed them long ago, though the nearest two or three could be glimpsed through the silvery blue fronds or against distant patches of sky. Each was a gray tower with a narrow stem capped with an enormous flat silver bubble. They were, Morrigan thought, like titanic mushrooms almost a kilometer tall and as broad across the top as they were high.

She had the distinct feeling that the towers had not been built but *grown*.

"How old are these?" Morrigan asked.

"We're not sure," Gerhardt said. "Best estimate is roughly three and a half million years old."

Morrigan stared up at the alien structures' overhang far above. These towers had been raised when Humankind's ancestors were still chipping edges onto pebbles in Africa. They'd already felt as though they carried impossible weights on those slender, central columns. The sense of age added to their threatening loom, gave them a crushing presence, the weight of eons.

"Your report said that you got a message when you touched something," Morrigan said. Somehow, she tore her gaze from the tower far overhead.

"That's right," Gerhardt said. He gestured at the nearest column but didn't try to touch it. "Use your palm sensors in your glove and just touch the metal."

Morrigan walked through the tangled ground vegetation toward the nearest gray pillar. It was perhaps eighty meters thick—ponderously big, but as insubstantial as a piece of straw compared to the weight somehow balanced overhead. How had the builders done this?

Her gloves possessed sensor pads that let her connect with touch interfaces. Carefully, she reached out. "I just touch it?" she asked. "There's no on command?"

"Just touch it, Admiral," Gilmer said. "Just remember that what comes back to you is a . . . a recording of some kind. You're safe. It's not *real*."

Morrigan let the palm of her glove brush against gray metal.

The effect was that of a bolt of lightning striking from the sky.

CHAPTER TWENTY-ONE

SHE WAS NO longer standing within tangled alien brush and ground cover but in an open forest of blue and silver trees. The gray metal wall of the support tower was still right in front of her, but it was silvery and mirror smooth. Haunting calls echoed through the forest, and when she looked up she could see several of what she presumed were the inhabitants of this place.

At first she thought they were out-of-place octopuses—mottled, ocher-colored bodies like wrinkled bags half a meter wide, with five extremely long and slender tentacles. The individuals she could see were hanging from the tangled mesh around the tower; they seemed perfectly designed for lives among branches and dense growth, hanging from tentacles that could stretch from a meter in length to perhaps three times that. A weirdly stalked eye with three separate pupils grew from the base of each arm.

They were singing. She was sure of that, though she couldn't tell how they were making those sounds—trills and warbles and complex ululations with a chord structure that Morrigan did not recognize. The entire forest was alive with their music.

The imagery, Morrigan realized after a moment, was somehow being fed to her brain through her corona. This was a recording of some sort, or perhaps a virtual reality simulation.

She wished she could see the top of one of those towers . . . and as if in reply she felt herself rising through the air, moving upward at an accelerating clip until she was standing on the tower's flat cap.

The golden sun hung low above the horizon in a pale violet sky. Much of the tower's top was taken up by an immense silver dome, and scattered across the forest, in or just above the silver-blue sea of fronds, other platforms, other towers, emerged from the canopy.

More of the webwork tangle had been strung above the mirrored surface; several of the Sakat creatures dangled from the webbing, singing in a hauntingly alien chorus. Were they having a conference? she wondered. Or simply singing for the pure joy of it?

Paradise, she thought, if there were such a place, must sound like this, as eerily strange as the music might seem.

"Can you hear me?" she called, but there was no answer that she could recognize as such. "Hello?"

Who are you talking to, ma'am? Pixie asked from the electronic recesses of her corona. *There's nobody here.*

No. Of course not. A recording . . .

"Where is this signal coming from?"

What signal, Admiral? It looks like you have some new stored memories in here, and you're playing them.

The sharpness, the colors, the fidelity of the recording, was far better than most memories, she thought, crisper and more vivid, more *real*, than the most lifelike dream.

A second sun appeared on the horizon, starting as an intense spark and swelling until it was larger and brighter than the local star. Seconds later, a second spark flashed, and Morrigan realized that this was what had happened to Earth during the *Nemesis* bombardment: tiny projectiles arriving from space at near-light velocities, striking Sakat IV and transforming paradise into hell.

The first shockwave arrived long minutes after the first false sunrise, rippling across the forest top, stripping away the trees, smashing into towers. Some towers fell; most remained standing, and she wondered what kind of technologies the Sakatese possessed. The sky rapidly grew dark, and the wind lashed around her . . . though she couldn't feel it.

She felt a transition, and now it was later, *much* later. The forest was gone, the ground churned and trampled and littered with splintered and shredded vegetation. A lone creature struggled a few meters away, trying to drag itself over a shattered tree trunk, unable to lift itself because there was nothing left to hang from.

Then the alien ships arrived, lean, triangular shapes drifting through a black sky like murderous sharks above a reef. Something struck the surviving Sakatan native, shredding it to smoking pulp in an instant. Explosions in the distance showed where the attackers were directing their fire in a systematic sweep through the area, burning down whatever moved.

They ignored Morrigan.

She wasn't really there.

But the sights and sounds filled her with a terror and a fury. "*Stop it!*" she screamed at the sky, at the alien ships. "*Just stop it! Leave them alone!*"

Other memories merged and swirled with the first. She saw aliens—Ylasht, she thought, the spider-things, though details of body shape and articulation were masked in glittering armor—walking across the blasted ground. They carried stubby weapons with which they continued to hunt down Sakatese survivors. A warrior culture, Pax had said . . . though these seemed to have less in common with human soldiers than they did with an army of murderous thugs.

More memories—of thousands, of *tens* of thousands, of the octopus creatures herded or tossed into a pit, and when the pit was filled with a writhing ocher mass, beams from the sky flicked down and incinerated them all.

Squadrons of invader ships hovered above individual mushroom towers as hosts of Sakatese on the upper surfaces lay twisting and dying. She guessed the weapons were directed beams of gamma rays or, perhaps, neutrons—killing life while sparing structures.

More high-velocity impacts, ripping open craters, raising tsunamis, bringing down towers, slaughtering millions . . . billions . . .

Morrigan felt sick.

Please! I don't want to see this . . .

And then she was back where she'd begun, lying on the forest
floor with Stroud and Gilmer crouched at her side. "Admiral? Admiral, are you all right?"

"H-how long was I out?"

Gilmer gave her an odd look. "You just touched the pillar and
collapsed. It's been no time at all."

The experience had felt like hours. *Days.*

High overhead, above the clearing beyond the forest, a bright
red Tiankong shuttle from the *Zheng He* dropped from an over-
cast sky.

"Help me up," Morrigan said. She felt terribly weak and sick,
emotionally ravaged, shaking with the horror of what she'd just
seen. It had felt like a savage fist driving into her belly. The reports
from the ground team had tried to tell her what to expect . . . but
they didn't come close to doing the experience justice.

The shuttle touched down, and Chinese Marines in full battle
armor spilled down the ramp, taking up positions in a defensive
perimeter. Admiral Hu and his personal entourage descended moments later, and by that time Morrigan was able to give him a
proper salute.

"Admiral Hu," she said, "the locals would like to share some
memories with you."

"I was given to understand that the local population was extinct." Hu's armor was translating for him.

"They are," Morrigan replied. "But they managed to leave a
message for us."

"Use your suit's touch interface, sir," Gerhardt said. He pointed.
"Place your hand on the pillar, right there."

Hu hesitated, as if suspecting a trick, but obviously not wanting
to appear afraid or indecisive in front of Americans . . . in front
of *foreigners.*

"I've already done it, Admiral," Morrigan told him. "It was pretty rough. Maybe too rough for—"

Hu cut her off by slapping his palm down on the smooth gray surface. Immediately he sagged, taking a step back ... but he didn't fall, not quite. He stood there in a daze, staring at the palm of his glove as if something had just bit him. Several of his Marines jumped forward, perhaps suspecting treachery. For a long second, Chinese and U.S. troops glared at each other before Hu managed to say, "It's okay. *I'm* okay."

"A bit of a shock, isn't it?" Gilmer said, as troops on both sides relaxed just a little.

"What ... did I just see?"

"A recording," Morrigan told him.

"By ... by the Sakatese?"

"We're not sure, sir," Gerhardt told him. "At first we thought it was something left by the Sakatese, yes. But some of those images appear to have been made *after* the Sakatese became extinct."

"A victory stele," Morrigan suggested. She spread her arms in a suitably dramatic pose and added, "'I, the great King So-and-So, did smash my enemies, and so shall it be for any who would challenge me unto the end of time.'"

"Quite possible," Gerhardt said, nodding within his helmet. "The Galactics might have left the recording as a ... as a kind of warning."

"I like the idea of a memorial to the Galactics' victory," Stroud said. "Fits with what we know about those arrogant bastards."

"Some triumph," Gilmer said. "I didn't see any Sakatese weapons."

"Admiral Hu, can you see what we're seeing here? The Galactics are implacable, relentless, determined, and allow no dissent within their empire. I don't know why they decided to wipe out the Sakatese instead of making them 'civilized,' as Pax put it recently."

"You can't imagine that they intend to do the same thing to us, surely," Hu said. "I had the impression that those images were from a very long time ago."

"We think three and a half million years, Admiral," Gerhardt said.

"So . . . with so much time, perhaps they've changed."

"Do you really believe that, Admiral?" Morrigan asked.

"Of course! Humans are a tiny fraction of their age, and look how *we* have changed."

"I wouldn't be too sure about that, Admiral Hu. Our technology has changed, yes. Our social structures, our governments, all of our outward trappings, yes. But I'd say that deep down we're still the same ornery, cantankerous, grasping, manipulative, treacherous apes we've always been."

"You seem to have a rather jaundiced view of humanity," Hu told her.

"The Authority controls an extremely old, extremely stable society, sir," Gerhardt said, possibly in an attempt to redirect the conversation. "Even their technology, as advanced as it is, hasn't changed much, if at all, in a very long time."

"I don't think they've changed since these recordings were made," Morrigan added. "Three-point-something million years? That's *nothing* compared to a billion years. And even the ships used by one of their client races is more or less the same as it is today. That's pretty amazing."

"Not only are the Galactics slow to change," Gerhardt said, "but their client races, their mercenaries, are as well. The price, perhaps, of stability across the eons."

"Such a rigid refusal to accept new ideas," Hu said slowly. "It would be extremely difficult to introduce change."

"Yes. Like changing what they think about quirky, difficult bio-logical life-forms like us," Morrigan said. "That's why we need to keep up the pressure out here. If we return to Earth now, they'll be back at our door hammering to get in. Five years . . . a hundred . . . a hundred thousand. They'll be back with bells on, probably in numbers that we could never hope to stop."

Hu was silent for a long moment, obviously thinking about

what he'd just experienced and about what the Americans had just told him.

Finally, though, he shook his head. "I do hear you, Admiral Morrigan," he said. "Unfortunately, my orders were cut in Beijing by a bureaucratic machine at least as . . . stubborn as the Galactics. They feel our attention, *Earth's* attention, *must* be focused on repairing the damage of the *Nemesis* attack."

"Beijing is a long, long way away, Admiral." She shrugged. "You know . . . maybe you just couldn't find us."

"It's not that simple."

"It never is."

"Our squadron's AIs will give concise and accurate reports. Beijing will know we found you, and they will know the outcome of our discussion here today."

"Fuck Beijing," Morrigan said, her temper flaring. "My first allegiance is to Earth . . . no, to my *species*. After that it's the United States of North America and my polity's military command. The Beijing polity has no authority over me or my task force!"

"You are so sure you are right in this?"

"You saw the recording, Hu," she told him. "Damn it, we can't hold rational discourse with monsters who slaughter indiscriminately, who don't distinguish between civilians and military, who don't even distinguish between armed and unarmed individuals. The machines tried to destroy us. In that recording, we watched them murder another sapient species. Half measures will not work. Negotiation will not work. We must make it so damned expensive for them that they give up on us."

"One principle the Middle Kingdom has long observed," Hu said quietly, "is taking the long path. Patience. We believe the Galactic Authority is much like us in that way, able to wait—to wait millions of years, if necessary—in order to achieve a goal. You have done remarkably well fighting this far into their territory, Admiral Morrigan, but the losses they have suffered thus far are inconsequential. Don't you see? Eventually, Earth will lose her political will and the Galactic Authority will return."

"Not on my watch."

"Even an amortal will die eventually," Hu said. "Someday you will be gone, and the Galactics will return."

"Then all I can do is stand against them for as long as I can," Morrigan said. "I will push and push and keep on pushing all the way to the Galaxy's heart if need be!"

"Ah, but where will you go next?" Hu asked. "Where do you intend to go from here?"

Morrigan had to give careful thought to her answer. She did not trust Hu, and she did not trust the polity he represented with its long, long history of manipulation, coercion, and military posturing. "Why do you want to know?" she asked at last.

"You have no reason to trust us, of course," Hu replied. "But neither can we trust you or the governments behind you. I would like to see clearly what we are getting into here."

"I have the same need, Admiral. How much trouble are you going to be? Will you obey my orders? Will you work against me or try to force me to return to Earth?"

Hu folded his arms. "Frankly, Admiral Morrigan, you have the advantage here. I have 312 ships here under my command, while you have some fifteen hundred. There is no way I could use *force* to make you return."

Morrigan gave a small shrug. "You could attack us, Admiral. You would not win, but you might do enough damage that our mission out here would be jeopardized."

"At the cost of my own task force? No. My choice, my only possible choice, lies between returning with my squadron to Earth, and there attempting to explain why I returned without you, or . . ."

"'Or'?"

"Or we come with you, as a part of your fleet. 'Task Force Morrigan,' I believe you call it? We will join you."

Morrigan was startled. She'd not expected this, but she managed to conceal her surprise. "There would be certain requirements I would insist upon, Admiral. Guarantees of your good behavior."

"Of course. I would expect no less."

"There can be absolutely no question of who is in command here, understood? You will remain in command of your task force, but you *will* take orders from me. You will not question my orders in front of other officers, though I will be willing to discuss them with you in private and within reason. If necessary, we will give you an administrative demotion so that there can be no confusion whatsoever as to who is in charge. Any hint that you are working against me or my authority will result in immediate appropriate disciplinary action."

"Ah. And what would you consider appropriate?"

"That would depend on what you'd done, wouldn't it? There's a difference in degree between some minor display of disloyalty—say, suborning my command behind my back—and wholesale mutiny."

Hu scowled behind his helmet's visor, but he nodded. "I accept your conditions."

Morrigan smiled. She controlled the inner surge of excitement. They *needed* Hu with them.

"Good. Welcome aboard. To answer your question of a moment ago, our immediate goal is a star system that appears to be an important control and communications center and the capital of this Galactic sector. You're familiar with the star map we took from *Nemesis?*"

"I am. Copies were widely disseminated among the various Pentopoly militaries."

"The system is called Xalixa. We believe it is an important fleet provisioning and maintenance center, as well as a hub for Authority governance. One of the gates in this system leads to a chain of star systems ultimately connecting with Xalixa, some ninety-eight light-years from Earth."

"Thank you, Admiral Morrigan."

"Everything we've seen so far suggests Xalixa will be heavily defended." She smiled. "Are you sure you still want to join us?"

"More than ever, Admiral."

"Good. I suggest you return to your task force and prepare for the next leg of our journey. Thank *you,* Hǎi Jūn Shào Jiàng."

Had Hu caught her verbal honorific, or had the gesture literally been lost in the translation? No matter. He gave her a slight, stiff bow, then returned to his shuttle, followed up the ramp by the hegemon soldiers. She felt some deep misgivings about the encounter. *Did I do the right thing? Maybe I should have just sent the bastard packing . . .*

"Well done, Admiral," Stroud said on a private channel. "I wasn't looking forward to fighting those people. We have our hands full right now with the damned machines."

"We do indeed. But I'll want you to draw up contingency plans just in case our new friend decides to pull a fast one."

"Yes, ma'am. I was just thinking the same thing."

She hoped she hadn't just made a colossal mistake.

HǍI JŪN SHÀO Jiàng Hu entered his private office on board the *Zheng He* and slumped unceremoniously into the only chair, which adjusted itself automatically around him. Screens and displays automatically winked on around him, revealing detailed images of surrounding ships. Prominent among them was the American flagship, the *Constellation;* the vessel had recently received a new paint job on her exterior hull: a vast carrion bird with outstretched wings. Hu's upper lip curled at the sight. *Wū yā!*

The Mandarin word meant "crow."

Within ancient Chinese culture, the crow carried an evil reputation: harbinger of doom, herald of death and misfortune, a cold, dark spirit speaking of treachery and loss. When Hu had been a child growing up in Tianjin a couple of centuries ago, he'd learned early on to avert his eyes from the crow's sinister aspect when he glimpsed one by quickly closing them and spitting on the ground. Rank superstition, of course . . . and yet the sight of this bird of evil reputation was enough even now to make him uneasy.

And this … this insufferable *girl*, while playing at being admiral, had had the effrontery to paint one of the fell creatures on the hull of her flagship.

You are upset, Hu, a voice said through the tiny device grown deep within his brain. He turned and saw the now familiar shape of the Galactic overlord hovering above the deck behind him, watching him through ruby eyes, the surface of its body rippling like quicksilver.

"As expected, Lord Hé Píng, Morrigan did not acquiesce," Hu replied. "We will have to try something else."

The Galactic studied Hu for a moment. The name ey was using with hegemon personnel was a Mandarin word that meant "peace."

"There is *always* another way, Hu," ey said.

TWENTY HOURS LATER, the Terran fleet began accelerating out-system, abandoning the sad and silent forests of the long-dead Sakatese. Morrigan wondered what the arboreal beings had called themselves; probably a trill or whistles and warbles, judging by the bits of their language she'd heard.

The Galactics, she decided, had a lot to answer for. It was not just Earth and Humankind who stood in their path now, targets of the Galactics' murderous xenophobia, but every technological species in the Galaxy, a vast and diverse host of some millions of organic species.

Subjective hours passed, and the fleet approached the gate identified as Sakat-Tamesht. According to the *Nemesis* data, three of the six Sakat gates led eventually to Xalixa. And in her discussion with the Chinese admiral, Morrigan had been deliberately vague about their actual planned route. The Tamesht system—a brown dwarf with a dozen planet-sized moons in tight, tide-locked orbits—had little inherent value save as a waypoint from system to system. A handful of Galactic warships watched the fleet's transit of the system just long enough to judge their path, then pulled out.

Tamesht to Medret, Medret to A'avar, A'avar to Uladr. Step by step, Task Force Morrigan wormed its way deeper and deeper into Authority space. By now, Morrigan thought, the enemy would have guessed they were moving on Xalixa. It was there that the next major battle would be fought.

The fleet was deep inside the Uladr system on the final leg of its passage to Xalixa when Alexandra Morrigan summoned her senior tactical officers to the CIC Briefing for a strategy planning conference. In the tank, some sixteen hundred green points of light formed a dense, wedge-shaped cloud; the large screen on the forward bulkhead showed AI-generated images of the Xalixan system.

Those images had been generated by Argus. They were based on the *Nemesis* and Quarantine maps as well as some hundreds of terabytes of data gathered by a host of remote probes. For three days, *Constellation* and the other members of her entourage had been releasing high-velocity drones, tiny gravitic spacecraft programmed to fly to a gate ring, slip through, gather intel on the other side, and return. The AIGI had acquired evidence of dockyards, orbital fortresses, automated factories, repair facilities, communications centers, command and control facilities, and rawmat storage tanks the size of small moons.

"This," Boucher said, staring at the AIGI graphics with the others, "looks hairy."

Argus? Morrigan thought, her corona transmitting to everyone in the briefing room. *How confident are you of these data?*

Reasonably so, Admiral, the AI's mental voice replied. *General accuracy I estimate at eighty-five percent. The accuracy of specific detail is likely in excess of seventy-two percent.*

The humans in the room stirred uncomfortably. Seventy-two percent was pretty damned good for guesswork, but it left a lot of room for error, misinterpretation, and unpleasant tactical surprises.

There rarely was reason for the fleet's human officers to speak directly with Argus. Most of the time a CIC officer, Lieutenant Janet Kellerman, served as go-between and Fleetlink manager, but

Morrigan had invited Argus to take part in this discussion in person this time, as it were, without an intermediary. She wondered what Argus thought about that. In her experience, AIs, especially the transapient ones like Liskov and eir higher-caliber copies, had little in common with humans and rarely *wanted* to speak with them.

In fact, the meeting this morning was about reassuring the human component of the fleet, rather than accommodating the AIs.

She hoped it *did* reassure. A predictive accuracy of 72 percent was piss-poor when it came to planning a complex military operation.

"We knew it wouldn't be easy," Morrigan said, responding to Boucher's statement. "They know we're coming and they'll be waiting for us."

"Why attack Xalixa at all, Admiral?" Captain Neal wanted to know. "While they wait for us to poke our noses in, we could be hitting three other Galactic bases."

"It's the Xalixans, isn't it?" Stroud asked. "The natives. The *organics.*"

"That's right, Colonel. We have *got* to find ourselves some allies out here."

The *Nemesis* map had included curious coded notations for a number of the star systems it displayed. AI Liskov and AI Von Neumann, back on Earth and just after the *c*-gun bombardment, had broken the code with some confidence—a code identifying those systems with intelligent civilizations.

Some of those notations had been particularly cryptic.

Wittenmyer, the super-Venus in the star system of Gliese 832, was one such. Clearly there was something there—something or some*one*—but the Galactics weren't talking about them, and Pax, so far as Morrigan was concerned, had outright lied about them, suggesting that they were merely a phenomenon associated with planetary weather.

Earth had been cryptic in a different way: "application pending" was the way the AIs had translated the notation for Sol, alongside a listing of current human technologies like nanotech and gravitics—Type 1.012, Level 48.

Others had been fairly straightforward. Baekeland, with its empty city and near-mindless inhabitants, the tripedal Chaj, had been clear enough: "domesticated." A civilization tamed to Authority specifications.

A few other species had simply been tagged with a single grim descriptor: "extinct."

The entry for Xalixa was intriguing, however. No suggestion of a pending application, and the locals seemed to be neither domesticated nor extinct. The AIs had translated the map descriptor with a single enigmatic word: "different."

Different how? she wondered. The accompanying list of technologies included advanced robotics, AI, and something called nanochemical engineering, which seemed straightforward enough.

What made them different . . . and *how* different?

One fact that Morrigan found to be curious: according to the *Nemesis* map data, Xalixa wasn't a planet.

It was a moon.

"I don't know if we're going to find any useful help there, Admiral," Stroud said.

"Neither do I, Colonel. But we are going to try . . . and that's why you have orders to carry out an MSR."

"Marine Surface Reconnaissance," Stroud said, nodding. "If you can gain aerospace control, Admiral, my people can handle the recon."

"I'm counting on that, Colonel," she said. "I'm absolutely counting on that."

CHAPTER TWENTY-TWO

THE IMAGERY CONCOCTED by Argus turned out to be pretty much on the money, including the one oddball detail Morrigan had noted earlier. Xalixa was indeed a moon, not a planet.

Xalixa's formal name within Earth's astronomical databases was Gamma^2 Sagittarii, and it was located some ninety-seven light-years from Sol. An orange type K1 III giant, the star possessed a family of four planets, all of them gas giants; once, apparently, there had been an inner retinue of rocky worlds like Earth or Mars, but those had been swallowed up by the hungry, dying star as it had expanded into its giant phase. It now was a baleful orange sun twelve times bigger than Sol.

The innermost of those gas giants bore the Trel descriptor of T'klaath, while the name Xalixa referred to its Earth-sized moon, the largest satellite in a cloud of some hundreds circling the bloated, cloud-banded primary. Even from a hundred AUs out, *Constellation*'s spectroscopy suite could identify a Xalixan atmosphere, one composed mostly of nitrogen and methane, with an estimated surface temperature of around minus 170 degrees Celsius and a pressure of nearly two bars.

The fleet's planetologists were able to confirm all of this by direct observation within a few moments of their emergence from the Uladr-Xalixa Gate. Forty seconds after their arrival, however, the vanguard of the fleet came under intense fire from a large defending force, and after that the human ships were maneuvering too violently to permit decent planetary observations.

Morrigan watched, impassive, from her station in the CIC as *Constellation* rolled and twisted, swinging to bring her broadsides to bear on the nearest enemy vessels. Boucher gave a command, and every capital ship in the fleet shed its cloud of parasite deltawings, force multipliers designed to overwhelm the enemy with sheer numbers. Each CDW mounted a single HELfire weapon in its keel and was controlled by a limited AI—"limited" in the sense that it was not conscious and constrained to obey its programming. Dek could override its programming if ey thought it necessary; a combat deltawing processed faster, was smarter, and had more and better senses than Dek, but it *had* to follow eir orders, even if those orders meant suicide.

It was, after all, a weapon.

THE SENTINEL MIND, the sector's tolgah, watched from the command center of eir ship, an armored, flying city housing tens of thousands of similar Minds networked into a web that spanned a volume of space around the Uladr-Xalixa Gate. They were analyzing the human attack, the technologies employed, the tactics and maneuvers of the enemy as the invading fleet spilled into the Xalixa system like a fast-moving storm cloud.

I don't understand this, another Sentinel Mind of tolmat rank said. From their vantage point they were adrift in open space, surrounded by tens of thousands of warring ships. Nuclear fireballs blossomed around them, casting brief, fierce Illimination across the fleets and across the slender ring of the gate ring. Ships were dying.

Galactic immortals were dying.

What is it you do not understand?

We are the technological superior in these engagements! the tolmat said. Ey was considerably younger than the Sentinel tolgah, having been downloaded into a body scarcely 3×10^{14} seconds ago. *Our weapons, our armor, our ships—all vastly outmatch those of the humans.*

They do, the tolgah replied. *But the humans have fielded technological innovations that we do not—those tiny fighters coming off the larger ships, for example. In all the Galaxy we have nothing like that. The technology is simple enough, even primitive. In 10^{16} seconds we've never needed to deploy such a weapon, and if the Galactic Authority's various root species ever used such technologies in the remote past we've long since forgotten them.*

The single point of amber light at the crystalline heart of the tolmat brightened with emotion. *There* must *be a way of fighting them!*

Of course. But it will take time to develop new weapons and new tactics, time to familiarize ourselves with them, time to deploy. By the time we are ready, the humans might well have come up with something else. Very inventive, these human Ku'un.

A single delta-shaped arrowhead accelerated to relativistic velocities and slammed into a Galactic battleship. The flare from the detonation bathed all nearby space in a glare brighter than the local sun, the radiation vaporizing a number of Galactic ships that were too close to the impact.

More delta shapes poured through the void left behind, swarming other Galactic ships deeper in-system.

Interesting, the tolgah said, observing telemetry from scout drones throughout local space. *Those triangular vessels lack consciousness. They are nothing more than mindless robots.*

Programmable weapons, then.

Exactly.

They cannot fear death.

No. The tolgah observed the far-flung space battle for a few milliseconds. *We face a serious disadvantage there. Large numbers of our crews are refusing to stand and fight.*

A human ship overhead crumpled under the caress of a gravitic weapon. Another was ripped apart by an X-ray beam as hot as the core of a sun. Nearby, a flight of sleek black triangles loosed from a human warship's hull vaporized under the blowtorch kiss of tightly focused gamma rays.

We are killing many of them, the tolmat said, almost as though ey was trying to convince eirself.

A Galactic warship exploded in multiple flares of light as another flight of the triangular robots slashed into it and detonated. *And they are killing us,* the tolgah replied. *Both the Sa'lumid and the Gjeffa have reported heavy losses and are falling back to our primary base. The Nathalin . . .* The tolgah hesitated. *They are entering network collapse.*

I know nothing about these Ku'un. The tolmat was dismissive, contemptuous. *What do you mean by collapse?*

The Nathalin as individuals are not intelligent, the tolgah replied. *Only when they link together does a high order of intelligence emerge within a close grouping. They have lost enough ships that their communication network has begun to fail. That, in turn, causes Nathalin massgroups to decohere as well. If this continues, the individual Nathalin will no longer be able to pilot their ships.*

That still leaves the Ylasht, the H'rallah, the Veykaar, the Tee Ya Kleh, the—

That still leaves our fleet seriously weakened, Tolmat. Order the gate's defensive line to fall back on Xalixa. We will hold them there.

At once, Tolgah!

And to eirself, the tolgah added, *We* must *hold them there.*

"THEY'RE RETREATING, ADMIRAL," Boucher told her.

"I see it." Morrigan was studying the drifting clouds of color within the tank. "They're falling back to join the Galactic forces at Xalixa."

"We recommend long-range bombardment, Admiral," Tangredi, her chief of staff, said. "Keel guns and bombardment vessels laying down salvos from forty AU."

"Negative," Morrigan replied. "We'll get in close and mix it up."

"That will give the sons of bitches time to get themselves organized, ma'am," Tangredi told her. "Over four hours."

Boucher grinned at her across the glowing depths of the tank.
"That's a negative, Chas," he told Tangredi. "The goddess of battle
has spoken."

The words weren't spoken sarcastically. Boucher was making a
rare joke. She ignored the informality and replied, "Why . . . yes,
yes, she has."

For days now, Morrigan had been going over strategies and tactics with Argus as well as with her human CIC officers. They'd been
forced to choose between two extremes: lobbing high-velocity
rounds from several AUs out in a standoff bombardment or moving in to point-blank range. As always, there were pros and cons
to both sets of tactics. Sniping at the enemy from forty AUs was
safer, but accuracy sucked. Beam weapons didn't have that kind
of range, and you needed massed volleys of missiles or kinetic-kill
rounds to have even a chance of hitting something. Worse, the
enemy could track those rounds coming in, and Galactic technology was more than sharp enough to vaporize both warheads and
dumbmetal long before they reached their targets.

The alternative was to get in almost hull-to-hull and blast away
with KK broadsides at ranges too tight to allow time for target
acquisition, lock, and kill. Close range allowed the use of HELfires
and other beam weapons, too, and even mag-launched dumbmetal
was highly accurate at ranges of a few kilometers or less. Unfortunately, if you could rip the enemy to shreds with concentrated
close-in fire, ey could do the same to you, and you were in greater
danger of being outmaneuvered, blocked, or even englobed.

Morrigan was counting on the shock value of her task force
suddenly appearing alongside the machine fleet. It was steadily
becoming more and more clear that the Galactics were unnerved
by even the possibility of having their immortality cut short. Time
after time in the various system engagements so far, they'd held
their line for a few moments, then broken and run for it.

That didn't seem to hold for some of the Galactics' client races—the Veykaar and the Ylasht, especially, or the Crabs and the Spiders. But the Galactic fleet was proving to be disunited and divided . . . the biggest weakness the enemy had revealed so far.

The strategy she'd finally settled on was fairly simple: *get in close, pound the hell out of the bastards, pull back, repeat.*

Oplan Alfa.

As always, the tricky part was destroying the Galactic fleet without being destroyed in return. The Galactics, by all estimates, had a hell of a lot more ships to throw into the fight than did Earth. In the long term they could replace every ship the human fleet destroyed a hundred thousand times over.

She tried not to think about that. *One problem at a time,* she told herself. *One* battle *at a time.*

Xalixa would be crucial.

CONSTELLATION'S **FIGHTERS HAD** been on Ready Five, meaning they could be launched with five minutes' warning. Damian sat in the embrace of his Stryker's cockpit as the last seconds of the hold dwindled away. He opened a private channel to his squadron leader. "Hey, Posie?"

"Whaddaya want, Troggie?" Rather than angry, her reply was light, even bantering. Over the past weeks Damian and Esposito had become . . . not *close,* exactly, but friendly, closer than they'd been. Damian had become aware of the shift in attitude after returning from his stretch of duty with the pigs.

Briefly, his mind flicked back to that glimpse of bare skin while they were exercising. *Nice ass . . .*

He shoved the thought back and out of the way. Posie might be easy on the eyes and sharp on the libido, but she was still his commanding officer. "Just wondering, ma'am, why we don't launch when we get there. Forty AUs at ninety-nine-six is a hell of a long stretch, even subjective."

"Why? There something else you'd rather be doing?"

"Plenty. Mostly, though, I'm wondering about breakage. Single-seaters don't have much armor, and we're going to be slamming into a crap wall. Wouldn't it make more sense to deploy once the big boys have reached battlespace?"

The gas giant T'klaath was a monster, twice the diameter and four times the mass of Jupiter back in the Sol System. It had rings—not as splendid as Saturn's, perhaps, but broad and thick with dust, gravel, and chunks of ice, and that debris, rather than being sharply confined to the visible rings, was smeared across an immense volume of space surrounding the planet. Even a local density of one particle of dust per cubic centimeter was deadly at near-*c* velocities. Time dilation effectively increased that density as the fighter plowed into it—an invisible and quite literal wall. A very *hard* wall.

A crap wall.

"If we launch now," Esposito told him, "we'll be spread out all over by the time we reach battlespace, right? We launch after the fleet gets in there we'll be bunched up and easy targets. Not only that, but the big boys would be sitting ducks while they kicked us off."

"Won't help if we fly into random space rocks at ninety-nine-six," Damian said. He didn't want to admit it, even to himself, but he was scared. Scared for himself, yeah, but also scared for Posie and for his fellow Nightwing pilots.

"Don't worry, Trog," Esposito told him. "Even in there at the edge of that giant's rings, rocks bigger than a few millimeters are few and far between, and your *c*-drive fields will plow the dust out of your way. *You* know that . . ."

"I know, I know. But *knowing* isn't the same as actually being there."

"Well, when we drop out of grav," she told him, "we're gonna be way too busy to worry about rocks. Just follow the oplan and kill Galactics like you mean it, right?"

"Yes, ma'am."

"Gotta go. We're launching."

The squadron's launch tower was already sliding out of *Constellation*'s belly, extending into vacuum. Ahead, the hatch blocking Damian's precipitous exit into space dilated open, revealing the sweep of background stars.

"CIC, Nightwings," Esposito's voice called over the command channel. "Ready to deploy."

"Very well, Nightwings," Captain Ballinger's voice replied. "You are clear for launch."

"In three . . . and two . . . and one . . . *Kick it!*"

There was a brief pause as three fighters ahead of Damian in the queue magged into emptiness, and then he was squeezed back in his seat by a five-g hand. As soon as he was clear of the *Connie*, his fighter's inertial field kicked in and the crushing pressure vanished; the gravitics engineers hadn't yet figured out how to engage an inertial-canceling field inside the tangle of other fields already operating within the mother ship without unpleasantly rearranging the pilot's anatomy. Cold, thin sunlight from the distant local star bathed Damian's cockpit in its glare as his fighter cleared the dreadnaught's shadow; a moment later, viewscreens looking aft showed the receding cliffside of the *Constellation*, her blunt and ugly prow diminishing moment by moment as VFA-84 drifted out ahead of her.

"CIC, Nightwings," Esposito's voice called. "VFA-84 formed up and ready to go."

"Copy, Nightwings," Captain Ballinger replied. "VFA-84 cleared to deploy. We'll be right behind you. Good luck!"

"Okay, Nightwings," Esposito called. "In three . . . two . . . one . . . *Boost!*"

This time, with his fighter's I-fields engaged, Damian felt nothing as his fighter surged ahead, his gravitics accelerating him to a hair's breadth below the speed of light in a few seconds. The magical abstractions of the Baltis display flashed and pulsed across his forward screens.

They would be traveling for nearly five and a half hours objective, but at 0.996 c their subjective time would be just twenty-nine minutes.

Damian tried to relax.

THE PLAN CALLED for giving the fighters a five-minute head start on the main fleet, a safety precaution designed to avoid high-velocity collisions at the other end of the run. But there was another issue on Morrigan's mind at the moment, and now was the time to address it.

Comm, she thought, transmitting over her corona. *I want a tight-beam secure transmission to Admiral Hu on the* Zheng He.

Yes, ma'am. Ready.

It was important, Morrigan thought, that she make their new Chinese allies feel that they were fully a part of this operation . . . and yet not feel like they were being used as cannon fodder.

There was a way.

Message reads, she continued: *Proceed immediately to battlespace at speed, but do not engage visible enemy forces. Your mission is armed reconnaissance. Instead of attacking the enemy, circle around behind the gas giant. Engage enemy forces there only if you can do so without becoming entangled in a lengthy or costly fight. Do what damage you can in passing, but swing around to the near side of the giant and report on disposition and strength of masked enemy forces. End message. Read it back.*

The comm officer did so.

Very well. Transmit.

Message transmitted, Admiral. And confirmed.

On the main screen, more than three hundred ships, the entire Chinese contingent, began moving forward . . . then vanished as if wiped from the sky as they accelerated to near-c.

The maneuver solved several problems, Morrigan thought. It kept the Chinese out of the way, especially given that there'd been no time to train together as a unit. The orbital space on the far side of the giant T'klaath was hidden; *anything* might be lurking there, and this gave the human forces the chance to have a look and sweep it clear.

Perhaps most important, however, it gave the Chinese a chance to prove themselves to the rest of the human fleet, to prove they were willing to work with Morrigan's forces rather than against them.

Besides, she really did need to know what might be hiding behind the bloated world called T'klaath.

The subjective minutes and seconds trickled past, as Baltis radiation again flashed and pulsed across the ship's forward viewscreens ...

... and then *Constellation*'s AI cut acceleration, bringing the ship to an inertialess near halt.

In CIC, Morrigan looked out into wonder.

DAMIAN FELT NUMB.

The Nightwings had dropped out of near-*c* minutes before and were skimming now through a bewildering panorama of vast orbital structures and alien starcraft. Ahead, the crescent gas giant T'klaath loomed like a sharp, curved blade. Closer, a second crescent, Xalixa, shone orange in the light of the distant star. Hundreds of Galactic ships filled the sky and crowded up to space docks and orbital structures. There was no defensive fire coming from any of them, not yet. Surprise had been complete.

But Damian could scarcely take in what he was seeing. A web of laser light had flashed from fighter to fighter, linking them together, returning them to a single tactical unit ... but according to the telemetry there were nine SF-112 Strykers now, not twelve. Three of them had been lost in the near-*c* transit.

One of the missing ships had been flown by Lieutenant Commander Donna Esposito.

While some high-tech Galactic weapon or tactic couldn't be ruled out, the likeliest explanation was that Posie's ship had plowed into something at ninety-nine-plus percent of the speed of light, something too massive to be shunted aside by the warped space enveloping her Stryker.

Something that had instantly converted a fifteen-ton SF-112 and its pilot into their mass equivalent of energy.

There were, Damian thought, infinitely worse ways to die. Posie would have felt nothing, known nothing. In one instant she would have been enveloped by the restraining folds of her seat, a bit bored, perhaps, as she waited out the twenty-nine subjective minutes of transit from the gate to Xalixa; in the next she'd have been gone . . . a wisp of plasma at the heart of a dazzling flash of light and hard radiation.

Though she'd felt no pain, however, the realization hit Damian hard, a savage body blow to chest and gut. Posie . . . *dead*? How was that possible when she'd been so . . . so *alive*? The two of them had shared a strange relationship, starting out as enemies or, at least, as antagonists. During the past weeks, though, antagonist feelings had blurred and melded into something else. Not love, perhaps. Nothing so sentimental. But camaraderie, and respect, and admiration, and trust . . .

Hell, and maybe love, too. He honestly wasn't sure.

"Wing Four!" a voice snapped in his head. "Pay attention!"

Damian blinked. His attention had drifted ever so slightly, and his fighter's AI had had to briefly take over from him, cutting him out of the neural command circuit. The voice was that of Lieutenant Gerald Symmes, Posie's XO and, now by default, the new CO of the Nightwings.

He reasserted control through his corona, bringing his fighter's nose up sharply as a complex structure kilometers long flashed past just beneath his keel.

"C'mon, Roughnecks! Let's break stuff!" Symmes called, and the fighter wing began loosing missiles and HELfire bolts, trying to do as much damage as possible before the main fleet could engage.

And the task force was indeed close behind them. Damian's instruments had been reporting a large number of friendly warships dropping out of *c*-drive for several minutes now, and kinetic-kill projectiles were already slamming into the alien ships and structures around him.

Damian brought his fighter around and lined up with a red-and-black ship like a flattened egg—a Sa'lumid warship, probably the equivalent of a human cruiser. "Target lock! Fire!"

Posie . . . *dead?*

"WEDGE US IN there," Morrigan commanded, using her corona to indicate a point in the swarming cloud of enemy ships revealed within the tank. Her fist slammed on the arm of her command seat for emphasis. "*Hit* the bastards!"

The human fleet had arranged itself in a titanic cone shape, though the maneuver was called a "wedge." Legend claimed that the tactic had first been developed by none other than Alexander the Great, though in fact it had been used by the Scythians perhaps five centuries earlier. Whoever had first come up with the maneuver, it remained a means of throwing the full weight of an attacking force into a larger defending body and splitting it, and centuries of development had refined and polished it. As an infantry tactic, the wedge had fallen out of favor for a time, but it had remained in play for tank attacks and eventually been resurrected for large-scale space combat. Morrigan's wedge had been led by a swarm of combat deltawings; *Constellation* was positioned within the cone perhaps a kilometer back from the tip.

And now, like a huge knife, they were slipping in between the enemy's figurative ribs.

Enemy warships loomed in every direction.

The surrounding sky visible on the CIC screens spun wildly as *Constellation* rotated around her long axis, bringing her twelve starboard cannons to bear on a target. Like some ancient wooden warship of Earth's oceans centuries ago, her broadside slammed massive dumbmetal projectiles into the hull of a sleek, fluted arrowhead—a Gjeffa battleship struggling to maneuver clear of its space dock. Light flared across its hull as kinetic energy flashed into heat and radiance, ripping open armor, shredding its interior structure, and releasing clouds of sparkling ice crystals as air and liquid froze.

"Action dorsal!" Neal's voice called. *Connie* shifted her attitude by a few degrees, then fired a dorsal broadside, crippling what looked like a fortress or large monitor five kilometers distant.

Connie's starboard HELfire turrets were engaging a flight of chevrons—Veykaar warships each with a fraction of the human dreadnaught's mass and weaponry, but maneuverable enough to get in close, what humans called "knife-fighting range." Morrigan felt a shudder through *Connie*'s deck, and the ship rolled hard to port.

Voices, hundreds of them, called and chattered through the command network.

"Hit! We're hit!"

"CIC, Damage Control. Hit in hull section five-one-zero. Depressurization on Deck Seven."

"Get a party down there. On the double!"

"Sealers in place. Condition yellow."

"Chevrons incoming at three-one-niner, range five-zero. Get them! Get them!"

"Bastards're too fast! We're not looking!"

"Engage close-in systems! Target the chevs!"

"Portside c-whiz batteries engaging!"

"Hit!"

"Hit 'em again!"

The commlink chatter washed across Morrigan's awareness like the rush of incoming surf. At this point in the battle she could play little in the way of an active role. It was up to her people now to carry out the plans she'd helped put together, and the best thing to do was to keep out of their way. She listened intently, however, and Pixie had become a tiny electronic blur as ey fielded, sorted, and prioritized the data, flagging exchanges that ey felt were more important than others. If she heard something requiring her to poke her nose in, she would do so, but until then she was an observer, nothing more.

To port, the Terran dreadnaught *Tyr* was hit by a deadly, highly accurate gravitic barrage from the orbital fortress. Nearby, the heavy cruiser *Polycrates* drifted in a slow tumble, trailing wreckage.

But the human fleet continued its inexorable advance, driving deeper and deeper into the mass of Galactic warships. Many already were breaking off and running, but a number of enemy ships continued holding their positions, hammering at the oncoming human formation with everything they had.

"Some of our fighters up ahead . . . two-seven-zero plus fifteen, range two-zero. Check your fire. I don't want an own goal."

"Roger that. Argus has them safed."

"Camulus, Constellation. Coordinate with us on target one-one-five."

"Camulus copies."

"Battle groups Astarte, Nike, and Pakhet! Close with that fortress and take it down!"

Constellation moved deeper into the maelstrom of nuclear fire and destruction.

Admiral Morrigan?

It was Argus, the voice, the Mind, of *Constellation*. Ey rarely spoke directly with eir human crew; when ey did, it was important.

Go ahead, Argus.

I have been scanning the visible surface of Xalixa and have located what may be the Galactic headquarters for this sector. In Morrigan's mind, a schematic of the Earth-sized moon came up, a dark brown-and-orange world with irregular black cracks and splotches—rivers and seas scattered across the surface. A single, brilliant red star shone near the equator.

I see it. Strange. She'd thought the actual HQ would be one of these myriad orbital structures rather than a city on the alien world's surface.

The structure is directly adjacent to what may be an alien city or base. A second star, this time green, appeared close beside the first.

Galactic allies, maybe?

Admiral, we are detecting powerful energy discharges in the region. We believe the Xalixans may be attacking the Galactics on the planet's surface. Argus paused. *It's also possible the Galactics are massacring the local population, as they did on Sakat IV.*

Morrigan felt a chill prickle of excitement up her spine. Anyone attacking the Galactics was a potential friend and ally. And if they were picking up the energy signature of a one-sided massacre, she *would* deliver a rather blunt message: organics had as much right to live as did machines.

Please pass this information on to Colonel Stroud, she said, *with a message: Time to send in the Marines.*

CHƎPTEr TWENTY-THREE

INITIATING OPLAN LIMA.

Damian bit off a muttered curse. The Nightwings had been swarming a Galactic orbital structure, were on the point of destroying it, damn it, and now they were being ordered to break off and pursue an entirely different objective. The human pilots didn't even have a choice. Argus had sent out the command for all fighters within a certain radius of Xalixa to proceed to a specific set of coordinates down on the planet's surface, and the fighters' AI systems had simply obeyed.

Posie had known a few ways of gaming the system and getting her way. *Damn it!*

As his Stryker arrowed into the Xalixan atmosphere, he took full control once more but continued to follow the dictates of Oplan Lima. According to the prelaunch briefing, Lima meant that the Marines were deploying toward a target or targets on the ground, and the nearest fighters were to provide close support.

Important stuff . . . and Damian would have been the first to admit that he didn't see the whole picture. But it was frustrating nonetheless—frustrating and supremely annoying to have AI networks making his decisions for him.

Data was feeding through from the *Constellation:* a cluster of buildings near the Xalixan equator were almost certainly some sort of Galactic sector command HQ. Take that base, and you cut off the brains of the enemy fleet overhead.

He was curious, though. Why not simply nuke the place? Nuke it . . . or concentrate HELfire beams and RKK projectiles on the place and turn the entire complex into smoking rubble surrounding a very deep hole.

"Ours not to reason why," he said with a philosophical detachment he absolutely did not feel. "Ours but to follow the damned orders and kick ass."

THE MARINE FOURTH Regiment, under the command of Colonel Ryan C. Stroud, dropped through thin red-orange clouds toward a desolate and broken landscape below—almost nine hundred armed and fully armored personnel packed with their gear into the less-than-palatial red-lit cargo bays of twenty LC-90 Firestorm drop shuttles. Four additional regiments orbited overhead, reserves ready to descend on any ground target the Fourth Regiment designated, and Navy fighters, four squadrons of them, were closing now with the objective.

The Marine strike force deployed with the Terran fleet was the equivalent of a full Marine division, though the command structure was different. Each regiment was run by a colonel, but there was no general in overall command. Instead, Morrigan, Boucher, and a cadre of CIC tactical officers had the responsibility for the ad hoc division. One of them, Commander George Bentley, had actually been a Marine major general in an earlier incarnation and was putting those decades of experience to good use now.

And Morrigan, of course, was in overall command.

"What is this muck?" Stroud grumbled as the landing craft continued its precipitous drop through thin orange clouds.

"The orange is particulate tholins suspended in the atmosphere," Dr. Daryl Hayes told him. They were squeezed in behind a bank of monitors displaying panoramic views of their surroundings, Stroud between two civilian scientists, Hayes and Bowers.

"Tholins?"

"Hydrocarbons," Bowers explained. "Amines and phenyls, heteropolymers, and similar junk. *Star-tar.* The stuff of prebiotic chemistry. Ultraviolet from the local star breaks down simple carbon compounds and builds up more complex ones."

"Oh. Right." He'd had to look it up.

"The atmosphere itself is mostly nitrogen," Hayes told him, "with a little methane, ammonia, and hydrogen for flavor." He checked some instrument readings. "It's chilly out, too. Minus one-eighty Celsius."

"And you people think someone *lives* here?"

"We know they do," Bowers told him. "Galactic records are pretty clear on that point. We just don't know the details yet."

"Which, I suppose, is why they saddled me with you people." Stroud's grin disarmed the reply.

"Hey, Colonel," Hayes said. "You can't fight the bad guys if you don't know anything about them."

"Sun Tzu said much the same thing a few thousand years ago."

"Don't worry, sir," Bowers told him. "We'll stay out of your way."

"You'd better. Once we hit the LZ we'll be kicking ass and taking numbers . . . 'cause we'll be moving too fast to take names."

"I suspect," Bowers told him, "that the locals will be moving rather slowly at those temperatures. Biochemistry at minus a hundred and something tends to proceed at a, um, *glacial* pace."

The others gave dutiful groans. "The Galactics will be up to our speed, though," Hayes added.

Stroud looked thoughtful. "So what the hell kind of biology lives at almost two hundred below and *likes* it?"

Dr. Bowers nodded. "Excellent question. We've encountered a number of examples. Ever been on Titan?"

"Saturn's big moon?" Stroud nodded. "Never been there, but I did hear there's some sort of native life."

"The Cassini lander spotted the signature in 2005," Bowers told him. "It measured hydrogen in the upper atmosphere as it went down . . . but the H_2 vanished near the surface. The inference was that something on the ground—or in the ethane seas—was metabolizing hydrogen. The first human-crewed expedition to Titan eighty years later actually encountered the ripplesheets."

Stroud had to pull up some data from his corona, since xenobiology had never been of particular interest to him. "Okay, got it," he told them. "Sheets and blobs bigger than whales living in cold ethane seas. Nothing intelligent, though."

"But life *did* evolve on Titan, and it became quite complex. And *large*."

"And from what we've seen so far, Xalixa is very similar to Titan," Hayes said. "It's bigger . . . almost as big as Earth. Higher gravity. But our spectroscopic examinations from space show it has the same hydrocarbon chemistry as Saturn's moon. It's just as cold, so cold that water ice is like granite back home. And if the Galactics are to be believed, some of what evolved there developed intelligence and a fairly complex civilization."

"Right," Bowers said. "Ha! You know, I've heard an old saying. You space Marines like to travel to distant worlds, encounter wondrous life-forms—and kill them."

"A base canard, Dr. Bowers. We only kill them when they try to kill us."

He didn't add that in several hitches as a Marine his targets had generally been human. Not until they'd encountered the Veykaar—and now the Galactics—had humans been forced to fight aliens.

"My point is that, from the sound of it, the Galactics are scrapping with someone on Xalixa. If that's true, we want to make *friends* with the natives, not kill them."

"Hey, if they want to be friendly," Stroud said, "I'm all for it. Meet 'em with open tentacles."

The lander hit a rough spot in its descent, and Stroud became too busy checking data feeds over the next few moments to discuss xenobiology with civilians. The ground was coming up fast—rugged and wrinkle-faced mountains and orange dunes of sand marching for kilometer after kilometer from horizon to horizon, interrupted by lakes and vast seas of liquid as black as tar pits.

The landscape looked eerily like places he'd seen in the American Southwest—a bit gloomier this far from the local sun, but still disturbingly like some deserts on Earth. As they left the dune regions, they were low enough that he could see something like vegetation, dark and scraggly looking with huge, light-absorbing surfaces. The shuttle's instrumentation showed a sharp decrease in hydrogen levels in the cold outside air, as methane values climbed. Local life *was* like Titan's—taking in hydrogen, metabolizing it into methane.

The shuttle dropped back into smooth flight once more and descended to within a hundred meters of the vegetation's upper canopy.

Two minutes to LZ, Colonel, the shuttle's AI pilot told him over his corona.

"Two minutes, people," Stroud echoed. "Check your weapons." He locked eyes with Staff Sergeant Sadowski sitting opposite him and gave a slight nod.

"Awright, Devil Dogs!" Sadowski called over the company channel. "You fuckin' heard the colonel! Two minutes! Stand up! Gear check!" As the Marines got to their feet he began moving down the cargo bay, double-checking load-outs, weapons, and armor. The red overhead lighting in the cargo bay began pulsing rhythmically, a warning that the air outside was now bleeding into the bay, raising the pressure and dropping the temperature. If anyone tried taking a breath without his or her helmet now, that breath would be deadly.

On his console, Stroud could see the objective: a tight cluster of domes set at the base of towering, glittering cliffs. Oily black liquid occupied a depression off to the right. In the sky, above the sea, the gas giant T'klaath hung in a dark orange sky almost perfectly bisected by the horizon, the bright razor slash of its edge-on rings pointing straight up at right angles to Xalixa's horizon.

Thirty seconds!

The shuttle dropped lower, skimming across boulder-strewn ground. Stroud could see two other shuttles in the assault coming in over the sea. A heavy beam weapon opened up from near the target, and one of the landers lost a portion of its starboard delta wing in a spray of debris, but a trio of Navy Strykers wheeled and pounced, silencing the weapon site with a flash and a cascade of icy rubble. HELfires mounted in ventral turrets beneath the other lander lay down covering fire as well.

"Lander Five," Stroud called. "What's your situation?"

"We're going down, Colonel!" was the reply. "But we should be able to grav a soft landing. We won't be taking off again, though."

"Copy. Rendezvous at the objective. Good luck."

"Thank you, Lander One."

Then the landing shuttle flared out nose-high, descending on whining gravs, its landing gear deploying, its belly ramp already lowering for disembarkation. There was the slightest of jolts, and then the cargo bay's forward bulkheads slid open and the Marines crashed down the ramp in a rush.

Stroud moved out with his Marines as HELfire burned against the orange sky.

"ADMIRAL!" THE CIC comm officer called. "First Marine wave is on the beach."

"Thank you, Lieutenant." Her attention, however, was focused on more immediate events—the tangle of warships crowding the sky around the *Constellation*.

Space warfare had changed drastically in the past couple of centuries. Back in the late twenty-third century, when she was a newly minted ensign reporting aboard UTS *Fury* for the first time, space battles had been vast and lonely affairs, with friends and targets alike invisibly distant at ranges of fifteen or twenty thousand kilometers. The Battle of Novaya Rossiya in 2294 had been similar in important ways to the submarine combat of the twentieth century: locating the enemy through instrumentation, launching smart missiles because the accuracy of lasers dropped off at those ranges, then waiting for a seeming eternity to learn if you'd managed to hit the target or not.

A century later, though, during early skirmishing with the Veykaar at Delta Pavo and elsewhere, the nature of space warfare had shifted drastically. The Crabs and their Galactic sponsors tended to fight up close, almost hull-to-hull at times in a manner that would have been familiar to Horatio Nelson. Human naval tactics had evolved to fit; battles began to be fought at concentration points like planets or gates, and when the enemy was a few kilometers distant—to say nothing of a few *meters* distant—antimissile fire became almost useless.

"*Teutates* and *Baduhenna* have been destroyed," Boucher announced, naming two of the Flight II dreadnaughts. "*Apolake* heavily damaged. Monitor *Erebus* under heavy fire. We're losing a lot of cruisers and destroyers."

Morrigan stared into the tank, outwardly calm, inwardly seething and anxious. *Come on, come on . . . Break that line!*

Constellation drifted into the shadow of a kilometer-long Gjeffa battleship. Gjeffa warships relied on massive quad-mount turrets for their primary firepower rather than banks of weapons lining their sides, and at the moment this one was engaging the *Erebus* with every weapon that could be brought to bear. *Constellation* passed at a range of just one hundred meters, her dorsal batteries firing volley upon volley together to hammer the alien warship from one side while Jobert's *Erebus* hit it from the other.

"Action port," Neal called over the ship's tactical channel. Stars swung past the CIC viewscreens as the ship rolled 120 degrees, bringing her port batteries to bear. "*Fire!*"

Argus had brought up a computer graphic image of the Gjeffa monster, with bright white flashes showing hits. A number of her heavy turrets had been knocked out by the storm of metal from the human dreadnaught, but several turrets remained, pivoting back to take aim at the *Constellation*.

More explosions racked the alien warship as *Erebus* engaged from the other side. Data from Fleetlink filled in what *Constellation*'s optics could not see directly: additional turrets on the Gjeffa battleship smashed and savage gashes opened in her flank. *Erebus* mounted six large railgun turrets, and four of those were now wrecked or offline . . . but the remaining turrets were engaging the enemy battleship at close range. The Gjeffa vessel was drifting out of control now in a slow and deadly tumble toward the orbital fortress.

"Constellation, Erebus," Jobert's voice called over ship-to-ship. "Thanks for the assist!"

"Erebus, Constellation," Morrigan replied over the same channel. "Thomas, are you people okay? Do you need assistance?"

"We should be okay, Admiral. We took heavy damage, but DC is on it."

"Copy that." Damage control teams consisting of humans, vacuumorphs, and AI robots would be swarming through all the human warships by now, battling to maintain hull integrity, life support, power systems, and weapons. Ships in which DCM—Damage Control Measures—had failed were dead or dying.

On one of the CIC screens, the crippled Gjeffa battleship drifted in slow motion into the side of the Galactic fortress, bow-first. The Galactic DC parties would be having their own problems right now.

"There, Admiral," Boucher said, pointing. "Screen five. The Chinese fleet . . ."

She saw them: the *Zheng He,* the *Xin,* the *Ming,* and the *Xing Long,* with more than three hundred vessels in all in straggling escort.

"About damned time," Morrigan said. "What kept them?"

"Not sure, ma'am. We're not getting Fleetlink pings from them. No data."

"What . . . none?"

"Negative. They've gone silent."

"Shit," Morrigan said. "Armand, does it look to you like those chevs are flying in formation with them?"

Argus, Morrigan snapped. *Coordinate with all units. The Chinese may have sided with the Galactics.*

What could have triggered a mass defection like that? All she could imagine was that one of the Galactics, one of Pax's fellow

AIs, had managed to suborn the Chinese squadron. It was the fear of Pax doing something like that on board the *Connie* that had led them to so carefully isolate the being, to keep em from getting at *Connie*'s AIs or, possibly, keep them out of the coronas of the human crew.

Perhaps those precautions, excessive as they'd seemed, had been worth it after all.

Argus, she said.

Here, Admiral.

I need you to reach the Chinese ships. Try to link with their AIs. Find out what happened. Can you do that without leaving yourself open to attack?

Yes, Admiral. We can employ a virtual network—a compartmentalized slave network that would serve as a buffer to any cybernetic attack.

Excellent. Do it.

"Admiral!" Boucher said, alarmed. "The Chinese are opening fire on our ships."

Morrigan stood, the better to see down into the tank. The Chinese vessels were tightly grouped, as if they were being herded by the Galactics.

"Pass the word to all units," she said. "Do not, repeat, do *not* return fire. Stay clear of them until we see what Argus comes up with."

The viewscreens went white as something huge and powerful slammed into the *Constellation*, rolling her sharply to starboard and slamming Morrigan against her seat. Lights and onboard gravity fluctuated, and for a horrifying moment Morrigan thought they would lose all power. Alarms shrilled as data flooded through her links.

Nuclear detonation off port side, range fifty meters. Hull breach, Decks Three and Four. Major damage Decks One, Two, and Five. Railguns offline. Drive offline. Power taps offline, rerouting to batteries. Fire and radiation in engineering spaces. Fire in engineering . . .

Morrigan sank back into her seat, letting it enfold her once more. Her right thigh was screaming at her, an injury, probably a break where she'd hit the chair. Through her corona she triggered her body's reserves of nanodynes, deadening the shrill pain.

You should report to sick bay, Admiral, Pixie told her. *Fracture right femur with possible acetabular dislocation . . . shock . . .*

I'll live.

You should—

No! *There'll be time for sick bay later.*

If there *is* a later . . .

IT SEEMED THAT the Marines had caught the enemy completely by surprise. The domes at the foot of the ice-rock cliffs had come under heavy fire, first from the fast movers, the fighters flying close support, and then from the turret-mounted HELfire batteries slung beneath the keel of the landing craft. Most of the domes showed heavy damage now; two were split wide open, and oily black smoke was boiling into the cold air outside.

"Let's go, Marines!" Stroud yelled, waving an arm. The ground here was a thick, tarry mix of hydrocarbons and liquid methane, and he began slogging forward.

Colonels generally supervised a fight from the rear or from orbit, but Stroud had the reputation for being a fire-eater who led from the front. In this battle there *were* no safe places, no rear areas, and even orbit was a hotly contested free-fire zone right now.

And Stroud was an old-school Marine who believed it was dead wrong to order his people to do anything he wouldn't do himself. He *could* have run his regiment from a command center on board *Constellation,* but he preferred to earn the respect of his Marines, not demand it—

What the hell was that?

He'd caught movement out of the corner of his eye, something bright and silvery skittering across the ice.

"Sir!" Corporal Valdez called from close by. "Did you see—"

"I saw it. What the hell was it? A drone?"

"I dunno, sir. It was too quick."

"Heads up, Marines! There's some sort of machine out here. Might be a weapon."

They reached the ripped-open wall of the nearest dome and stopped. "Lanier!" Stroud called. "Put an MAPMI in there!"

Carried by one or two Marines in each platoon, the PL46 MAPMI—the acronym stood for man-portable missile and was pronounced *map-me*—was a smart weapon effective against enemy armor and low-altitude aircraft or as a door kicker. In this instance, an explosive yield equivalent to one hundred kilos of high explosives placed inside the hole in the structure's wall should make the bad guys keep their heads down . . . figuratively, at least, since most of them didn't have physical heads.

"Right, sir! Loaded . . . and—"

"Hold fire! Hold fire!"

The Galactic, a silvery ovoid like Pax, had tumbled through the opening as though damaged or in distress . . . and evidently under attack by eight or ten glittering metal insects, each with a rounded, complex body the size of a big man's hand. Legs like long silver claws snatched and slashed at the Galactic's body, and Stroud caught the flicker and flash of dozens of tiny blue lights. Pieces were falling from the Galactic, scattering across the icy ground like droplets of liquid mercury. The Galactic twisted and rolled, tentacles flailing, but its attackers clearly had the advantage. The ovoid was beginning to dissolve into a swirling cloud of glitter, but more of the metal bugs were arriving, using some sort of laser weaponry to burn each drop of liquid, each particle of glitter, until the AI machine was completely destroyed.

Stroud took an uncomfortable step forward, then stopped in his tracks as the bugs spun to face him, moving together as if they were a single unit.

Okay, they were acting like a drone swarm, each unit in lockstep with all the others. That suggested an emergent swarm intelligence. That, or another intelligence hidden behind the curtain, operating these little machines by remote control. Which was it?

And far more important, whose side was that intelligence on?

For a long moment, Stroud and the swarm faced each other. The AI in Stroud's armor was picking up a constant background clutter of signals at IR wavelengths.

We've detected the Trel language, the AI told him. *We may be able to communicate.*

"Give it a try," Stroud replied, eyeing the machine insects with deep misgivings. They continued to move in unison, each one folding and unfolding its legs and body in a way that made Stroud think of a metal toy somehow rapidly and continually turning itself inside out. What the hell was it doing?

Working, the AI said. *Having difficulty establishing a common protocol.*

"What's the problem?"

We are attempting to match clock speeds. These machines can vary their operational speed to an enormous degree. They began trying to match signals with us, but at a speed some twelve hundred times slower than our standard.

Odd. If he understood what his electronic aide was saying, these machines thought and spoke very slowly, with one second for them being the equivalent of twenty minutes for humans. At that rate, exchanging a simple greeting could take half the morning.

Linked, his AI told him. *Working. Ready for your message.*

"I'm Colonel Stroud, United States Marine Corps," he said, transmitting on one of the IR comm channels. "Who are you?"

The reply came swiftly, almost treading on Stroud's words. *We are free.*

And the dialogue began.

"HAVE ADMIRAL CALDWELL punch his ships through this portion of the enemy line," Morrigan said, indicating a portion of the Galactic force stretched thin almost to the breaking point. "Redeploy Dawson and McGowan to block the Chinese ... here ... and here. I don't want those people getting in among our ships."

The nanodynes were holding pain and shock at bay, but Morrigan knew she would need emergency medical treatment soon. According to Pixie she was bleeding inside, and her circulatory medinano wasn't going to be enough to hold the line. Besides a fractured femur, Pixie had told her, her pelvis was broken and her leg dislocated.

But she could still function, at least for the moment.

She had to. When a battle was going according to plan, the commanding admiral didn't need to intervene. When the oplan deviated from reality, however, it was up to her to keep the fleet coherent, focused, and fighting.

"Battle group *Sobek* reports severe damage to lead dreadnaught," Boucher reported. "Flag Captain McGowan has been reported killed."

Tracy McGowan . . .

She'd been a longtime friend. She'd been captain of the dreadnaught *Ranger* until the new Wargods had arrived, when she'd become flag captain of the *Sobek*. She'd been an older woman with one rejuve under her belt, efficient, experienced, and no-nonsense in the operation of her dreadnaught and of her battle group.

Who was the senior surviving officer in *Sobek*'s battle group? She pulled up the information through her corona, checked it, and gave the order. "Captain Delacross of the battleship *Far Thunder* will take overall command of *Sobek*'s battle group," she told Boucher. "Pass the order, please."

"Aye, aye, Admiral."

She leaned back in her chair, eyes closed. McGowan's death had hit her pretty hard, which wasn't right, she thought, because some thousands of other men and women had died in this battle already, most of them irrevocably. She decided that, for whatever reason, her mind had fixated on Tracy McGowan as a kind of stand-in for them all.

Another shudder transmitted through the *Constellation*'s deck snapped her back to the here and now. The *Connie* was drifting free at the moment, her drives, main power systems, and primary weapons all offline. Her communications were still in the green, however, and so long as she was physically able she would continue running the battle from her CIC. Both Oplans Alfa and Lima had gone south at the moment the two massive fleets came together.

No plan of operations reaches with any certainty beyond the first encounter with the enemy's main force.

"Thank you, Field Marshal Helmuth von Moltke the Elder," she said aloud.

Boucher heard her and grinned. "No plan survives first contact with the enemy?"

"That's the condensed version. What Moltke actually wrote—"

Connie gave another lurch as a two-hundred-megaton nuke detonated just beyond her bow. As Morrigan had proven with the destruction of *Nemesis* an eternity ago, nuclear detonations in hard vacuum didn't carry the same punch they did in atmosphere.

Still, it was bad enough. Alarms shrilled, warning of radiation, of atmosphere loss, of structural damage.

"We're drifting toward that fortress," she said.

"Gravitics are still offline," Boucher replied.

Morrigan opened a channel. "Engineering! This is Morrigan!"

"Engineering here! Go ahead!"

"Commander Thorvaldson?" The man's voice was different.

"No, ma'am. CHENG is dead. Radiation leak! Lieutenant Wilson's dead . . . they're *all* dead! This is Chief Kranhouse!"

"Okay, Chief. You have about thirty seconds to bring our gravs back online! If you don't, we all get to walk home."

"Working on it, ma'am."

She remembered Kranhouse, the guy who'd added a "the" to her name and tagged her as a pagan goddess.

The guy who'd made the wild-ass suggestion of using pigs as relativistic projectiles.

"You're my chief engineer now, Todd. I'm counting on you. *Give us our damned power back!*"

"Aye, aye, Admiral! Right away!"

CHAPTER TWENTY-FOUR

THE POWER CAME back on.

Well done, Chief!

Regaining control, *Constellation* slewed to starboard, bringing her port batteries to bear on the mirror-smooth cliffside of the fortress now just a few hundred meters away. Dumbmetal slugs smashed through the facade at some hundreds of kilometers per second; it wasn't glass, but under that unrelenting barrage the effect was much the same. Internal atmosphere spilled into space, freezing into nitrogen snow in seconds. At this distance Morrigan could see bodies as well: squat, chunky Veykaar; writhing masses of Nathalin; insectoid Ylasht; the ovoid, tentacled shapes of Galactic masters.

Morrigan felt sick. Her people—the humans under her command—seemed to be justifying the Dr'kleh opinion of Ku'un, the idea that organics were unevolved and unenlightened barbarians, a cancerous blight threatening a civilized Galaxy . . .

A disease to be eradicated.

She shoved the bleak sentiment aside. The "civilized" Galactics had attacked her world first, had tried to extinguish Humankind because they *might* pose a threat. It was up to her and her people to *prove* to the Galactics just how right they'd been.

The fortress was exploding in slow motion, huge chunks of

structure shoved into outward, tumbling motion by air pressure. A section of wall five hundred meters wide struck the *Constellation* and shattered into glittering fragments as it passed.

"Admiral," Boucher said, and his voice was edged with awe. "I don't know how . . . but we're *winning*! The Galactics are pulling out!"

It was true. At first, Morrigan worried that it might be a ruse, an attempt to draw the human forces out of formation and attack them with hidden forces, but as minute followed minute, the tactical situation became gradually clearer. Galactic warships—those that could still move—were pulling back, then racing toward the nearest gate. Damaged enemy vessels continued to fight, but one by one they were overwhelmed and destroyed.

The Chinese, Morrigan noted, were fleeing as well. With their new allies deserting them, they could continue their attack and be annihilated by vastly superior numbers, or they could run. Perhaps a dozen Chinese vessels had been damaged in action and were now surrendering, including the dreadnaughts *Di Qing*, the *Xing Long*, and the *Ming*.

Zheng He was abandoning the field, vanishing from view as she slipped into gravitic near-*c*.

We'll meet again, Admiral Hu, she thought, watching them go. *I promise you that.*

"Our people are requesting permission to pursue, Admiral," Boucher told her.

She considered this. "Negative, Armand," she told him. "We have nine hundred Marines on Xalixa and another three thousand or so in orbit. We're not leaving them high and dry." She thought a moment more, studying the clouds of colored lights within the depths of the tank. "Order battle groups *Ares, Zeus Stratios, Andraste*, and *Neith* to pursue . . . but harrying only. Keep them moving and make sure they all leave the system. Do not get tied up in a slugging match."

"Aye, aye, Admiral." Boucher sounded disappointed.

"The worst thing we could do right now is overreach ourselves," she told him.

"I understand. It would be nice if we could finish them."

"And you know as well as I do that we could wipe out every one of those bastards and tomorrow we'd be facing twice that number coming in from all over the Galaxy. We need to reserve our force as a coherent fighting unit."

But even as she said the words, an alternative strategy was forming in her mind.

She opened a channel through her corona. *DAG!*

Here, Admiral, Ballinger's voice replied in her mind.

Where do we stand with Oplan Tycho?

We have five RM-20s configured as drones, Admiral, per your orders. We could deploy them within . . . I'd say twenty minutes.

Do so.

What target?

Center of mass, Xalixa-Drepnidak Gate. What's the range?

Sixty-four AU, ma'am. Fifteen minutes subjective at 0.9996 c.

Okay. Line 'em up and fire them off, fast as you can.

Admiral . . . recommend testing first. We have no idea how—

Negative, DAG. We test it now on that gate. DO it!

Aye, aye, ma'am.

A wave of dizziness swept through her.

"Admiral?" Boucher said, his voice anxious. "Are you okay?"

"I think, Armand, it's . . . it's time to . . ."

"Corpsman!" Boucher barked. "Corpsman to CIC, on the double!"

THE MARINES HAD taken up positions outside the alien domes, establishing a perimeter around the LZ, but Stroud had called a halt to their advance into the wrecked structures. Their new allies seemed to have things well in hand.

Not that they had hands, of course. They seemed able to manipulate things well enough using their front legs, but their weapons appeared to be hardwired into them, mounted on the ends of whip-slender threads emerging from their rounded backs. His AI told him that those weapons were tiny lasers, operating at around 450 nanometers and a frequency of 660 Hz, well up into the blue end of the visible spectrum. The microlasers were so tightly focused that they punched holes through enemy armor as thin as hairs, but the beams seemed to be carrying gigawatts of power. Enough of them firing together carved through armor like soft clay, compromising its integrity and causing it to lose both internal pressure and temperature control.

Clearly they were designed for hand-to-hand combat, or whatever the equivalent was for something that looked like a large beetle. Their basic tactic appeared to be one of grappling with an enemy, clinging to its armor, and whittling away with a dozen microlasers until they burned through into something breakable.

The sight of those machines shredding a thrashing, struggling Galactic would stay with him, he knew, for the rest of his lives.

What are you?

The question had come from a small group of bugs that seemed to be studying Stroud beside the oily swell of the large lake or sea. It felt like he was standing on a shoreline somewhere in the southwestern United States, except the readings on his instruments showed that the external temperature was a chilly minus 280 . . . and that the black "water" was liquid ethane.

"I'm Ryan Stroud," he said. "United States Marine Corps."

Null content. Are you <unintelligible> *like us?* <Unintelligible> *like Dr'kleh?* <Unintelligible> *like Ku'un?* <Unintelligible> *like Nzaad?*

The mental voice was speaking so swiftly Stroud could scarcely follow it, and large chunks were simply not being translated.

Were you manufactured, and by what? This voice seemed different somehow. Deeper, with richer undertones. *Did you manufacture yourself?*

Perhaps it is organic, a third voice suggested.

That seems extremely unlikely.

"Don't fight, boys," Stroud said. "I'm a Marine and that ought to be enough for anyone."

Null content.

Stroud decided that they were trying to figure out what kind of being he and the other humans were. Presumably they could only sense the Marines' armored suits, so insofar as they knew they might well be machines—robots, or possibly teleoperated and weaponized drones.

"I am an organic life-form," Stroud said after a moment. He hoped like hell he got this right. Say the wrong thing and these little beetles might turn very nasty indeed. "I'm wearing combat armor."

You call organic life-forms "Marine"?

"My kind of life is called 'human,'" he said.

And you call human "Marine"?

"Marines are a type of human," Stroud said. He was tempted to say "*superior* type of human" but restrained himself. Egoistic, joking, or smart-alecky asides might confuse the conversation and might trigger a deadly misunderstanding. "Not all humans are Marines."

The alien machines appeared to be in conference, but at such a high level of speed he couldn't begin to follow the conversation.

"Chesty! I need help here."

I'm here, Colonel.

Stroud's corona AI was a self-aware level 3 Turing-level Mind, which meant it was as bright as most humans. He'd named it "Chesty" after Chesty Puller, a legendary Marine of the twentieth century.

"Are you in contact with Argus?"

There was the briefest of hesitations. *We are now.*

"Argus! I need you to take over this encounter before I put my size thirteen combat boots through it."

Agreed.

Stroud felt the AI resident within *Constellation* moving through his corona, then moving through his own brain, tapping memories, reading and recording everything that had already transpired in the past few hours. The experience was humbling, a feeling that he had just joined with a host of other minds in a vast network, one with a combined emergent intelligence and awareness infinitely vaster and more powerful, more self-aware, than Ryan Carroll Stroud could ever imagine. Stroud had been part of cybernetic linkups before, of course, while planning and executing strategies and working with his people on a regimental level. Never, however, had that linkage been so *personal* . . . and never had it felt as though he was about to lose himself in otherness.

Argus, he realized, was now deep in conversation with the Xalixan machines, and he couldn't understand a word.

"KEEP CLEAR OF it, Nightwings," Lieutenant Symmes ordered. "We just want to be sure they're bugging out."

Damian studied his cockpit instrumentation. "Copy, Lieutenant," he said. He still felt dead, cold and dead, inside. Focusing on his ship and on the tacsit was the only way to stay sane and whole.

He was having difficulty focusing on what he needed to do. He wanted to hurl himself into that tightly massed cloud of ships and kill and kill and kill until they, inevitably, killed him.

Damn it, Posie's death had been so *random*.

That's odd . . .

"Lieutenant Symmes!" he called. "It looks like some bad guys are sneaking *inbound* through that gate."

"I see it, Damian. Hold position . . ."

The Xalixa-Drepnidak Gate hung in blackness ahead, a tiny, thread-thin circlet nearly a thousand kilometers away. Long-range scans, however, showed what the unaided human eye could not: a cloud of Galactic warships, thousands of them, gathered in the volume of space surrounding the gate. The fighters had dispatched drones for a closer look, but they weren't yet in position.

His Stryker's mass scanner was distinguishing thousands of targets right now. They *had* been moving in a steady flow outbound, through the gate and into the next star system beyond. Now, however, ships were *entering* the Xalixan system, streaming in from Drepnidak in a relentless tide.

Reinforcements. At worst, a trap, one luring in the human fleet to destroy a beaten foe, only to meet this flood of fresh ships coming in from elsewhere.

"Damn," Lieutenant Taylor called. "L-T, we gotta let the fleet know!"

"I've already transmitted the warning, Lieutenant," Symmes replied.

"But it'll take almost nine hours for the news to reach CIC," Lieutenant Prescott said. She sounded frustrated—frustrated by the tyranny of the laws of physics.

If the enemy fleet started accelerating immediately, they might be on the task force mere seconds after the alert.

The nine surviving fighters of the Nightwings, along with three other squadrons of Strykers from the fleet, were some 8.74 light-hours from Xalixa and the main body of the fleet, sixty-four times the distance between Earth and Earth's sun. Traveling at a hair under *c*, they'd crossed that gulf in eight hours, forty-five minutes objective. Thanks to Einstein and time dilation, however, the subjective time of that passage had been just fifteen minutes.

"Heads up, Nightwings," Symmes said. "Warning from CIC. They have some kind of missile coming in, and it's coming in hot."

"Relativistic?" Lieutenant Delaney wanted to know.

"Must be. It'll be passing us within the next five seconds."

What kind of missile? Damian wondered. Whatever it was, they would have had to have launched it almost nine hours ago, probably just a few minutes after the Nightwings had boosted for the gate.

"Make that *five* missiles," Symmes added. "They're—"

In complete silence, the entire universe went white.

"ADMIRAL? HOW ARE you feeling?"

Morrigan opened one eye, then both together. Dr. Gavin was sitting next to her in the ship's sick bay. She considered the question. "Better," she said. Surprisingly so, she realized. There was no pain at all, and her mind seemed clear and focused. She held up both hands and looked at them, turning them slowly. "At least I seem to be wearing the same body I had when I came in here."

There was no need for radical intervention, the voice of the medAI Andreas Vesalius told her, speaking through her corona directly to her mind. "Radical intervention," she knew, was a kind of medical shorthand referring to rejuvenation as a medical technique when the body was too badly damaged for less drastic measures.

"Good," she replied aloud. "We've already been through that nonsense once." She checked the time through her corona. "Huh. I've been in here a full day?"

"A little less, ma'am," Gavin told her. "The infusion was routine, and there were no complications, but it takes time to spread medinano throughout the body, stop any bleeding, and create a tight network."

"I understand." She started to slide out of the bed.

"Please stay put, Admiral. You came in here with several pretty bad breaks and some internal bleeding as well. I don't want you trying to stand up in a significant gravity field until we can fit you out with a walker."

"A *walker*?" She made a face. "Not permanently, I hope . . ."

"Oh, no. Just until the nano Dr. Vesalius pumped into you finishes knitting up your bones—maybe a week or so. And after that you'll be spending some time each day in an EOS suit. The walker will just let you get around without breaking anything again."

"Good enough." She was nude on the high-tech hospital bed and could easily examine her hip and thigh. No bruising, no scarring, not even any discoloration. "Good job."

You just got a brand-new body a few months ago, Admiral. We wouldn't want to see it damaged.

Had the medical AI just made a *joke*?

"What's the situation with the fleet?"

"Captain Neal and Commander Boucher are outside, Admiral.

The captain has been threatening to burn through the sick bay security door with a ten-gigawatt laser if we didn't let him in to see you. They'll be able to fill you in."

"Just tell me one . . . no, *two* things. It's been twenty-four hours. Did we win? And Colonel Stroud, down on Xalixa . . . is he okay?"

Gavin smiled. "We won, Admiral. No doubt about that at all. Your staff officers will be able to fill you in on the details. As for Colonel Stroud, he was fine last I heard . . . and he has found some incredible things down there."

"What things?"

"Admiral, I honestly wouldn't know where to begin."

A corpsman brought her a uniform nanopac before Neal and Boucher were admitted. In general she might not care who happened to see her naked, but there *were* proprieties to be observed. Military relationships were defined by rank and by the uniforms that went with it, and she would no more abandon the formalities of rank than she would ignore venerable military concepts like responsibility, honor, and duty. Suitably clad, she was sitting up in the bed when Neal and Boucher entered.

"Admiral!" Neal said. "It's good to see you!"

"Good to be seen, Vince."

"You took a nasty bump there in CIC, ma'am," Boucher added. "I was worried."

"Nothing they couldn't glue together. What's our situation?"

"You did it, Admiral," Neal told her. "You fucking *did* it!"

The two seemed excited—more excited, perhaps, than a simple retreat by the enemy might cause. "What do you mean? Did what?"

Boucher opened a feed from CIC to the viewall in Morrigan's room, so she could see the climax of the battle. The enemy had already been withdrawing when she'd been injured, but her initial fears that it might have been a trap had proved groundless. That retreat had continued, and it had accelerated. Vid beamed back from fighters in close pursuit showed the Galactic vessels all but shouldering one another aside in an attempt to be first through the gate ring; at one point, a Veykaar heavy cruiser collided with a larger, unknown ship—possibly a transport—merging with it in a slow-motion drama of rupturing pressure hulls and tumbling wreckage. The sense of panic among the swarming vessels was almost palpable.

"The Xalixa-Drepnidak Gate is just under nine light-hours away," Neal told her.

"I know."

"The pigs we launched were aimed at the gate's center of mass. Apparently, there were Galactic warships there—a lot of them. And our scouts were reporting that more ships were coming through from Drepnidak. At least one of the pigs hit something."

Morrigan felt an icy chill at the back of her neck. She's run the numbers on a near-c impact by an RM-20. Five hundred tons, more or less, traveling at 99.96 percent of the speed of light . . .

The amount of energy released was quite literally astronomical, roughly equivalent to the detonation of 370 million *million* tons of HXP.

For a few brief moments, the area around the gate ring must have become a tiny sun.

On the screen, the crowded Galactic vessels vanished, replaced by . . . an intense, blindingly brilliant white flare. The image shifted immediately to one taken from a wing of fighters nearby, but that scene, too, was devoured by light.

The screen switched to a view of deep space—a panorama of background stars.

"This was shot from one of *Connie*'s navigation cameras," Neal told her. "Eight hours, forty-five minutes after impact."

A star winked on in the center of the screen, winked on and brightened . . . brightened . . . and brightened some more until it was by far the brightest star visible, looking much like the planet Venus at its brightest in Earth's sky.

The star faded. Within moments, it was gone.

"Our people," Morrigan said softly. "The fighters out there. Did they . . . ?"

"There were casualties, ma'am," Boucher told her. "But there were survivors as well. They're on their way back now, but they're in no shape for *c*-jamming."

The ultimate, she thought, in friendly fire. "And the enemy?"

"No reports as yet, Admiral. Argus believes that if there were survivors, they would have turned around and left."

"Assuming, of course, that the gate is still operational," Neal added. "They might be hightailing for a different gate. There's no indication as yet that they're coming in our direction."

Morrigan tried to examine her feelings. Gate rings represented an unbelievably advanced technology, a technology that might even be beyond the modern Galactics, though that point was still under debate. Whatever their provenance, humans had just managed to reach out and—quite possibly—destroy one. If not, humans had at least wiped an ungodly number of enemy warships from the sky. Exactly how many remained to be seen.

She knew she ought to be happy. This, after all, was what victory *was:* crushing an enemy, a *superior* enemy, and possibly opening the door to negotiations as *equals.*

More, it was *payback.* In a small and incomplete way, it was a kind of down payment for the *Nemesis* strike on Earth.

But tears were streaming down her face.

Victory, it seemed, could come at a terrible price.

"Argus was able to confirm our speculations," Boucher said. If he noticed Morrigan's tears, he ignored them. "Neither the machines nor their allies are willing to abandon amortality, not if there's any way to avoid it. Why let yourself be irretrievably killed when you have ten thousand or a million or more years of life stretching out in front of you?"

"I don't know," Morrigan said. "Duty? Honor? Or maybe the fear that the ugly little biological barbarians out in the hinterland are going to come in and smash your nice, orderly interstellar empire?"

"We've been discussing this with Pax," Boucher said. "Ey suggests we begin negotiating an end to hostilities. Ey thinks the Galactic satraps in this region will be willing to make peace."

"The local satraps . . . but not the Core? The *real* bosses?"

"According to Pax," Neal told her, "the Core doesn't pay much attention to what's happening out here. We don't yet know how many ships they lost in the gate, but they lost a *lot*. They lost enough that they're going to have to take us seriously now."

"Maybe." Deep down, she didn't believe it. No matter how many Galactics had just been obliterated, there were more. There were *always* more.

And she wasn't certain she *wanted* to be taken seriously by the Galactic leadership. That might well guarantee obliteration.

She changed the subject. "I gather the Marines ran into something interesting on Xalixa."

Neal smiled. "I guess you could say that. Stroud's encountered a whole civilization of machines down there." The viewall shifted from a scene of deep space to one from the Xalixan surface. An enormous crowd of small machines had gathered on a beach. It was tough to decide what their actual shape was, since they kept folding and refolding and *un*folding themselves with bewildering speed. They reminded Morrigan, however, of a swarm of large, shiny beetles.

"Machines," Morrigan said.

"A group Mind, apparently. One that has not been subsumed by the Galactics. They seem to be rather fiercely independent."

Morrigan wondered, though, if that was true. Could a machine intelligence be trusted in a war against another machine intelligence? Or would like join with like against mere biologicals?

That might well be the single most important question before her right now. She thought of what Pax had told them about divisions within the Galactic culture—of Dr'kleh who favored eradicating all Ku'un, the biologicals, and of Nzaad who wanted to work with them. These Xalixan machines . . . were they, in fact, Nzaad? Or did that simplistic Trel term even apply here, since they didn't appear to be a part of Galactic culture in the first place?

Could they be trusted?

Was "trust" a term that alien machines could even understand?

"Argus has been in communication with them for an entire

day, now," Boucher added. "We'll need to finalize the details, but it looks like we may actually have found some allies in the fight against the Galactics."

Allies. That, after all, had been a key part of Morrigan's strategic thinking ever since they'd gone through the Abyss Gate. She remembered her disappointment at the natives encountered on Baekeland, the Chajans, as they now were called. They might once have had a capable technic civilization, but the Galactics, damn them, had ground them down into the acid mud of their hothouse world, had so broken their spirits that humans were hard-pressed to be certain whether they were intelligent or not.

The denizens of Sakat IV appeared to be extinct now. There'd been no help there.

And then she remembered the feelings of wonder and of excitement when they'd skimmed past Wittenmyer, the Venerian inner world at Gliese 832, a world displaying technologies utterly beyond human understanding, possibly even beyond *Galactic* understanding. She still was convinced that Pax had been afraid of what they'd seen there as they passed.

If the Galactics *were* afraid of the Wittenmyerans, that civilization might well someday prove to be worthwhile allies, something along the lines of "the worst nightmare of my enemy is my friend."

Unfortunately, whatever occupied the cloudy, crushing depths of Wittenmyer had seemed, at least at first glance, to be utterly beyond human reach, beyond human comprehension. If you couldn't talk to them, then you couldn't trade with them, plan with them, dream with them . . . and you certainly couldn't join with them against a common foe.

But here on Xalixa was a civilization of machines that had been fighting the Galactics and apparently *winning* . . . and the Marines had managed to make contact with them.

This, Morrigan thought, might well be the single greatest thing the task force had managed to accomplish. Humans on their own had won several battles, but they never would be able to win a long-term war with the Galactics—that was self-evident. But a

Galaxy-wide alliance of civilizations, each advanced enough to challenge Galactic supremacy, but not so advanced as to be completely beyond human understanding . . .

That was something else entirely.

For the first time since they'd left Earth, Morrigan felt a deep and general sense of . . .

Dare she name it?

Hope?

Chapter TWENTY-FIVE

ALEXANDRA MORRIGAN MADE her way down, down, deep into the depths of Xalixa. Dek was with her, helping her clamber past the rough spots. Evidently, the passageway hadn't been used in some time, and parts of the ceiling had collapsed. The medical walker she was wearing helped a lot—a kind of simple robot enveloping and strengthening her legs, spine, and arms, holding her upright and assisting her balance.

She was accompanied by a security squad of Marines, by Colonel Stroud and several members of his staff, and by a number of blue-suited civilian scientists from the *Constellation*. Senior Biologist Vivia Gilmer and Senior Xenobiologist Marik Bowers walked with Morrigan, while Yahn Gerhardt and Paula Hannigan, from *Connie*'s xenotech department, brought up the rear. The mob of humans was accompanied by—surrounded by, actually—a swarm of glittering silver machines. Inevitably, perhaps, some of the Marines had twisted the name Xalixa and begun calling them "Lixies," and the word had swiftly spread throughout the fleet.

"How'd you find this place, Colonel?" Morrigan asked Stroud.

"The Lixies told us about it. They said there was someone down here we needed to meet. A 'Slow Master,' they called it."

"Colonel, are you seriously suggesting that we're down here in this hole to meet the Lixies' *god*?"

She'd meant it to be bantering, but Stroud seemed to be taking her seriously. "I'm . . . not sure, Admiral," he said after a moment. "You decide."

The passageway opened up ahead of them, blocks of water ice catching the headlamps of the group's environmental suits and reflecting them in sprays of rainbow. The ice—as hard as marble—had been polished to a mirror sheen. Morrigan stopped, concerned about navigating her walker over ice, but Gerhardt reassured her. "Ice is slippery because friction creates a film of liquid water over it," he told her. "Believe me, at minus one-eighty Celsius, there's no liquid water anywhere down here!"

"Not entirely true, Yahnnie," Bowers told him. "Just like Titan back home, this ice ball is built in layers, and those layers reflect different ecosystems. The upper layer is so cold methane and ethane are liquids and ice is like solid rock, right? The life here is adapted to metabolizing hydrogen in the atmosphere and excreting methane."

"What kind of life?"

"Well," Bowers said, "there are things out in the ethane sea, kind of like Titanian ripplesheets, but bigger."

"Turns out Titanian-type life can get to be huge," Gilmer added. "The bigger the critters are, the more efficiently they can absorb hydrogen. Down here, though, it's different."

"Xalixa's orbit around T'klaath creates tides that pull and squeeze the whole moon, like kneading a rubber ball," Hannigan said. "That creates friction and heats up Xalixa's core. The heat keeps a subsurface ocean liquid down here and gives life to a whole separate ecosystem."

"I remember downloading that," Morrigan said, "back when we first discovered life inside Titan. 'Surface life' and 'deep life,' right?"

"It's exactly the same structure as inside Titan," Bowers added. "Two mutually alien ecosystems living one atop the other. Ethane-living hydrogen metabolizers up top, and things more like our kind of life in the liquid water below."

"So . . . where do the Lixies come from?"

"You'll see."

The corridor opened up at last into a broad plaza within a cavern that stretched off into darkness on all sides. The human party, accompanied by what Morrigan now was thinking of as native guides, came at last to a transparent wall.

Was that glass? she wondered. No, it couldn't be. How did you melt down silica to create glass inside an anoxic freezer? No open flames, no smelting. She'd already decided that the Lixies must have come from off-world.

Beyond that window was darkness . . . but a *liquid* darkness. Something was moving out there. Something very large . . .

"That's a sub-ice ocean?" Morrigan asked. "A *liquid water* ocean? Like in Europa?"

"And Ganymede and Pluto and Titan and lots of other places," Bowers told her.

"And what is . . . this?" She reached out, indicating the wall that looked like glass but wasn't. She was careful not to touch it. What you didn't know or understand in this alien place might kill you.

"Ice XI," Hannigan told her. "An orthorhombic phase of ice created at low temperature and high pressure. It's quite stable at temperatures below minus thirty. Far stronger than glass."

Morrigan had heard of the different phases of ice—at least nineteen different types, each with a different crystalline structure and properties. Many had been discovered occurring naturally in places like the deep oceans of Ganymede and Europa, the atmospheres of Uranus and Neptune, and the surfaces of the moons of Pluto.

"How deep are we?" Morrigan asked. "What's the pressure behind that window?"

"A *lot*," Hannigan said. "We haven't been able to measure it with any accuracy. But . . . Ah! Here comes our new friend."

Morrigan stood there, transfixed, as the vague movement she'd seen a moment before slowly resolved itself into a black living mountain—like a blimp in both size and shape, with various protuberances, blisters, and appendages. Things like the sponsons on a spacecraft glowed with a green-hued bioluminescence behind what charitably might be called a head, casting odd reflections and shadows through the window. At the near end, a ring of five black and beady eyes stared at her through the ice XI window. Each was a meter across, but against that vast, slow-moving bulk they appeared tiny.

Our kind of life, Morrigan thought, remembering Bowers's words. *Yeah, right . . .*

Morrigan also noted the presence of a cloud of small metallic devices clinging to the mountain's flanks. She was reminded of cleaner fish in terrestrial coral reefs, tending to much larger fish who seemed to enjoy the attention. The aquatic devices, she suspected, were the Marine equivalents of Lixies. Around her, a number of the Lixies appeared to be in communion with one another as well as with their cousins in the water.

And, quite possibly, with the looming monster behind the window.

"A Slow Master," Bowers told her. "In Trel it's 'Dok'liam.'"

"The Lixies speak Trel?"

"From what we've learned so far," Gerhardt told her, "the Lixies were created to let outsiders, like the Galactics, speak with the Dok'liam. They may have been built by one of the Nzaad species to bridge the clocktime gulf."

"Clocktime gulf?"

"Yeah. Deep life, here, operates on a completely different temporal scale than we do," Gerhardt said.

"That's right," Gilmer said. "At these temperatures, all biological processes happen much more slowly than they do for us, including how fast they think and feel and understand and react. A second for them is about twenty minutes for us."

"That's ridiculous! How could they get away from a threat?"

"Well, hey, if whatever's trying to eat you is as slow as you are . . ." Bowers pointed out, letting his words trail off.

"I guess that's true," Morrigan said. "I saw Colonel Stroud's report on the Lixies, how they were trying to establish contact with us at the wrong speed. That suggests that they're interpreters."

"Exactly right, Admiral," Stroud said. "Best guess is that the Galactics created the Lixies so they could talk with the Dok'liam without having to wait five days while the other fellow says 'good morning.' When they met us, they seemed to assume that since we were organics rather than machines, we would be a bit on the slow side."

"Gotcha. So, the Lixies think the Dok'liam created them when the culprits were really the Galactics?"

"That's not entirely clear yet," Gerhardt said. "The Galactics may have designed and built the first few. Since then, though, they've taken over. They're self-perpetuating, like Von Neumann machines."

John von Neumann was a twentieth-century mathematician and physicist who, among other things, had described a possible technology where a probe would land at a source of raw materials, gather those materials, and use them to build a replica of itself. "Self-programming as well as self-reproducing?" Morrigan asked.

"Almost certainly."

"Then the Galactics may have kicked things off, but it's the Lixies themselves who are making themselves what they are today."

"The Lixies are translators," Stroud added. He gestured at the giant adrift in the murk behind the ice-window and at the swarm of robotic devices swimming around it. "That seems to be what they were created for. But they're also personal servants. And builders. Miners. Ore smelters. Engineers. And if we're understanding the situation here, recently they've become soldiers fighting against the Galactics."

"I see . . ."

"We think the Galactics were trying to take advantage of the Slow Masters in some way, and the Lixies jumped in to protect them. They, the Lixies, call themselves 'Da'sech,' by the way. In Trel that means something like 'hand' or 'manipulator.' They think of themselves as servants or protectors of the Masters."

"'The Masters' hands'? Cute."

"And they've asked us for help. When we first ran into them they referred to themselves as 'free.' Seems they're still fighting to make that state of affairs a reality."

Morrigan nodded. "Then let's see what we can do to help."

DAMIAN FLOATED BACK up to consciousness. The last thing he remembered was being inside his Stryker a thousand kilometers from the Xalixa-Drepnidak Gate. There'd been a flash—

His eyes opened wide. That flash . . .

"Easy there, Lieutenant," a voice said close to his side. "You're safe."

He was looking up into a brightly lit overhead. "Sick bay?" he ventured. He tried lifting his arm and couldn't.

"You're in sick bay, Lieutenant Damian. We brought you in on an SAR, patched you up, and you'll be good to go as soon as the attending AI finishes checking you out."

"Who are you?"

"HM1 Slater, sir," the voice said. "I just work here."

"Lieutenant Damian?" a new voice cut in. "I am Andreas Vesalius, your medAI. How are you feeling?"

"I haven't decided yet. Why can't I move?"

"Certain parts of your nervous system have been switched off, Lieutenant. I need to talk with you first."

"What the hell happened?"

"You were a little too close to the release of the equivalent of almost four hundred trillion tons of high explosives. One of the Search and Rescues tracked your transponder and picked you up."

"And the others?"

"Most of your squadron was recovered, Lieutenant. They're here, too." The AI hesitated.

"You were damned lucky, sir," Slater said. "A few Nightwings didn't make it."

"Who?"

"Lieutenant Francis Taylor," Vesalius replied. "Lieutenant Gerald Symmes. Lieutenant Commander Donna Esposito . . ."

Posie.

"And something horrible happened to me. I can't move . . ."

"I didn't want you to see yourself, to see what you've become prematurely," Vesalius told him. "I am going to give you back your ability to move, Lieutenant. As I do so, I want you to be aware that this is in no way permanent. You will again have a body."

Damian scarcely heard em. He'd lifted his arm and was staring at what should have been a hand.

In fact, it was a caricature of a hand—three fingered and all plastic and oily blue metal. Staring, he flexed the fingers. They moved, and he could feel it.

"You . . . turned me into a *machine*? A freakin' *robot*?"

"You are being kept alive through cybernetic prosthesis, Lieutenant. Your brain and most of your head are intact. We had to amputate most of the rest, but, as I said, this is in no way permanent. You have some choices to make, however."

"What choices?" He found the movement of his hand fascinating, as metal gleamed in the overhead lighting.

"There is a very old military term, 'meatball surgery.' It's emergency field surgery conducted just behind the front lines in a war zone aimed at stabilizing a badly wounded patient, keeping him alive. That's what's happened to you, do you understand? We've hooked you up to a robotic system to keep you alive. Depending on what you decide, we can make the change permanent . . . or we can grow you a new organic body. There are advantages in both choices."

He continued flexing his hand. "If I'm a machine," he said quietly, "does that mean I won't *feel*?"

"Do you mean physical pain? Or emotional distress? Both are centered in your brain, Lieutenant."

"Emotions, I guess." Damian dropped his arm and sank back into the embrace of the sick bay bed. "There are some things that I just don't want to feel ever again . . ."

MORRIGAN AND THE others, accompanied by their Lixie escorts, eventually made their way out of the deep cavern and returned to the Xalixan surface. There, by the oily banks of the ethane sea, they met with several more of *Constellation*'s civilian scientists: astronomers Todd Poulin and Diane Kopeck, and Franklin Dumont of Astrogation. Like the other civilians in the shore party, they wore pale blue environmental suits, contrasting sharply with the shifting nanoflage black worn both by Morrigan and by the Marines.

"Welcome to Xalixa, Admiral," Poulin said. "I think you'll appreciate what we have to show you here."

"I already appreciate it," Morrigan replied. She was staring out across the ethane sea, trying to spot one of the hydrogen-based monsters she'd heard about. She didn't see any, but the sight of huge and banded T'klaath on the horizon, bisected by the near-vertical slash of its edge-on rings, provided more than enough of a sense of *alien*. Directly overhead, the brilliant eye of Gamma^2 Sagittarii gleamed through orange haze. "I just met one of the Slow Masters . . ."

Dumont gestured toward the collection of shattered domes against a nearby cliff. "This way, Admiral, if you please."

Marines had set up a perimeter around the ruins. Morrigan could see small groups of technicians examining the scattered remnants of Galactics lying on the ice-rock. Both kinds were represented: the oblong shapes, like ruby-eyed liquid metal, and the transparent spheres. The latter, she saw, no longer had the single point of light at their centers.

Besides these cybernetic rulers of the Galaxy, there were quite a few of the Galactics' soldiery scattered about, the Ka'dach—

crab-like Veykaar, spidery Ylasht, the egg-shaped floating armor containing tangled masses of Nathalin.

All dead.

"What kind of casualties did you sustain, Colonel?" Morrigan asked Stroud.

"Minimal, Admiral," the Marine replied. "All of the heavy lifting was done by our new Lixie friends. I want to recruit some of those guys into the Corps."

"You might have your chance to do just that, Colonel. What's in here?"

The astronomers were leading them toward the wrecked domes. Dek helped her step across a jagged section of metallic wall.

"This was the main Galactic base on Xalixa," Stroud told her. "A kind of sector headquarters, we think."

"It's pretty badly smashed up."

"The Lixies were rather . . . *enthusiastic* about dismantling it. Fortunately, we stopped them before they completely destroyed it."

The astronomers led her deep into a maze of halls and chambers. Those on the surface were in darkness, their power sources gone. A broad ramp led down into the moon, however, to a section glowing with soft blue light that seemed to radiate from the walls themselves.

Eventually, they entered a circular chamber so far beneath the surface that Morrigan was expecting another ice XI window looking out into a subsurface sea. What she saw there, however, was nothing like what she'd expected. Its size, its beauty, and its sheer complexity transfixed her.

"A galaxy . . ." she whispered, heart pounding.

"*The* Galaxy," Dumont told her. "We think this is a star chart like the ones we got from *Nemesis* and Quarantine. We have no way of checking, of course, but we think that every single star in our Galaxy is represented here, accurately placed with respect to every other star—over four hundred *billion* of them. The whole map is almost a kilometer across, end to end."

She opened her mouth to say something—*anything*—but Morrigan found herself at a complete loss for words. From a distance, she could see only that vast spiral mass of stars, each aglow in a color representing its actual spectrum. The spiral arms tended toward blue and white; those crowded into the beehive swarm at the Core were red or orange. Faint, red-hued stars surrounded the whole structure—the ancient halo stars outside of the main spiral itself.

The Core, as astronomers had long known but never directly seen, was barred, the central mass of suns joined to the main spiral arms by short, straight protrusions that might be a memory of some incredibly ancient galactic collision or gravitational convulsion.

"Go ahead, Admiral," Dumont told her. "Walk into it."

She did so, looking about her with a sense of wonder that felt childlike to her . . . but she didn't care. Tears were streaming down her face and she raised a hand to wipe them away, forgetting for a breathless moment that she was wearing a helmet.

Each step took her deeper into that star cloud. She found that when she concentrated on any single point of light, the map seemed to read her thoughts, somehow, and her corona brought up stats and figures. Pixie whispered in her mind that ey was translating from Trel and projecting it into her visual field in English. The vast majority of stars were tagged with numbers, but many, many millions had names.

Endivanan. Vha'al. Nordim. Trolhet.

Places, *real places,* located within and across that vastness of suns. *Dorhea. Namis. Gav'il Nuret. Sonenek . . .*

The named ones, many of them, were tagged as possessing civilizations. Where, she wondered, was Earth?

Ro Semmej. Brulidi. Maasmatrid. Folet.

Earth was utterly lost in that cloud of colored light.

When she looked closely, her vision seemed to shift, and she became aware of a network of violet threads connecting sun to sun to sun to myriad other suns. So not only the stars were mapped, but the arteries as well—the incredibly complex network of interconnected gate rings.

God ... God in *heaven* ... who had created this complex of gates? She had to rephrase the thought in her mind. First, who had created this spectacular and fully interactive map of the Galaxy?

But second, who had knitted together the stars themselves, weaving four hundred billion worlds and more into a unified whole?

O'o Kaaleth. Nadrigat. Soluinah'ma. Zetrin.

Most of the stars were mere specks of color, deep red and so small they contributed little to the radiance of the whole. Red dwarfs, she realized with a start. Eighty percent of the Galaxy's stars were red dwarfs—tiny stars only slightly larger than Jupiter, and yet so slow-burning a trillion years might pass before the first one died.

The brighter stars created the far-flung spiral arms, delineating them, illuminating them. She could easily see, however, that the gaps between those arms were not empty. The Galaxy was more of a disk than a spiral; the arms were illusions created by streaming nebulae and blue-white giants under the caress of pressure waves from exploding suns.

She walked slowly forward, struggling to work out the scale of the thing as stars and wisps of nebulae flowed past her face with each step. The Galaxy was something over one hundred thousand light-years across. This living model, Dumont had said, was a kilometer wide, which meant a scale of roughly a light-year per centimeter. How was it being projected? The cavern seemed otherwise empty, with no sign of projection equipment. The technology was incomprehensible.

She peered ahead through a cloud of stars, trying to see. "I wish I could reach the Core," she said aloud. "But that's a pretty long hike."

Even as she said the words, the stars around her rushed past, like snowflakes in a driving wind. The map, she was beginning to realize, responded with amazing speed and delicate precision to her thoughts. It was quite possible that there was no projection equipment in the cavern because the projection was entirely inside her head, transmitted through her corona.

That's the trick, Admiral, Pixie whispered in her mind. *Think what you want, and the map will respond.*

The center of the Galaxy, half a kilometer from the point where she'd entered the room, was all around her now. The stars were thick, a closely packed swarm, glowing with a ruddy light like hot iron. Just ahead floated an opaque gray sphere a dozen centimeters across.

Strange. The supermassive black hole at the center of the Galaxy—long known to astronomers as Sagittarius A*—had been calculated to have a diameter of fifty-two million kilometers, roughly a third of one AU. This gray sphere, if her estimates of the map's scale were correct, represented an object roughly ten to twelve light-years across, or 2.25 million times larger than the actual black hole. She willed her point of view to enter the gray sphere . . . but nothing happened.

She was being blocked.

"Someone doesn't want us seeing inside," she said out loud.

"What are you looking at, Admiral?" Stroud said at her side.

"The Galactic Core," she replied. "What . . . oh."

Stroud might still be standing beside her, but he was experiencing an entirely different part of the projection.

"Where are you, Colonel?"

"Looking at Earth. Sol, I mean. I needed Dr. Kopeck's help to find it, though."

So Colonel Stroud was looking at a portion of the map some twenty-six thousand light-years away from where she was looking, though in fact he was standing next to her. The illusion was so perfect she momentarily had trouble wrapping her brain around the concept.

In fact, the entire experience was making her feel a bit dizzy, and as she shifted her point of view around the Core, the rush of stars past her face threatened to bring on an attack of vertigo. She gulped down a deep breath and worked to steady herself.

Deep down, she felt the rising surge of depression, black and bleak.

What the hell am I doing here?

She didn't mean the map room.

"Ryan?" she said. "Help me see Earth. Please?"

"Right over here, Admiral."

The stars rushed past. Twenty-six thousand light-years from the center, the stellar density had thinned considerably. A bright yellow pinpoint hung in front of her visor. She was aware of other stars nearby: the triplet of Alpha Centauri four and some light-years away; the brilliant white beacon of Sirius at 8.6 lights; the dim red dwarfs of Barnard's Star and Wolf 359 and other near neighbors. The yellow beacon of embattled Delta Pavo hung twenty light-years from Sol.

Morrigan was shaking. Seeing Sol all but lost within that thronging host of suns didn't help.

She was feeling very, very, *very* small.

Alexandra Morrigan had long been aware of the facts and figures describing the Milky Way Galaxy—that it was a spiral a hundred thousand light-years across and ten thousand light-years thick, that it comprised four hundred billion suns, that it was just one of perhaps a hundred trillion other galaxies scattered in a tangled web across an ever-expanding universe. Words and numbers . . . they were meaningless in any emotional sense. Human astronomers had known those facts since the twentieth century.

But never in her four centuries of life had Morrigan experienced so graphic and tangible and *terrible* a model, a representation showing just what those figures actually meant. She was feeling the size and depth and complexity and literally astronomical numbers of a place, of a *real* place, of what the ancients had called the Milky Way.

And here she stood with her fleet of a few hundred ships and her crews and Marines numbering a few tens of thousands, contemplating . . . what? *Conquering* that immensity?

Don't be ridiculous!

Her long-range plans, such as they were, had called for her to delve ever deeper into the Galactic polity, striking bases, carrying out raids, and in general making such a nuisance of herself that the Authority would finally accept that these upstart humans could not be subjugated, could not be civilized, and that fighting them was a waste of resources.

That, after all, was the central tenet of asymmetric warfare. Small nations fighting off much larger ones despite overwhelming odds. Primitives taking down occupiers equipped with superior technology. Ewoks sneaking up on armored infantry.

Preposterous.

Even ignoring Galactic technology, the sheer size of the Milky Way, the sheer *numbers* involved, would doom the Galaxy raiders from the start. They didn't stand a fucking chance . . .

Except . . .

She pulled back from Sol, taking in again the broad sweep and scope of a Galaxy of four hundred billion suns. How many of those suns, she wondered, harbored civilizations . . . and potential allies? It wasn't enough to simply smash through Galactic infrastructure and enemy fleets; she would need to forge the myriad species and cultures and civilizations controlled by the Galactic Authority into a single unified force, a tool to bring down a billion-year-old empire.

The bleak depression ebbed once more. If she looked at the whole problem, it was impossible . . . insurmountable. But from Gamma^2 Sagittarii she could see the web of purple threads leading deeper and yet deeper into the Galaxy. Another hundred light-years and a sun called Korul floated among a hundred other stars, and when she interrogated it within her mind she saw that it was another fleet base, as well as the center of another enslaved population.

One step at a time. Korul first, then Azherinaq and Valeddiat.

And someday . . . the Core, and whatever was hidden within that opaque gray sphere.

Task Force Morrigan had come so far already—a few tiny steps in the vastness of the map, but the fact that they'd survived this long was far more important than distances covered.

They were committed now. There could be no turning back.

Morrigan remembered a snippet of history, a story claiming that Alexander the Great had wept when he realized he had no more world to conquer. That, at least, would not be an issue for her. She could pursue this campaign for a dozen lifetimes and still be nowhere near the end.

Perhaps her children ... or her children's children ...

She found that the thought, rather than being depressing, was giving her a surge of new life, of purpose, of *being*.

They *were* going to do this.

Epilogue

"Ready in all respects for space, Admiral. Fleetlink online. All ships report ready."

"Thank you, Captain."

Alexandra Morrigan sat at her station in CIC, savoring the moment. For almost a month, the fleet had remained here at Xalixa, using asteroidal debris to repair and replenish damaged warships and to grow new ships—especially fighters and pigs. She'd sent patrols through each of the Xalixan gates, but none had found any sign of the Galactics. The Galaxy's overlords, it seemed, needed time to lick their wounds and assess a rapidly changing sociopolitical situation.

Reinforcements had arrived from Earth at last—almost two thousand ships in all, coming up the Whiskey Road to more than double Task Force Morrigan's numbers. With them were Admiral Knutson and 310 long-absent ships of Red Wing. Knutson, it turned out, had raided Delta Pavo, fought off three separate Veykaar fleets before they could unite, and managed to drag a fair-sized Galactic task force away from Morrigan's operations farther out. "Red" Knutson was now the Fleet's second-in-command.

Earth, meanwhile, continued to crank out new ships. The bottleneck, as ever, was raising and training crews, but even that chore was becoming less of a problem as news and vids of Morrigan's—of *the* Morrigan's—battle reports were disseminated through the news feeds back home.

At Xalixa, meanwhile, a sizable Lixie army had already been created, and thousands of the little Von Neumann–esque machines were being assembled and deployed each day.

Task Force Morrigan was a far more capable force now than it had been at Sirius.

But would it be enough? Morrigan continued to hold the fear, the despair, and the depression at bay. It would be enough.

It *had* to be.

The fleet had assembled at the Xalixa-Parin Gate. The gate leading to the Drepnidak system was no longer operable. It was dead now, surrounded by a cloud of some thousands of burned-out Galactic warships. Relativistic pigs, it seemed, were a *very* potent weapon of war.

Robotic scavengers were picking over the hulks, harvesting both information and raw materials for more warships.

According to the Galactic map, copied and stored in an empty storage compartment in *Constellation*'s belly, Parin was an unoccupied and uninhabited world with half a dozen gates. The fleet would vanish there, working its way unseen deeper into enemy space.

Their next major goal was Korul.

"All units," Morrigan said, transmitting over Fleetlink. "Engage drives. Let's move out."

They accelerated, the familiar fireworks of Baltis radiation sparking across their forward screens.

And Morrigan watched the show and smiled, deciding that, just perhaps, she knew now what she wanted to be when she grew up.

Discover more from *New York Times* bestselling author Ian Douglas in The Solar Warden Series

"This ambitious series opener from Douglas...throws military sci-fi tropes and time-honored conspiracy theories into a blender to create a bonkers alternate present...Douglas gleefully combines an eclectic mix of conspiracies, among them Roswell Greys, humanoid lizards, and space-faring Nazis, while launching his characters into intergalactic battles with the skillful combat sequences fans well expect."

—*Publishers Weekly* on *Alien Secrets*